DARK WINTER

Also by William Dietrich

Fiction
Ice Reich
Getting Back

Nonfiction
The Final Forest
Northwest Passage

DARK WINTER

WILLIAM DIETRICH

WARNER BOOKS

An AOL Time Warner Company

This book is a work of fiction. Names, characters, places, and incidents are the product of the author's imagination or are used fictitiously. Any resemblance to actual events, locales, or persons, living or dead, is coincidental.

WARNER BOOKS EDITION

Cover design and illustration by George Cornell

Warner Books, Inc.
1271 Avenue of the Americas
New York, NY 10020

Visit our Web site at
www.twbookmark.com.

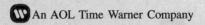 An AOL Time Warner Company

Printed in the United States of America
Originally published in hardcover by Warner Books
First Paperback Printing: December 2002

10 9 8 7 6 5 4 3 2 1

To the men and women who go to the ends of the earth for science.

Station Roster

The Beakers

Mickey Moss: astrophysics
Harrison Adams: astronomer
Carl Mendoza: astronomer
Gina Brindisi: astronomer post-doc
Dana Andrews: atmospheric science
Gerald Follett: atmospheric science
Hiro Sakura: magnetic fields
Alexi Molotov: aurora australis
Jed Lewis: meteorology
Lena Jindrova: botanist
Eleanor Chen: science technician
Robert Norse: psychologist

Station Support

Rod Cameron: station manager
Nancy Hodge: medic
Abby Dixon: computers
Doug "Pika" Taylor: generators
Wade "Cueball" Pulaski: cook
Jimmy "Buck" Tyson: vehicle mechanic
Gabriella Reid: berthing and administration
Linda Brown: logistics and galley
George Geller: maintenance
Steve Calhoun: carpenter
Hank Anderson: carpenter
Charles Longfellow: electrician
Gage Perlin: plumber
Clyde Skinner: radio and communications

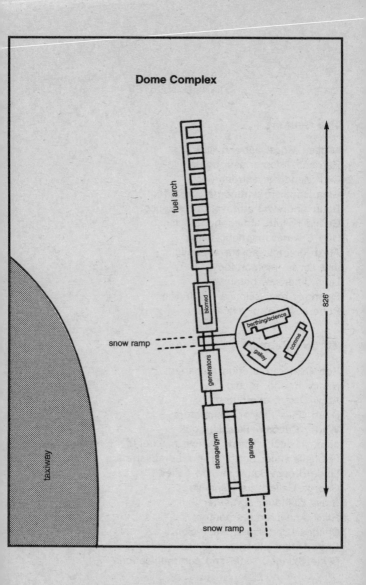

Dome Complex

fuel arch

biomed

snow ramp

berthing/science

comms

galley

generators

storage/gym

garage

snow ramp

taxiway

826'

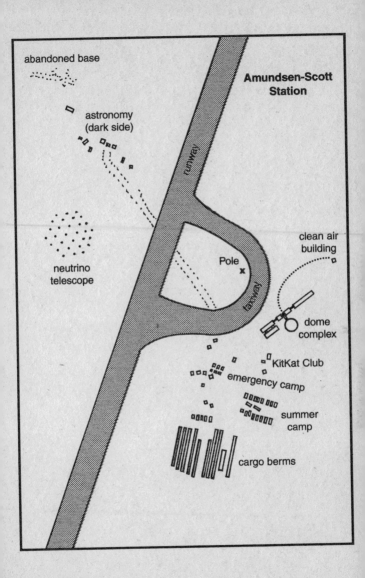

DARK WINTER

CHAPTER ONE

Sometimes you have to go into nothing to get what you want.

That was the Jed Lewis theory, anyway. West Texas oil patch, Saudi, the North Slope. Hadn't worked for him yet but one kind of extreme had led to another, one kind of quest to its polar opposite. Sometimes life patterns like that, when you keep changing your mind about what it is you *do* want. So now he'd come to the very end of the world and was peering over its edge, too late to turn back, hoping that in the farthest place on earth he'd finally fit in. Atone to himself for his own confusion of purpose. Belong.

Maybe.

"The Pole!" Jim Sparco had seduced him. "Feels closer to the stars than anyplace on earth. It's high desert, a desert of ice, and the air's so dry that it feels like you can eat the stars. Bites of candy." The climatologist had gripped his arm. "The South Pole, Lewis. It's there you realize how cold the universe really is."

The money had almost been secondary. They'd understood each other, Sparco and he, this longing for the desolate places. A place uncomplicated. Pure.

Except for their rock, of course. That raised questions. It was their pebble, their tumor, their apple.

The world is round but it has an edge. A cold crustal wrinkle called the Trans-Antarctic Range runs for more than a thousand miles and divides Antarctica in two. On the north side of the mountains is a haunting but recognizable landscape of glacier and mountain and frozen ocean: an Ice Age world, yes, but still a world—our world. To its south, toward the Pole, is an ice cap so deep and vast and empty as to seem unformed and unimagined. A vacuum, a blank. The white clay of God.

Lewis crossed in the sinking light of an Antarctic autumn. He was exhausted from thirty hours of flying, constricted by thirty-five pounds of polar clothing, and weary of the noisy dimness of the LC-130 military transport plane, its webbed seats pinching circulation and its schizophrenic ventilation blowing hot and cold.

He was also entranced by beauty. The sun was slowly dipping toward six-month night and the aqua crevasses and sugared crags below were melodramatic with blaze and shadow. Golden photons, bouncing off virginal snow, created a hazed fire. Frozen seas looked like cracked porcelain. Unnamed peaks reared out of fogs thick as frosting, and glaciers grinned with splintery teeth attached to blue gums. It was all quite primeval, untrodden and unspoiled, a white board on which to redraw yourself. The kind of place where he could be whatever he made himself, whatever he announced himself, to be.

The Trans-Antarctic Range is like a dam, however, holding behind it a plateau of two-mile-thick polar ice like a police line braced against a pressing crowd. A hundred thousand years of accumulated snowfall. A few peaks at the edge of the ice plateau bravely poke their snouts up as if to tread water but then, farther south, relief disappears altogether. The glaciers vanish. So do ridges, crevasses, and theatrical light. What follows is utter flatness, a frozen mesa as big as the contiguous United States. When the airplane crossed the mountains it entered something fundamentally different, Lewis realized. It was then that his excitement began to turn to disquiet.

Imagine an infinite sheet of paper. No, not infinite, because the curve of the earth provides a kind of boundary. Except that the horizon itself is foggy and indistinct with floating ice crystals, suspended like diamond dust, so that the snow merges without definition into pale sky. There was nothing to see from the tiny scratched windows of the National Guard transport: no relief, no reference point, no imperfection. When he thought he saw undulations in the snow the load master informed him he was merely looking at the shadow of cirrus clouds far overhead. When he thought he saw a track across the snow—left by a tractor or snowmobile, perhaps—the load master pointed to a contrail being left by an outgoing transport. His track was the shadow of that dissipating streak across the sky.

Lewis moved among the pallets of cargo from window to window, waiting for something to happen. Nothing did. The plane lumbered on, cold slithering along its fuselage.

He checked his watch, as if it still meant anything in a place where the sun went haywire, and looked out again.

Nothing.

He looked out a different window. No movie would start on the blank screen below. No progress could be discerned. He searched a sky and plateau that seemed blank mirrors of each other, vainly searching for some rip, some imperfection, some reassurance that he was *someplace.*

Nothing.

He sat on his web seat and chewed a cold lunch.

After a drag of time the Guardsman cuffed his shoulder and Lewis stood again, looking where the sergeant pointed. Far away there was a pimple on the vastness. A tiny bug, a freckle, a period with a white runway attached to make a kind of exclamation mark. Amundsen-Scott base! Named by Americans for the Norwegian who got there first in 1912, and the hard-luck Brit who froze to death weeks later after seconding at point zero. Lewis made out a bottle-cap of a dome that sheltered the South Pole's central buildings and an orbit of smaller structures like specks of sand. From the air the human settlement was remarkable only for its insignificance.

"The buildings fit in a circle about a mile wide, altogether," the load master shouted to him over the roar of the engines. "Doesn't look like much, does it?"

Lewis didn't reply.

"You staying the winter?"

He shrugged.

"Glad it's you and not me!"

They buckled in, the snow seeming to swell up to meet them, Lewis's heart accelerating during that disquieting gap between air and ground, and then with a thump and a bang they were down, swerving slightly as the skis skidded on the ice. The plane shuddered as it taxied, continuing to vibrate when it stopped because the pilots didn't dare shut down the engines.

Lewis stood, stiff and apprehensive. He was the only passenger, the last arrival of the season. An anti-migrant, swimming against the tide of humans fleeing north. Well, his timing had never been the best. The cargo ramp opened to a shriek of white and the cold hit him like a slap. It was palpable, like a force you waded into.

"We had a fly stowaway from New Zealand one time," the load master shouted, his military mustache almost brushing Lewis's ear. The propellers were still whirling so the hubs wouldn't freeze, and the National Guard sergeant needed this intimacy to be heard. "Buzzed like a bastard for three thousand miles! When we opened the doors it flew to the light and made it three feet! Three feet! Then the fucker dropped like a stone!" The man laughed.

Dizzy, Lewis walked out. He couldn't get a proper breath. There was a crowd of orange-parka people at the edge of the runway, waving but fidgety, anxious to get away. The last of the summer crew, going home. Snow from the prop wash blew over them, hazing them as if they were already being erased. Awkward from his duffel and enormous white plastic polar boots, Lewis staggered toward the group in seeming supplication. A figure detached from the crowd to meet him. The man's hood was up and all Lewis could see were goggles and frosted beard, framed by a ruff of fur. Lewis had been given the same government-issue parka. He'd been told it cost seven hundred dollars and a sacrificial fox.

"Jed Lewis?" It was a shout, above the noise.

A nod, his own goggles giving the Pole a piss-yellow tint.

The man reached, not to shake hands but to shoulder the duffel. He turned to the others. "Let's move, people! Let's get this cargo off so you can all go home!" His goggles rotated across their rank, taking mental roll. "Where's Tyson?"

There was a long moment of silence, goggled heads turning, a few smiles of unease and amusement. In their cold weather gear everyone looked alike except for strips on their coats with block-letter name tags.

"Sulking!" someone finally called.

Lewis's greeter stiffened. There was another silence beneath the drum of the engines, someone shrugging, his guide sucking in unhappy breath. "Well, someone go the hell and find him and tell him to get the damn sled up here so we can get this plane off! He's got eight long months to sulk!"

The others shifted uncomfortably.

The man turned back to Lewis, not waiting to see if anyone followed his command. "This way!" They set off toward the central aluminum geodesic dome, half buried now by drifting snow, their pace briskly impatient. Lewis looked back, parts of the orange-clad group now breaking off to troop to the plane. Then ahead to the dome, an upended silver saucer, dramatic and odd, like surplused flotsam from a World's Fair. He'd read the dimensions: fifty-five feet high, a hundred and sixty-four feet in diameter. An American flag snapped at the top, its edge ragged, its gunshot stutter audible now above the idle of the plane. Streaks of snow dust curved across the top of the dome in neatly drawn parabolas.

Lewis's nose hairs had already frozen. The cold ached in his lungs. His goggles were fogging up and his cheeks felt numb. He'd only been outside a few minutes. It was worse than he'd expected.

They descended a snowy ramp to a dark, garage-sized entrance at the base of the dome, Lewis mincing in his Frankenstein-sized boots so he wouldn't fall and slide on his butt. His guide paused to wait for him and let their eyes adjust to the dimness inside the door. Two cavelike corrugated steel arches extended into gloom to his left and right. "BioMed and the fuel arch that way, generators and garage over here." Lewis had a shadowy impression of walls and doors of plywood and steel, unpainted and utilitarian. Before he could peek into the arched tunnels he was led straight ahead. "The dome where we're quartered is this way."

The overturned bowl shielded the core of the South Pole base like a military helmet, keeping warmth-sucking wind and blowing snow off the metal boxes where people lived. Three of these boxcar-shaped structures, colored orange, sat on short stilts under its shelter. Since the base was built on snow, the powder didn't stop at the entrance but formed the dome floor, drifting over wooden crates and mounding against the orange housing units. Dirt and grease had colored the snow tan, like sand.

"It never melts," his guide said, scuffing at it. "The ambient temperature in here is fifty-one below."

Lewis tilted his head back. There was a hole at the top of the dome that let in pale light from a remote sky. The entire underside of the uninsulated structure was covered with steel-gray icicles, pointing downward like a roof of nails. It was beautiful and forbidding at the same time.

"You didn't finish the roof."

"Ventilation."

Someone bumped Lewis and he staggered to one side. It was another winter-over, rushing a crate of fresh fruit to the galley before it could harden in the cold. "Sorry! Freshies are like gold!" They followed the hurrying man to a freezerlike door and opened it for him. To get inside you pulled a metal rod sideways and tugged at a slab like a wall. Lewis realized that the freezer wasn't *inside* here, it was the outside: Anything not carried into the orange housing modules would turn hard as a brick. They followed the fruit bearer. There was a vestibule hung with parkas and beyond it a galley of bright fluorescent light, warmth, and the excited chatter of more people saying goodbye. Their duffels were heaped like sandbags. People were packed to go.

His guide let Lewis's gear drop with a thud and pushed back his goggles and hood. "Rod Cameron. Station manager."

"Hi." Lewis tried to fix the face but the men in their parkas looked alike. He had an impression of beard, chapped skin, and red raccoon lines where the goggles cut. Lewis was wondering about the absentee at the plane. "Someone not show up for work?"

Cameron frowned. He had a look of rugged self-confidence that came from coping with cold and administration, and a hint of strain for the same reason. The Pole wore on you. "Egos in kindergarten." He shook his head. "My job is to herd cats. And I'm having a bad day. We had a little alarm last night."

"Alarm?"

"The heat went off."

"Oh."

"We got it back on."

"Oh."

The station manager studied the newcomer. Lewis still looked smooth, sandy-haired and tanned, with the easy tautness of the recreational athlete.

It would pass.

"You got your file?"

Lewis dug in his duffel and fished out a worn manila envelope with employment forms, medical records, dental X rays, and a list of the personal belongings he'd shipped to the Pole in advance of his own arrival. His new boss glanced inside, as if to confirm Lewis's presence with paper, and then put the folder under his arm. "I've got to go back outside to see this last plane off," Cameron said. "I'll show you around later but right now it's best to just sit and drink."

Lewis looked around the galley in confusion.

"I mean drink water. The altitude. You feel lousy, right? It's okay. Fingies are supposed to."

"Fingie?"

"F-N-G-I. Fucking New Guy on the Ice. That's you."

Lewis failed at a grin. "Latecomer."

"Just new. Everybody's a fingie at first. We know we're lucky to get you last minute like this. Jim Sparco e-mailed about you like the Second Coming."

"I needed a job."

"Yeah, he explained that. I think it's cool that you quit Big Oil." Cameron gave a nod of approval.

"That's me, man of principle." Lewis had a headache from the altitude.

"Course, we need their shit to keep from freezing down here."

"Not from a wildlife refuge, you don't."

"And you just walked out."

"They weren't about to give me a helicopter ride."

"That took some guts."

"It had to be done."

Cameron tried to assess the new man. Lewis looked tired, disoriented, chest rising and falling, half excited and half afraid. They all started like that. The station manager turned back to the door, impatient to get away, and considered whether to say anything else. "I've got to go get the plane off," he finally said again. "You know what that means, don't you?"

"What?"

"That you can't quit down here."

A stream of people followed Cameron out, some looking at Lewis curiously and others ignoring him: the winterovers going to off-load the supplies and the last from summer flying home. The Pole had a brief four-month window when weather permitted incoming flights, and then in February the last plane left, fleeing north like a migrating bird. In winter it was too dark to see, too windy to keep the ice runway clear, and too cold to risk a landing: Struts could snap, hydraulics fail, doors fail to open or close. The sun set on March 21, the equinox, and wouldn't rise again until September 21. From February to October the base was as remote as the moon. There were twenty-six winterovers who retreated under the dome to maintain its functions and take astronomical and weather readings: eight women and eighteen men this year. It was like being on a submarine or space station. You had to commit.

The galley had emptied and Lewis took a place at a Formica table. The room was low-ceilinged, bright, and warm. A bulletin board was thick with paper, a juice dispenser burbled, and in the corner a television monitor displayed outside temperatures. It was fifty-eight below zero near the runway, the breeze lowering the windchill to minus eighty-one. The reading was an abstraction except for the freezer door he'd come through. That was old, and cold leaked around its edges to rime its inner face with frost. The frost reached all the way across it in stripes, like fingers. The pattern reminded Lewis of a giant hand, trying to yank the door away.

"Drink as much as you can. Best cure for the altitude."

Lewis looked up. It was the cook, bald except for a top-knot that hung from the back of his head. His skull looked knobby, as if knocked around more than once, and he had a gray mustache and forearms tattooed with a bear and eagle. Here was somebody easy to remember.

"It doesn't look high."

"That's because it's flat. You're sitting on ice almost two miles thick. Our elevation is ninety-three hundred, and the thinning of the atmosphere at the Poles makes the effective altitude closer to eleven thousand. Walking out of that transport is like being dumped on the crest of the Rockies. Your body will adjust in a few days."

"I feel hammered." The short walk from the plane had made him ill.

"You'll be racing around the world before you know it."

"Around the world?"

"Around the stake that marks the Pole." He sat down. "Wade Pulaski. Chief cook and bottle washer. Best chef for nine hundred miles. I can't claim any farther because Cathy Costello back at McMurdo is pretty good, too." McMurdo was the main American base in Antarctica, located on the coast.

"Jedediah Lewis, polar weatherman." He shook.

"Jedediah? Your parents religious?"

"More like hippies, I think. When it was a fad."

"But it's biblical, right? You're a prophet?"

"Oracle of climate change by temporary opportunity. Rockhound by training. And it's actually just another name for Solomon. 'Beloved of the Lord.'"

"So you're wise."

His head was pounding. "I take my name as God's little joke."

"What do you mean by rockhound?"

"Geologist. That's my real job."

"So you come to the one place on earth where there aren't any rocks? Doctor Bob will have a field day with that one."

"Who's Doctor Bob?"

"Our new shrink. NASA sent him down to do a head job on us before they plant too many people on the space station. He's wintering over to write us up while we mess with each other's minds. He thinks we're all escapists."

Lewis smiled. "Rod Cameron just told me we can't quit."

"That's what I told Doctor Bob! It's like being paid to go to prison!"

"And yet we volunteered."

"I'm on my third season." Pulaski stretched out his arms in mock enthusiasm, as if to claim ownership. "I can't stay away. If the generators stop like they did last night we've got maybe a few hours, but we always get them running again."

"Why'd they stop?"

"Some moron turned the wrong valve. Rod went ballistic, which meant nobody was in a mood to confess this morning. But it was a stupid annoyance, not a threat. And you're going to learn that as long as you don't freeze to death things are really good down here, especially now that the last of summer camp is leaving and the bureaucrats are ten thousand miles away. I give you better food than you'd get back home and there's no bullshit at the Pole. There's no clock to punch, no bills, no taxes, no traffic, no newspapers, no nothing. After today everything calms down and this becomes the sanest place on earth. Cozier than most families. And after eight toasty months you come out with your head straight and your money saved. It's paradise, man."

Lewis reserved agreement. "You got any aspirin?"

"Sure." The cook got a bottle from the kitchen and brought it back. "You feel like shit right now, but you'll get better."

"I know."

"You even acclimate to the cold. A little."

"I know."

Pulaski went to the counter where food was passed. He bent under it to get a commissary-sized soup can, its label stripped and its inside cleaned to a bright copper. "Here, your arrival present."

"What's this for?" Lewis realized he felt stupid from the altitude.

"You'll drink all day and pee all night, this first night. It's your body adjusting to the cold and altitude. This can saves you about three hundred trips to the real can."

"A chamber pot?"

"Welcome to Planet Cueball, fingie."

CHAPTER TWO

Lewis's room was windowless and just ten feet long. He could span its width with lifted arms, his fingertips brushing each wall. It was one of a row of cells on the second floor of the science building, another orange metal box that claimed its grandiose title by virtue of having a small computer lab downstairs. His room looked every day of its quarter-century age: scuffed, faded, and leaking. The insulation had become soaked and frozen on the outer wall and there was another mold of frost inside, a white reminder of how thin their protective shell was. A few inches inside the wall the temperature was kept near seventy degrees by a blowing heater. The air was very dry and smelled faintly of fuel from the base generator. The mechanical drone was like being on a ship.

"The dreaded Ice Room," said Cameron, who'd brought Lewis here after the plane left. The station manager looked tired but was trying hard to be welcoming. "Being on the end of the building sucks, but last come gets last pick."

Lewis put his hand against the wall, the clamminess cold as aquarium glass. "What if my butt freezes to this during the night?"

"We bring a blowtorch every time you're late for breakfast." There was a pause, for timing. "Just don't roll over the other way."

Lewis dutifully smiled. Sometimes you go to prison as a means of escape, he thought. Sometimes the very worst places offer the most possibility.

"Now, we call this floor Upper Berthing, jargon left over from the Navy days. It's perfect for you since you're a beaker. You can crunch your data downstairs."

Beaker was polar slang for scientist. Lewis had already encountered this caste designation in New Zealand, where he was issued a punching-bag-sized duffel of cold weather gear at the American warehouse in Christchurch. "You get the shitty nylon because you're a beaker," the clerk had informed him, handing him insulated bib overalls. "The workers get Carhartt." This alternative looked like tough canvas.

"Scientists are workers," Lewis had protested.

"Scientists don't spend twelve hours fitting pipe. You get the nylon."

Now his place in the hierarchy had dictated assignment of a room. Like a runt piglet jostling for a teat, he was on the outer end. Also growing out of his orange box were appendages that included an electric substation, hydroponic greenhouse, and closet full of fire-fighting gear. Fire was the most feared enemy at the Pole.

"Homey," he offered.

"A leaking derelict," Cameron corrected. "The whole base had a life expectancy that expired five years ago and it's slowly falling apart. A recent inspection turned up two hundred safety deficiencies, which means we really have to stay alert just to stay alive. The National Science Foundation wants to replace everything—in summer they fly in congressmen like a D.C. shuttle—so we're under pressure here to show some results. Practical benefits from basic research. You'll find people are under a little strain. Still, the good news is that the Ice Room is warmer than outside, half private—your one neighbor will still hear more of you than they want to—and the government is past complaining about tape or tacks on the walls. Just don't put up a centerfold: We're politically correct now."

"You admit you weren't?" His question was wry.

"It was so macho that the Navy guys had nudes laminated into the tables. Only way to remember what females looked like. Gone with the wind, man, and better for it. Things are more civilized now that we have women."

"What happened to the tables?"

"They're still in the old base, abandoned in '75 when they built this dome. It's snowed over and slowly being crushed by the ice. Unsafe and strictly verboten, but a fascinating depository of cultural archaeology. Beer cans. Frozen hot dogs. America at her zenith."

"But you've seen it."

"Winter-overs have been known to explore. Big Brother left on the last plane, you know. Except for *moi*. Which reminds me." Cameron beckoned him down the hall and pointed toward the shared bathroom. "Our biggest shortage is melted water. That means the most onerous rule concerns the showers. No more than two a week, two minutes of running water each. You wet, turn it off, soap, turn it on, rinse off. We're sitting on seventy percent of the world's fresh water but it's so hard to melt we might as well be in the Sahara. It's rationed." He stopped, listening. They could hear the clumping sounds of someone inside.

"No shower for three or four days?" Lewis leaned back in exaggeration.

"It's so cold and dry you don't sweat much here." He was talking to Lewis but his attention was on the door. He sounded distracted. "Or if you do, people get used to it."

"Splendid."

The door opened and a lumbering bear of a man shambled out, naked except for a towel around his waist, his hair wet. He was bearded, hairy, and huge, a veritable Sasquatch. He stopped in surprise at their presence. "What's this, a line to pee?" The voice was deep, the eyes hard and squinty.

"Just rising to join us, Buck?" Cameron's look was of dislike.

The man scowled. "Just cleaning up after trying to make some room for all the crap that came in."

"We had trouble getting the plane off on time."

"It got off."

"We're both stuck here now. I need you on time."

"It got off. And I need *you* to stop nagging and let me do my job." The two men held their gaze for a moment, a mutual glare, and then the big man's slid away and he looked past the station manager. "Who's this?"

"The new guy, Jed Lewis. Getting the tour."

"Another beaker fingie? Great." He didn't offer a hand. "You getting the Ten Commandments from Ice Prick? Learning how to fill out work requests?"

There was an undercurrent of resentment that Lewis felt unsure how to respond to. What was the beef of this guy? "Just looking."

"Well, don't look the fuck at me." The man pushed past them, lurching down the hall, his fist clutching his towel to maintain some dignity.

"Buck, we're on a team," Cameron said after him. "Lewis here is part of the team."

The bear turned. "It ain't a team, it's a caste, and it's beaker glory on G.A. frostbite. If I could have waved good-bye to this zoo I would've been on time for *that*." He sized up the newcomer, who was wondering what G.A. meant, and pointed a stubby finger. "You watch your ass around here, *Lewis*, because it's cutthroat island among the beakers whenever someone throws grant crumbs our way. You got any sense, you'll look out for Number One. And don't pay any attention to all the brown-nosing, middle-management, ass-kissing bullshit, either." His finger swung to Cameron. "I'll take a fucking shower when I fucking want to." He went in one of the rooms and the door slammed.

The station manager was looking after the man unhappily, his mouth working as if he were still deciding what to say.

"Who the hell was that?"

"That was Tyson. Our mechanic." It was a mutter.

"The guy they said was sulking?"

"Don't pay any attention to him." Cameron shook his head unhappily. "He fought to get hired down here and has bitched about it ever since. He's a malcontent and a loser." The station manager frowned at his own candor. "He'll come around." Cameron glanced at his watch, suddenly losing interest in the tour. "Listen, I'll finish showing you around tomorrow, including where you work. You'll be up for it then. For now, just take it easy, try to get used to the altitude, get over the jet lag, and unpack. Okay?"

"Is that guy having a bad day, or what?"

"Every day's a bad day for him."

Lewis went back to his room, sat on his bunk, and scratched the frost, watching a strip peel off under his fingernail. Pulled into the path of heat, the crystals began to melt. *Welcome, fingie.*

He decided to remain philosophical. First of all, he'd volunteered for this. Walked out of his oil patch job and straight into unemployment in a fit of righteous environmentalism and self-doubt. It was a miracle he'd met Jim Sparco and fit his emergency need for a polar research assistant. A miracle he'd been given a purpose again. There was no question he was meant to be here. Expertise, desire, and opportunity had all neatly fit.

And second, he knew, sailors, inmates, and astronauts had certainly endured worse. Despite the spongy outer wall, his room was toasty enough—except that he couldn't use the word *toast.* That was Antarctic slang for burn-out, that late-season time when the monotonous lack of color and smell and sound and variety left a winter-over with an Antarctic stare, the mood of the condemned, and the social skills of roadkill. They'd warned him about it at the headquarters of the National Oceanic and Atmospheric Administration in Boulder, the agency that employed him. *Toast, toasty, toasted, crouton.* Not a nice thing to be. So let's just say *warm.* Cheery. Anticipatory. Nervous. And someday, even if not *toast,* perhaps depressed, bored, loopy, horny, hungry, sleepy, and dopey. They'd warned him of all those things, the list sounding like a casting call for *Snow White.*

At least he had his own room, a polar luxury. The winter-overs had cheered and whooped when that last LC-130 roared away, its engines burning so rich in the cold that they left four black streaks of soot on the snow. The departure meant independence, room, a tiny cell of privacy. Lewis understood the reaction. They were beginning! The plane lifting off left him feeling both trapped and satisfied,

newly secure. He'd made it! All the way to the South Pole!
Every problem he'd ever had was temporarily gone, lost
across a no-man's-land of ice. Every relationship was a
fresh start. With just twenty-six souls, every person was
important. Vital. Even that grump Tyson. Lewis had an important job with clear parameters, unique opportunity, and
no everyday hassles for the next eight months.

No escape, either. No backing out.

He liked the finality of it.

"My fellow fingie!"

Someone new filled the door of his room, smiling. Clean-
shaven, but a skull as distinctive as the cook's: close-
cropped stubble except for a darker Mohawk streak on top.
Despite this bizarre choice he was a handsome man a decade
older, Lewis judged, late thirties, with bright blue eyes that
flicked curiously around the barren chamber like a detective's. Nothing much to see yet, of course, so they came
to rest on Lewis. "Robert Norse." He put out a hand. "Recent arrival and resident shrink."

The two men had to stand at the foot of the bed in the
cramped quarters, squeezed too close. "Jed Lewis." He took
the offered hand, hard and dry.

Norse pumped vigorously. He looked fit, muscular, his
frame erect with an almost military tautness. There was an
intense energy to his friendliness. His teeth were perfect,
his eyes assessing, his smell of aftershave. The scent made
Lewis realize how little there was to smell at the Pole besides what people brought with them. By the end of the
winter he'd know everyone's smell, he supposed. Their
voice, ticks, expressions, inflections, and flaws. Their past
and intended future. It had to be a psychologist's paradise.

"Except everyone calls me Doctor Bob. Nicknames are

endemic here, and you'll get one, too. I only arrived a week before you."

Lewis looked pointedly above Norse's brow. "A psychologist? So explain the haircut, Doc."

Norse smiled, running a hand along the crown of his head. "I got this at McMurdo on a dare. Polar plunge sort of thing. Supposed to add to solidarity. I'm hoping it helps me fit in. Be one of the gang."

"Isn't that the kind of thing you do in junior high?"

"People try to fit in from preschool to the mortuary, without exception, instinctually. Basic monkey behavior. Everyone wants to belong without ever asking why. You do want to belong, don't you?"

"I guess." Lewis thought about his answer. "I want my life to stand for something. I'm willing to join a team to do that."

"An idealist!" Norse grinned. "And you think before you talk! A self-examined man!" He nodded. "I'm impressed. Maybe." He pretended to consider the issue. "Or are you simply a joiner? A conformist? A follower? Is the way to self-realization through society? Or inside yourself?"

"I've got a feeling you've got the answer."

"I came down here to *get* the answer. And being a shrink is like being a cop or a priest or a journalist. Everyone tenses up. So I have to adopt camouflage." He knocked the top of his skull. "A haircut. And, unlike tattoos, this goes away."

"We'll probably tattoo each other, too. The cook said we've volunteered for prison."

Norse nodded. "'Then the Philistines seized him,'" he suddenly recited, "'gouged out his eyes and took him down to Gaza. Binding him with bronze shackles, they set him to grinding in the prison. But the hair on his head began to grow again . . .'"

"Say what?" Norse was quite the gabber.

"Story of Samson. Ever read it?"

"I think I caught the movie."

"Instructive story. Watch out for Delilah." He winked.

"Is there something religious about this place? The cook asked about my name."

"Oh no. Just literate."

Lewis sat on his bunk to get some space. The guy seemed friendly enough, but he didn't know what to make of a psychologist. Especially one who so blandly gave himself away. "I heard about you. I was told you'd want to analyze me."

Norse took half a step back, as if exposed. "Really? Analyze what?"

"That I'm a geologist in a place with no rocks."

"A geologist? On an ice cap?" Norse nodded sagely, considering, and then leaned forward like a mock confidant. "I'm sure the Freudians would have something to say about *that*. So. Why *are* you in a place with no rocks?"

"Because it has no rocks." Except it did, of course, but Norse didn't need to know that.

"I see." Norse mulled this over. "Makes perfect sense. Like a shrink in a place with no complications. You're quite sane, aren't you?"

"I'd appreciate a professional opinion."

"Ah. That will cost you. And I didn't bring a couch. So . . ." He thought. "Do you have a piece of paper?"

Lewis looked around.

"Wait, I think I've got one." Norse pulled out a sheet of folded paper from a pocket inside his sweater. It was blank. "I carry this around to make notes. Dumb idea, because it scares the hell out of people when you do. Anyway, sign your name. Instant handwriting analysis."

Lewis was curious and did so, handing the paper to Norse. The psychologist studied it. "Oh dear. My quick and dirty judgment is that you'll fit in with our group quite well."

Lewis smiled. "So what are *you* doing here, Doc?"

"Me? I'm using us all as guinea pigs for a future trip to Mars. The Pole is like a spaceship, NASA hopes. Communal. Also confined, hostile, and dark. Months of isolation. How does that make us feel?"

"I feel nauseated."

"That's the altitude. Took me three days to adjust. Some never do—I think it was your predecessor who rotated out a few weeks back. And mentally? I'm still adjusting. Will be for eight months, I suppose. That's why I dropped by. Antarctic veterans have one perspective, newcomers another. I'm hoping you'll share your observations as the winter goes on."

"Observations of what?"

"Whatever goes on."

Lewis shook his head, bemused. "I heard the power went out."

"Somebody goofed, which was great for me because it injected a variable." Norse smiled. "It's like having a lab where I didn't have to build the rat maze. I was planning a briefer visit but I got delayed in New Zealand and then the medic, Nurse Nancy, said she could use some help over the winter. I had a sabbatical leave, an opportunity to observe. . . . The fates conspire, no?"

"So that's what's to blame."

"Yes, destiny." Norse said what Lewis had just thought.

"Destiny and free will. A little of both, I think. And we're the two newcomers here, you and me. Right?"

"I guess so."

Norse nodded. "So, Jed. I want to be your first friend."

Lewis met most of the others at dinner, a confusing blur of fresh faces. Twelve scientists and technicians and fourteen support workers to keep them alive. Lena Jindrova, their greenhouse grad student, was the youngest, at twenty-three. The oldest was the man Lewis had been quietly sent by Sparco to meet, sixty-four-year-old Michael Mortimer Moss. The astrophysicist wasn't in the galley and no one seemed surprised.

"Mickey Mouse is determining the fate of the universe," an astronomer named Harrison Adams told Lewis when he asked. "Far too important to eat with we mortals. So he takes Twinkie-type crap out to the Dark Side and broods, the god on Olympus. It will all sound ennobling in his autobiography."

"Mickey Mouse?"

"Nickname." Adams chewed. "We call him that behind his back because he's pretentious. Not a bad guy, really, but the Saint Michael stuff gets a little old when you have to work with him. Although I will concede, he's the quintessential OAE."

"OAE?"

"Old Antarctic Explorer. Decades of Ice Time."

"Jim Sparco knows him," Lewis said. "Seems to admire him. Told me I should meet him."

"Yes, you should. Mickey Moss built this base. He made it all possible, as he'll remind you at every opportunity. But Jim Sparco doesn't have to hear those tiresome reminders, like I do. Or compete with him for grant money, like Carl Mendoza does. Or put up with his bullying, like our dear ineffectual station manager Rod Cameron does. Or jump to his orders, like our G.A.s do."

"Someone else used that. G.A., I mean."

"General Assignment. Assistant. Grunt. Serf. Supporter. Except you never find one when you need one. They're the people who really run this place. It's like officers and noncoms. We outrank them in everything except what really counts."

"I detect some worldly cynicism."

"You detect polar realism. You've joined a family, Jed, and like all families ours has some history."

"Am I going to regret it?"

"Not if you fit in."

Lewis got some food, taking a tray and nodding at the cook. Pulaski was being helped by a plain but friendly woman named Linda Brown. She looked at the tiny helpings on his plate and laughed. "First-night fast." She patted her ample hips. "Even I remember. Dimly."

He took his meager meal and sat down. If Adams seemed a bit sour, the rest seemed to be laughing and joking. Everyone was exclaiming about the shipment of fresh food. Lettuce! Tangerines! There was a vigor to the group, a buzz of energy and camaraderie that Lewis found appealing. They were excited at the departure of the last plane, which marked the true start of winter. Yet there was also a social sorting as they ate, he noticed: four of the women together in apparent defense against male attention, other females mixed casually with the men; scientists tended to congregate at one table, maintenance personnel at another. Those at Lewis's table made jokes about his pallor. They remembered what arrival was like.

"When do I stop being the fingie?" he asked, knowing full well that no one newer was coming until October.

"When you're so cold that your face is beginning to frostbite, your balls have shriveled to peas, and your hands feel like shovels," Carl Mendoza, an astronomer, told him.

"I think I've got an inside job."

"I know what you do. Wait until you commute to work."

"But you get acclimated, right?"

"You get frozen so many times you're incapable of thaw." Mendoza pointed with his head. "Like our Russian aurora expert."

"What cold?" Alexi Molotov said, reaching for the butter.

"Or when you join the Three Hundred Degree Club," said the medic, Nancy Hodge. She was in her late forties, a thin and once-pretty woman with the kind of lines that suggested she'd seen a little too much of life. Her welcoming smile had a twist to it. No ring, but a white mark where one had been.

"What's that?"

"You'll see."

The others were excited about the fresh food, loud about their plans for the winter, and excited by the new responsibility of being cut off. Lewis picked at his own food but as he tired he realized he couldn't fully share the mood. He was exhausted from his journey, and in his weariness the crowd became cloying and the galley air hot and steamy. His appetite had deserted him and he couldn't concentrate. The plan after the meal, he was told, was to watch *The Thing,* a perennial Polar ritual.

"It is this American movie about an outer space being infecting the bodies of Polar scientists and killing them, one by one," Molotov summarized with relish. "It is very funny. They fight back with guns and flame throwers. Boom! Boom! Yet this"—he held up a butter knife—"is as wicked as it gets at real Pole." He laughed. "Everywhere else in life your body *is* taken over, by bosses, by advertisers, by government, by nagging wife. Here, no."

"Yet you watch it anyway."

"It is, what you call it . . ." He made a squeezing motion on his arm with his fingers.

"Inoculation," Nancy Hodge said.

"Yes! Yes! Inoculation against the fear. The scare of being left here, for the winter. You know? The veterans know all the lines by heart. You will see. It is lots of fun."

But Lewis was so weary he felt in danger of falling into his plate of food. The thought of enduring a movie appalled him. After embarrassing himself twice with dull responses that made him sound like a half-wit, he finally excused himself to bed.

The others nodded without surprise. It took time.

"If you wake up and you are the last one left," Molotov called after him, "don't be surprised. Then you know the outer space being, the creature—it is *you*."

CHAPTER THREE

Lewis's sleep was ragged, his body periodically jerking awake as he gasped for breath. Each time it did so he'd have to roll out of bed to urinate, ridding himself of bloat. By morning his soup can was full and his breathing was easier. He felt his body beginning to adjust, his red blood cells multiplying, but when he went to the galley all he wanted for breakfast was toast and coffee. The maintenance worker sitting next to him looked at his plate with disbelief.

"You'll starve on that bird feed." The man shoved more food into his mouth, talking as he chewed. "George Geller, G.A. I'm serious, you gotta eat more."

Geller was consuming a four-egg ham and cheese omelet, hash browns, two steaks, a bowl of cereal, and three tumblers of orange juice. The gluttony renewed Lewis's nausea.

"How can you hold all that?"

"This? Hell, I still lose weight in the cold. You better have more than that, man. The Pole devours calories. You eat against it."

Lewis put aside the last of his toast. "Not today."

Geller shrugged. "You'll see."

"I'm just not hungry."

"You will be."

Geller attacked his meal with a steady industry, like a steam shovel excavating a foundation. Lewis was half hypnotized by it. "You came here for the food, then."

The maintenance man broke his pace enough to smile. "Pulaski ain't *that* good. I came here to get away from it all. So did everybody."

"The urban stress of turn-of-the-millennium life?"

Geller speared a piece of steak. "The Minnesota stress of a fucked-up marriage, nowhere job, and pressing debt. Same problems as the guys who went with Columbus."

"I've got a Visa balance, too."

"My creditors are a little heavier than that, man." He chewed. "Truth be told, this is the Betty Ford Clinic for me. Cold turkey from the track and cards. I had an affair with Lady Luck and the bitch dumped me, so these loan sharks who looked like the missing link came calling and said highly disturbing things about accumulating interest. Down here they can't reach me. I'll make enough this winter to start over."

Lewis nodded. "You're here for the money."

"Fuckin' A." Geller nodded. "Everybody needs money."

"Is the money good down here? For you guys?"

He shrugged. "Same as a beaker. A long work week and no expenses. The wage scale's no better than back home but it's like forced savings: There's nothing to buy. I might even save enough to *not* go back. Keep my money for myself and chill out on some tropical island. Buy a boat. Who knows?"

Indeed. The Pole offered possibility.

Cameron came into the galley and stood over them, assessing. His air of authority had come back but there was also a hesitant uncertainty to it, Lewis thought, the betraying experimentation of someone new to command, never quite sure how the others would react, still caring what they thought. Cameron was in his late twenties, younger than many of those he supposedly supervised. "How's it hanging?" the station manager asked.

"Didn't freeze," Lewis said.

"You ate?"

"A little."

Cameron looked dubiously at the toast. Fingies. They all had to learn. "All right, then. Looks like you're ready to see the homestead. Let's saddle up."

"Yippie-ki-yay."

Suiting up to go outdoors was as laborious as donning armor. Heavy long underwear and two pairs of socks. Sweater. Fleece vest, pants, and insulated nylon bib overalls. Neck gaiter, goggles, stocking hat, white plastic "bunny" boots, glove liners, mittens, ski gloves in case dexterity was required, and finally down parka with hood. Lewis felt as padded as the Michelin Man and awkward as an astronaut. He was roasting.

"Up to a point, there's no such thing as cold," the station manager said. "Just inadequate clothing."

"Up to a point?"

"If you put too much on when you're working you can actually sweat," Cameron said. "That's dangerous when you cool down, or because of dehydration. At the other extreme, nothing will keep you warm when the wind comes up."

"What do you do then?"

"Tough it out. Up to a point."

"I can't walk in these things." Lewis pointed to his boots, inflated with air for insulation. They looked like white melons.

"You'd be walking on frostbitten stubs without them. Dorky, but they work."

Lewis clumped along the floor. "Like wearing weights."

"One year some pranksters started pouring sand into a guy's bunnies where the air goes. Little bit each day. By the end of the season they weighed about seventy pounds. Pretty funny."

Lewis shook a boot, listening. "Ha."

Stepping out of the berthing unit into the gray light of the dome was like stepping into a freezer. Lewis was jarred again at the nearness of such cold, just outside the door. The icicles hung overhead from the dome as before. And yet he was so hot from the dressing that the change felt good at first. Refreshing.

The snow ramp from the dome exit led upward to the plateau surface and a bright cold that was more telling. This was a chill that wasn't confined to an enclosure but was the single salient fact of his new world. He stood a moment, letting himself adjust. The sky was overcast, the light flat. Even with a mild breeze he could feel the temperature sucking at him, trying to drain him of heat. The cold got into his lungs and palpated his heart.

He pulled his gaiter over his nose and mouth, the moisture of his breath immediately starting a growth of frost. Goggles shielded his eyes and forehead. His hood kept a thin cocoon of slightly warmer air near his face. He took a moment to practice breathing, as if he were underwater.

Okay. He wasn't going to die.

Lewis looked around. The snow was flat and, beyond

the cluster of human structures, utterly empty. Nothing moved. There was no natural feature to catch the eye.

"First of all, stay close to the base," Cameron lectured, leaving his neck gaiter down so he could be heard clearly. "Even when it's not snowing the wind can kick up surface powder into a blizzard six or seven feet high. The blowing snow is just high enough to put any human who isn't in the NBA into whiteout conditions. So, if you do go somewhere, sign out, take a radio, and take some bearings. Pay attention to where you are, where we are. Start memorizing the layout. People have died in Antarctica a dozen feet from shelter. Temperatures can drop fifty degrees in ten minutes."

Lewis nodded.

"Second, we're marking the most frequently used routes with flags." He pointed to long poles with pennants on the end. "In the dark that's coming you just follow one flag to another to get back to a building. One route goes to astronomy, which the beakers call the Dark Sector because lights aren't allowed out there: It screws up their telescopes. Everyone else calls it the Dark Side. Another goes to Clean Air, where you'll work. It's away from the generators and any air pollution. A third goes to Summer Camp, which is shut down now." He pointed at distant buildings. Summer Camp was a row of Korean-War-vintage canvas Quonset huts. "A branch goes to Bedrock, those little blue huts there. That's our emergency shelter if anything goes wrong in the dome."

"Goes wrong?"

"Fire. Generator failure. Battery explosions. Well poisonings. The usual." He smiled.

Cameron also pointed out antenna towers, telescopes, construction materials, supply crates, drifted-over vehicles,

and random jetsam, everything raw and jutting from the
snow like the debris of some midair collision. Lewis thought
the place looked like a dump but wasn't surprised. All the
treeless places he'd worked in had the same look: Where
could you hide the mess? The chaos represented logistical
evolution.

"Third, pay attention to your body. It's sort of like being
an astronaut where you pay attention to your air. Are you
staying warm? Are you still alert? Are you losing energy?
If you start to feel frozen, get back inside for a while.
Capisce?"

"Yeah. Common sense."

"You'd be amazed how quickly that can disappear around
here."

Lewis looked out at the foggy horizon. "How far can
we see?"

"About six miles, three in each direction. A few more if
you get up on a tower."

The sun was low, a white disk behind fog like a dim
headlight. It circled the horizon every twenty-four hours,
each day settling lower, like a marble rolling down a fun-
nel. On March 21 it would be gone.

"You been to The Ice before, Rod?"

"Four times."

"So you like it."

"I love it."

"Even the Pole?"

"Especially the Pole. It's like no place else on earth.
Come on, I'll show you."

They started walking toward the astronomy complex that
squatted three-quarters of a mile away, crossing the ice taxiway. Just beyond was a stake jutting two feet out of the
snow.

"Here it is. Go ahead, walk around the world."

"This is the South Pole?"

"Yep. Bottom of the planet. When it gets dark I come out here sometimes on a clear night and lay down to watch the stars and the aurora. Sometimes I do feel upside down, like I'm about to float off and drift into the sky. It's spectacularly beautiful then, and the vertigo makes me high."

"I thought the Pole would look like something more."

"In summer there's a ceremonial pole over there." Cameron pointed vaguely. "We took it down for the winter a couple weeks ago. It looks like a Santa Claus pole— you know, with barber stripes and a silver globe on top? We put the flags of the Antarctic treaty nations around it and the VIPs who fly in for a few hours pose for pictures. But this stake is the real pole. The ice cap moves, flowing toward the sea, so every January we have to drive a stake about ten meters from the last one to keep pace." He pointed out a line of older stakes marching away across the snow, marking where the Pole had been. "Eventually the dome will roll right over it, except maybe we can win funding for the new base and the dome will be dismantled."

"Everybody needs money," Lewis recited. He trod a circle around the stake. "Around the world. I read that Admiral Byrd said it was the middle of a limitless plain. You get here, and that's all. He said it was the effort to get here that counted."

"That, and getting away. But Byrd said that back in the 1920s, way before the base started in '58. Nowadays it's the staying that counts. We're here for a purpose. Your job is important. Mine is important. They're all important. Scientifically. Politically. We're at a place that no single nation owns, dedicated to knowledge. I think that's pretty cool."

"Cool." Lewis brushed the frost on the ruff of his hood.

"You know why people like it down here, Jed?" Cameron was looking directly at him, but with the goggles on the effect was odd, like being looked at by an insect.

"Why?"

"Because the purpose of life is to *learn*. That's why we exist, to learn. That's my belief, anyway. That's why the station exists. Moss and Adams and Mendoza have the world's best window on space. Jerry Follett and Dana Andrews are deciphering the atmosphere. Hiro and Alexi are trying to understand the aurora, which is one hell of a show. You do climate, Lena hydroponics . . . it doesn't get any purer than this."

The hood against Lewis's ears made everything like listening through a blanket. "So how do we tell direction down here?"

"We make our own grid. The Greenwich Meridian is grid north; the opposite way south. Mostly, though, we point. There's nowhere to go, so it's like being on a small island. Disneyland. Come on, let's go see where you'll work."

They trudged toward the Clean Air Facility, a brown metal box a half mile from the Pole. It was elevated on stilts and festooned with instruments and antennas. As they walked, Lewis felt as if he'd gained a hundred pounds. His feet felt hot and heavy and his lungs were unhappy with air that remained too thin, too dry, too cold. His neck gaiter had become a muffler of ice, scratchy and smothering. He swatted at it, breaking some bits loose, but more clung to the fabric. At the same time he realized he was sweating.

The snow squeaked as they walked, dry and powdery, a

loose coverlet on harder blue-white ice. Wind blew this skin into small, shin-high drifts that Cameron called sastrugi. "Alexi says it's the Russian word for eyebrows." It was laborious to lumber over or through them.

"What's his story?"

"There's no money in Russia. He's one of the top aurora experts in the world. So we gave him a posting here."

"He said he liked that movie *The Thing*."

"I think there's something in that film that gets to our ex-Commie. The fact that no one can trust anyone. I think he was into some pretty heavy science politics in the old Soviet. Down deep he's pretty serious, you know, kind of quietly ambitious. He'd love to accomplish something down here to bring credit to Mother Russia. Point of pride to bring out something new. But he's also a lot of fun. So's Hiro."

"They the only foreigners?"

"Dana's a Kiwi and Lena emigrated from the Czech Republic, but nobody's a foreigner, not down here. Antarctica is the only place on earth where you don't need a passport and you don't go through customs. No single nation owns anything. That's pretty cool, too."

There was the distant chug of the generator but no other sound. No bird call, no rustling leaves, no distant shout of children, no drone of highway noise. Lewis pushed back his hood and pulled down his gaiter a moment to listen, ignoring the bite of cold, his exhalation a puff of steam.

There was a quiet whisper behind him.

He turned his head. No one there.

They kept walking, puffing over the drifts.

Again the whisper.

Lewis turned completely this time. Odd. The snow was empty. What the hell?

The station manager was watching him with amusement.

"I thought I heard something."

"It's your breath, fingie. The moisture freezes as you walk and crackles behind your ear as it sprinkles down. Weird, isn't it?"

"My breath?"

"The vapor cloud."

"Oh." He puffed and listened as his exhalation floated away like fairy dust, with an audible crinkle. "You notice the noise," he conceded. "There's nothing else to hear."

"Just the voices in your head."

An outside metal staircase led up to the Clean Air Facility, perched on its columns like a heavy bird. Inside were instruments he'd been briefed on at Boulder by NOAA. Windows looked out at the flat bleakness of the ice cap. The elevated structure was here because air at the South Pole was thousands of miles from human industry, and hence the most unpolluted on earth. Lewis's primary job was to sample that air for evidence of global warming. He actually had to keep track of thirty-five separate measurements, some of them automated and some requiring manual sampling of air, snow, sunlight, and atmospheric ozone: temperature, carbon dioxide concentrations, wind, snowfall, pollutants, barometric pressure. *My job is important.* If the planet was heating, it would perversely show up here first, just like the ozone hole had. If their ice plateau melted, it would drown the world's ports. Antarctica was a global trip wire, warning humans if industrialization had gone too far. Jed Lewis was this winter's Paul Revere.

"Kind of cozy," he commented. Indeed, the elevated building felt like a tree house. A boy's fort.

"You've got good duty," Cameron said. "Your job forces

you to get outside each day so you don't become a dome slug, and you get some privacy and independence out here. It's the closest thing to a vacation condo this side of the KitKat Club."

"The what?"

"An old balloon-launching shack. We don't need it anymore because the balloons have gotten smaller and lighter. A carpenter turned it into a getaway pad with carpeting, heat, stereo, and VCR TV. Since then it's seen more consummations than Niagara Falls. Not that we station managers approve, of course."

"There's a lot of nooks and crannies to this place, aren't there?"

"Oh yes indeedy."

"And this building is a rendezvous as well?"

"People come out to Clean Air sometimes to break the monotony and party. Carl Mendoza is promising to cook up some dome-brew."

"He'd better not spill beer on my instruments."

"Nah, they spill it over here." The station manager walked out on the platform ringing the building and pointed downward to a yellow-stained cleft in the snow. "Our Grand Canyon is the pee crevasse. It's a long run to the john in the dome so guys just piss over the rail here. It's quite a sensation when the wind's blowing."

"Clean air, dirty snow?"

"We don't take our drinking water from here, needless to say. Storms cover up the evidence each winter."

"What do women do?"

Cameron laughed. "Who knows what women do?"

"You certainly don't," a female voice said.

They turned. A young woman about Lewis's age was standing in the doorway, nylon windpants over her legs but

her feet in wool socks and her upper half clad only in long
underwear, which showed some nice shape to her. She was
holding a screwdriver and seemed oblivious to the cold.

"We look for a leafy bush," she confided to Lewis. The
closest one was two thousand miles away.

"Hello, Abby," Cameron said.

"Hello, pig," she replied pleasantly.

"You were hiding under one of your computers."

"I was getting our planned obsolescence ready for our
newcomer." She looked at Lewis. "Please pay no attention
to Ice Pick. He's flunked every chance at being a New Age
sensitive type of guy since assuming his exalted post and
all the women on station are preparing a lawsuit against
him. Or maybe just ritual castration."

"Hey, I'm sensitive. And I like women."

"Exactly the problem."

Cameron made the introduction. "This is Abby Dixon,
our resident computer nerd. Abby, Jed Lewis, our new
weatherman."

They stepped inside and Lewis shed his mittens to shake.
She had long, slim fingers and a firm grip. Her hair was
short and dark, her features tomboy pretty, her smile wide
and welcoming. Not bad.

"I didn't see you at dinner," he said.

"Sometimes I eat on the job. Especially when we have
fruit. An apple, a PC, and me. Heaven."

"You don't miss our companionship?"

"Machines are good company. Especially compared to
some of the alternatives." She cast a mischievous glance
at Cameron.

"Abby's an elusive one," the station manager said. "Pretends to have some geek boyfriend stashed elsewhere in

Antarctica. Our isolation and my charm, however, are breaking down her reserve."

"I'm positively gregarious compared to Jerry," she told Lewis. "Jerry Follett. You'll work with him, too. His idea of small talk is atmospheric dynamics. He'll want some help launching his balloons but he's loud as a mollusk. Don't be put off by it."

"So you work out here, too?"

"Just when you need me. I heard you'd arrived and thought I'd better get the busted one up and running. It's been on my list after your predecessor broke it."

"I hope he didn't spill beer," Lewis said.

"Probably threw up on it. Had a tough time with the altitude." She turned to Cameron. "So, we going to name this guy Snowman, too? He's collecting it."

"No, everyone needs their own nickname. Polar tradition," he explained to Lewis. "I'm Ice Pick, because I can be a prick when I have to be."

"He's just fussy," Abby said. "Picky. He fails at being mean."

"I'm just nuts from coping with twenty-five other eccentrics in a place that demands conformity. Everyone wants to make their careers in six months and solve their life problems while they're at it. When they don't, it's the station manager's fault."

"Maybe we should call you picked-upon," Abby teased.

"Picked apart, anyway. Cotton-pickin' crazy. Now." He considered Lewis. "Abby's Gearloose, for her vast technical skills. And you are . . . maybe . . . Krill."

She laughed. "Oh dear!"

"Krill? What does that mean?"

"Zooplankton," Cameron replied smoothly. "A tiny, translucent shrimp that makes up much of the marine biomass off Antarctica. Vital to the ecosystem."

"I look like a shrimp?"

"It's worse than that," Abby said. "He means you're at the bottom of the food chain. The new guy."

"The fingie," Cameron said cheerfully. "Nobody newer for eight toasty months."

"I don't think so," Lewis said slowly. "How about something flattering?"

"Not allowed," the station manager said.

"What about the grumpy shower guy? Tyson? What's *his* nickname?"

"Buck to his face, because he's big and into knives. But we spell it with an *F* behind his back."

"And Island," Abby said. "As in, 'No man is'? Every winter there's one guy so weird that he runs the danger of being ostracized. Tyson seems to crave the honor."

"Not me. *I* came down to get along." Embarrassingly, his stomach chose that moment to growl. As Geller had predicted, he was hungry, fiercely hungry. "And eat."

Abby took pity. "Don't think you *look* like a shrimp."

"Thanks. I am almost six feet." His stomach rumbled again.

"In fact, aside from his rude noises, I'd call him an Antarctic Ten." She smiled slyly, head tilted judiciously. They were still making fun.

"A what?"

"An Antarctic Ten is a member of the opposite sex who'd be a Five anywhere else," Cameron explained.

"Ah. Very flattering. Great."

"We all look better and better as the months drag on."

"Terrific."

"You *could* be a Six." Abby winked. "The women will have to vote."

"I'll look forward to that."

"But Krill is too cruel for him, Rod. He's right. Maybe Ozone."

"Maybe Sediment. He *is* a rockhead."

"A what?" she asked.

"Geologist. Running from rocks."

"Rolling Stone, then."

Lewis shook his head. He'd have to find his own name. *And if I could make Six, you could be an Eight,* he judged, watching Abby laugh. *Even a Nine after a few months at the Pole.* Things were looking up.

A telephone rang and Cameron answered it. "Hello. . . . Yeah, he's here." A pause. "Okay, Mickey. . . . Right, I'll tell him." He hung up.

"Who was that?" Lewis asked.

"Our estimable astrophysicist, Michael M. Moss. Pooh-bah of the Pole. He'd like you to come by astronomy later today." He pointed to the other building on stilts, three-quarters of a mile away. "You can do that?"

"After lunch." His stomach growled again.

Cameron was looking at Lewis curiously. "Mickey usually isn't this welcoming. He can't remember half the names on the base. But he asked for you."

"I'm flattered."

"It's interesting that he'd want to see you so soon."

"Maybe he likes fingies."

Cameron shook his head. "No, he doesn't. He's a snob."

"Well," Lewis said, enjoying finally knowing something the others didn't, "maybe he likes geologists."

CHAPTER FOUR

N ine-tenths of the universe is missing, Lewis. My job is to find it."

Michael M. "Mickey" Moss leaned back in his desk chair in the astronomy building and waited to be asked for clarification, his hands making a tent in front of an expression both regal and watchful. Despite a Disney nickname that had dogged him from grade school—or perhaps because of it, in compensation—Moss looked nothing like a cartoon. He instead maintained an Aristotelian aura with his mane of white hair and beard, raw pink skin, and eyes both bright with intelligence and as dark as obsidian marbles. Lewis was sure the look had been cultivated: Moss was the kind of scientist who could command the lectern of an academic gathering on appearance alone.

"I wasn't aware we'd misplaced the universe," Lewis said on cue, playing straight man to the lecture. Moss would get to the point of this visit in his own good time.

"Exactly! Exactly the problem!" The scientist bounded out of his seat and theatrically pointed toward the ceiling. "People marvel at the sky. All those stars! And yet those trillions of suns represent only a tiny fraction of the matter that has to be out there, judging from the rotational speed and placement of galaxies. There should be ten times as much stuff. A hundred times, maybe. So—what else? Dim stars? Dark planets? Or something we don't even suspect? That's what we're looking for." He pointed at the floor. "Down there." He smiled as if posing a riddle.

"Sparco told me you're building a telescope in the ice."

Moss looked mildly disappointed at this shortcut in his lecture. "You're familiar with neutrinos?"

"Never seen one."

The astrophysicist nodded wryly. "Precisely. Far smaller than an atom. So small that billions are passing through our bodies right at this moment without effect. So small that a neutrino can pass through the entire planet without hitting anything. The most inconsequential objects imaginable. Chargeless. Massless. Yet what if they *do* have mass, however slight? There are so many of them they could represent a substantial fraction of our missing universe. If we could find and count them and tell where they come from, it would bring us a lot of information. It's the finding that's the problem."

"Which you've done."

"Which we're in the process of doing. Statistically, a very few neutrinos do collide with the particles of an atom as they streak through the earth. When this happens there's a tiny explosion of sorts, a spark, a kind of radiation—a point of light, if you will. We can't see these flashes in rock. But sensitive instruments can see them in transparent mediums such as tanks of water. Or, ice."

"Ta-da," Lewis said.

"Drill holes deep enough and the ice becomes so compressed that all the bubbles and color are squeezed out of it. Ice becomes clearer than glass. Clear as diamond. Instruments can detect these flashes for a thousand feet in all directions. We've drilled holes a mile deep to spot neutrino light. It's the best place in the world, really. If it works. If it works."

"There's been problems."

"No! Not problems. Scientific realities. Impatience by funding agencies. Because they have no idea of the conditions down here. No idea! I'm staying this winter to try to keep things on schedule. Because we might find something so unexpected that it changes all our understanding of gravity, matter, energy . . ."

"You *did* find something unexpected."

"Yes." Again, Moss resented the prompting. "As a by-product of a lifelong search. A search *here,* at the harshest place on earth."

"The Pole is pretty awesome."

"You're privileged to be here. Men have been trying to decipher the heavens since Babylonian priests climbed their ziggurats. Like pilgrims and holy men, they've gone to the mountaintops. Now they've come to the farthest mountaintop, the South Pole. The farthest place! After this, the next ziggurat is space!"

"And you *have* something from space." Lewis was trying to be polite but he was growing impatient to see what he'd been sent for.

"Yes." Moss gave up on his preamble. "You have some expertise?"

"A little from college. I'm not kidding myself about why Jim Sparco picked me. I wasn't the best, I was convenient and unemployed. I was interested in his research. And he thought I was principled, which meant he thought I could keep my mouth shut."

"Yes, I'm interested in your principles." Moss studied him. "You've signed on to look for global warming, correct?"

"As part of the weather readings."

"And yet you're a petroleum geologist, right?"

"I was."

"Which *contributes* to global warming."

"Maybe."

"No maybe about it."

"Oil also keeps us alive down here. So *you* can find the universe."

"Conceded."

"Besides which, I quit."

"Yes, that intrigues me. Sparco told me the story when I e-mailed him about my rock. I'm sure Big Oil paid well. So you've made an interesting choice, haven't you? Everyone comes to the Pole for something."

"I came to help out. I came to work for the good guys. If I make some small contribution toward your discovery, I'm excited."

Moss nodded. "Fair enough. Fair enough." The idea of a fingie wanting a piece of Michael Moss's reflected glory obviously pleased him. Made sense to him. "I admire your dedication. Someday your help may be credited. In the meantime, however, the need for discretion, as you said, is paramount. No one knows of this discovery. No one *will* know, until I choose to tell them. Agreed?"

Lewis nodded. It's what Sparco had told him to expect.

"I haven't decided what to do with it," Moss explained. He nodded again.

Slowly, the scientist stood up, moved to a file cabinet, and opened a drawer. "It's interesting how compelling a rock becomes in a place that doesn't have any. I've touched this thing a thousand times. Wondered where it came from. What might be inside." He lifted his arm, hefting a dull brown rock the size and shape of a large, lumpy baking potato. "It's remarkably ugly."

Lewis took the stone, dense and heavy. Eight, ten pounds. The rock was burnt and glassy on one side. *My God.* "How many people know about this?" he asked.

"No one, really. I confided in Sparco because we've spent so much time down here together. He persuaded me this might represent a life-changing opportunity. But I couldn't risk even transmitting a picture of it on the Internet. It was he who suggested finding someone like you to make an initial judgment. I think he'd already met you, at Toolik Lake. Fortuitous, no?"

"And you found it . . ."

"A few months ago, when drilling Hole 18-b. Just happened to strike it. Dumb luck, I admit. About a thousand years down as measured in layers of snowfall."

"And thought it might be a meteorite . . ."

"Because why else is there a rock in the ice cap? If there's a stone at the Pole, it has to have come from the sky."

Lewis nodded, looking at the tarlike crust. Evidence of heat from a fall through the atmosphere. Which meant . . .

He looked at Moss.

The astronomer was watching him expectantly. "Well?"

"Superficially, at least, it fits." Lewis set it carefully on some papers on a desk.

"Then you think it's from space?"

"Probably." He paused, considering what to say. "As you said, the fact that there's thousands of feet of ice between this and bedrock suggests it fell from the sky. That's why Antarctica has become a prime hunting ground for meteorites of all kinds. They stick out like a sore thumb. But all the others have been found on the surface around the Trans-Antarctic Range, where flowing ice hits the mountain barrier and breaks upward to carry buried meteorites to the surface. The wind blows the last snow away. To strike a buried one with your drilling is pretty lucky. Amazingly lucky."

"It could have been salted by some joker, I suppose," Moss conceded. "Dropped down the hole when I wasn't looking. But why? No one has confessed and it looked like the real thing to me. We use hot water to melt holes in the ice, drilling downward with what amounts to a big shower head. A camera showed something was sticking into one side of our tube. I gave the crew a break, paused to melt a bulb of water to free it, and then hauled it up."

"And kept quiet about your find."

"I wanted to be sure."

"You understand I'm no expert?"

"You're as close as we could find, at short notice, to come down here like this."

"Yes. And, as Sparco suspected, I don't think this is your average meteorite. Have you noticed it's basaltic?"

"I've noticed it's plain."

"Exactly," said Lewis, now the lecturer. In geology he wasn't the fingie. "Compared to many of the metallic meteorites, this looks boring to us. Ordinary. That's because it's a common kind of rock found on earth but a rare kind to come from space. Most meteorites have more iron and nickel. They date from the dawn of the solar system. This one came later in history, after the place of its origin had experienced some kind of heating and melting and igneous rock had formed, like the earth's crust."

Moss was nodding. He was eager for confirmation.

"That suggests it didn't come from the usual source like asteroids or comets," Lewis went on. "It probably came from the moon. Or Mars. Blasted into space eons ago after a bigger meteorite, maybe a mile across, slammed into the red planet. Ejected and captured by earth's gravity like the one they found in the Allan Hills, the famous one they thought might have fossil evidence of Martian microbes."

Moss allowed himself a hint of eagerness. "Could this one have fossils inside?"

"There's been no agreement they exist in the other one. But this kind of meteorite is rare and even the remotest possibility makes it pretty valuable. We can't be sure what this is at all, of course—not with me. I don't have the instruments and I don't have the expertise. The way they confirmed things in Houston was by analyzing ancient gas trapped in the meteorite and finding it matched the Martian atmosphere."

"It may not be Martian at all," Moss allowed. He wanted more hope.

"No. Only sixteen have been found worldwide. But . . . it looks possible to me," Lewis gave him. "An achondrite, the kind of meteorite that would come from a planet or the moon. Sparco says you have a spectroscope down here and I brought some stuff to reduce a sample for a gas-spectrum analysis. I can also slice a small cross section and look at its composition under the microscope. I'll test for oxygen and oxidized iron isotopes. Check its magnetism, which indicates how much ferric iron. If it's a simple plagioclase-pyroxene basalt, or maybe olivine, it will be promising. Radioactive dating of a young age will persuade even more. We'll need some photos and a statement to authenticate its place of origin. And then you take it to Houston, or wherever."

Moss nodded, watching him. "Yes. Wherever." He hesitated. "Jim told me I could trust another question to you."

Lewis had been waiting for this. "Its commercial value?" This opinion was Sparco's price for his being allowed to come down here. He was to assess, and then keep his mouth shut. He'd wanted purpose, and this was his ticket.

"As another measure of its importance."

"Private collection of scientific artifacts is booming," Lewis said. "Having a living-room museum has become cool among the ultra-rich. The mere possibility this could be from Mars will be enough for some buyers. The chance it could hold evidence of extraterrestrial life trumps all. That rock could be worth a lot of money."

"How much money?"

Lewis had researched this. "Pieces of Mars have sold for twenty-five hundred dollars a gram."

"Which makes this rock worth . . ."

"Several million dollars."

Moss nodded solemnly.

"Pieces of the moon are even rarer and have fetched ten times that. The Apollo rocks turned out to be from a concentrated region of unusually high radioactivity, so lunar meteorites tell us more about the moon than what the astronauts brought back. They've fetched twenty-five hundred times the price of gold."

"Astonishing," Moss said. He didn't seem very astonished.

"But everything here is the property of the American government, right?"

"If they know about it," the scientist said, looking evenly at Lewis.

"It's an American base. American taxpayer dollars." No

one was allowed to hunt for souvenirs in Antarctica, Lewis knew. They told you that up front.

"Is it?" Moss asked. "To you, just stepping off the plane, looking at that ragged flag, I suppose it is. But to me . . ." The scientist pointed to the wall above his desk. It was papered with pictures of himself with a stream of celebrities: visiting congressmen, presidential science advisors, adventurers, network anchors, movie stars, foreign dignitaries. Mickey Moss as polar landlord. "It's not American land. Not American ice. It's nobody's ice, except the people willing to come down here and pioneer it."

"And you pioneered it."

"Exactly."

"But at government expense, right?"

"At personal sacrifice!" Moss took a breath. "Listen, young man, I know I look like an old egghead to you, sitting here in my warm office, surrounded by vinyl and plastic. But I was doing science down here when you were sucking at your mother's tit. I was doing science when we slept in plywood barracks and ate out of tin cans and didn't get a letter or a radio call for months at a time. I did science until I was frostbitten so bad that when I came back inside it felt like my face was being held to a hot iron."

"I understand."

"No, you don't. You can't. No one can who didn't do it. And I gave the testimony that helped build this building. I dragged the Washington bureaucrats down here kicking and screaming and got them to see that this place—*this* godforsaken place—was the best place for certain kinds of science in the entire world. The Pole was the ringside seat when that comet plowed into Jupiter in 1994. It's going to help us remap the universe, decipher our magnetic field, understand our atmosphere. We've got telescopes out in the snow that can see in half a dozen ways the human eye is blind to. Because for half the year the sun never sets and for the other half we have a constant dark sky. Because I, Mickey Moss, showed them the way."

"I think everyone respects that."

"Do they?"

"Sure."

"I used to think respect was enough." He sat down, looking at the rock.

"They'll probably name something for you."

"When I'm dead." He picked up the meteorite. "They scoff at me now, you know. Geezer Mouse. Don't think I don't know."

"They're jealous. Academic rivalry."

"They don't understand my project has to have priority. Priority! To justify the Pole. To justify the new South Pole station."

Lewis waited.

"I'm just saying that I've paid my dues."

"I'm not arguing, Doctor Moss."

The scientist turned the meteorite over in his hands. "I've made no decisions," he said softly. "It's just that I'm getting old. I had to fudge my medical exam to get down here last time. I don't have endless time anymore. I haven't put a lot away. My family . . ." He glanced up. "Are you surprised to find me human, Lewis?"

"No." Lewis shifted uncomfortably. He *was* surprised, actually. It didn't fit his stereotype of a grand old man of science. "It's just that Jim Sparco wanted a rough evaluation. He didn't talk about keeping it."

"Nor have I! Nor have I." He looked at Lewis warily. "Don't jump to conclusions. Don't start rumors that aren't true. I've got a reputation, and in the end a reputation is all a scientist has. Thirty *years* in this place, and that's all I have. And then at the end a missive from space, a stroke of luck. . . . Why?"

Lewis couldn't answer.

"Well. The first step was to get your opinion, correct? Now we've got some thinking to do. What's best? What's right? What's fair? That's always the question, isn't it?"

"The unanswerable one, sometimes."

"Yet you must choose an answer." Moss stood and put the rock back in his filing cabinet. "The funny thing is, there're almost no locks on this base. That's why you can't breathe a word of this to anyone."

"Don't you want to kick this around with the other scientists?"

"No." He looked depressed. "Word would leak, misinterpretations would be made. They're jealous, like you said. They'd use this against me."

"I could be wrong about the meteorite, you know."

"I understand that."

"It really needs some tests."

"Of course. But in the meantime I'm going to put this where others won't find it." He looked intently at the young geologist. "And then decide the right thing to do."

CHAPTER FIVE

Jed Lewis had a theory about life. Life was hard. Complicated. Life was a long, meandering slog up a very steep mountain and if you didn't have good friends to help point out the way, it was pretty easy to choose the wrong path sometimes. (Lewis didn't think Mickey Moss had many friends, just admirers. Rivals.) And even after choosing, you could go miles, years, before knowing whether your path was wrong or right. Moreover, everybody had their own route and their own schedule. So Jed was slow to judge how people made it up the slope. You didn't know where they were coming from. Couldn't know, as Moss had said. Didn't know where they were going. Lewis had examined the meteorite and would probably test it, but the fate of the rock was really none of his concern. Let the old scientist make his own lonely way up the peak.

Lewis himself was tired of being alone.

By the time he got back to the dome he was ravenous again. Geller was right: The polar cold almost snatched food out of your mouth. When Lewis yanked open the freezer door and stepped into the galley vestibule, he was salivating.

The galley was crowded and a table of beakers was almost full. Lewis, curious to sample the station's social spectrum, decided to sit with some of the support staff who kept the place running. He plopped next to Geller, who was working on another mountain of food. Next to him was a smaller, quiet, mouselike man he'd noticed earlier, keeping his head down as he ate.

"A beaker joins the rabble," Geller greeted.

"Just trying to meet everyone."

"And your appetite's improved." He nodded at Lewis's tray. Stroganoff, fresh green beans, cobbler, all heaped high. Pulaski and Linda Brown could cook.

"I was on tour. The cold really burns up your reserves."

"That ain't cold. Sitting out eight hours in the wind trying to fix equipment some moron beaker busted—*that's* cold."

"Are there always no scientists at this table?" Lewis asked.

"Mostly. We get along great but they tend to eat with their own, we tend to eat with our own. They bitch about us, we bitch about them. Works better that way."

"I thought segregation was against the law."

"It ain't segregation, it's fucking high school." It was the growl of a new voice and Lewis looked up. The grump from the shower, Tyson. He sat heavily, spreading his arms and legs to claim a substantial portion of the table. His manner was one of fingie instructor. A heavily muscled forearm boasting a tattooed snake pulled his tray against his torso. A fork was held upright in his other fist like a flagstaff. He'd unconsciously made a tiny fort of his food. "Like the jocks and the nerds, remember? We got more cliques here than Hot Pants High."

"I think you're exaggerating a little, Buck," Geller said mildly.

"The hell I am. You got us, and you got the beakers, and you got the smokers, and you got the singles, and you got the women. The science side is all rank and show-off, with know-it-alls like Mickey Moss lording it over grad students and postdocs. And then even the tweezer twits get snobby when they want something done."

"Yeah, but everyone gets along. Better than anyplace I've ever been."

"We *gotta* get along, or we fucking *die*. But that don't mean people don't cluster with their own. Look around this room. Planet of the Apes, man. We're monkeys." The phrase jogged a memory. Hadn't Norse said something similar?

"Buck Tyson, resident sociologist," Geller introduced.

"Yeah, me and our new shrink." He nodded to Lewis.

"We met at the shower."

"Yeah, I remember. That wasn't about you. That was about Ice Prick."

Not exactly an apology, but not hostile, either. Maybe Tyson was okay. "You like to analyze?"

"I just see things like they really are. My day job is master mechanic. I make our go-carts go. You need a snow Spryte, a D-6 Cat, you come to Buck Tyson. But at night I think about our loony bin. Me thinking for myself makes some of the beakers nervous. You nervous?"

How to respond to that? "You like Doctor Bob?" Lewis deflected.

"I like where he's coming from. I like that he stays in shape. I talked to him already and I think he sees through the bullshit like I do. We're into the same shit: self-reliance. The importance of Numero Uno and thinking for yourself. He's got all these ideas from NASA about whether this place suggests what you need to make starship troopers. It's cool, what he's trying to do. Not the touchy-feely crap of the other shrinks that come down to The Ice." He turned to Geller. "You know what they did to a shrink at Vanda, over in the Dry Valleys?"

"No, what?"

"Ran over his gear with a tractor." Tyson laughed.

There was a silence, the others digesting this.

"I guess Buck is your nickname," Lewis finally said. "What's your real name?"

"James," Geller quickly interjected.

"Jimmy, you dumb fuck. You know I hate James. English faggot name."

"James Bond ain't a faggot."

"James Bond is the biggest goddamned English pansy there is! He carries a girl's gun and dresses like a fucking bridegroom! I like big guns, and big guys. I like guys who go it alone and kick butt. Like Clint Eastwood. And John Wayne. And Bruce Willis. And Rambo. And Ahhhnold. Except *he* married the fucking Kennedys."

"Everyone calls Tyson Buck because he's into knives," Geller explained. "And guns. And commando crap. And every other bit of militia weirdness."

"No, I'm not. I'm into *sufficiency,* which is more than a little important way down here." Tyson pointed his fork at Lewis. "Don't take this 'all for one and one for all' crap too seriously because when it's dark and blowing and people are freaking out, you gotta know how to take care of yourself. Right? The government likes to jabber on about our happy little commune, but in fact it's just a bunch of fucked-up overachievers. They may have a doctorate, but they manage to bring down every goddamn neurosis there is."

"Buck doesn't like people," Geller summarized.

"That's not true. I'm eating with you assholes. I even like some of the beakers like crazy Alexi, our Russian cocktail. He tells it like it is, 'cause he's out of the gulag, man. Hiro's kind of funny, like a Jap cartoon. But some of them are humorless know-it-alls, like Harrison Adams. *Harrison.* Not just Harry. Pompous twit. Or weirdos like Jerry Follett. I watch my backside around that faggot. Or Mickey Mouse out there in the Dark Side. Our head rodent needs his ears pinned."

"You're talking about Saint Michael," Geller said with humor.

"Pope Moss can kiss my you-know-what." Tyson turned to the other man at their table, who'd been eating silently, and clapped him on the shoulder. "The one you want to stay friends with is this guy, who runs the power plant. We try to keep *him* sober and sane."

The small man looked up like a blinking mole. He was balding, with pinched features and a brushy mustache. "Pika," he mumbled as introduction.

"What?" Lewis hadn't understood.

"Pika," Geller said. "Like the animal."

"What's a pika?"

"Sort of a rock rabbit," Tyson explained. "No one can stand to hang around with Pika 'cause he whistles while he works, like those dwarves. Remember them? Drives us all nuts, like Muzak. His real name is Doug Taylor but we call him Pika, which is sort of like a marmot. Critter that whistles?"

Lewis slowly nodded. "Got it."

"Pikas sort of squeak," Geller said. "But we liked the sound of the word."

"Makes sense to me."

"See, Mickey Moss can collect all the medals he wants to but what it comes down to is the guys like Pika," Tyson said. "We're at the outer edge of the envelope down here. They don't like to tell us that, but it's true. The generators stop, and we're dead. The well gets fucked up, and we're dead. A good fire gets started, and we're dead. This place is the easiest place in the world to sabotage. Any of us could kill all of us in about three nanoseconds. And then they send down a shrink? How does *that* make you feel?"

Lewis tried to smile. "That I better stay friends with Pika."

"You better believe it. Some idiot shut off the heat the other day. It was this little guy who got it back on." Tyson nodded in approval.

"Don't touch my machines," the small man mumbled. He didn't look at Lewis, just mildly kept eating his food.

Lewis wondered what his story was. "Okay."

"Just leave my machines alone."

It was quiet for a moment.

"So you're the new weather dude, correct?" Tyson finally asked.

"Yeah."

"So how do you like the magic kingdom?"

"It's pretty interesting."

"Damn right it's interesting. Absolutely fucking fascinating. For about three days." Tyson snorted. "After that, it's *Groundhog Day.* You seen that movie, where they repeat the same day over and over?"

"I've seen it."

"That's winter at the Pole."

"Don't listen to Buck too much," Geller said. "He whines like a mosquito."

"I *whine* because that fucker *Cameron,* and the bureaucrats he *fronts* for, won't get off my back. Have you seen our work schedule? Do this, do that, blah blah blah: More work on that list than you could do in three winters! Give me a fucking break. They're just showing off."

"Buck believes the world is out to get him," Geller interpreted.

"Screw you. It *is* out to get me."

"Carries a chip like a cross."

"I carry the station, man. I do the shit. You know how many people work here?" he asked Lewis.

"How many?"

"About half." Tyson laughed again.

"So what are you doing down here?" Lewis asked Tyson.

"What's that supposed to mean?" He took it like a challenge.

"It's volunteer, right? You wanted to come, right?"

"Hell yes, it's volunteer! Until they spend six thousand bucks getting each of us down here with no replacements in the pipeline. Then it's like, 'Oh, you don't care for our little utopia? Seems we've lost your return ticket until next October. Gosh golly darn. Have a great winter.'"

"It'll go faster with a positive attitude, Buck," Geller advised.

"It'll go faster when Cameron lays off me, man. Maybe I can't quit, but I don't have to jump through his work-schedule hoops, either. They may not like me, but they can't touch me." He grinned. "Not down here."

Pulaski had found them a pet. By treaty, animals weren't allowed in Antarctica in order to preserve its pristine environment. Unaware of this agreement, a small slug had smuggled its way onto the continent in a head of freshie lettuce. Lena, their greenhouse horticulturist, adopted the creature and put him in a jar with clippings from the hydroponic tanks. She called the slug Hieronymus and announced he was good luck. She was a botanist on green card from the Czech Republic, and to her everything seemed charmed in this new world. "I feel that all the time I am on vacation," she told Lewis.

"Someone should have told you about Hawaii."

"And now we have a pet!" she enthused.

"Somebody said something about a dome slug," he remembered.

"Those are people. That's what you become if you don't get outside."

"And if you do get outside?"

"Then you are a . . . Popsicle!" She smiled at her own knowledge of the word.

With some ceremony the slug was designated the official mascot of the Amundsen-Scott drill and dart team, which designated itself the Fighting Gastropods. Twice a week the loose assemblage played a match with the New Zealand winter-overs on the coast, keeping score by crackling radio. The Kiwis relied on their countryman Dana Andrews to keep the Yanks honest as they reported score. A caustically humored redhead with the build of a fireplug and an opinion on everyone, Dana complied. The Americans at McMurdo lent their own monitor, who hiked over to the New Zealand base for the matches in return for Kiwi beer.

Lewis was invited to join. "We're a classier team now that we have a mascot," Geller told him. "There's a real status to it now."

"I'm not much on darts." He sat down to one side as they shoved aside tables in the galley.

"You can't be any worse than Curious George," coaxed

another woman. Gabriella, her name was, and she was a more effective recruiter, as sensual as Dana was stolid. She was slim, dark-haired, her skin the color of butterscotch, her eyes large, and her mouth arrested in a wry curl. She moved with a self-conscious liquid grace. Not pretty like Abby so much as alluring. Dangerously so.

"I suppose not," Lewis agreed, watching while Geller put three darts wide of the bull's-eye.

The maintenance man was frowning at his own volley when Gabriella brought Lewis to the line. Geller gave them a knowing look. "I see you've managed to let yourself be drafted. You found this dame persuasive?"

The woman gave Lewis a glance.

"More so than you," Lewis allowed.

"That isn't even a compliment," Gabriella complained.

"I like the mascot."

"That's no better! I hope you're more adept with darts than words!"

In truth, Lewis had never played the game. But he was determined to socialize down here and so he threw, managing to hit the board. Then he watched as Gabriella toed the line and cocked her slim arm, the dart balanced in her fingers like a feather. She was a male magnet and knew it, reeking of femininity and pheromones. "Who is she?" he murmured to Geller as they watched.

"Gabriella Reid, gal Friday. She does berthing, assignments, time cards, records, and all that administrative crap. Not to mention keeping men on red alert."

"I heard that, George." She didn't seem very offended, arching her body up on her toes as she threw.

"We call her Triple-A," Geller whispered after she threw a near bull's-eye and went out of earshot to retrieve the dart. "Anybody, anytime, anywhere."

"Ouch."

"She'll put out for you if you want. Looking for love in all the polar places. Easier to warm up than Ice Cream."

"Ice Cream?"

"Abby Dixon. We keep the ice cream here outside and it comes in so rock-hard we have to microwave it to eat it. The joke is that Dixon needs thirty seconds in the box, too."

"She seemed friendly enough."

"Everybody likes Abby. She's just not as friendly as our teammate there. Abby's got a boyfriend somewhere and pretends it still matters at the Pole."

Gabriella took aim again. She could tell they were watching her, talking about her, and thrived on it.

"Reid's really a good kid. Fun-loving. If you're looking for that kind of thing."

"I'm still getting over altitude sickness."

Geller laughed.

Gabriella hit the bull's-eye again.

"She's good," Lewis observed.

"Coordinated," Geller said, loud enough for her to hear.

The woman pulled the dart out. "Coordinated enough to keep my thumb out from under a hammer, which is more than I can say for you, George."

"I know. I worship you, babe."

"And I'm indifferent to your existence." She winked at Lewis.

"What brings you to the Pole?" Lewis asked her.

Gabriella considered that one more seriously. "Time. Money. Fun. It's kind of a do-over, you know?"

"Do-over?"

"I was in a cubicle next to three thousand co-workers and not a single real friend. None of it was real. Nothing

I was doing counted. Nobody seemed genuine. There was too much . . . noise. So I decided to see if I could get a new start down here."

"Quite a change."

"I hope so. Everyone comes down here with a lot of baggage. Armor. Everyone knows they're going home. So some people are here but they're not really here, you know what I mean? You can just wait the winter out if you want to. I don't want to wait, I want to *live* life. *Here. Now.* How about you?"

Lewis shrugged. "I guess I'm still a fingie on that one."

"Not for long, maybe." She was flirting.

He decided on caution. "There's some interesting personalities at the Pole."

"Oddballs, you mean."

"Characters. Individuals."

"It wouldn't be worth being here if there weren't. Would it?" She held out the darts. "Your turn again."

"And why the Pole?" Lewis asked her, toeing up to the line.

"Because it's a powerful place. Where all lines converge. Point zero. You're on sacred ground, Jed Lewis."

"Sacred snow, isn't it?"

"Just give yourself the luxury of feeling."

Their medic, Nancy Hodge, came in and was cajoled into taking a turn. Her stance was firmer, legs apart, head cocked back rigidly, dead serious. She missed the board completely and everyone laughed.

"That's the way she gives shots!" Geller called.

Nancy pulled the errant dart out good-humoredly. "Watch what you say, George. My charts tell me you're due for a prostate exam."

"I'd rather get cancer."

Nancy lined up again, mouth pursed in concentration, and this time managed to hit the edge of the board. Dana radioed the scoreless result.

"Now we know why we won the America's Cup," the Kiwis radioed back, the comment buzzing with static.

"I guess athletics aren't Nurse Nancy's forte," Lewis observed.

"Not after teatime anyway," Geller murmured again. "If you need something checked, try to see her in the morning. She's steadier then."

"Booze?"

"Ah, I don't know. She's just not big on the hand-eye coordination thing, which ain't too cool if you need brain surgery."

"Our sole physician."

"You get the best and worst at the Pole. Missionaries and escapees. How many good doctors can walk away from their practices for a year? It's like the old naval surgeons. They all tend to have interesting stories. From the lines on her face, she looks like she's got more than one. My bet is she busted up with someone and came down here."

"To lick her wounds?"

"Or to find somebody else. This can be Lonelyhearts Club sometimes, goofily so. Hell, even somebody as ugly as me gets lucky sometimes."

"I don't know if I believe that one," Lewis said, playing straight man.

"It's true. The pilots brought in a crash dummy once and even he scored."

"But Nancy's not competent?"

"I didn't say *that*. She's smarter than any of us. We have a lot of fun with each other, kidding around. Just seems kind of rattled sometimes, like she's anxious to get rid of a patient. Like she's afraid of making a mistake."

The darts were fun and unworldly, performed to the background buzz of a radio linking them to a base across eight hundred miles of ice and snow. The Kiwis were intrigued by the new American mascot and Dana insisted the slug was doing gyrations every time the Yanks scored a point. Players drifted in and out, Lewis holding his own for a while. With the Americans down three matches to one, however, he excused himself and walked up a flight of stairs to the upstairs bar, the only place on station where alcohol could be consumed. It was the one nutrient they had to pay for.

Norse was there and Lewis joined him, nodding at the psychologist's beer and getting one of his own from the fridge, putting a mark on a tab for later accounting.

"Feeling better, I see," Norse observed.

"Just drinking after realizing what I got myself into."

"Miss your rocks already?"

"At least the ones ground into sand on a sunny beach."

Norse looked at Lewis with amusement. "It's interesting that they picked a geologist to do your job."

"I was available."

"That's *their* reason. What's yours?"

It sounded like a shrink question. "I trace it all to my mother."

"Ah." The psychologist nodded in defeat. "Okay. Confession some other time." He sipped his own beer. "I heard you met the estimable Doctor Moss."

"He granted me an audience."

"Interesting that you two got together so quickly."

Lewis wanted to deflect this line of questioning, too.

"He's friends with my mentor, Jim Sparco. And it's fun to talk to God. He says we're all down here for Science."

"Well, that's the party line," Norse said. "We're the cannon fodder of the National Science Foundation, you know. They see us all as a means to an end: knowledge."

"And you don't?"

"I see knowledge as a means to us: as a way to develop as people. It's a subtle difference, but an important one. Are we here to save civilization or is it here to save us? Some historians see all of human history as the triumph of the group over the individual. But one of my questions is whether it isn't the extraordinary individual who defines the group. If the *group's* purpose isn't to make possible the occasional exceptional human being. The Einstein. The Jefferson. The Alexander."

"You're looking for Einstein at the Pole?"

"I'm looking for character. Integrity. Individuality. I sense some of that in you, Jed. You have a certain center of gravity. And then determining if that kind of person functions in a tight, almost claustrophobic society like the Pole. Is smothered by it. Transcends it."

"I'm just trying to keep my butt warm."

"Exactly."

Lewis smiled. Norse seemed more interested in who Jed really was than in helping him fit what the Pole wanted him to be. "Lots of individual characters here," he said, "and I like that. But it can be lonely being *too* individual."

"Thinking of someone in particular?"

"Well, I heard Buck Tyson's real name is Island."

"That doesn't mean he's lonely."

"He said at dinner that you two think alike."

Norse laughed. "Did he? Well. My belief is that no two people *do* think alike, contrary to popular belief. The Western god is rationality, and a communal kind of sanity: all of us agreeing on reality, and pulling along the same track. This social scientist is squishier, I'm afraid, theorizing that each of us is a prisoner of our own beliefs, fears, perceptions. That we live in different worlds. So to me the fundamental question is whether the kind of knowledge we gather in places like this leads to real sanity or some view of the universe that, in its very rationality, is truly insane. Does it lead to happiness? Well-being? Does it solve anything at all?"

Lewis considered. "Isn't knowledge worthwhile just for its own sake? Rod Cameron told me the purpose of life is learning. Aren't we all down here because we sort of believe that, in an unconscious way?"

"Do you believe that?" the psychologist asked.

"I don't know. It's nice to have a goal."

"Whose goal? Yours? Or the group's?"

"Both."

"No. Cameron just gave the goal to you."

Lewis was irked now. "What do *you* think we came down here for?"

"I don't know," the psychologist admitted. He sipped again. "That's what I'm down here to find out."

"Make a guess."

"I don't guess. I'm a trained professional." It was self-deprecating.

The psychologist had his own evasions, Lewis saw. "Not good enough," he persisted. "What's *your* reason, Doc?"

"Okay. I came down here to see if we should be here at all." The psychologist nodded, as if to confirm it to himself. "Do you know that America spends two hundred million dollars a year in Antarctica? Two hundred mil on the altar of knowledge! That's a goodly chunk of change. But what if rationality is a fraud? What if sanity—the idea every-one should think the same way, share the same reality—is a fraud? What if *science* is a fraud? That what pretends to explain everything in fact explains nothing to animals like ourselves, that NSF stands for a myth, that the druids and pagans and witches were right and that the true knowledge, the real insight, is in the dark wood—is in ourselves? What if the outermost veneer of civilization we represent is no thicker than the aluminum on this dome? What if at some point in our explorations we reach not revelation but utter mystery, a whole new pit of the indescribable, the un-knowable?" He was looking at Lewis, his eyes bright. "What do we do then?" That intensity again.

Lewis shrugged in self-defense. "Well, golly. Open an-other beer, I suppose." He got one and did so. "You're say-ing you're getting your ass frozen off for no reason?"

Norse laughed, as if that were a huge joke. "I hope not!"

"But you think we're nutcases because we believe in sanity?"

"No, no. I'm rambling." The psychologist studied his beer. "Drinking. But in an age when the machines are bend-ing us to become like them, to become part of them, I'm curious what it still means to be human. To stand for your-self. Here, at the most inhuman place on earth."

Lewis left the bar more wound up than when he entered it, still unable to sleep as his brain tried to make up its mind about his new home. He impulsively decided to walk outside. No dome slug he. The suiting up took fifteen la-borious minutes and when he surmounted the ramp he saw the same pale sun at midnight that he'd seen that morn-ing. Weird. The constant light was disorienting, the circuit of the orb dizzying. His own brain was swirling with impressions, new faces, glib philosophies. Individuals, every one. But a group, too. Which was what he'd come for.

Wasn't it?

Maybe Doctor Bob's problem was that he'd never been truly alone.

Lewis felt alone now, the station still, the breeze mild. Yet when he listened for the whisper of his freezing breath he realized he was not. There was a distant whining noise of a moving machine and he gradually recognized it as a snowmobile. Tyson? Someone, at least, was out driving at the witching hour. He began walking in a broad loop around the dome, still puffing from the altitude, looking for the source of the noise. Finally he saw a speck in the distance, an orange dot on a black one, someone driving out onto the featureless plateau. He had no idea who the driver was: old or young, man or woman. Odd at this time, but then scientists kept odd schedules.

Where was there to go?

The sound seemed to connect them like a thread and his eye remained fixed on the receding traveler, because there was nothing else to see.

Then the snowmobile slid out of view, as if entering a dip, and a few seconds later the noise grumbled away. Silence.

Lewis waited awhile for the pilgrim to reappear, but nothing happened.

The plateau was empty. He got cold and bored and turned back inside, exhausted enough now for bed.

What Came Before

I called him Fat Boy.

Not to his face, of course, because by law and custom and administrative directive the university was so politically and sexually and racially correct that those of us grubbing for a check were expected to be as unctuous as undertakers: prissy, constipated, and afraid. But in my mind he was Fat Boy, a lagging drogue of blubber, a leech, a handicap, a brake, an anchor, a limit, a curse.

I honor people who achieve the ultimate of what they can be.

I despise those who pretend to be what they can never be.

Fat Boy could never be a mountain climber.

Let me tell you about climbing. It is the most sublime of all human activities. First, because it is difficult. Second, because it is dangerous. Third, because it has a tangible goal and there can be no mistaking if that goal is reached or not: You summit, or you don't. Everything else is bullshit.

Fourth, because it is revealing. A mountain brings out the truth in a man. Or woman.

And fifth, because it is beautiful.

Our doomed little party started out at three minutes past midnight, the temperature fifteen degrees and the stars an orbiting city past the great dark silhouette of the Cascades volcano that was our goal. When the moon rose at three it turned the glacier into a bowl of milk and our route into a clean kind of heaven. It was early enough in the season that the crevasses were mostly filled with snow and so we made good time. Fifteen college students, two instructors, and myself tagging along on each climb because I actually knew what the hell to do on a mountain. It was a real class, Professor Kressler getting paid to pursue his hobby, Fleming in his shadow like an eager puppy, the kids getting credit for sweating in the snow. For me it was an excuse to go climbing. Schmooze. Brown-nose. Connect. You know the drill.

We were roped in three parties of six. The kids were quiet, in awe of the mountain, and I mostly just heard the clink of equipment and the rasp of nylon. It was good that way. The pant of their breathing was like a team of horses. The plan was to summit an hour after dawn and then glissade back down before the rising spring sun turned the snow to mush. It was the last climb of the semester.

I'd expected Fat Boy to drop the class by now. He wasn't just obese, he was weak. He wasn't just weak, he was incompetent. He could never remember the knots, never keep track of his gear. And he wasn't just incompetent, he was stupid. Twice he'd dropped off a route to catch his wheezing little breath, and once I'd had to go back down myself to find him. He hadn't been apologetic, he'd been surly. I'd told him the sport wasn't for him. He'd shown up the next class anyway. I should have shaken him, slapped him, shamed him into recognizing his own limitations. But we weren't allowed to do that. And at that time I was still weak. I was still willing to believe that others, the kind of morons that wind up in administration, might know what was best for me.

The warning signs were there. Fat Boy was last to climb out of his bag. Last to dress, last to eat, last to gather his equipment. He'd farted, stumbled, spilled. After three months of classes he still needed help with his crampons! Still needed help with his line! Almost put another student's eye out with his ice ax! Whining, defensive, apologetic. In a realistic kind of world—a just one—his kind of genetic fluff would be combed away in an instant.

But the world carries its cripples now, doesn't it?

For a while I thought we could pull him along okay, like a goat on the end of a wagon. Fleming, the other prof, knew how much I hated the kid and so put him on his rope, last in line, and managed to cajole rather than curse. The man had the patience of a saint. And for a while I could forget Fat Boy was with us. We topped the glacier, made Sullivan's Saddle, and pushed on up the central cone, only half an hour behind schedule. The boy had blubbered a bit, nose dripping, pack awry, one mitten lost who the hell knew where, but he was keeping up with a frantic gasp and if we finally made the damn summit I think I'd have been almost ready to forgive him. My contempt wouldn't fade, but my anger might.

I was actually in a good mood that morning. I still had a life. The sky was pinking. The Cascades were turning from black to deep blue shadow, and we could see the glint of the cities along the Sound. The air was cold and so clean it washed you out, laundered your brain, and I could taste the top, we were so close. Clouds were building in the west, an approaching storm, but I thought we could beat it. I was ready to forgive Fat Boy anything if we could just finish and be done.

But then there was a shout and the party came to a jerking, unsteady halt, the students gasping gratefully for breath in the respite, confused calls running up and down the line.

I unroped and sidestepped down the snow, trying to find out what was the matter. Minutes ticking on. The sun approaching to the east. Overcast from the west. The summit waiting. We had a tight window. We had to summit and get down.

Of course, I knew what I'd find before I even got down to the last team. Fleming pointed in the light of the dimming moon and I followed the rope with my eye to where its end trailed on the snow like a dead snake, empty of anything.

He'd spoiled it, of course, for all the others.

He'd spoiled it for me.

Fat Boy had untied himself and was gone.

CHAPTER SIX

Lewis sniffed Abby Dixon's approach before he saw her. Not perfume. Her breath.

His new instruments at Clean Air alerted him. So sensitive was the carbon dioxide sampler at detecting changes in the surrounding atmosphere that the tracking pen jumped from the contribution of her lungs. Other meters logged the dying sunlight, chlorofluorocarbons that could attack the earth's ozone layer, ozone itself, and water vapor. It was like gaining new senses. He'd come back inside after a brisk thirty minutes of collecting snow samples and was still warming up in front of his machines when she stamped her boots in the vestibule by the door.

"Gearloose," he greeted her.

"Rockhead," she replied cheerfully, pulling off her parka.

"I'm thinking of a nickname a little less descriptive," Lewis said. "Vaguely heroic, perhaps. Like Stormwatcher. Skywalker."

"It will never catch on." She hung up her coat. "Too nice."

"Doesn't anyone have a flattering nickname?"

"Neutral is the best you can hope for."

"How did the tradition get started?"

She plopped into a chair, shivering slightly as the tension of being in the cold outside was shed, her cheeks pink, her dark eyes bright. She seemed confident in this environment and he liked that. Her strength. Her energy. "I don't know. The Navy, maybe. Or the parkas. When we're outdoors it's hard to tell who's who: Everyone looks like an orange traffic cone. So they came up with name tags, except people didn't like that—it felt like we were at a convention—so some put them upside down. Names seem part of the world we've left behind. So people got tagged for their occupations. And it evolved, in the perverse way things do around here. You *have* noticed how perverse this all is?"

"Wade Pulaski told me it's paradise."

She laughed. "Cueball would say that."

"That's his nickname? He called this place Planet Cueball. I thought he was referring to the terrain, not his head."

"Rod says he looks like Queequeg in *Moby Dick*. I'd go with Jesse Ventura, or an old Yul Brynner movie. He's actually ex-military, which he doesn't talk much about except to hint he was into some extreme stuff. Scuba, climbing, biting the heads off chickens. Whatever. Apparently he didn't fit into ordinary life very well so he came down here."

"Odd alternative."

"Better than winding up a mercenary in Angola. I guess you could say that about all of us."

"The South Pole saved you from Angola?"

Abby smiled. "The South Pole saved me from being ordinary."

There was silence as he considered this. Of course.

"It's interesting I could detect your approach by your CO_2," Lewis finally said. He pointed to his sampler. "It's like I have superpowers down here."

"By the end of the winter you'll wonder if the instruments are an extension of you or if you're an extension of your instruments."

The observation seemed to echo what Norse had said about machines. Had he made the same ramblings to her? "To what do I owe this visit?"

"The official reason is that I wanted to check to make sure the broken computer is performing okay."

"Wow. Every technician I've ever spoken to—after forty-five minutes on hold with excruciating music—wanted to get off the line as rapidly as possible. None ever called back to see if things actually worked."

She smiled again. "You're in paradise, like Cueball said."

"And what's the unofficial reason you've come for a breath of Clean Air?"

"I wanted to check how you're getting along. It isn't easy being the fingie, and everyone's curious about you. So . . ."

"Curious?"

She looked at him wryly. "It's unusual to come down on the last plane like you did. And you're a geologist, not a meteorologist, which is kind of odd. And you quit some oil company, apparently. And . . ."

"You came for the gossip."

"I came for the truth. It's a small town, Jed. People talk. Speculate. If they don't know about a person, things just get made up."

"Ah. So they send a comely lass to worm my secrets out of me. A spy. A temptress. A—"

She wrinkled her nose. "Please."

"But it's more than your undeniable fascination with me."
Lewis grinned disarmingly. He was enjoying this. "You're
an emissary of espionage. You were elected. Someone sent
you."

She looked disappointed. "It's that obvious?"

"I'm just used to being ignored by women."

"I doubt that." She paused to let him mentally log the
compliment. "Actually, Doctor Bob suggested I visit. He said
he's trying to write up a sociological profile of the base:
who we are, why we're here. Then he'll track our attitudes
over the winter. At the end—"

"We're all toast."

"Yes."

"The good doctor already asked me to explain myself,
you know," Lewis said.

"He told me that," she admitted.

"And?"

"He said men will tell things to women they won't tell
to men."

Lewis smiled as he looked at her, her neck high, ears as
fine as shell, eyes large and guileless. He could guess why
Norse had recruited this assistant—she could attract any
man on base—and wasn't surprised she'd agreed to be recruited. It was indeed a small town. People would make
fast friendships, and they'd rupture even faster. He'd noticed the undercurrent of flirting and competition almost
immediately. What was it Cameron had said about women?
We're more civilized now. Well, maybe.

"For a spy, you're pretty blunt. You might want to work
on that."

"The truth is, I'm not very good at the whole human in-
teraction thing."

"Who is?"

"I guess that's what Doctor Bob wants to know."

"So, do you want me on a couch?" he asked. "Should I blame it all on my parents? My unhappy childhood?"

"Did you have an unhappy childhood?"

"Dismayingly, no. Middle class, middle brow, middle life."

"Me neither. Wealthy parents, but nice, too. It's so annoying."

They watched each other for a moment, smiling slightly.

"Damn," Lewis finally said. "I don't know what Doctor Bob is going to find to do all winter."

"Well," she said, "you're not *entirely* normal. We're all wondering what a geologist is doing on an ice cap."

"Ah. Jim Sparco was desperate for a replacement. He's studying oscillations in polar climates spaced over decades and my predecessor took sick, as you know. Reading the thermometer is not that hard a job."

"What did your family say?"

"My folks are dead, actually. Accident."

"I'm sorry."

"It happened after I left home, quite a while ago. Anyway, I was pretty much alone. Job gone. Friends fleeting. No warm and fuzzy relationships."

"No significant other?"

He took her curiosity as a good sign. "I never stayed in one place, so girls didn't stay, either. There wasn't a lot holding me."

"Still," she persisted, "it's hard to find people to come down here sometimes, especially at the last minute."

"Yes. I was desperate, too."

She looked at him with honest curiosity. "What happened?"

He paused to remember. What had happened? The tu-

mult of emotions he'd experienced was only slowly being
sifted by his mind into a coherent story. "I went into geology because I liked explanations," he finally said. "Rocks
were a puzzle out of the past, a trip back in time. They
were also stationary and organized and understandable,
compared to people. I liked mountain climbing, so it meshed
with my hobby. But to make a living in geology I had to
concentrate on one kind of puzzle: where oil is hidden.
That was fine for a while. Exciting, even. Texas, the Gulf,
Arabia. But then I wound up on the North Slope of Alaska,
puzzling in a place we weren't really supposed to be, just
in case Congress changes its mind someday about opening
up the wildlife refuges to drilling. We were pretending to
be backpacking tourists, but we were setting off shock
waves to probe for oil."

"And you began to question what you were doing."

"No . . ." he said slowly. "It was like there was never
any question, and then suddenly there was no question
about quitting. The tundra did that to me."

She waited for him to explain.

"It's a place something like this one. Not snow-covered,
not in summer, but treeless and stark with this low, ever-
lasting light that seems to reach inside you. And yet it took
me a month before I really noticed that. My mind was underground. Finally there was a rainstorm late one afternoon, dark and furious, driving us into camp, and then
rainbows, and finally a plume, like smoke, curling over one
ridge under that prism of light. At first I thought it was a
fire, but how could a fire burn in a place that damp? Then
I realized it was caribou. A drift of life in a place so empty
that suddenly everything hit me like adrenaline. All my
senses suddenly came awake. Do you know the feeling?"

She nodded, cautiously. "Maybe. Like falling in love?"

The analogy hadn't occurred to him, and he cocked his head. "Maybe. Anyway, what I was seeing was the Porcupine River herd. I'd seen animals, of course, but never animals in numbers like you see numbers of people—never animals to make you question everything you thought you knew about whose world this truly is. They came over a ridge and down to the Kavik River. I stood there in that light watching them for hours. And that was it. Suddenly the idea of spending my life looking for a pollutant struck me as profoundly unsatisfactory. Sneaking onto a refuge seemed wrong. People told me my dinner was getting cold, but I ignored them, and then that *I* would get cold if I stood out there all night, but I ignored that, too. It wasn't even night, of course, the sun never fully set. I didn't feel the cold at all. Everything just got rosy and soft. Finally, when everyone else was asleep, I pulled together some gear and started walking after the herd. I left a note so they wouldn't worry about me."

"What did it say?" she asked. She was looking at him appraisingly, finding herself liking a man who could be affected so profoundly by caribou.

His smile was wry. "I *quit*."

"I'm sure that did reassure them."

"One of the things I realized is that I didn't truly know a single person in that camp. Had never thought deeply about what I was doing."

"Nothing to hold you, like you said."

"Nothing to care about. Nothing to be proud of. I walked two days before I hit the Haul Road that runs from Fairbanks up to Prudhoe Bay. It was the loneliest two days I've ever had, and two of the best. They turned me inside out. Then some scientists came by in a Bronco and gave me a ride. I stayed at an ecological research camp at a place called

Toolik Lake and that's where I met Jim Sparco. He was doing climate measurements in the Arctic and he's one of those rare omnivores interested in all kinds of science. We hit it off, talking about weather, geology. Climate and oceans come from rocks, you know. Volcanoes run the planet. We stayed in touch while I bummed around Idaho. I was running out of money, deciding what to do next, when I got a package from Sparco's lab in Boulder. It had a T-shirt inside that read, 'Ski the South Pole. Two miles of base, half an inch of powder.' Plus his telephone number. I called and the rest, as they say, is history."

"He sent it to a geologist."

"Yes, because he knew me."

"And because of Mickey's rock."

He was surprised. "How'd you know about that?"

"I told you there're no secrets here. It's a small place. Mickey went weird at the drill site one day last fall, evasive, and people have wondered ever since if he found something unusual. He seemed pretty excited for a guy whose project is over budget and behind schedule. Then a geologist? It's not hard to put two and two together. What else could he find in the ice but a meteorite?"

"He told me no one knew."

"People guess. There's always a lot of buzz about everything because there's nothing else to do. The question is, why did you come all this way to see it?"

"It's more like I agreed to see it in return for getting to come all this way."

She leaned forward, looking expectant. "And?"

"And what?"

"Is it significant?"

He stalled, wondering what to say. "Don't I get seduced first?"

"Sorry. Just twenty questions."

"You're the worst spy I've ever seen." He knew she was pumping him and that he should muster some annoyance, but he actually enjoyed the attention. "The fact is, he asked me to keep quiet about it. I'm not supposed to talk."

She nodded, her interest confirmed. "He wouldn't bring you down here if it wasn't important."

Lewis smiled like a sphinx. "Women are so snoopy."

"Women *listen.*"

"Sparco is a friend of Moss's. Our astrophysicist wanted an opinion from a rockhound. I was unemployed. That's all there is to it. I haven't even done any tests yet."

"But what you saw is worth testing."

"We'll see."

"If it's the right kind of meteorite it could be big."

"For Mickey's reputation."

"That's not what I mean. You *know* that's not what I mean."

"What?" She was too damn smart, and he liked smart women.

"If it's a meteorite, it could be worth a lot."

The wind came up as evening approached. When Lewis walked back to the dome from the Clean Air Facility he felt the first true bite of winter. The temperature still hovered at sixty below but a rising wind pushed the windchill to minus one hundred. Dry snow undulated in ragged sheets across the ice, the flakes rasping at the fluttering nylon of his windpants. They stung the bits of skin that were exposed, his upper cheeks and temples. The wind made a low moaning sound as it blew, a discomfiting change from the earlier quiet, and when he followed the fluttering route flags to the dome he found the big bay doors had been closed against the first drifts. He yanked open a smaller door to one side and the wind pushed him as he stepped in, so that he had to lean back against the door to shut it. As he caught his breath he regarded the gloom of the dome with new gratitude. Inside felt safer. He could still hear the hoarse scratching of Antarctica. The blowing snow made it sound as if the aluminum dome were being sanded.

Lewis didn't see Norse at dinner and so went looking for him afterward, guessing the weight room attached to his berthing module. The psychologist was the kind of guy who would try to stay in shape. Norse wasn't there but Harrison Adams said he'd just left, heading for the sauna. The astronomer was working out in faded trunks and gray, baggy T-shirt, grunting as he lifted with his white, stringy muscles. Adams was a sharply intellectual man, obsessed with the sky, and it was odd to see him like that. "Can you take a minute to spot me, Lewis?"

Lewis wasn't anxious to. He found Adams prickly, the kind of scientist who did not suffer fools gladly and who thought everyone who wasn't interested in what he was interested in was a fool. "I need to find Doctor Bob."

"He'll cook for a while. Come on, spot me first. Tyson certainly won't."

The big mechanic was lifting in a corner, an enormous weight across his back as his knees bent and straightened like thick hairy pistons, his lungs whooshing like a surfacing whale. He looked at them balefully, as if offended by their mere presence. For a man who claimed a crushing workload, he seemed to have plenty of time and energy to lift weights.

"What do I have to do?" Lewis asked Adams.

"Stand over me on the bench here, while I press. Just so I don't pin myself."

"Why can't Buck do it?"

Tyson pushed himself erect, exhaling. "I'm busy."

"He's always busy," Adams said, moving to the bench. "Too busy to grade the trail to the Dark Sector. Too busy to fix the Spryte. Too busy to move the cargo for my scope repair before this wind came up. Too busy to give me any hope of meeting schedule."

"I'm not your servant, Adams." The weight clanged heavily down, Tyson's arms dangling after it like an ape's. "The world doesn't revolve around you."

The astronomer lay down on the stained weight bench. "We're not serving *me,* are we, Mr. Tyson? We're serving the research. We're justifying our time and expense. The world *does* revolve around this Pole. Except too many of *us* have to wait on *you.*"

"Screw you." Tyson stretched. "Shoulda let me go home when I had the chance, if you don't like me. And get in line. Tell Cameron to back off on the other stuff he wants me to do if you're so anxious for my help."

"You use too much water, too. You ignore the rationing. People resent it."

"Let them drink beer."

"I'm talking about the showers."

"Let them shower in beer."

Adams gripped the bar of the weights. "At the end of the winter, Buck, there's going to be a review for bonuses and recommendations for future employment."

Tyson took two fifty-pound weights and began hoisting them like a crane. "Is that a threat, Harry?" He knew Adams hated the common nickname.

Adams began lifting, too, grunting. "Simply a reminder of how things are," he gasped.

"I'm thinking how things ought to be."

Adams was growing red from the exertion. "Maybe you ought to think about where you are right now, Buck. Your future. Your lack of it." His arms were shaking with the final lift.

"Maybe I *am* thinking about my future. Maybe I'm not the moron you think I am. Maybe errand boy here is starting to think for himself."

The astronomer gasped and put the weight to rest, sitting up. He was sweating, angry, frustrated. "You can't go through the winter like this, Buck. You can't sulk for eight damnable months. You've got to get along."

"Really? And who says?" Tyson racked his own weights with a thud. "Who says I have to get along with anybody? The truth is, Adams, you need *me* but I don't need *you* for a single fucking thing. I could care less about the sky. I could care less about you, or the fingie there, or Cameron, or any other moron stupid enough to like it down here. I do my job at my own pace, mind my own business, and count the days until I get out. And if people were honest about it, everyone else does that, too."

"No, they don't."

"Like all you beakers are best buddies? You know Moss pigs out on the grant competition. You know you're in a race with all the beakers to get papers featured in *Science* or *Nature*. You know the competition is about as collegial as a convention of Mafia dons. And you know that all you want from me is a broad back and compliant brain. Two weeks after the winter is over you won't remember who I am."

"Dammit, that's not true. This is the one time in your life to contribute to—"

"So you can take that bonus of yours and cram it up

your ass. Because down here I don't have to take no shit from nobody." The big man walked out.

Adams shook his head, looking after him. "Now, there's a project for Doctor Bob," he muttered to Lewis.

"Doctor Bob might think Tyson has a legitimate point of view."

Adams snorted. "Shrinks think everything is a legitimate point of view."

Lewis went to the sauna. Cameron had told him the cedar box was both a morale booster and a safety feature, adept at warming people up after too much exposure outside. It was also supposed to relax them, bringing them together in communal contemplation. It worked well enough to be heavily used.

Lewis shed his clothes, wrapped a towel around his middle, and stepped into the red-lit dimness inside. He recognized Norse's muscled form and Mohawk crew cut through a veil of hissing steam and sat down on a cedar bench. The psychologist lazily raised a hand.

"Adams and I were just talking about you," Lewis greeted.

"In flattering terms, I hope."

"About putting Buck Tyson on the couch. Making him into Mr. Rogers."

Norse smiled. "As if therapists could make anyone into anything. The best they can do, I'm afraid, is help people come to grips with who they are."

"I think Buck's already come to grips with himself as a self-centered, shower-hogging, antisocial, dysfunctional, butt-ugly son of a bitch."

"So, good for him." Norse threw some water on the sauna rocks, releasing a hiss of steam. The psychologist leaned back, uncharacteristically quiet.

"Who am I, Doc?"

For a minute he thought Norse wasn't going to answer. Then: "That's what I'm working on, remember?"

"I talked to your spy today."

"Spy?"

"Abby came out to poke into my past. Said she was working for you."

"Oh yes." He sounded unembarrassed. "She's already reported back."

"And?"

"Said you were 'desperate.' I think that was the word. It's in my notes." His tone was amused.

"Is that description accurate, do you think?"

"I suppose it is," the psychologist said. "Of everyone. What's the phrase? Lives of quiet desperation?"

They were quiet again. Then: "What the hell are you really doing down here, Doc?"

"I already told you."

"Trying to get into our brains is just going to piss people off."

"I'm not trying to do that."

"It's one thing to trade life stories. It's another to be pinned like a bug to a wall for some shrink's research project. I don't care for it, and I don't think anyone else is going to, either. I know you've got your job to do, but nobody asked for a psychologist and it's going to be a long winter. Head collecting isn't going to make you popular."

Norse turned and looked at Lewis directly for the first time, his features indistinct in the shadows. He seemed to be considering what to say. "Questions bother you, don't they?" he finally tried.

"I just don't think I have to explain myself."

"Nor do I." Norse thought a moment. "Okay, look. First

of all, I'm not a psychiatrist, I'm a psychologist. I'm an observer, not a therapist. I don't change people, I only study them. But your point is well taken. I've got not only the most unpopular job, I've got the most difficult one. So, do you know why I'm *really* here?"

"That's what I'm asking."

"Because we're about to leave this planet, Jed." He waited for a reaction.

"What the hell does that mean?"

"Childhood's end, as Arthur C. Clarke would say. Space travel is inevitable. Maybe we'll eventually find some new Eden, or be able to build one way out there, but the first voyages are going to be in conditions like we have at the Pole: hostile, crowded, uncomfortable. A ship of strangers. Maybe a ship of fools. Who is going to go out there? Why? Can they function when they do?"

"This place does."

"Which is *exactly* why I'm here. You think your job is important, and it is. All the jobs down here are important. But of equal importance is the mere fact of your existence: that you're here at all, surviving, cooperating, feuding, an unwitting guinea pig at the beginning of the next era. The Pole is at the edge of space: cold, dry, clear, deadly. It doesn't even have normal time. Can we adapt to that? We have to, somehow. Earth isn't going to last forever. The National Science Foundation and NASA are as interested in our simple existence as in our research product. Uncomfortable result: me."

"I don't want to be written up as some misfit."

Norse laughed. "Misfit! I wish it were that simple."

"Meaning what?"

"Meaning that misfit is a cop-out word: Everyone fits, but each in their own way, from admiral to hermit."

"But you called us guinea pigs, right? Rats in your maze?"

"That's what I'm trying to explain," Norse said. "I'm not allowed to build a maze. Not as an observational psychologist. Sociologist. It's bad enough I'm here at all, an observer who changes things slightly by the simple act of observing. Manipulating events would discredit my entire study. It would ruin my winter. No, my issue is different. What drives people to places like this is one of the greatest mysteries of human history. Why did we ever leave Africa? Why do we risk at all? Do you know that when Shackleton came down to Antarctica just before the First World War to drag his men through several circles of hell, his advertisement to attract fifty-six recruits promised only low pay, abysmal conditions, hardship, and danger? And do you know how many applicants he attracted?"

"Plenty, I'll bet."

"Five thousand."

Lewis didn't want to admit his surprise. "Humans like adventure. They get bored."

"Adventure. Change. Escape. And yet when they get to a place like *this* they get all the visual stimulation of a cement wall. I mean, come on! It's Amundsen-Scott base that's pinning us like bugs to a wall. We're a little island, with tedious routine. The very people who *most* want to come to the Pole may be the *least* qualified to coexist here. At least that's one theory. Do we need *commandos* in space? Or accountants? That's the question. When the heat went off the other day some reacted smoothly and some had a little panic. Not necessarily the ones you'd expect. I'm in the prediction business, like you. You're trying to forecast the climate, and I'm trying to forecast human nature. We both look at patterns to do it."

"You're going to list twenty-six rational reasons for being here?"

"What's rational? Wasn't that our discussion at the bar? When the First World War finally started, with Shackleton's ship trapped and sinking in the ice, the Germans launched a massive attack through Belgium toward France. They did so even though they knew, mathematically, that their attack couldn't succeed. Their own planners had calculated they could not move enough troops on Belgium's dirt roads in the time available to beat the French once they got there. The whole idea was doomed. But they did it anyway, producing a monstrous four-year stalemate that slaughtered millions, and do you know why?"

"Why?"

"Because it was the best plan they had at the time." The psychologist waited, watching Lewis. Did Norse believe a thing he was saying, or was this a calculated game to elicit reaction? He tossed another cup of water on the hot stones, obscuring himself with steam. "*That's* human motivation for you. The best plan we have, given our tangled past, messy emotions, confused logic, and vain hopes. *My* issue is, is that good enough? Can we rely on each other, becoming stronger than the sum of our parts? Or does it all fall apart somewhere on the way to Pluto?"

Lewis thought back to the argument in the weight room. "Your conclusion?"

"Would be premature. That's why I'm spending the winter. But corporate and government America worships groups. Teamwork. The committee. Modern historians have abandoned the importance of the individual leader and embraced economics and sociology and biological instinct. They worship the anthill. One of *my* questions is whether that worship is appropriate in extreme circumstances. When does a team become a herd, and then a mob? How important is the individual and self-reliance? Can a single person, like yourself, or Buck Tyson, change the chemistry of an entire community? Were Pericles and Caesar and Napoleon and Lincoln the product of their times, or the creators?"

"How the hell are you going to tell that down here?"

"By watching what happens to *us,* when the first real tests come."

Lewis was acclimating to the Pole. His first nights in his "Ice Room" hadn't frozen him to the wall as he'd joked but they'd been uncomfortably restless as his body adjusted to the dryness and altitude. His dreams were turbulent and he'd jerk awake suddenly, gasping for air, alternately parched or prodded by a full bladder. Yet slowly his breathing and pulse slowed. He found himself regularly using lotion on his hands and face for the first time in his life, fighting the dryness. Pulaski told him to smear his nostrils with Vaseline before venturing outdoors to protect the lining of his nose, and he began to associate the smell with the snow. Inside the dome he noticed the rarity of smell. When he took one of the last fresh oranges from the galley to the computer lab and peeled it, Abby was drawn from a machine she was fixing like a moth to a flame. Each strip of skin released a puff of scent, intoxicating and tropical, that drifted on the currents of ventilated air. Hiro Sakura came, too, sniffing, and so did Nancy Hodge. He playfully offered them sections of fruit, juicy and elastic. Together they bit and sucked with wistful glee. Ambrosia.

Abby was becoming a friend. He told her about the drift of the continents, and how Antarctica had once had forests and dinosaurs. She talked about the history of communication, and how the Internet was like a melding of brains, an accelerator of thought, as potentially revolutionary as the printing press. How machines might outsmart them all.

Once she took him to the garage and they checked out a snowmobile, Abby demonstrating how to use it on a runway that was beginning to drift. In the coming dark it would be too cold to use them. They skittered around the Quonset huts of summer camp, her arms around his waist, shouting directions into his hood, the air cutting so fiercely that they had to give it up after half an hour.

His "nights" had turned deep and dreamless, his body sapped each evening by the toll of cold. He set an alarm to keep on schedule and when it went off he'd jerk awake, disoriented and groggy. The sky didn't help him to tell time.

When his door slammed open in the middle of one sleep then, lights blazing on, his shock and confusion were profound. He jerked in his blankets, panicked at the chance of fire, and then before he could collect himself Cameron and Moss were crowded into his room, jostling his bed, rifling his things.

Lewis sat up in his underwear, dumbfounded. Norse was there, too, he realized, hovering just outside the door.

"What the hell?"

Moss was pawing through his duffel in frustration, and Cameron leaned over his bed, pinning him in place. "Relax, Lewis. We're here to help."

"What?" His heart was hammering in confusion.

"The quickest way to remove suspicion is to do a search. Mickey insisted."

"Get him the hell out of my things!"

"No can do."

"Bob?" He appealed to Norse, who was watching from

outside the door. The psychologist reluctantly stepped into the room, glancing around. "It's for your own good, sport."

Moss swore, backed out from under the bed, and stood up, winded. "Nothing." The astrophysicist looked disgusted, at Lewis and at the world.

"What in the hell is going on?"

The three others looked at each other, confirming, and then Norse spoke. "That's what we want to ask *you*. Mickey's meteorite is missing."

CHAPTER SEVEN

W hat we have here is a fascinating sociological situation." Robert Norse was enjoying their dilemma.

The others looked at the psychologist sourly. Mickey Moss and Rod Cameron hadn't slept and Lewis was still groggy from having been awakened. The four were crowded into the station manager's office next to Comms, the radio communication center of the base. It was tight, hot, and electric with tension.

"Fucking swell," Cameron muttered.

"What time is it, anyway?" Lewis asked blearily.

"Three-thirty."

"Three-thirty in the morning?"

"Stop whining. The sun's up." It was a sour attempt at levity. The sun was always up, until it went down in a couple of weeks and stayed there. Already the outside was a world of blue shadow.

"Something of uncertain value," Norse went on, "disappears in a tiny community from which there is no possibility of a getaway. Why? Who? How?"

"The why is obvious," Moss rumbled. "Our newest member, Mr. Lewis here, somehow called attention to my find after I sought his expertise. The motive is money."

"Money?"

"He confirmed that I'd discovered a scientifically important meteorite. The right kind can be valuable."

Norse turned to Lewis. "Is that true, Jed?"

Lewis looked at Moss warily, miffed that the scientist had searched him. "I agreed it might be important. I hadn't even started the chemical analysis yet." How much should he say? "Rich people will pay a lot for a piece of outer space. It's a fad."

"What kind of money?"

"Throwing figures around will only encourage thievery," Moss cautioned.

"I'd say the thief's already encouraged," Norse countered.

Lewis looked uncomfortably at Moss. The astrophysicist shrugged gloomily. "One entrepreneur put tiny slices in Lucite cubes and sold them on the Home Shopping Network," Lewis finally said. "Hundred bucks each."

"Nice payday."

"An intact one, from the South Pole, that could come from Mars or the moon . . . who knows? Thousands per gram."

"Which means . . . ?" Norse prompted.

Moss was looking at the floor. Lewis shrugged. "Five million dollars?"

"You're kidding," Cameron interjected.

"Maybe more."

"No way."

"If there's any microscopic fossil evidence of life, the value becomes . . . astronomical. Pun intended."

"Jesus." The station manager thought a moment. "But

that's not an issue, not down here. By treaty, you can't sell anything found in Antarctica. It's against international law."

Lewis's tone was flat. "That's good to know."

"People down here don't care about money."

"Glad to hear it."

Cameron looked at Moss. "You knew this?"

"In theoretical terms," the astrophysicist said blandly. "The price is irrelevant to the science. When Sparco said he'd be willing to use a geologist who could also give a quick judgment on my discovery, I was delighted. It seemed useful, and Lewis here said he needed a job. But perhaps he concluded he could earn more another way."

"Meaning what?" Lewis asked.

"That you're the thief." Moss looked at him squarely, waiting for denial, and then waiting for any kind of response at all. Lewis refused to give it to him.

"I'm sorry, young man, this may be completely unfair," the astrophysicist finally went on with less certainty, "but I prefer not to be oblique. You have the knowledge to market such a rock, the skill to assess its true value, and possibly the need and bitterness as a fired petroleum engineer to hock it. When the rock disappeared I was forced to think about it from your point of view. To come down to study weather is a detour from your primary career. To come down for a meteorite from Mars or the moon, discovered at the South Pole—that's very good pay for enduring a single winter."

Norse was looking at Moss with amused interest.

"Stealing something when you can't get away makes no sense at all," Lewis said slowly. "And I wasn't fired, I quit."

"That's what *you* say. My point is, we don't really know

what your story is, and its disappearance is coincidental with your arrival."

"The common knowledge that there *is* a meteorite apparently came with my arrival, but not from anything *I* said. People were speculating about what you found for months. Inviting down a geologist simply confirmed it."

"And how do you know that?" Moss demanded.

"Because *his* emissary"—Lewis pointed to Norse—"told me so. Abby Dixon."

"Who?"

"The computer technician," Cameron explained.

Moss thought. "Oh yes. The cute one." He squinted at Lewis. "You're saying *she's* the thief?"

"No, I'm saying *anyone* might have known enough to lift it from your file cabinet."

"Aha! But it wasn't in my file cabinet! I'd hidden it!"

Lewis threw up his arms in exasperation. "Then how could I or anyone else have taken it?"

Moss opened his mouth and then closed it, looking troubled. "I thought you'd seen me. And guessed."

"Seen *what*?"

"That he drove out to the solar observatory on the plateau at midnight when it was closed down for the season and there was no scientific reason to go there," Norse said quietly. "It appears Doctor Moss, in trying to hide his find, betrayed it."

Lewis was surprised. So it had been Moss he'd seen.

Moss turned to Norse. "*You* saw?"

"I heard about it at breakfast," the psychologist said dryly. "I don't know *how* many people saw you, but your snowmobile trip so soon after Jed arrived set tongues wagging. You might as well have buried it with ceremony at the Pole stake."

"I thought people were supposed to sleep," Moss groused. "I informed my colleagues I had to double-check the winterization."

"Well, the general consensus is that your excuse was bullshit."

The astrophysicist looked embarrassed for only a moment. "So you told Abby Dixon about its value," Moss suddenly accused Lewis.

"You're not getting the point. It was more like she told me."

"Mickey, did you e-mail colleagues in the States about your find?" Cameron asked.

"Just Sparco."

"Who could have e-mailed who knows who, with word bouncing back down here?"

"I don't think so."

"But it's possible."

Moss frowned. "Yes." He didn't like the suggestion he was somehow at fault. "And irrelevant. Word leaked. The issue now is the theft."

"So what do you want?" Cameron asked slowly.

The astrophysicist took a deep breath. "We know Lewis here didn't hide it in his room, and I'm not surprised. But a thief had to hide it somewhere. I want to search the station. Every bed, every handbag. Anyone who is innocent shouldn't object. If the culprit wishes to confess and give it back, I'm prepared to end the matter for the winter: We all have to live with each other. If not—then I want it found." He waited.

"He doesn't have probable cause to search anybody," Lewis objected.

"Yes, I do. This is a very tiny village, young man, and

I have the certainty that my meteorite is in the hands of *someone* in our colony of twenty-six souls."

"That doesn't make you the Gestapo."

The astrophysicist was miffed at this challenge to his authority. "Nor do you have the right, as a raw newcomer, to call names! Your obstruction is exactly the tactic of a trapped thief!"

"Hey, time out!" Cameron lifted his arms, looking tired. He was irritated with Moss's accusations, but there was a subtle issue of rank here. Rod was station manager but Michael M. Moss was the quintessential Old Antarctic Explorer: an astrophysicist who'd been doing work at the Pole since the 1960s. The National Science Foundation respected this kind of longevity. They liked the guys who came back. Ignoring Moss was a political risk because word of any snub would get back to Washington. The man had become cranky and vindictive as he aged, and it was dangerous to cross him.

"Mickey, we all operate on mutual trust down here," Cameron tried. "You know that. We depend on each other for survival. Making accusations of thievery is like throwing gasoline on a fire."

"So is stealing. I've been here longer, and trusted longer, than anybody."

"Well, I didn't take your rock," Lewis said. He was disappointed that Cameron was allowing himself to be bullied by the headstrong scientist. It wasn't right.

"Then I want this place turned over until we find out who did."

Cameron groaned. "Mickey . . ."

"I'm not going to let this pass, Rod."

"Are *you* going to be searched?" Lewis asked.

Moss snorted. "Me! I'm the victim here!"

"How do we know that?"

"You're presumptuous, fingie!"

"Not as presumptuous as you!"

"I'm afraid Lewis has a point," Norse interjected quietly.

Moss looked at the psychologist with annoyance. "Pardon?"

"That *you* have the plainest motive of all. If the rock seems to have disappeared, you could smuggle and sell it without arousing suspicion. If you have a grudge against someone, like Lewis here, all you have to do is hide the rock and accuse him of stealing it. In fact, you could plant it on him, or anyone else. Maybe you're looking for sympathy. Maybe you've decided the meteorite is actually worthless but still want recognition for what you almost had. I can think of a thousand reasons to suspect you." He shrugged.

"You have a devious mind," Cameron complimented.

"He's full of shit," the astrophysicist corrected.

"Thank you," Norse said. "Occupational requirement."

"What you've suggested is ridiculous," Moss went on.

"I'm just saying that we're dealing with Pandora's box here. You throw accusations around and human emotions begin to burn like gunpowder. We need to think about this carefully. A disappearance occurring in a group small enough for everyone to be searched and questioned, if it comes to that. Does the thief wish to be caught? Did he hide the meteorite where it can't be found? Do we arouse suspicions? A dilemma as old as the first sailing ships, I'm sure."

"I'm glad you're having so much fun, Doc," Cameron said.

Lewis's mind was whirring. Moss? Abby? Who had the most plausible motive?

"Investigating this could prove a nightmare," Norse said. "However, it's just the kind of emotional dilemma I was hoping to explore."

"Then maybe *you* stole the rock," Cameron said with a sigh. He was visibly aging.

"Indeed. I should be among the first searched, if we decide to take that step. And Doctor Moss. Just as we searched Jed. Anyone with knowledge or motive. If we truly want to investigate this we're going to be making a list and checking it twice. So, the question is indeed, Who? Who knew about the meteorite?"

The others looked uncomfortable, thinking. "Well, I did," Cameron conceded. "I was skeptical about the Lewis hire, a geologist in a weather job. Mickey filled me in, sort of. I probably should have locked up the damn thing. Except there's no place to lock it."

Norse made a checkmark in the air with his finger. "Yes, of course. Lewis?"

"I didn't tell anyone. But Abby said it was common knowledge. Or at least rumor. The meteorite craze is no secret. I'd look for someone who needed money."

"People down here don't care about money," Norse quipped, quoting Cameron.

The station manager scowled. "I heard Geller's got some debt," he allowed. "Tyson's talked about money. Alexi doesn't have any in Russia—"

"Prestige?" Norse interrupted.

The station manager shrugged. "That's wide open. Any scientist. Anyone jealous. Anyone who doesn't like Mickey. . . ."

Moss looked annoyed.

"Which means that Lewis here could actually be a fall

guy for the real thief," Norse concluded. "They wait until he arrives and lift the meteorite. Voilà, the fingie gets fingered. By accusing Lewis, you might be playing into their hand."

Moss looked at Norse with frank dislike. "I despise your profession, you know."

"And I think you're close to retirement after an arduous career that has yielded you little fame and less money. We have no idea what you intended to do with the rock."

Moss jerked as if stung. Lewis was surprised at the psychologist's apparent willingness to make a powerful enemy. Willingness to come to Jed's aid.

"So, Doc, do we turn over the mattresses?" Cameron asked the psychologist, his tone strained by the sparring. "Strip-search the inmates?"

"That's your decision, of course. I'm just the observer. But we can consider the pros and cons. The danger of any search is it accomplishes nothing while pissing people off. The advantage is it could recover the meteorite."

"How much does that opinion cost?" Moss asked sarcastically.

Norse ignored him.

"Maybe we should sleep on it," Cameron said.

"No!" Moss objected. "That just gives the thief time!"

"I don't advise that, either," Norse said. "Make a decision. We should all pledge ourselves to secrecy about this discussion, of course—but I guarantee the dilemma will be all over the base anyway inside of an hour."

"You don't have a very high opinion of us."

"I don't have a very high opinion of human nature."

Cameron looked gloomy. He was thinking of the station report he'd have to file. "Would a thief really be stupid enough to put it in his room?"

"Yes. Because he might not be after a rock, or money, so much as to satisfy some other psychological need. Criminals betray themselves with regularity. A surprise search could work. Failure, however, might simply encourage our troublemaker. There's no right answer."

"We could just forget about the damn rock," Cameron said.

Norse smiled. "Yes. Forget about several million dollars."

"I don't want to turn the station upside down."

Moss glared. "If you don't, I will. There's science at stake, too, if that rock really hails from Mars. Or even if it doesn't."

Cameron closed his eyes. "People are going to go apeshit, Mickey."

Moss looked implacable. "*I* already have."

"Perhaps there's another solution," Norse suggested.

"What's that?" the station manager asked gloomily.

"Jed Lewis here represents opportunity." The psychologist nodded toward the newcomer. "He's a geologist. Our resident expert on all things stony. He should be motivated to clear his name. So I propose two things. First, that with his permission, we search his workplace as well. I don't think we'll find anything, even if he's the thief, but it simply eliminates one of the variables. Then search each of the rest of us in turn, right now, with all four along. Let's not have suspicions linger that any of us have anything obvious to hide."

His eyes polled the others. No one spoke to object.

"Second, let's enlist Lewis as our detective."

"What do you mean?" Moss said slowly.

"Lewis simply tells the truth. He admits he was brought down partly to check out the meteorite. He quietly lets slip it's missing and asks for guidance on likely suspects. These

are people who've been together for four months. They
know each other by now. Perhaps a suspect emerges."

"I'm going to be a private eye?"

"A discreet investigator. You're going to be yourself, with
a newcomer's curiosity. It's not Rod, laying down the law.
It's not Mickey, looking like a steaming bull. It's you—
asking a few new friends for help. If you handle it right,
no one will be upset."

What friends? "Another of your spies," he clarified.

"Mickey's spy."

Lewis looked at the others, considering. Poking around
was unlikely to make him very popular. Yet if he didn't,
he'd be hung with Moss's presumption that he had something to do with the disappearance. A lousy choice. "What
do I get if I find it?"

"Your good name back," Norse said.

"I never lost my good name."

"Your name and a recommendation for future employment," Moss said.

"No." Lewis shook his head. "There's no reason I
shouldn't get that anyway. I'm doing my job. I didn't take
your damn rock. I want something else."

"What, then?" Cameron asked.

"An apology for dragging me into this." He pointed at
Moss. "From him."

The astrophysicist scowled. Moss was not the type to
apologize to anybody. "Find it first," he said grudgingly.

"An apology for rousting me out of bed."

"Find it," Moss growled, "and I'll be fair."

"And what does that mean?"

"That you don't want me as an enemy."

CHAPTER EIGHT

Now what, Sherlock?

Lewis stood indecisively at the junction of tunnels near the entrance to the dome. Two corrugated steel archways, both completely buried under the snow, branched at either arm. To his left were the generators, gym, and garage. Bio-Med, the sick bay, was to his right, tucked into the same arch that held the station's fuel supply. The tunnels were like a huge half culvert, cold and dimly lit, and a scuffed layer of dirty snow coated their plywood floors like old sawdust. The medical facility was a windowless metal box the size of a truck trailer. Inside this makeshift hospital Doctor Nancy Hodge dispensed everything from useless advice on the inevitable polar crud—"We can't escape each other's viruses; deal with it"—to better-appreciated pain-killers, stitches, and antiseptics. If seriously hurt, their lives were in her hands. If desperately ill or wounded, there was probably little she could do.

It was a place to start. By necessity, Hodge knew every-body.

Lewis wanted to find the meteorite. Not for itself so

much as to find who'd caused him this trouble. Any thief must have known the fingie would be suspect. And of all the people on base, he was least equipped to probe because he *was* the fingie, the outsider. He really knew no one. Which the thief knew, too.

"You can be more objective because you're new," Cameron had told him.

Bullshit. It was a sop to Mickey Moss and a thankless job for Krill, low man on the totem pole. But he'd do it to save his winter.

And if he found the rock, he'd be tempted to keep the dang thing.

But first he had to find it. Find someone who knew people's secrets.

The four men who'd met in Comms had searched each other's rooms in the quiet hours before breakfast and found nothing of interest except Moss's fondness for a box of scratched vinyl LPs he'd shipped with an old turntable, a barrel-shaped kit telescope that Norse was assembling to look at the winter stars, and a shelf of pathetic how-to-be-a-boss books next to Cameron's bedside. Norse had a chess set, Cameron a jigsaw puzzle, Mickey a book of crosswords. Lewis wasn't surprised at the lack of smoking guns. No one was going to put the rock under his pillow. But it had satisfied him to rifle through their belongings as they had his. Served them right.

Now he pulled open the door and stepped into BioMed. "Doctor Hodge?"

The medic looked up with a start. A small pharmacy of pills was scattered on the wool blanket of the sick bay bed. Nancy was bent forward from a chair and going through it, sorting drugs into piles. The doctor jerked at the intrusion and some of the pills went awry.

Nancy hastily rolled them back. "Don't you knock?"

"I didn't know we were supposed to."

"Sometimes I have patients."

"I thought you'd use the lock."

She was slightly mollified. Lewis was new, after all. "We never use it because someone might be in a hurry in an emergency. Looking for stuff when I'm not around. Is this an emergency?"

"Not exactly."

"Then knock next time." She began scooping up pills and putting them into bottles. "So. You got the crud?"

"No." He glanced around. There was an examining table and the single bed. "Just wanted to pick your brain."

The doctor straightened and leaned back in her metal chair, looking curious and mildly wary. She got tense and excitable when patients showed up, a lapse in bedside manner that had already made base personnel reluctant to seek her care. Had there been some kind of malpractice back home? Or was she still just adjusting to the Pole? Now she gestured toward the bed as if there were a need to explain. "Look at all this medicine that's accumulated over the years. Antibiotics, aspirin, laxatives, even seasick pills. Some are pretty potent. I'm trying to sort it out." She held up two pills. "One to make you bigger, and another to make you small."

"Your own pharmacy."

"I could market on street corners." She smiled slightly and he realized how rarely Nancy mustered amusement. She wasn't dour, but she was serious. Tired, maybe. Thin, her face beginning to line, her hair to gray, her eyes to lose their optimism. Late forties and tough as horn. "Not something we'd advertise to NSF."

"That's the odd thing, isn't it?" Lewis said. "That in theory we could do anything we want down here and nobody would ever know."

Nancy shrugged. "That's the theory. The truth is that everyone is such a blabbermouth that sooner or later the feds in D.C. know everything. Which probably is just as well." That half smile again. "Keeps the place from exploding."

"I'm wondering if *you* know everything."

"What does that mean?"

"About the people who come down here. You get their records, and you might have some insight as to what makes them tick."

She laughed. "If you mean their organs, yes. If you mean their heads, no. That's Doctor Bob's business."

"He's too new. You've been with everybody for four months."

"As their medic, not their mother."

"I just need somebody who might have insights."

That slight smile again, and a sigh. "Lewis, you're looking at a woman who realized not long ago that she doesn't know anything about anybody." She held up her left hand, displaying that white streak on her ring finger. "A medical marvel who just happened not to notice that the man she'd lived with for eighteen years had taken up with one of her own nurses, drained her savings, and eloped to Mexico— until he sent a 'Dear Jane' letter from a Guadalajara cyber-café. You want medical advice, maybe I can help. You want to understand people? There's nobody more clueless than me." She nodded toward the door.

He stood his ground. "Well, you're the only person I can think of to start."

"Start what?"

"Getting Mickey Moss off my back."

She regarded him speculatively for a moment. Finally she pushed away from the pill-laden bed. "What's the problem?"

"Doctor Moss found this meteorite in the ice. Now it's missing."

"So?"

"It's been stolen."

Nancy looked skeptical. "Stolen? Why?"

"It's probably worth some money."

The medic barked a laugh. "Not down here it isn't. Who are you going to hock it to?"

"But later, outside . . ."

"No, that doesn't make sense." Nancy's mind was quick, everyone admitted that, and she was instantly engaged by this mystery. "I mean, steal it now and sit on it all winter? No, no, no. A prank, maybe. A borrowing. When was it missed?"

"I don't know. Couple days ago. I took a look at it because I'm a geologist and Mickey hid it out in the solar observatory and now it's gone."

"Not that long after the last of the summer crew?"

"Yes."

"Then *they* took it, don't you think? It's gone. Forget about it."

"No, I saw it after they left."

"Saw *it*? Or a fake? What if Moss swapped rocks? It's an alibi, see. Send the real rock out, bring in a fake, have the fingie tentatively authenticate the phony, and then get rid of it before he can really tell."

Lewis looked at the doctor in surprise. Hodge seemed to have certainly considered the problem in a very short time. "You've heard about this before."

She smiled, a certain grimness to her grin. "About the rock. Everyone has. If *I* was in charge, I'd start with *you*."

"They already did. I was searched last night."

"What'd they find?"

He kept his face straight. "A bag of white powder, a wallet full of prophylactics, and an Aryan Nations membership card."

"Told ya you didn't have it."

"My *Hustler*s they simply confiscated."

"I would have let you keep them."

"So who does have it? Nancy, I need help here. I come down, take a look at a meteorite as a favor, and it disappears."

"So you're questioning me?"

"I need to know who I *should* question."

"Maybe no one. Maybe you should tell Mickey to go fuck himself. Snooping around isn't going to make you very popular, you know."

"Moss is the station's eight-hundred-pound gorilla. I can't have *him* on my case all winter, either."

"True," she conceded. "I feel your pain." She thought a moment. "Well. Any number of people need money. Greed is universal. Cameron has no real career except as polar junkie, Linda Brown has a loser boyfriend back home who might marry her if she came with sufficient dowry, Gabriella Reid would be a gold digger if she could find anyone with any gold. . . ." The medic shrugged. "Take your pick."

"See? You do know things."

"That's stuff everyone knows. *I'd* swipe it, if I could."

"Do you need money, too?"

"I already told you I was pillaged by the son of a bitch I was married to. The bottom line, however, is it would be stupid as hell to take the meteorite at the start of winter.

Why have to hide it for eight months? Hocking something from the Pole wouldn't be all that easy anyway. The whole thing makes no sense. Why not wait and steal it in the spring? Mickey is smart, and old, and cranky, and I think he's somehow messing with all of us. Either that or . . ."

"Or what?"

"If it's one of us?" She thought some more. "I think it was taken not to sell, but to send a message. Make a point. Zing Mickey Moss. Relieve the tedium. Create a joke. Screw him. Screw *you*."

"But why?"

She shrugged. "Who knows?" She pointed to the door again. "But I wouldn't look for someone greedy. I'd look for someone pissed."

Lewis stood back under the intersection of archways again, more frustrated than ever. *Take your pick.* Well, hell. This kind of interrogation was really Rod Cameron's job but the station manager had been all too eager to palm the job off on Lewis. Nor was Cameron about to tell Mickey Moss to bug off. Harrison Adams had told Lewis that Moss had been down too long and was worshiped too much. He pushed everything too far, giving the Pole an importance it had never quite lived up to. It was rash to promise discovery and yet Moss promised incessantly, and bragged on work half done, creating pressures for performance that became obnoxious. "It's true he brings in research money and charms when he wishes," Adams had told him. "I've watched him schmooze a whole planeload of government VIPs who fly down for an hour to get their picture taken at the Pole. But he can also be as vain and vindictive as hell. Rod's afraid of him, and probably you should be, too. NSF can yank the old scientist's chain whenever they want to but they never will: Michael M. Moss is their polar god, the eminent graybeard poster boy. Don't cross him."

Yet someone had. Who had the balls to steal Mickey's rock?

One beneficiary of the mystery was Norse. He was an outsider, too, and the theft was exactly the kind of thing that played with their heads and gave the psychologist more to write about. Except that a stunt like that, the deliberate introduction of an artificial variable, would discredit the reliability of his entire study. Norse had said himself that he couldn't build a rat maze. Besides, the shrink had been surprised at the meteorite's value and was almost as new as Lewis, with no obvious ax to grind against Moss or anyone else.

A beaker, on the other hand, would recognize that any meteorite had value. A beaker might be jealous of Moss. Beakers were insanely competitive, boasting about hours worked, sleep forgone. They could be jealous, even petty.

Yet a scientist risked his career and reputation with any theft, while support personnel risked . . . what? There was no law or court or jail at the Pole. Theirs was a job, period, and a hard and thankless one at that. Put in a year and get out. There was little the scientists did that the cooks and mechanics and carpenters and safety specialists didn't know about. Some, like Buck Tyson, were openly contemptuous of what amounted to a two-tier system: the intellectuals and the grunts. If you wanted to annoy the eggheads you didn't throw a wrench into the power plant, because that hurt everyone. You . . . created another kind of turmoil. Like this.

And who was the station sorehead?

Lewis crossed to the archway on the other side and went down its dim half cylinder, the corridor's string of caged lights punctuated by pools of gloom. Pipes and conduit, years past their projected life, extended like rusty ropes on either side, wrapped in fraying, frosted insulation. In two places there were memorial pools of brown frozen water where sewage lines had ruptured before emergency repairs could be made. Sand had been thrown across the puddles until the dirty ice could be chipped out. Someday.

He went through another door to the generator room, more brightly lit and noisy. There were three generators here, one rumbling like an urgent drum, another in emergency readiness, and a third being overhauled. Pika Taylor, the plant manager, was bent over its black interior with ear protectors on, his head down inside his machine like a rabbit entering its burrow. He didn't hear the geologist.

Lewis considered the generator mechanic. Sometimes it was the quiet guys who blew. *Look for someone pissed.* Pika seemed awfully possessive about his machines. Yet he also seemed as mild as the animal he was named for. What did he have against Mickey Moss? The two were probably unaware of each other's existence. Pika's tuneless whistling hum was the sound of the bubble of preoccupation the man carried with him. He lived in a machine world, largely oblivious to the gossip, intrigues, friendships, lusts, jealousies, and alliances that swirled around him. His myopia was enviable, in a way. Unfortunately, Lewis wasn't allowed to share it.

Without interrupting Pika, he went on.

The gym beyond was the old garage, dark and low, with a frayed net that divided the space in two. It was the site of "volleybag" games, so named because an ordinary ball could be hit too easily up to the arched ceiling. A bundle of rags was used instead. Only a single light was on there, in line with the plea for constant energy conservation. There was no fuel resupply until the end of winter and the resulting twilight was spooky. Empty during the work shifts except . . . He started when he saw a shadowy woman sitting in the corner.

She ignored him.

"Hey, there," he tried.

No response.

Oh yeah. The woman was a mannequin he'd already been introduced to, the doll dubbed Raggedy Ann that had been brought down to practice CPR on. She was a mascot in the gym the way their slug Hieronymus was in the galley. Now she watched him from the gray twilight, slumped and somehow mocking. Hey yourself.

He turned left through another corridor that led to a second archway that had been added to replace the old garage. Inside was the station's motor pool, such as it was: two aging D-6 bulldozers whose rust had been arrested only by the arid polar air, two tracked exploration vehicles called Sprytes, and four beat-up snowmobiles, including the one he'd tried. It was becoming too cold to use the machines routinely and the main doors had been shut against the growing dimness outside. Blowing snow had made a small drift through the crack where the barn doors joined.

The garage was more brightly lit than the gym but still had a dungeon feel. Chains hung from overhead tracks used to hoist engine blocks, the red paint of their steel hooks flaked and faded into a semblance of dried blood. Metal racks built against the walls of the arch held a shadowy armory of spare and abandoned metal parts, intricate and mysterious. Pegboard above workbenches held racks of tools, heavy and sharp. A steel mesh floor laid across the snow was slick with dripping oil. The air stank of fuel fumes. A blowing heater kept its temperature barely above freezing.

A thousand places to hide a rock.

There was a screeching rasp and shower of sparks behind one of the parked Sprytes and Lewis made his way in that direction. He had no better plan of approach than with Nancy Hodge. *Gee, Tyson, you got the meteorite? You being so disliked and all.*

"Hey, Buck!"

Tyson glanced up from the spinning grinder with impatient annoyance and reluctantly turned, bracing himself against the likelihood of another work request. As he took his foot off the grinder pedal, its whir died away.

"Yeah?" It was a grunt.

"How's it going?"

Tyson squinted. "It's going."

Lewis looked at what the mechanic had in his hand. Flat metal, shiny and sharp. It was an opening. "I heard you made knives."

Tyson glanced around. "So?"

"As a hobby? You sell them back in North Dakota?"

"So?"

Maybe this was the wrong time to draw him out. The mechanic was on shift, and obviously not working on whatever he was supposed to be working on. He was probably afraid Lewis would tell Cameron. Lewis cast about for a revealing question. "Where do you get the material?"

"What?"

"For the knives? Where do you get the metal?"

The mechanic looked at him as if he were blind. "We've got enough scrap to build a fucking battleship. Every bit of useless junk you can think of except what we really need."

At least he was answering. And he took things. "What do you use for handles?"

Tyson considered his visitor. What was this about? He had no illusions about people who came into his garage. They all wanted *something,* and screw them. Still, he answered. "Metal. Wood. Bone. Hard rubber. Plastic. Why?"

"I'm thinking of buying one."

The mechanic looked wary.

"For Christmas presents. We'll be home by then."

Tyson waited for more.

"How much?" Lewis asked.

"What?"

"How much for a knife?"

The mechanic considered. "Hundred bucks."

"For a knife!"

"Handmade and engraved at the Pole." He deliberately huffed out a cloud of vapor, a plume like cigarette smoke. "I put up with a lot of shit to make these."

"Would you consider fifty?"

That baleful look again. "No." Then he reconsidered. "Maybe seventy-five."

"I'm on a budget, Buck."

"So am I."

There was a long silence, each watching the other. Tyson didn't act like an imminent millionaire. Another dead end. "When will they be finished?"

"Long before you get home." He grinned at that.

Lewis smiled falsely. "You got some I could look at?"

The persistent interest softened Tyson slightly. He shrugged. "In my locker in my room. Maybe I could show you later."

"My dad might want one, too."

"I don't care who wants them."

"He likes crafted stuff."

"Show me some cash. Then we'll get serious." Tyson turned back to the grinder.

Lewis glanced around again, spotting nothing of interest. The mechanic might be a grouch but there was none of the evasion expected of a thief. Lewis turned to go, thinking he might try Abby next and worrying she'd be more annoyed than helpful.

He was no investigator. This entire fiasco was a waste of time. . . .

"Tyson!"

Rod Cameron was stalking into the garage toward both of them, looking sleepless and angry.

"Jesus fuck . . ." The mechanic turned, stiffening. The mechanic's grip on the blade tightened and Lewis could see the knuckles whitening. He looked at Lewis accusingly, as if he'd led the station manager here, and Lewis shook his head in denial. What the hell was this about?

Cameron strode up and stopped, rocking slightly on his ankles, his mood stormy. "What the hell are *you* doing here?" he asked Lewis.

"Talking with Buck while my computer defrags." He raised his eyebrows, trying to prod Cameron's memory. The investigation.

"Oh." He looked at Lewis curiously and Lewis shrugged again. Nothing. "Well, go poke around somewhere else, Lewis. I need to have it out with Tyson." The manager's eyes darted back to the mechanic. He was gathering himself for a fight.

"Sure." Lewis took a step back.

"You don't have to leave, fingie," Tyson said quietly. "No secrets here."

Lewis hesitated. He was curious. Cameron glanced at

him, waiting for him to go, but Lewis thought Tyson might let something useful slip. "Maybe I can help."

Cameron blinked. It might help to have a witness. "Okay. No secrets." He turned to Tyson. "What're you doing, Buck?"

Tyson looked sourly at his boss. "Stuff."

"You get this Spryte fixed?"

"The machine's a piece of shit."

"We need it anyway."

"It's fucking dangerous if it breaks down."

"It's fucking all we've got. And I thought you were a good mechanic."

Tyson looked from Cameron to Lewis, wondering how belligerent he could afford to be, and spat, deliberately, the spittle hitting the floor. "I'm working on it."

Cameron looked at the big man's fist. "What's that, then?"

Tyson looked at the metal in his hand with apparent surprise and then held it up, the sharpness glinting in the light. "Piston rod," he said, deadpan.

Cameron looked at the hoisted knife and then back at Tyson. "I looked at the water budget this morning. Do you know the daily ration is off fifty gallons?"

"Why no, boss, I don't."

"It's because of your damn showers, isn't it?"

"Beats me."

"I do. I've been timing you."

"Then you've got more time than I do."

"You're using as much water as six other people!"

"So melt some more."

"You know the Rodriguez Well is slow!"

"Two months ago you were complaining I was too dirty."

"That's because you stank every time you came to meals!

You'd clear an entire table, like some goddamn wino! Are you insane, or what?"

"Don't you wish you'd sent me home?" Tyson smiled.

"You know I couldn't find a replacement, you goddamn butthead!"

Tyson pointed at Lewis. "Sparco did. You could, too. There's *still* time to get a plane in here, maybe. For an emergency. I feel appendicitis coming on."

"I'm warning you, Buck . . ."

"Because *I* wish you'd send me home." The mechanic tossed the knife aside onto the metal workbench, where it rang like a bell. He raised his big hands. "You want to compare hands, Rod?"

"Don't you threaten me."

"You want to compare those soft, white, thin-fingered paws of *yours,* which hardly ever get out of your warm fucking office, with *mine,* which get so hard I gotta soak 'em in Vaseline and wear gloves to bed? You want to spend a day under this Spryte or the Cats, where the metal's either so hot from the stinking engine, spewing carbon monoxide, that I burn my hands, or so cold that I burn 'em again? You want to work on shit so brittle that it shatters like glass, and string extension cords so stiff they snap like a twig?" He glowered as he spoke, like a looming thunderhead. "Don't talk to me about your fucking precious water! It's the only damn thing keeping me sane!" His volume had grown to a roar.

Cameron instinctively stepped backward. The big man was at the barest edge of control. The station manager was sputtering. "I've about had it with you."

"No, you haven't, you ineffectual snot!" The mechanic seemed to expand with frustrated rage, like an inflating balloon. He filled the garage, dark and hairy, and Lewis felt nervous, too. Tyson was losing it. "You haven't *had* it with me for another eight, fucked-up, gloriously boring months! You can't get away from *me,* and I can't get away from *you,* and so you can take your lunatic work calendar and cram it like a suppository up your soft supervisory ass!" The mechanic waited defiantly for a response, quivering with rage, and yet there was none, Cameron momentarily speechless at this outright defiance. The station manager had gone rigid. Then Tyson turned arrogantly back to the workbench, picking up the knife.

"That's outright insubordination!" Cameron finally managed.

"You need me, I'll be in the shower."

Cameron looked at the mechanic's back with a mixture of disbelief and hatred. "This time you've gone too far," he choked, trembling with outrage.

"So fire me."

"I'm writing you up in my e-mail report."

Tyson laughed. Cameron looked bitterly at Lewis, who was embarrassed at this exchange. The manager knew he couldn't let this one go. Couldn't risk losing control. Couldn't bear the humiliation.

"This time, Buck Tyson, you're *toast.*"

We Decide as a Group

Kids come out of their childhood thinking they'll be taken care of. Kids show up in college with this sorry-ass misapprehension of helplessness glued between their ears like slow-setting concrete, as hapless as clams, as dim as donkeys. Fix me. Be fair.

Fat Boy had been carried his whole life, I'm sure of it. Instead of being forced to get fit to survive, he'd always found a place on the team, always convinced the others to wait up, always whined his way into some kind of second-class acceptance. Fat Boy always got bailed out. And now he needed to be bailed out by me.

Who knows why the hell he unroped himself? To rest, to pee, to make the rest of us wait—what does it matter? He'd insisted on joining the group and was now slowing the group he'd joined, defining our chain by its weakest link. The end of his rope lay trailing on the snow like a foolish scribble. Somewhere he'd unleashed himself and was gone.

I looked at the summit, pink and swollen in the dawn light. I looked at the clouds to the west, which were beginning to mound into a grayish wall. If he cost us too many minutes, he'd cost all of us the climb. Unacceptable.

I wanted to take my team and Kressler's team up to the top. Let Fleming find him. He'd lost him. Why ruin it for everyone? Why ruin it for me? But Kressler sided with his friend and they insisted the entire class stay together. So down the tracks we went, the other kids grumbling and cursing, looking for the point where our chubby

*little moron had decided to wander off by himself, and
myself so potentially eruptive that I knew better than to
say anything. I half hoped Fat Boy had already found a
crevasse and was gone for the next ten thousand years,
frozen like the dense brick he was until a glacier spat
him out. Then maybe we could still make the top.*

I should be so lucky.

*It turned out that the idiot Fleming had lost him a full
quarter mile back, never having turned to check on the
end of his string. The weak-lunged half-wit! Couldn't say
that, either, of course, but Fleming was a lousy climber,
truth be told. Piss-poor instructor. He was too nice, always a mistake. Made me uneasy. There's a difference
between self-control and weakness. So back we went, a
quarter-mile backtrack, and sure enough footprints led
off the main trail we'd beaten and away in a meandering wander down one side of the saddle. What was Fat
Boy thinking? We hadn't followed his trail for fifty yards
when there was a break in the snow like a bite in a sand-
wich. The kid had obviously triggered a slide and been
carried over the edge with it. I can't say I felt much pity.
I frankly looked at the evidence with a certain feeling of
satisfaction. Life was just. Finis. Can we go to the top
now? But I bit my tongue.*

*Great surprise and consternation, of course. Wails,
tears, and so much phony emotion I thought the sheer
weight of the pathos would trigger another avalanche.
As if anybody really liked the dumb kid! But of course
we had to do the right thing, and the right thing was to
clamber up and around, risking us all, and getting so
close to the edge of Wallace Wall that we all might soon
join Fat Boy in Paradise. I kept looking for a place to
plant my ice ax once the class started the slide over. Ex-*

cept we didn't, and then, wonder of wonders, we heard a frightened scream.

Fat Boy wasn't done with us.

As the one instructor who really knew what he was doing, I had the other two belay me and edged down-slope for a look over the cliff where Fat Boy had fallen, leaning so far that the rope was taut as piano wire. At first I couldn't see a damn thing in the dim predawn light but then I made out movement on a ledge about three hundred feet below. The kid had slid down a chute, bounced off into space, and then by a miracle had some-how fetched up about three thousand feet shy of the real bottom. He saw my silhouette and started screaming to beat hell. The smart thing to do would have been to leave him right then and go get help.

Except that the storm was coming.

Kressler and then Fleming had to take their turns edg-ing down to see, minutes ticking by, our window closing. It was a mess, all right. A right royal snafu.

The triumvirate met. My advice was to get the rest of the kids off the mountain. Better to lose one than fifteen. Lower a bag down to Fat Boy and come back with a chopper and a medic unit when the weather allowed. Let's not be heroes now.

Kressler didn't like it, and I knew why. It was his class, really. We were assisting. A rescue would get in the news-papers and questions would be asked about why our dumb blubber buffalo had been allowed to wander off into an avalanche chute. Wouldn't look good for our fear-less leader to have allowed such an elementary mistake. Kressler was up for department chair and the competi-tion was vicious, as it always is in the ivied halls of acad-emia, where so many fight so relentlessly for so little.

His rivals would use this embarrassment against him. Silly, but there it is. Careers have turned on less. He'd really rather just bundle the kid down the mountain himself, if it was all the same to us. Come back a hero, smelling roses. It was the political thing to do.

No way, José.

But then Fleming, willing to brown-nose an up-and-coming department chair with the best of them—in order to grease his own skids toward tenure—sided with the ambitious idiot. The pair was convinced they could pull off this bit of derring-do.

Kressler was actually pretty good, technically, but Fleming was in over his head and didn't have the judgment of a flea. He trusted, always a mistake. And he trusted Kressler to be able to somehow snatch Fat Boy off that wall and save us all from an awkward morning-after of questions.

Stupid, stupid, stupid.

Except those clouds were coming. That was their trump card. I'd actually heard a little about the approaching storm—I'd volunteered to monitor the radio—but decided not to share it with the doomsayers the evening before because it might have cramped our try for the summit. In hindsight maybe that wasn't the smartest thing in the world to do but I thought we had time and I wanted the top, dammit. That was the whole point. We could have beaten the storm if not for the unroping of Fat Boy. Now the other two used the weather to justify our immediate rescue of the idiot. Left alone, the bozo might actually die. And then what was now mere bad luck becomes major fuckup. Turns Kressler from rising star to object of inquiry. So here's the plan. We climb down to Fat Boy—all of us—and then continue down an "easy" route that Kressler knew on Wallace Wall. We all get down off the mountain pronto. Disaster turns into rescue. Fat Boy becomes a trophy save.

Jesus.

The voice of reason, being me, gently pointed out that the pack of amateurs we were leading didn't have the skills to do this kind of Matterhorn macho shit. I told Kressler that he could go down there while Fleming and I took everyone else back down the glacier. But Kressler said he needed Fleming, and Fleming said Fat Boy was so heavy they really needed two more young studs to help, and no one wanted to break up the party, and so in the spirit of eternal togetherness the decision was made, over my quiet objections, to take fourteen kids down the hard way in hopes of saving one and avoiding any awkward questions.

I'm sure they'd tell you it made sense at the time.

The kids were frightened. "We need your help on this one," the other two instructors told me. I caved. With more camaraderie than sense I put on a happy face, announced we were all making a brief detour, and agreed to take Kressler's dubious route, picking up our over-weight blubber baggage along the way. We'd look so smart when we reached the bottom!

Ah, togetherness.

A couple of the girls were weeping. A couple of the guys looked whiter than the snow. The sun was just cracking the eastern range.

We started down.

CHAPTER NINE

I think I need some help."

Lewis had found Abby in the greenhouse. It was little more than a closet with burbling hydroponic tanks, potted soil, and the smell of tomato vines, but it was brightly lit by grow lights and a refuge of steamy warmth. Lettuce, tomato, parsley, kale, and other greens struggled to maturity there, adding meager scraps of fresh chlorophyll to meals dominated by canned and frozen foods. While the greenhouse was more hobby than experiment, NASA scientists had visited twice to take notes on the facility as a model for future spaceships. Abby came regularly to help Lena Jindrova tend the plants and get an injection of artificial sunlight.

"I'm kind of busy, Jed," she told him. She was snipping dead leaves.

As he'd feared, his investigation was turning people cool. No one wanted a snoop. Lewis suspected Nancy Hodge had put the others on notice about his investigative efforts. Was their doctor the thief, trying to sabotage any inquiry? Or the enforcer of group propriety? Last night when he'd sat in the galley the conversation had muted. And this morning . . .

"Abby, I'm in a fix here and I don't know what to do."

She didn't look at him. "Why come to me?"

"Because you've been here longer than I have."

She took another snip. "So has everyone."

"Okay, because we're friends."

"A friend you said blabbed about the meteorite. That may have started this whole mess. That's what I heard."

Jesus. Ice Cream had turned hard again. "We were just discussing who knew about it. *You* pumped *me*."

She didn't reply.

"And I didn't come here to ask you about the meteorite."

"I'm disappointed I didn't make your list."

He stopped, exasperated. He'd crossed some unseen line at the station. Some unseen line with her.

At his silence she finally stopped trimming and turned to look at him, allowing some reluctant sympathy. "Maybe that wasn't fair," she allowed. "But I don't know about the meteorite, Jed."

"I came to ask you about something else."

"I don't have any suspects."

"No. Something else."

She let the shears drop by her side. "What, then?"

"Someone slipped this under my door this morning." He took a piece of thick paper from a pocket and handed it to her.

Abby unfolded a five-pointed star cut from yellow construction paper. On it were printed the words, "Deputy Dawg."

She frowned.

"I don't even know what it's supposed to mean," Lewis said.

She crumpled up the star and threw it in a recycling basket. The sorting of trash was a basic ground rule at the Pole. "It means to back off."

"Back off what?"

She looked at him impatiently. "Are you dense? You're the fingie, Jed. No one knows you yet. No one *trusts* you yet. But you're going around asking questions about Mickey's rock like a cop and implying that the rest of us are a bunch of crooks. Worse, you're doing Moss's dirty work for him. Nobody likes him, either, not really. It's the worst kind of way to try to fit in here, and somebody's trying to tell you politely to cut it out before you're toast for the rest of the winter. Why do you even *care* who took the meteorite? Nobody else does."

"Because *he* thinks *I* might have taken it."

She looked at him with impatience. "And what do you care what *he* thinks? He's not the person you have to eat with, *we* are."

"He's Sparco's friend and Sparco hired me and ... I'm just trying to do the right thing."

"Well, this is a great community of good-hearted people and you're doing exactly the *wrong* thing if you want to fit in. Mickey can be a bully and Cameron always feels pressured but those guys aren't the group. *We* are. And we're not a bunch of thieves."

"I'm just trying to feel my way."

"So do your job, keep your mouth shut, and watch. Learn. Listen. There's a society here and your winter will be miserable if you don't fit into it."

"Tyson doesn't fit into it."

"And is he happy?"

Lewis didn't have to answer.

"In fact, Tyson is an example of the risk you run. I ran

into Rod and he's so hot he's got steam coming out of his ears. I think he and Buck had some kind of run-in."

"They did. I saw it."

She looked at him in surprise. She was instantly interested, unable to mask her curiosity. "When?"

"I was in the garage when he told Rod to essentially go screw himself. That mechanic is unbelievable. He's nuts."

"He's got so much anger it's scary. It's not the Pole. There's something wrong with him. Some basic resentment of other people, or frustration with his own life."

"They should never have let him come down here."

She nodded. "I think Rod went to Doctor Bob for advice. Tonight he's called a meeting. And that's why it's not a good time to play Columbo, Jed. There's too much tension on station and the winter's starting poorly. Things are coming to a head."

"About the meteorite?"

"About water."

Amundsen-Scott station sat on a freshwater ocean, but it was frozen into ice that stayed a permanent sixty degrees below zero. Imported jet fuel ran a heater that melted a bulb of liquid water in the ice cap called a Rodriguez Well, but raising the temperature of the ice to the melting point was enormously costly. It took a gallon and a half of jet fuel just to fly in a gallon more for use at the Pole.

"Liquid water here costs more than gasoline at home," Cameron told the assembly in the galley that night. "Every drop we consume represents energy we can't use for heating or lights or to run our instruments. If we were on a nuclear submarine we could shower all day, but we're not. And we're using water faster than it's budgeted."

"How much faster?" Carl Mendoza asked.

"About fifty gallons a day."

Some of the others turned to look at Tyson, who was slouched in the shadows along a back wall. He looked determinedly bored.

"Are you listening, Buck?" Cameron called to him.

For a long minute the big man didn't answer. Then: "What? Hard to hear you, Rod. Might need to wash my ears out tonight."

There was an uneasy silence in the room. Tyson looked huge, surly, mean. Everyone was waiting to see what Cameron would do. What Cameron *could* do.

The station manager waited, letting the silence and uneasiness build. Finally he went on. "The reason we're using so much water is, of course, a mystery." There was a murmur of surprise, but Doctor Bob was watching Cameron expectantly, nodding slightly. "The one thing we *do* know is that if we're going to make it through the winter with a sufficient fuel reserve, we have to curb our excessive consumption."

"*One* person has to," astronomer Harrison Adams muttered.

"So," Cameron continued blandly, ignoring Adams, "I'm being forced to announce a new rationing policy. Effective immediately, showers are being cut from two to one a week."

"What?" Geller shouted. The crowd erupted. Several turned to glare at Tyson. He had straightened in initial surprise but now was grinning sardonically, enjoying their outrage, seeming to feed off it.

"That's not fair!" Dana Andrews protested.

"Rod, you can't do that to the maintenance crew," station carpenter Steve Calhoun objected. "We get dirty, man. We stink. Once a week is too long in between."

"And I'm not going to lose my privileges to accommodate that blowhard baboon!" Mickey Moss thundered, pointing at Tyson. "He's a bully!"

"Sticks and stones, man," the mechanic mocked him.

"I'm going to break you!" Moss shouted at Tyson. "Not just here but after, when we get home! Your performance is going to dog you the rest of your life!"

"Fuck you, Mickey Mouse."

Moss was seething, fighting for self-control. "The rest of your life, Tyson."

Cameron held up his hand. "This rationing is temporary until water consumption appears to be coming back into line with projections. I'm leaving it up to the rest of you to figure out how to make sure that comes about."

There was quiet again, everyone looking speculatively at Tyson. He looked back at them defiantly, saying nothing.

"This is *your* fault," Lena Jindrova finally hissed, standing up to look at the big man, who topped her by a good foot. "You are the pig who is making the rest of us suffer."

"Fuck you, too, Lena."

"You are the pig like the old party bosses in Czechoslovakia, pulling everything to themselves, caring for no one."

"This whole water-rationing crap is bullshit. We've got plenty of fuel. More than we can use."

"You're wrong, Buck," Cameron said quietly.

"You are like a worm that cares only for itself," Lena went on heatedly. She pointed to the galley serving counter, where a glass mason jar held a leaf of lettuce and the curled form of Hieronymus. "Our mascot has more heart than you. More soul."

Tyson scowled, the resentment in the room toward him

so palpable it made the air they breathed like syrup. You could smell the sweat, the electric tension. In a moment Cameron had turned everyone against him. "That slug?" the mechanic growled ominously.

"More brains, more work, more everything."

"Little Hiero?" The mechanic pushed himself away from the wall and made his way around the folding chairs where the others sat, his work boots ringing on the floor as he walked. He was supposed to have taken them off, as well, before entering the galley, and they left a trail of snow and grease. The others watched him warily, resentfully, none quite daring to interfere with whatever he chose to do next. He walked up to the counter and picked up the mason jar with the gastropod. "This slime sucker here?"

"Don't you touch him!" Lena warned.

Tyson held the jar up to the light. "Oh yeah. I see what you mean. He's cuter than any bitch in this room."

"Buck, put it down," Cameron commanded. He now looked worried. Tyson's open defiance hadn't been planned.

"Cool it, Tyson." Pulaski stood up, too, muscles tensing.

"I'm cool, Cueball." Then the mechanic made a sudden violent swing of his arm and brought the jar down on the galley counter with a crack. The glass shattered and Lena screamed. The slug slid a short distance on the stainless steel, braked by its own slime. Tyson flicked a couple of pieces of glass off the animal and gingerly picked it up between two fingers, holding it up in front of the crowd.

"Is this what you prefer to *me,* Lena?"

"You put him down!" she cried.

Norse had become rigid, his gaze flicking around the room, taking it all in.

"Do you think I give a flying fuck what any of you think of me?" Tyson asked them, turning in a slow half rotation to give everyone a clear view of the slug. "Do you think I give a diddly damn about any of *you*? We're all down here for bucks and glory and to punch the time card home, man. I don't give a shit about the science, I don't give a shit about the station, and I sure as hell don't give a shit if the rest of you don't get a single shower for the rest of the fucking winter. Here's the bottom line. I don't *need* you. I don't *want* you. I sure as hell don't *like* you. I ain't *afraid* of you." He held the slug closer to his face, scrutinizing it. "And this is what I think of this little guy here."

He opened his mouth.

"Buck, if you do that you're bloody dead on station!" Dana Andrews cried.

"Suck my dick, Dana." He crammed the animal in.

"No!" Lena shouted.

"Jesus Christ," Pulaski said in disgust. The crowd groaned.

Tyson chewed twice, his look wildly defiant, and then swallowed, the gulp audible. There were flecks of slime on his beard. He deliberately belched.

"Why in the name of God did you do that?" Cameron breathed, his look one of horror. He took a shaking step toward Tyson, and Norse put a hand on the station manager's arm.

"Here's another rule for you ass-kissers," Tyson said, wiping his mouth. "No pets in Antarctica."

Lena was looking at him in hatred. Pika regarded the mechanic in disbelief.

"This your idea, Bob?" Tyson asked the psychologist. "Turn everyone against me? Well, surprise, surprise, they already were. So fuck you, too."

Norse, composing his expression into something opaque, didn't answer.

"I'm crazier than you thought, aren't I?" Tyson persisted.

"You're setting yourself alone, Buck," the psychologist warned quietly.

"You're right on that one." He waited for another challenge, his look amused, but none came. "Okay? We done here? Gotta hit the showers, man."

The quiet was as thick and cold as the ice cap.

He left.

Lewis could hear the bubble of the juice dispenser in one corner.

"One shower," Cameron finally said shakily.

The others looked frustrated, furious, sick.

That night, someone nailed a piece of burnt toast to Buck Tyson's door.

It was two nights later that Jed Lewis was roused from his bed once more, again in the early hours of the morning. Cameron burst into his room and flicked on the light.

"What? What?"

"Get up, we're organizing a search."

"Now?"

"Sooner than now. Get your ass in gear." The station manager looked sick.

"What's going on? Is it the meteorite?"

"Screw the meteorite. Now something's really wrong."

"What?"

"I can't believe this is happening to me."

"What, dammit?"

"Now Mickey Moss is missing."

CHAPTER TEN

This is what it's like to be dead, Lewis thought.

The searchers had stopped on the polar plateau three miles from the dome, clambering gratefully down from the Spryte to take a break from the snow tractor's ungainly lurch and guttural growl. It was a tiring vehicle to ride in, noisy and slow, with treads like a tank and a cramped, wedge-shaped orange cab. But it could also straddle small crevices, snort its way up forty-degree slopes, and clamber over pack ice. If Mickey Moss was lost on the plateau, the tractor should spot him.

He wasn't.

There was nothing to see. Distant radio towers appearing as fine as spider silk marked Scott-Amundsen base, its dome a bump on the horizon. In all other directions the whiteness was as empty as heaven and as frozen as hell. It was amazing how far they seemed from the station. The effect was strangely dreamlike, Lewis feeling as detached as an astronaut cut from a lifeline. He didn't like being out here, unprotected and cold.

Moss's body could have been covered by drifting snow,

of course. But why would the astronomer walk out here?
There was nothing to walk to: no hillock, no wrinkle, no
vale, no stop. They'd gone first to the tiny solar observatory buried in the snow a mile from the dome, its ramp
the place where Lewis had seen Mickey's snowmobile disappear that lonely midnight. It consisted of another metal
box sunken in snow, its interior housing a small solar telescope boxed for the winter. No Mickey, no meteorite, no
tracks. Beyond that, all destination disappeared once you
left the polar station. There was only the wind.

"This is stupid," Tyson said.

The mechanic was their driver, pressed into reluctant
service after the three hours that it took him to get their
one operable Spryte in running condition and warmed up.
If Moss was out here he was already dead, Tyson had
reasoned, and if he was dead they'd probably never find
him. The blowing snow would bury him. So what was
the point?

"Do it anyway," Cameron had said quietly. No one else
had said a word. Tyson had hesitated and then finally
shrugged and obeyed.

A disappearance was serious.

Pulaski had been picked to accompany Tyson because
of his military background. Lewis was drafted because of
his unwanted association with the whole mess. Norse had
come along on the theory he might guess where Moss had
gone and could help manage the volatile Tyson.

Cameron wouldn't get on the same machine with the ostracized mechanic and so he was leading the others in a
systematic search of the buildings. If Moss wasn't *there* he
had to be out *here*. By crackling radio, they were confirming he was neither.

"Didn't he go off by himself all the time anyway?" Lewis asked.

"Just over to the Dark Side with his junk food," Pulaski said. "You could phone him. Never went off like this before."

Snow skittered up to their knees, blowing so fast that any tracks were erased within minutes of being made.

"So what'd they teach you about this in the Army?" Tyson asked Pulaski. It was an honest question, not a mocking one, and a tentative effort toward reopening some kind of communication with the group he'd scorned. Tyson had seen the piece of toast on his door and was quietly reconsidering his defiance. He was tired of the Pole but it was spooky how nobody was talking to him. Maybe he'd gone too far. Besides, the mechanic respected the cook's mysterious military past.

Pulaski let a silence hang for a moment, just to let Buck know where he stood, and then answered. "Have clear objectives. Inform your superiors. Maintain communication. Prepare for the unexpected." The cook squinted into the wind. "Doesn't look like Mickey did any of that to me."

"Anybody ever vanish like this before?" Lewis asked.

"The program's been pretty safe, considering. I mean there's been a lot of American deaths in Antarctica—more than fifty since World War II, if you count all the ship and plane injuries—but mostly industrial accidents. We've never lost a beaker at the Pole. And a guy as experienced as Mickey . . . it's weird, man."

They shuddered in the wind. The uncomfortable orange cab was beginning to look good again.

"So do we just keep driving around in circles?" Tyson demanded. "I'm about to go snow-blind."

"I'm betting he's not out here," the cook agreed. "Unless he was suicidal or something. And this is a tough way to go. It's like swimming out to sea—all of a sudden the station looks very far away and you turn back. Any sane man would do that."

"Was Mickey sane?" Lewis asked. Suddenly it seemed like a fair question, given the man's long association at Amundsen-Scott.

"This place was his life."

"And why would Big Rodent be suicidal?" Tyson added. He looked pointedly at Lewis. "The way I heard it, he was about to come into big money."

"Maybe *that* was the problem," Norse said quietly.

The others didn't reply. Everyone on station was contemplating the coincidence of Moss vanishing shortly after the meteorite disappeared. Everyone, Lewis was sure, was thinking about how his own arrival had brought bad luck.

"Maybe Mickey has fled or left or escaped the station on purpose, going somewhere else," Norse suggested.

Pulaski barked a laugh. "Where?" He gestured at the blank plateau. "There's no place to go to, Doc."

"Yeah," Tyson muttered. "Except Vostok."

"Where?" Norse turned to the mechanic.

"The closest Russian base," Tyson explained. "It's across the plateau, which means it's basically flat. No glaciers, no crevasses. Nobody in their right mind would want to go there but it's the one place you might actually drive to. People have joked about it."

The psychologist was interested. "You think Moss could have gone there?"

"No. It's seven hundred dick-shriveling miles. You'd need a vehicle, extra fuel, and I'm the guy in charge of the motor pool. Mickey didn't check anything out."

"Is it hard to drive a Spryte?"

Tyson looked at the psychologist dubiously. "It ain't hard on your brain. It's hard on your butt. But I'm telling you, we ain't missing a Spryte."

"But someone could *do* it."

Tyson contemplated the Spryte. "With that piece of shit? Maybe. You'd have to want to get there very, very bad to risk it. But it could be done, if you were lucky."

"But Moss *didn't* do it," Pulaski clarified.

The mechanic nodded. "No way. Dollars to donuts he's within five miles of where we're standing. And frozen stiffer than the poker that's up Rod Cameron's ass."

The station manager called another meeting in the galley that night. Lewis came last and sat in the back, depressed by the mood of bad feeling. Abby glanced his way and then turned her head, looking troubled. He'd said hello to her earlier, hoping she'd warmed, but she'd flitted by him in distraction, not wanting to talk. "It's not you, it's Mickey," she had muttered. Something about Moss's disappearance had hit her hard.

Norse sat to one side of the room near the serving counter, again scanning the crowd. They needed a shrink now, didn't they? Yet the psychologist looked somber, no doubt remembering Tyson's blow-up at the last meeting. Lewis bet that slug eating hadn't been in his script. Now Lewis watched Norse catch Abby's eye once and give her a look of reassurance as if to say, *I understand.* Had their psychologist become her confessor? Lewis found the idea irked him.

His own mood was gloomy. He'd come to the Pole for a fresh start and instead his counseling on the meteorite had dragged him into the middle of a serious crisis. *You can't quit down here,* Cameron had told him.

Well, hell.

The station manager got up from his chair and stiffly faced the group. His movement left two chairs empty, Lewis noticed. Pulaski without thinking had set out twenty-six, and Moss's was conspicuously vacant. Everyone eyed the extra seat uneasily. It was an accusation, a plea, a warning.

Cameron looked haggard. He hadn't slept in thirty-six hours and the e-mailed heat he was getting from Washington, D.C., was enough to set his terminal on fire. First he'd had to tattle on Tyson's water-rationing violation instead of simply fixing the problem himself. Now the possible death of Michael M. Moss would be shocking the polar establishment. Moss was Mr. South Pole. Worse, the people on station were family and now he'd somehow lost one of them. Cameron had apparently failed in the most fundamental way: at keeping them all alive. He was in no mood to forgive himself. At the sight of his drawn face the group's anxious chatter died away.

"I'm not very religious," the station manager began, his voice hoarse. He stopped, looking confused. Pulaski got up and poured Cameron a glass of water, handing it to him with the gravity of communion. The station manager drank, and the simple act seemed to steady him. He tried again.

"I'm not very religious, but I'd like to start this meeting with a prayer—not mine but our own prayers, each of us individually, from our own hearts. I don't know where Mickey is but let's acknowledge the central truth—that whatever our relationship to him, he was—is—the soul of this station. So I'd like a minute of silence to pray for *his* soul, which I hope is alive and which I fear is somehow, inexplicably, dead. At least none of us have seen hide nor hair of him for more than twenty-four hours. We've looked and looked and are going to keep on looking, but right now I think we need the help of a higher power. So, for just a minute, please, send our sonofabitch Old Antarctic Explorer your best thoughts."

He bowed his head. Lewis did too, trying to think what Moss might have been thinking, or where he might have gone. It made no sense. Nancy Hodge was looking with sad sympathy at Cameron: She knew a tragedy like this would threaten to erase whatever professional advancement the station manager had hoped to gain by coming down here. Norse was calmly letting his eyes scan the group, as if someone would betray themselves. And Buck Tyson looked uncertain, as if the possibility of Moss's death were making him reconsider his intransigence. Self-sufficiency was one thing, exclusion another. Tonight, everyone had shifted their chairs away from his.

"Well."

Heads came up and Cameron continued. "I've let NSF know our situation and that we're doing everything we can. They send us their best and urge us to keep searching. I'm going to launch another perimeter search around the station tomorrow and go through the buildings again. I don't . . . I don't know what else to do." He hesitated, looking gloomy. "Maybe he had a heart attack."

"He was strong as an ox," Pulaski said.

There was quiet.

"Strong people die, too," Nancy finally amended.

"In any event," the station manager went on, "we're getting our winter off to a stressful start and it's at times like these that the group has to hang together. Together!" He looked at Tyson worriedly. "It's hard to lose anybody, but especially Mickey. Damned if I know what happened. Could have been illness. Could have been an accident. Could have gotten lost. You probably have your own ideas. I pray to God he'll just show up, but we all know how cold it is outside."

Several faces turned to check the television monitor. The temperature was sixty-one degrees below zero. A rising wind had pushed the chill factor to minus ninety-two.

"Why don't you tell us what this is really about, Rod?" a voice demanded. It was Harrison Adams, the astronomer. "As a scientist, I don't believe in coincidences."

"What does that mean?"

"The rumor is that Mickey found a meteorite in the ice. Someone apparently took it. He demands an investigation. Then he disappears. I mean, come on."

"What are you saying, Harrison?"

"That five million dollars makes this more than a simple missing person."

There was a murmur through the crowd as speculation suddenly became baldly stated fact.

"Five million *what*?" Pika asked in confusion.

"Take your ear protectors off once in a while, doofus!" Geller chided.

"Now, hold on," Cameron cautioned. "We don't know that."

"Do the arithmetic," Adams said. "That's what it comes out to if this meteorite is really a chunk of Mars or the moon, and our fingie isn't blowing smoke. Right? So that's *my* question. What do we know? Not that Mickey had a heart attack. Only that we're missing a stone that some people—irresponsibly, I might add—have wildly speculated might be worth a lot of money. Next thing we know, boom. Mickey's gone."

"Jed Lewis just gave a professional opinion."

Adams swung to look at the fingie. "It's an amateur, un-scientific, seat-of-the-pants opinion and this problem started when Jed Lewis stepped off the plane."

"That's not fair, Doctor Adams." It was Norse. "Our meteorologist was asked to give a geologic judgment, based on his professional background, by Doctor Moss himself."

"That's right," Cameron said. "There's no evidence that anything's connected."

"And no evidence it isn't," Adams said.

"Jed said he was searched," Nancy Hodge spoke up. "What did you find?"

"Nothing," Cameron replied.

"Several of us were searched," Norse chimed in. "Including Mickey. Nothing was found."

Abby, Lewis noticed, had turned her face to the floor. Something was wrong. *Had* something been found?

"I want to emphasize here how little we know," the psychologist went on. "We don't know if the meteorite really had value. We don't know if it was lost or stolen. We don't know what happened to Mickey. Any conclusions at this point are premature."

Cameron looked at the psychologist with gratitude. Maybe Norse had his uses. An excited buzzing broke out among the group.

"So now what?" Gabriella finally shouted.

Cameron took a breath. "Now we decide what to do. Together. In trust."

"The only problem being that one of us may be a thief. Or worse." It was Pulaski.

"Exactly," said Norse, and heads turned back to him. "So a more realistic option is to work together in temporary *distrust*. To scrutinize each other carefully in order to get all bad blood out of the way."

"How do we do that?" Geller asked.

"Our real problem is lack of information," the psychologist said. "We're afraid because we don't know. Accordingly, I have a proposal to make. It's unusual, but this is an unusual situation. It has to be a group decision, not imposed from above. I was skeptical when Mickey himself first proposed it but it might be the quickest way to reinforce our belief in each other." He paused, his eyes polling the group, seeking permission to broach an idea. Physically and in personality, he was a more commanding presence than Cameron. His shower idea hadn't broken Tyson, but the mechanic's defiance was cracking. Norse seemed to have a better idea what to do.

"Go ahead, Doc," Geller prompted.

"I propose a broader search," Norse went on. "Not of the station, where we've been looking for Doctor Moss, but of our rooms, to look for the meteorite. I suspect we'll find nothing, but any discovery that would clarify this situation would help. Finding nothing, in contrast, might reassure each of us about each other."

"Our rooms are the only bloody privacy we have," objected Dana Andrews.

"I sympathize," Norse said. "I propose to limit the searchers to two people, myself and Doctor Hodge. I'll check the rooms of male personnel, she the female. As we've said, I've already been searched: I'm not asking anyone to undergo anything I haven't already experienced. We'll do it now, while the rest of you wait. If anything is locked, we ask for your keys. What we discover remains entirely confidential unless it has some bearing on the disappearance of Doctor Moss or the meteorite." He glanced at Cameron. "Agreed?"

"No!" Tyson yelled. "I don't want some self-appointed shrink searching me!"

"That's because you've got more phallic objects in that armory of yours than a nymphomaniac in a nunnery, bathing boy," Geller scoffed. The others laughed.

"Fuck you." Tyson glowered, his belligerence immediately returning in response to mockery. He was always ready for a fight.

"Nobody's afraid of a man who showers more than a teenage girl, Buck."

"Yeah? Try me sometime."

"My creditor friends tell me even the biggest goon can slip in the shower and not get up, if he stays in too long."

The group stirred uneasily at this threat.

"Enough, enough," Cameron said. The station manager was trying to look stern but was fighting the start of a smile at this needling Tyson was getting. The mechanic looked uncomfortable and scowled, avoiding anyone's gaze. It wasn't easy being toast.

"Is this going to work?" Alexi Molotov interjected. "You would have to be stupid to steal a meteorite and hide it in your room, no?"

"Who said people were smart?" Norse replied.

"You would be even more stupid to *find* the meteorite and not keep it for yourself," said Hiro. "Perhaps we should check the pockets of our two doctors at the end." The others laughed nervously. "Perhaps they hunt for themselves."

"You agree to a strip search, Doc?" Pulaski asked lightly.

"Only if you can hide a meteorite in there," Norse replied. Laughter again, the tension breaking slightly. "Look, everyone can come along but the idea is not to embarrass anyone. Nancy and I are used to handling things in confidence.

We're trying to eliminate suspicion, not create it. Trust us, this once, so you can trust each other."

With glances, the group polled itself in uneasy silence. Tyson looked angry but said nothing. Lewis had no sympathy for anybody. *I've already been probed,* he thought. *Now it's your turn.*

Adams spoke up. "I agree to this search," the astronomer said. "I have nothing to hide. But I think we also need to start using our heads as well as our feet. Maybe Mickey left other clues. Electronic ones. If I could get his passwords I could examine his hard drive."

Carl Mendoza wryly smiled, as if there were something more behind this idea than Adams was admitting. Geller smirked. Cameron looked questioningly at Abby, their computer technician.

"I have them," she said in a quiet voice. "It's privacy, again."

"I guess I'd draw the line at our hard drives," Norse said uneasily. "That's like reading our thoughts. We do need *some* privacy."

"I'm not talking about *our* files, I'm talking about Mickey's," Adams said. "I worked with the guy. Maybe he left a note. This is an emergency, dammit."

"It's for his own good," Mendoza added guilelessly.

Geller rolled his eyes.

"If Mickey's dead, so is his issue of privacy," Adams went on.

The psychologist opened his mouth to disagree again and then closed it, considering all the ramifications. "It's a group decision."

Cameron looked at the group. "Well?"

No one objected.

"Let's do it, then," the station manager said quietly.

*   *   *

Norse and Nancy Hodge left the galley to go through the berthing areas. Abby and Adams departed to open up Moss's hard drive. The mood of the remainder was somber. Cameron tried to lead a desultory discussion about outdoor safety but no one responded. Nobody wanted to talk about rules. The clock seemed to have stopped.

"What if we never even *find* Mickey?" Dana abruptly wondered aloud.

"We'll find him," Pulaski said. "Ten to one he had a stroke over this meteorite and got covered up by snow. Another good wind and his parka will pop back out."

"I'm not even willing to say he's dead yet," Cameron said. "But if he is, it's a lesson to us all. Sign out, take a radio."

"That's the third time you've said that," Geller groaned. "We learned that stuff way back in Denver and Mickey knew it, too. Look, can we continue this discussion upstairs? I need to clear my sinuses." Upstairs was the bar.

"Yeah," Steve Calhoun, the station carpenter, chimed in. "There are times when life needs to be dealt with through an alcoholic stupor."

"Getting drunk isn't very professional at a time like this," the station manager objected. He was worried how this would all look in the reports. Look back home.

"But it's damned rational," Dana rejoined.

"NSF wants us to keep our wits about us."

"Your Yank bureaucrats are ten bloody thousand miles away! For God's sake, Rod, we're going to bloody choke each other if we can't lighten up!"

The station manager looked at them gloomily. Tyson had already put everyone on edge, and now this. He was clearly outnumbered. "One drink each, then. That's all."

"Right, Dad." They pushed past Cameron and surged upstairs, crowding the small room like frat boys in a phone booth. All but Tyson, who remained downstairs, determinedly alone. Cameron hesitated, not wanting to wait in the same room with the mechanic. "I'm going to check on Harrison!" he called.

"We won't miss you!" Dana sang back.

Music came on. A few of the winter-overs began tapping to its beat, relieving some of the tension. It was creepy being searched. Creepy having their station manager be so morose. Creepy having Moss disappear.

Lewis got a beer. The elbow-to-elbow jostling made him feel less isolated and he began to cheer up a little. The music was cranked higher. He wished he could talk to Abby but she was off with Adams. He was curious about her now. There was something she wasn't telling.

Molotov came over instead, his water glass half full of vodka. "Now, Lewis," he said, clasping the American on the shoulder. "From you I need to know how to sell this rock. In America, where all the money is. Just in case I ever find it. Yes?"

"Too late, buddy. Secret's out. If we ever find it I'm afraid it's going to stay with Uncle Sam."

"Well then, let's spend the winter looking for another one!" The Russian grinned, showing a steel flash of old Soviet dentistry. "The jewel of Mars, no?"

Everyone was joking about what Norse and Nancy would find in their rooms. Lingerie. Sex toys. Marijuana grow lights. Offshore bank accounts. Jimmy Hoffa.

"It's like going nekkid," said Calhoun.

"Except the docs are the only ones to see us in our birthday suits," his companion woodworker, Hank Anderson, said. "And praise God for that. I see the crack of your ass too much already, every time you bend over to drive a nail."

"Didn't know you were lookin', Henry."

With nothing else to do while they waited, some people began dancing, awkward in the press of bodies. Lewis, still feeling isolated by his own clumsy investigation, maneuvered himself against a wall. He thought the bar was a good idea to break the tension but he wasn't really in a mood to talk. He felt like bad luck himself.

He watched Gabriella Reid slither through the press of people, teasing, taunting, a serial flirt, inviting attention. Eventually she came up to him, grinning at his wallflower stance, a beer in one of her hands. "You're all alone."

"People are learning to avoid me."

"It's unfair that people blame you."

"I guess it's because I'm new."

"I like new people." She rolled a long-neck on her lips, eyes dancing. "Antarctic Ten, I judge."

"I've heard what that is." He was wary.

She smiled mischievously behind the bottle. "Okay. Eleven, maybe. How about me?"

He smiled distractedly, glancing beyond her. Abby still hadn't come back.

"Don't bother with Ice Cream. She's frigid."

Lewis focused on the woman in front of him. "Frigid? Or careful?"

"She holds things in. Not me." Gabriella swayed in time to the music and handed him her beer. Turning a circle, she pulled her waffle-weave long-underwear top over her head. A silk undershirt beneath showed the line of a low bra and the bump of nipples. "Getting hot in here. Hot enough for the Three Hundred Degree Club."

"What is that, anyway?"

She smiled mysteriously. "The place where you learn where you really are."

The music cranked still higher and it became difficult to hear, the beat pounding against the walls. No one was obeying Cameron's admonition of one drink. The winter-overs were sweating. The air was rich and dark and heavy. The mood was tribal. Lewis allowed himself to dance once with Gabriella and then, when Abby didn't return, did it again.

She smiled at him. The invitation was obvious.

"What are *you* doing down here?" he stalled, raising his voice above the music.

"I like to be at the center of things."

"The Pole?"

"Everything comes together here. All the lines, all the numbers. It's a place of power. I worship natural powers, you know. Nature. Instinct. Emotion."

"What about science?"

"That's for beakers. What about feelings?"

"Beakers have them."

"No, they don't. They have to be drawn out."

She made him nervous. "I'll bet you're good at that."

"I can show you the way."

Christ. It was tempting. "Excuse me. I've got to check on something."

"Don't check too long."

He moved away, maneuvering toward the bar. He ducked behind as if looking for something and Geller sidled over. "Looks like you still have a friend."

"She makes me nervous."

"She'll make more than that, buddy. Until you lay off the meteorite and we figure out what's up with Mickey, she might be about the only friend you have."

Lewis looked at the maintenance man sourly. This place

was too damn small. "Why does everyone assume I'm to blame?"

"I don't." Geller sipped a scotch. "There's so many people sick of Moss that I won't be surprised if we never find him. Who wants to?"

"I don't believe that."

"You can bet Adams is going to use those passwords later to snare some of Mickey's data. Clues my ass. He's robbing the dead. And you noticed Carl Mendoza? He looks like he won the lottery. With Moss not undercutting him he might actually keep his grants."

"That's cynical."

"You lose money to the wrong people and you get cynical."

"Moss said he made everyone else's research possible."

"As long as they sucked up. Moss was also a Class-A prick."

"What do you think happened to him?"

"That he saved his reputation by dying."

It was after midnight. Then one, two o'clock. Everyone danced with everyone. Stocky Dana Andrews shook like a Maori, and Lena Jindrova turned an erect circle with a drink perched bizarrely on her head. Gabriella moved sinuously among the other men, her body a kind of social lubricant, erasing inhibition. Even Linda Brown, Pulaski's plain and overweight assistant in the kitchen, lost her stiffness and began to gyrate. The steaminess brought a kind of communion that relieved the anxiety over Mickey. For a blessed respite, the chill disappeared.

By the time Norse's head appeared at the foot of the stairs, then, they were drunk. He bounded upward and Nancy was right behind him, her eyes wide and dark, following with a hand on his belt. A ragged chorus of hoots and Bronx cheers erupted at their reappearance. "The underpants police!"

The crowd parted slightly to embrace them and pull them in, like an amoeba swallowing prey. "Who is it?" a drunken Pulaski shouted. "Which of us is the thief?"

Norse grinned reassuringly. "We found not a hint of scandal. You're all the most boring people in the world."

Now the crowd booed, clamoring for salacious detail. Who had the most secrets to hide?

"Our lips are sealed," Nancy said.

"Ply them with alcohol!" Pulaski cried.

A bottle of champagne erupted, fountaining over the two newcomers. Norse and Nancy ducked, but not quickly enough. White foam spewed over them, adding to the heady salt and sweetness of the room's cloying air. It ran down their clothes, making them sticky.

Norse staggered in the press of bodies and gasped, suddenly grabbing the neck of a bottle and taking a swig. He passed it to Nancy and grinned with relief at this enclosure by the crowd. His eyes swept them triumphantly and for just a moment Lewis thought he saw a wistful shadow in the psychologist's survey of the others, the same longing to belong that Lewis himself felt. Then commanding self-assurance replaced it, like a mask. Norse was the king of self-control.

Lewis could learn from him.

"What now?" Geller shouted.

"We've still got a mystery," Norse said, handing back a few keys they had been lent for personal lockers. He drank again. "We tried to put things back, but Carl, I accidentally broke one of your candles. Just clumsiness. I apologize."

"You didn't puncture my sex doll, I hope."

"No, but I had to inflate her to make sure she worked."

"*Do* we trust?" Dana asked.

Norse grinned. "Personal choice."

"Does that mean we're innocent?"

"It means you can choose to believe in each other."

"And how long do we keep partying, Doc?" Geller asked.

"Until I've drunk enough myself. Or until Harrison—"

As if on cue, though, the music abruptly cut. Everyone groaned. The lights came up and they were blinking, the communal mood shattered. It was Cameron, who'd come up quietly and slipped behind the bar. "Time to pack it in," the station manager said gruffly.

The group protested. "Rod—"

"Shut up. We've got something."

That silenced them. More footsteps, and Abby and Harrison Adams trooped up the stairs. They looked graver than Norse and Nancy and as they pushed into the hot room the crowd split apart from them, squeezing against the walls, as if *this* news threatened to be unwelcome. Everyone was suddenly uneasy again. It was deathly quiet.

"Did you find anything in the rooms?" Cameron asked Norse and Nancy from the bar.

"Nothing," Norse replied.

"Well, Harrison found something," the station manager said grimly. "Doctor Adams?"

"There's an e-mail on Mickey's drive," the astronomer said. "We're going to trace it if we can. Meanwhile, it points to a place we haven't looked."

"Which means I need a few men to volunteer now, pronto, and the rest of you in bed so I can have you tomorrow, half awake and not too hungover," Cameron said.

"What's going on?" Mendoza asked.

"It's a place I hadn't thought to look, frankly. We're going to go there now."

"Where?" Everyone was curious.

"Where even Mickey Moss had no business being."

"Where?"

"The abandoned base."

CHAPTER ELEVEN

Thin blue shadows bobbed ahead of the search party like anxious children, their silhouettes running ahead to get to the buried ruin. Lewis felt more hesitant. He was curious about the abandoned Navy base but he'd also been warned it was utterly dark and cheerlessly cold. The truth was, he was mildly claustrophobic. He didn't relish looking for a dead body down there.

The e-mailed message that Adams had found had been deleted from Moss's computer but Abby, who had some hacker skills, had been able to retrieve it from the encrusted history of his hard disk. *If you want your meteorite back, meet me in the old base at midnight.* Unsigned, of course, and dating from the evening before Mickey disappeared. She was trying to retrace its point of origin now.

Meanwhile, the elongated penumbra of their own bodies stopped at a womblike slit in the snow, its lips widened as if recently penetrated. Someone had passed this way not long before. The edges of the tiny entry glowed a cobalt blue that sank into the ink of a catacomb. It seemed the kind of hole that could close up behind you, not letting you out.

"It's the only place we haven't looked," Cameron said in response to the unspoken reluctance of the others. Everyone was tired and hungover. The cold worsened their headaches.

"Why in hell would a thief lead Mickey here?" Pulaski wondered aloud.

"Cheese to a mouse," suggested Geller, who'd pulled down his gaiter to bite on a candy bar. His beard began to grow ice crystals as he chewed.

"Which implies a trap," the cook said.

"Or an exchange," said Cameron.

Let's get on with it, then, Lewis thought. He was tired and uneasy and the half-mile walk from the dome had left him sweaty and cold. He wanted to crawl into bed. But volunteering to help this time seemed another way to get loose of the albatross of suspicion.

"This opening goes down to the old meteorology room at one end at the old base," Cameron said. "Stay tight and watch your step. The timbers are starting to buckle from the weight of the snow." He was carrying rope, an ice ax, and a small field shovel.

"Why'd they build it down there, anyway?" Geller asked dubiously, looking at the hole.

"They didn't. The snow just piled up around it. Eventually it buries everything."

"You don't even have to dig your own grave down here," Pulaski said.

"And a hundred thousand years from now the ice will have flowed enough to spit everything back out into the ocean," Cameron replied. "Sewage. Garbage. Remains."

"Won't want to be around when that iceberg melts out," Geller said.

They crawled through the opening, switched on flashlights, opened a hatch, and descended. Cones of illumination danced down old wooden stairs to a snow-dusted plywood floor. The wood was too frozen to exhibit any signs of decay. When they got to the bottom the four of them almost filled the low room, its ceiling bending ominously from the weight of snow above. Cameron let his beam play across the walls. There was a table with an abandoned military radio, its clunkiness suggesting decades of antiquity. A gray metal office chair. Another table with old meteorological charts. There was no decay and no dust, just a patina of frost. The air was utterly still and heavy with an ancient, undisturbed cold, somehow more cloying and penetrating than the brisker air outside. While the temperature was a constant fifty-five below zero, it felt colder.

"Well, I don't like *this*," Geller announced. "Would Mickey really come down here?"

"Moss once lived here, remember?" Cameron said. "He helped build it."

"Built a meat-locker morgue."

"It was different with the heat on."

Lewis played his flashlight along the floor, trying to ignore his claustrophobia. "Boot prints." His light slid along to a dark doorway. "Lots of them, going both directions."

"Doesn't mean anything," Cameron said. "There's no wind, and no fresh snowfall except what seeps through. Come down here and your prints last as long as on the moon. Until someone else walks over them, like us."

They went through the door to another room. There were crates and old cardboard boxes, empty. A few polar visitors had scrawled or scratched names on the walls. Nothing had decayed in the cold.

The men shuffled ahead, the gloom swallowing where they'd been and obscuring what lay ahead. Doorways appeared like the lids of pits, yawning a deeper darkness. Examination with the flashlights showed them to be merely old rooms, empty of any life. Walls canted crazily from the strain of the snow above.

"If these lights go out, we're in shit city," Geller said. "This place is like a maze."

"Exactly," Cameron said. "So don't wander off."

"Except maybe it would go faster if we split up."

"No splitting up," said Pulaski. "Mickey got into trouble because he was alone."

"I thought you was Rambo," Geller said. "One-man army."

"Rambo is horseshit. In the Army the idea is to get there first with the most, and most means you don't split up. Warriors who want to do their own thing are called dead heroes."

"Tyson says you have to look after yourself."

"Tyson's a butthead. You look after yourself by looking after each other."

They came into the galley. It was as if the old base had been suddenly evacuated, not shut down. There were dirty glasses, open beer cans and bottles, and a spill of old forks on the floor. Tables and chairs were askew. In the kitchen an abandoned refrigerator hung open to reveal a cascade of forgotten, frozen hot dogs. A bulletin board had meeting notices and cartoons from a quarter century before. Their lights flickered over an old bar, revealing the charms of a laminated Miss November. Geller studied her with a historian's interest. "They plasticized her," he said. "Look, she was before pubic hair."

"Did they pack or flee?" Lewis asked as he looked around.

"Some of this is crap from people who sneak down here to party," Cameron explained. "Nobody stays too long because it's too damn cold. It's just something to say you've done it, like sleeping in a haunted house. But yeah, the Navy pretty much just walked away."

"Why didn't they move their stuff?" Geller asked.

"Move it where? It was old and there's no place to store it. Cost a fortune to fly it out. So this has become a repository, like Scott's Hut at McMurdo. A thousand years from now some archaeologist is going to come down here and find those hot dogs."

"Not exactly King Tut," Pulaski said.

"But it's history. Just like the dome is history. That's what we're doing down here, making history."

"The way Mickey Moss is history," Pulaski said.

"Let's hope there's still a chance." Cameron lifted his head and shouted, "Mickey!" The call echoed away into the darkness, seeming to shake the old base as it did so. Somewhere a wall creaked in reply.

"Jesus, don't *do* that," Geller said. "You'll bring the whole place down on us."

"We gotta try."

They went into the next room, an old barracks. The bunks and mattresses were free of mold because of the cold. Not even bacteria could live here. The beds held frozen impressions as if bodies had vacated only hours before. Lewis felt like the place was inhabited by ghosts. He was freezing up from their slow pace.

"Are we near the end?"

"Halfway."

The ceiling on the garage and powerhouse had mostly collapsed, the trusses and plywood snapped and crumpled across an old generator. Cameron played his flashlight across the wreckage, looking for a clue. There was none.

They went on through a connecting corridor to the other half of the base, a gap of snow having been left between the two to help contain any fire. The short passageway was lit by a faint gray crepuscular light that penetrated the snow from the surface.

A beam creaked as they edged past.

There was an old recreation room with abandoned ping-pong table and bookcases. In a storage center were steel and paper drums, lined like sentries, their frozen dregs unknowable. The science room had been mostly gutted of equipment except for a lab bench. Calendars were dated 1974. Discarded trash was heaped in corners.

The last room was a small astronomical observatory. The clump of their boots on plywood was uncomfortably loud.

"They launched weather balloons here and took sightings of the stars," Cameron said. "End of the line."

"That's it, then," Pulaski said. "No Mickey."

"Where do those stairs go?" Geller asked, pointing to a set leading upward.

"Out, I hope. This is the other entrance to the base. We might have to dig a little if it's drifted." Cameron glanced around the barren room, clearly frustrated. "I can't think where else to look."

Lewis let his flashlight play about. Its beam was already dimming. "What's that?"

There was a small plywood door behind the stairs, its edge opened a crack. The snow at its foot was heavily scuffed.

"I think it's an old tunnel that goes out to pits used for earthquake and geomagnetic research. Probably collapsed."

"Except the door's been recently opened," Lewis said. He walked over and pointed. There were fresh splinters of yellow wood around the faded gray.

"Bingo," Geller said.

The door had frozen back in place and Cameron used his ice ax to once more pry it free. A tunnel just five feet high and three broad led into darkness. The wood ceiling bulged downward as if pregnant. The walls looked ready to implode. But patches of snow on its plywood floor showed a welter of tracks and scuff marks.

"Gawd," Pulaski said doubtfully. "Mickey would go in there?"

"Somebody did," Cameron said. "Not too long ago, either, I'm guessing. I think we'd better rope up. Who wants to lead?"

No one spoke up.

"Okay, I will." He peered down the tunnel uncertainly.

"I'll go last," Lewis said. "With the other light." The cold was stiffening his muscles and he didn't want to stoop-walk into that dark corridor. Last in, first out. The snow was pressing down like earth on a coffin. "I'll take the ice ax; I've used one before. If you fall, I'll brake you."

They moved in a half crouch, their boots echoing in the stillness. At one point the squeeze of the ice was so great that they dropped to a crawl, then stood again. Still a confusion of tracks went on. The two flashlights continued to dim. Lewis realized he was sweating and that made him shiver. His heart was hammering. It was impossible to see what was ahead.

"Shit!"

It was Cameron. There was a crack of breaking wood

and his light disappeared. The rope jerked taut, yanking the men to the floor and dragging them forward in a terrifying slither. Lewis frantically dug with the ax and it scraped along the plywood with a squeal. Then it caught on a joint between two sheets of wood and he jammed it down past the plywood into the ice. Their slide was arrested.

They were stretched like beads on their rope, their waists painfully squeezed.

"Rod! You all right?"

"I'm hanging in some damn pit! Can you back us up?"

"Pulaski and I can brace ourselves against the plywood walls," Geller grunted. "You pull on the ax, Lewis."

Slowly the three men who had escaped the fall began to retreat, hauling the station manager back up as they did so. Cameron got to the lip of the hole and worked his way over broken plywood to the top. They rested a moment, panting.

Lewis had the only light. "What happened to yours?" he asked, shining it on Cameron.

"Dropped it."

The station manager crawled to the edge of the pit and looked down. Lewis joined him. The fallen flashlight was still glowing feebly fifty feet below where the old study excavation hole ended, the pit's icy sides marked by meter sticks installed four decades before. The hole had been roofed over with boards and plywood, but someone's weight had broken through before them. Cameron had simply stepped too close and slid down the sagging wood into thin air.

"Ah, Jesus," the station manager now breathed.

A man was down there, curled in a fetal position in the cone of fading light. They had found Mickey Moss.

*   *   *

It took them an hour to lift the astronomer out. Pulaski had done some rock climbing in the military so they lowered him to the bottom of the pit to attach a line around the stiff corpse. Then he shimmied back up and they hauled, cursing when Moss's rock-hard limbs caught momentarily on the uneven edges of the broken wood. The scientist was heavy. Finally they got him up and over the edge of the pit.

They sat back, gasping. Moss's parka-clad body seemed to fill the tunnel.

Cameron dug out a water bottle he kept unfrozen by strapping it to his torso and passed it around. The water was actually lukewarm. "To Mickey. Drink all you can. Working in the cold is how you get dehydrated in Antarctica."

Lewis drank and shuddered. "I need to keep moving."

"We all do. My hands and feet are numb. I think we can sled Mickey from here."

They dragged the body unceremoniously, finding it skidded well. When they came through the door back into the stairwell they lifted Moss more gently, like pallbearers, and carried him to the aluminum-roofed observatory above. A ladder led to a wooden trapdoor, which they pried until it fell down, swinging on its old hinge. There was a roof of snow over the entrance, softly blue, and the men looked at the color eagerly. A few twists of Cameron's shovel and the snow cascaded down in a flush of gray light. They lifted and pushed Mickey's body up and surfaced, gasping as if emerging from underwater. The hole they'd come from looked pitch-black. Cameron reached down and pulled the trapdoor shut.

"That's enough of that."

Lewis looked at the horizon. Clouds were moving in, obscuring the low sun. The day was hardly more than a gloomy twilight and yet brilliant after the darkness below.

"Mickey didn't get the cheese," Geller said, panting. "No meteorite. No jillion bucks. Was the pit a trap?"

The station manager wearily got to his knees and examined the body. The astronomer's eyes and mouth were open, and they could imagine him bellowing for help. One leg was twisted unnaturally, as if broken. "Or an accident. It would be easy enough to just fall. I did." He looked at Lewis. "You were smart not to take point, fingie."

"I don't like dark places."

Cameron said nothing.

"It's weird," Pulaski said. "He could have been lured, pushed, dragged, whatever."

Geller lay back, blowing. "Not dragged. Too much work."

"Well, somebody shut the door behind him, right?"

"He could have done it himself. Or it swung shut. Who knows?"

"Can we just get back?" Lewis asked.

Cameron rocked Moss this way and that, looking for anything that could tell a story. "If anyone was aware of the dangers of the old base it was Mickey."

"We've got to get back or I'm going to freeze," Lewis insisted. His torso was beginning to tremble. He'd never felt such cold.

"I know." Cameron glanced at Lewis speculatively and stayed at a kneel, his hands searching. Moss's outer pocket held the usual gloves. Then the station manager yanked hard on the parka zipper, breaking a sheen on ice, and reached inside to a polar fleece pullover. There was something flat in a zippered pocket.

He pulled out a photograph and looked at it in mystifi-
cation, not showing it to the others. Then he tucked it inside his own clothes and took out his field radio, calling
Comms.

"This is Ice Pick," he radioed. "Harrison there?"

Clyde Skinner, their radioman, took a few minutes to
fetch the astronomer.

"Adams."

"You guys traced that e-mail yet?" Cameron asked.

"Dixon did," Adams said, his voice crackling. "Is Lewis
with you?"

"Yes."

"Then I'll tell you later."

Cameron looked at the fingie. "No. Tell me now."

There was a hesitation. "The message came from one of
the computers in Clean Air. Jed Lewis's password."

The quartet absorbed this. Then: "Roger that. Out." The
station manager put the radio away.

Everyone looked at Lewis.

"If I sent Mickey that message, would I do it from my
own machine?" he asked. "My own password?"

No one replied.

"Come on!"

"*Did* you send Mickey that message?"

"No! No." The others looked grim and tired. "Look, this
is crazy."

"It sure is," Geller said.

I'm being set up, Lewis thought, his heart hammering
with new paranoia. "So who was that picture of?" he asked,
pointing.

"Nobody."

"Hey, if someone's sending e-mail on my account, I get
to see what else is turning up."

Cameron considered and then slowly took it out. The others frowned.

Mickey Moss had been carrying a picture of the one person who knew all their passwords, who could read all their mail. A picture of Abby Dixon, next to his heart.

Fatal Confidence

Going down a new route is always harder than going up. It's risky to lean out far enough to properly see, and gravity conspires to short-circuit your decision making. People bunch up, hesitating and sliding, and inadvertently kick stuff down on each other. If the kids hadn't been a pack of scared-silly sheep, with implicit trust in our decision making, we'd never have gotten them started down the wall at all. Kressler kept telling everyone it wouldn't be bad after we got to Fat Boy. They were frightened enough to believe him. Once started, the students gasping in anxiety and their limbs trembling as they clutched the wall, it seemed even worse to have to go back up. Yet each step we took, each foot we descended, sank us deeper into the trap we were digging for ourselves.

Fat Boy didn't exactly help the mood. His pleas and moans and bitchy impatience were enough to put experienced climbers on edge, let alone a bunch of shaky kids. Then he cursed and whined at the rocks and snow that seventeen clumsy people inevitably knocked down toward him, hugging himself to the cliff wall and expressing all varieties of self-pity. I wouldn't have blamed his classmates a bit for pitching the blob off the ledge once we got down to him. But instead there were shouts of greeting and reconciliation and hugs and a hurried half-assed setting of his broken leg, Fat Boy roaring in pain. For a moment of excited triumph we were all united again, one for all and all for one, plucky and indomitable: in other words, so thoroughly deluded that I could have

*written the overblown feature story about our insane lit-
tle victory all by myself.*

*Except we were squeezed onto a ledge that was like
an overloaded, open-walled elevator going nowhere, cliffs
below and cliffs above, and the clouds were blotting out
the surrounding peaks. It was getting colder.*

*Kressler and Fleming were hearty as hell, of course.
Everyone was doing great, way to go, jolly good, pip pip,
and any other kind of bullshit nonsense that popped into
their heads. Me myself and I, however, happened to take
a tiny peek over the edge of our view terrace and didn't
see Kressler's easy way down at all. There was, in fact,
a several-hundred-yard drop down a soft-rock cliff before another ledge led sideways to a point where we
might sidehill on snow again—assuming we didn't trigger an avalanche. How we were going to get two hundred and twenty pounds of blubber boy and fourteen other
amateur climbers down this way, however, was not at all
clear to me and, it turned out, not at all clear to our
would-be department chairman.*

*Kressler, we now learned, had never been here at all.
He'd just read that it was climbable.*

Jesus. Oh, what a pack of veritable Einsteins we were.

*Let me tell you something about Cascade volcanoes.
You go up the right way, at the right time and season,
and most of the way it's a steady snow slog to the top,
exhausting but not terribly technical. Really dumb people have done it, and have the snapshots to prove it. Get
fancy about it, however, and you can face some of the
most treacherous climbing in the world. The mountains
are hot inside, active and full of steam, and the steam
leaches out through the lava rock of their cones and turns
their geology into a kind of Swiss cheese, crumbling and*

unreliable. The mountains are weak and have an alarming tendency to break, slump, or slide with no warning. The rock is about as firm as hardened snot, in other words, breaking off with pops and bangs with each rise of the spring sun, spitting out pitons and breaking loose handholds for anyone optimistic enough to try it. Skill can very quickly be trumped by bad luck. It was dawning on me that all our luck this day seemed exceedingly bad indeed.

I suggested we go back up and regain the normal route.

The kids wouldn't hear of it. Kressler had scared the shit out of them getting them down this far, and the idea of going back up the mountain when a storm was swirling in struck everybody but me as absolutely insane. I started arguing, me against the other two, and a debate in front of weeping Fat Boy and tired, shivering sophomores was probably not the brightest thing we could have done. Kressler was furious I'd even raised the question. He needed confidence and the group was losing it.

My two esteemed colleagues finally announced that they would show us the way while I babysat the classroom. Climb down to that beckoning snowfield and scramble back up, setting ropes, driving belay points, and generally building a super freeway for the rest of us doubters so we could get the hell out of here before we found ourselves in whiteout conditions.

There was long, doubting silence. They were all waiting for me to speak. Well, go for it, I finally told them. Oh Pioneers! Yep, you fellows go right ahead. I'll just bundle up with the coeds here and you all call when you're ready. Oh, and hurry it up, will you?

Didn't say that, of course. Just gave my in-the-face-of-adversity nod and said I'd try to fashion some kind of sling to lower Fat Boy. What choice did I have, as the lone voice of reason? I was being dragged down with them, doomed by the Original Sin of Fat Boy's unroping, and if we by some chance actually survived I'd sure as hell demand my share of glory for trailing along.

Idiots.

The doughty pair started down off the ledge. It was rock climbing, for which we were neither equipped nor prepared. We had stiff boots for crampons, not rock shoes, and the two instructors were weighted with too many ropes and carabiners and pitons because they wanted to fashion a near-ladder for the class. Even in the best of conditions it would have been difficult to descend that route. Now the sky was spitting snow. Fat Boy was groaning in discomfort, many of the others were snuffling, and when Fleming's head disappeared below the edge I have to confess that even I felt terribly alone.

If they'd made it, of course, everything would have been very different.

I crawled over to watch their progress. The wind was rising and nothing was audible, but I could see them slowly picking their way down. The more they descended the more they hesitated, and I could tell the descent was looking more and more impossible. Once Kressler stopped and looked back up at me for the longest time, as if realizing he was in over his head.

Come back up, you moron, I thought to him as hard as I could. I really did.

But he didn't hear my mental message, or chose to ignore it. A few hundred more yards and his mistakes could be transformed to rescue, the second-guessing trans-

formed to a good war story. His chairmanship might be secure. Can you imagine any goal more pathetic? So they kept going, fixing a line, and for one brief minute I began to concede they just might show me up. Get down, get the kids down, even get Fat Boy down. And they would have, too, if they were descending a wall with any kind of structural integrity.

But Wallace Wall is as unreliable as a lover's promise. One minute they were bolted to it, making our route, and the next moment a foothold gave way and Fleming, who was highest, slipped, fell, and bounced, hanging on his rope from a piton, suspended in terror, his ice ax sparkling as it whirled away downward. There was an awful pause, Kressler roaring instructions, and then the pitons popped off the steam-riddled rock like buttons in a Fat Boy squat. Ping, ping, ping! The rope curled out in space in a lazy arc, bright red against the foggy depths beyond, and then Fleming fell past Kressler and plucked him off his perch as neatly as you'd pick a grape.

They went screaming.

The students shrieked, too, an anguished wail that signaled their own sudden realization of mortality and doom. The instructors tumbled in a gray dawn light, orbiting each other in an embrace of line, and then hit rocks, ice, glacier, snow, setting off a small avalanche to accompany themselves and sliding down in their very own slurry of debris, the rope snapping. They settled out individually finally to lie still some infinity of distance below us, their broken profiles looking like discarded dolls.

They were dead.

The keening from my little mob of survivors was as mournful as the bitter wind. Snow was spitting at us, visibility failing, and we were trapped on a shelf of rock with about as much square footage as a king-sized bed. The easy route down had been exposed for the fraud it was, and our leaders for fools.

So now they clutched, pleaded, wept.

And turned to me.

CHAPTER TWELVE

The funeral of Michael Mortimer "Mickey" Moss, astrophysicist and Old Antarctic Explorer, took place the following morning at the stake that marked the South Pole. Or at least the clocks said morning. Lewis, still tired and sore from recovering the body, felt a groggy, growing disorientation from time. The sun ran around the base like a coin on a track, refusing to go up or down or acknowledge the normal succession of days. Geller had made a joke about it: "A cowboy riding into the sunset would get mighty dizzy here."

Under the dome, in contrast, was perpetual shadow. Brain chemicals that were normally triggered by the rhythm of darkness and dawn were beginning to misfire.

"It gets worse," Nancy Hodge had told him when he first complained about the problem. "They've found the Pole can mess up your thyroid and a bunch of other stuff. T3 Syndrome. Reports of depression date back a hundred years to the first explorers. A study a decade ago found two-thirds of winter-overs had trouble sleeping and half were depressed. It saps your energy, slows your mind. The best thing you can do is be conscious of it and stay focused. Scheduled."

"If I feel this toasty now, I'm going to be a charcoal briquet by October."

"Find a hobby. Gina is teaching Italian. Hiro is trying to learn the harmonica. Bob is building a telescope. Even Tyson is doing *something*."

"Right. Manufacturing knives."

But Lewis hadn't found a hobby yet and was feeling increasingly alone and misplaced. It had taken him two hours in the sauna yesterday to expunge the haunting chill of the old base and he'd left the hot room wrung out and exhausted. His sleep had nonetheless been troubled. Lewis had never seen a dead body before: By the time he got back from Saudi Arabia after his parents' death the funeral was over and they were already in the ground. At first the corpse had simply been a frozen weight, a piece of cargo. Pulled up on the ice cap, however, Mickey Moss had been recognizable as a once-dominant human being. Without wishing to, Lewis had caught a glimpse of the skim-milk pallor of frozen flesh, the obscenely open mouth, the bulging eyes. Moss had died in pain and horror.

And who was trying to blame it on Lewis?

The astrophysicist's shock was covered now by the plastic garbage bags used as a makeshift shroud for the body. Sealed with duct tape around the dead man's torso, the plastic rattled in the bitter wind like a playing card in the spokes of a bicycle. Lewis found the others stood a little away from him, and he thought the twenty-four other mourners looked like a cluster of orange monks, hooded and hunched. Their ski goggles and neck gaiters masked all expression, and the tendrils of their fur ruffs waved like the groping cilia of sea anemone. Blowing snow slid across the plateau, caressing the corpse with filmy waves.

The station manager led the group in an awkward recitation of the Lord's Prayer, Cameron stumbling haltingly through the words. There were normally no services in winter and no minister. Only Pika and Eleanor Chen, a science technician, sometimes allowed themselves to be seen leafing through the Bible.

The group needed a priest. What they had was a psychologist.

Norse, too, stood a little apart from the others, as if to watch both them and the body. Like everyone else, his expression was unreadable under his swaddling of clothes, his goggles giving him that black, blank-eyed stare of cartoon space aliens. Lewis was sure he was trying to figure the tragedy out. Figure them out.

"There's not much I can say and it's too cold to say it," Cameron began after the prayer, his gaiter pulled down and his beard beading with bits of ice. "We'll put Mickey's body out by the cargo berms until it can be evacuated in the spring. As you know, he fell down an old research pit and it's impossible to say if it was accident, heart attack, the meteorite, or what." He glanced at Norse, a mute acknowledgment of the possibility of suicide as well. Moss had found almost the only place on the flat Pole to fall any appreciable distance, and how accidental was that? "We'll probably never know, and maybe that's how Mickey would prefer it. I think he'd like to be remembered for what he lived for, not how he died. And he lived for this base. He lived for us. We might not be down here, having this unique opportunity, without him."

The group shuffled uncomfortably.

"Mickey was one of a kind, a sort of polar Miles Standish who helped pull this place together. He and I didn't always get along but I'll say this now, and I'll say it honestly—I'll miss him."

"Amen," Pika concluded.

Gabriella leaned forward with a plastic flower, liberated from a floral arrangement kept in a Coke bottle placed in one of the bathrooms that the women claimed as theirs. She put it on the body. The wind caught it and it flew off almost immediately, startling her. Norse stopped it with his boot and brought it back, sticking it upright into the snow. A red waxy rose.

"Pika?" Cameron prompted.

The power plant mechanic zipped down his parka, reached inside, and pulled out a small portable disk player. "I downloaded this from the Internet," he announced. He pushed a button and a mournful tune began, tinny and barely recognizable: the military ending known as "Taps." The military dirge played out, its long notes warped by poor recording and carried away by the wind.

Then there was quiet, except for the fluttering of the plastic shroud.

"Well, that's that, then," Cameron said. "We'll tow him over to the storage area. We made a cross for him out of black PVC plumbing pipe. The body will be rock solid perfect until we can ship it home. The berms of stored cargo will give him some protection from the wind."

"That's *not* that," spoke up Adams, his words muffled by his gaiter. "I said I don't believe in coincidences." His masked head rotated to look at Lewis and then Abby. "I'm not sticking Mickey in the snow and forgetting about him. We need to check his hard drive, his records, his papers, everything we can to find out why the hell he died down there."

Geller coughed. Lewis couldn't see past his goggles and the cloth that covered the maintenance man's mouth, but he imagined the smirk. Robbing the dead, he'd predicted.

No one said anything until Norse spoke up. "There's still that issue of privacy."

"I think group survival is a little more important than privacy," Adams righteously replied.

"It was probably an accident," Cameron said. "Probably a coincidence. But yes, of course we're going to try to figure out what happened."

"Who happened," Adams corrected. "You have to let me look through his things."

"We'll talk about it."

The group began to break up. Lewis heard a sound of snuffling and realized it was Abby, weeping behind her muffler. Any tears that leaked out would freeze.

Something was going on with her. Something about that picture. Why the hell had a geezer like Moss gone to his death with a picture of her on his chest?

Lewis watched as Norse stepped around the body and came to her, whispering something reassuring. Then the psychiatrist put his arm around her shoulder and led her toward the dome.

Lewis resented the intimacy.

No one else said a word to him. They'd heard where the e-mail had originated from. Guilty or not, he was bad luck. It wasn't even dark yet, the long winter still stretching ahead, and already he felt like toast.

At midnight, insomnia drove Lewis to the computer lab. Compiling weather numbers for Sparco was the one thing he'd found that was reassuring: If the sun would not finally go down, a necessary first step toward the eventual

return of spring, at least his data sheets grew day by day
with satisfying progression. Time was passing. He found
that entering the readings was relaxing, a precise but mind-
quieting task that could ready him for sleep. It was midnight and the station was still except for the ceaseless
murmur of machinery and ventilation.

He was not particularly surprised to find Abby there,
however, her face lit by the glow of a screen. She inhabited the nighttime lab like a specter, appearing at odd hours
and taking comfort in nursing her sometimes balky machines. He admired her mastery of them, the self-possession
her skill gave her when she burrowed into their innards.
He liked her curiosity.

Right now she appeared to be taking a minute for herself, not easy to do in an environment where the expectation from higher-ups was tireless work. Beakers were
desperate to get as much information as possible in their
allotted research time and their pace set an air of urgency
in research camps that was impossible to escape. Polar science was done at a dead run. But tonight her slim hand
moved a mouse casually. She was playing solitaire on the
computer.

He hesitated a moment in the doorway, watching her.
The flicker of light played across the fine features of her
face and made it float in the surrounding darkness as if
disembodied, a ghostliness that seemed doubly foreboding
after Moss's funeral. Suddenly everyone seemed vulnerable down here. Certainly Abby looked as lonely as Lewis
felt. He needed a confidant and they'd proven harder to
find than he'd hoped. Summoning up the courage to endure rejection, he walked in and sat next to her.

"Gearloose," he said gently.

For a minute he thought she wasn't going to reply. Then,

"I've thought of a nickname for you." She didn't look up from the cards on her screen. She was going to win, he could tell.

At least she was talking to him.

"Higher than krill, I hope."

"Enzyme. The agent that makes things change."

He winced. "A metabolic chemical? I'm not sure that's an improvement."

"It's true, though. Things are different since you came here."

He waited for her to elaborate, but she didn't. She won her round and the deck of cards began handsprings of laudatory joy.

"How so?"

"More complicated."

"I didn't send that message, Abby."

"You should have told him his rock was useless."

"Lied, you mean."

"Yes."

He sighed. Secretly, he agreed with her and it was costing him sleep. "I didn't know Mickey Moss was going to die. All I wanted was a job and a chance."

"A chance for what?"

"A chance to be at the Pole. To mean something. Fit in."

"You didn't fit in before?" She said it lightly but she doubted him now, his machine the source of that e-mail to Mickey, and she wanted to erase that doubt. She wanted to know that the newcomer she had trusted indeed deserved her trust.

How much of this would get back to Norse? He wanted to tell her anyway. Maybe even tell the psychologist. "Not very well. I didn't tell you everything that happened in Alaska, you know. It was more complicated."

"You're not just an environmental zealot?"

"I was a field geologist, but not exactly one of the boys. You get hard if you stay in the oil business and I was never comfortable with that hardness. I thought, I joked, I objected. I looked to them for family but they're not a family, they're a machine."

"You quit because Big Oil wasn't cozy?"

"I quit because I didn't have enough in common with the people I worked with. It bothered me, what we were doing. I left some documents at Prudhoe where a tour group from the Wilderness Society might find them. Sooner or later it was going to come out. I was just waiting for the ax to fall. I didn't like my boss. I wasn't really doing my work."

"So you came down here. To escape."

"I came down here to find some meaning. Is that so crazy?"

She bent her head. "No. Understandable. Admirable, even."

"It seems noble, all this research. But that damn rock . . ."

"Is it really so valuable?"

"Not that it's worth a life."

She dealt herself a new hand. "You're not unique, you know."

"Meaning?"

"We all came down for things."

"Money, I think Geller and Tyson have said."

"Yes. As well as fame, love, promotion, tenure, wisdom, self-understanding, and companionship." It was a recital.

"Belonging. Contributing."

"Yes."

"And you, Abby?"

She thought before answering. "I didn't fit in, either. The

thing that's spooky about us is that we're too alike. I got my first master's in marine biology and discovered I didn't like ships. They're male, cold, and force an intimacy with people you might otherwise not pick as friends. I don't make good friends easily. So I went over to computers. They're like pets. Much more controllable. Predictable."

"Not the ones I buy," he joked. "So here you are, a marine biologist, eight hundred miles from the sea. From ship to spaceship."

"Doesn't make sense, does it? Except . . . I wanted time by myself to know myself." She hesitated. "I . . . know another guy, a beaker, who I met at McMurdo and who's now on the coast at Palmer station. I didn't know if it was real or an Ice infatuation. The winter gives me some time to sort it out."

No wonder she was Ice Cream. Already booked. "What's he think about the separation?"

"That it will give *him* time to finish his dissertation."

"And have you sorted it out?" It was like asking her to hold up her left ring finger.

She swung away from the game to face him. "Not with a dead man having my picture in his pocket!" She meant Moss.

"You know about that, then."

"The whole base knew about it within twenty minutes after you guys got back. Same with tracing the e-mail to Clean Air. Everyone always knows everything about everything."

"Except why Mickey died."

"What if that's somehow *my* fault?"

He laughed bitterly. "I thought everyone was blaming me."

"Doctor Bob isn't."

"You sure like talking to Doctor Bob."

"He's a professional."

"Barely. He's a sociological researcher."

"He knows people and he thinks it's possible Mickey killed himself."

"Over you?"

"Over fear, somehow. Because the only thing a man like Moss accumulates is reputation and self-respect. Maybe the meteorite and . . . the picture . . . threatened that. That's Doctor Bob's theory, anyway."

"Where did the picture come from?"

"I don't know."

"Why would Mickey have it?"

"I don't know."

"Did you know Mickey somehow?"

"No." She sighed. "I don't like these questions."

"Did *he* know *you*?"

"I don't want to talk about it anymore right now."

"Okay." Lewis leaned back, cautious lest he drive her away. "I'm just trying to be a friend."

"So is Bob, so is everyone." She said it impatiently, rubbing her eyes as if the whole idea of solicitous concern was immensely wearying. They sat for a while, listening to the fan of the computer.

She laid a hand on his forearm finally, giving it a slight squeeze. "Why does everything have to be so hard?"

He tried not to betray the jolt that ran through his body at her touch. *You want more than a friend,* he admitted to himself. "It doesn't, Abby."

"I thought things down here wouldn't be complicated."

"It's full of humans."

"One less, now."

They were quiet.

"You know, an enzyme isn't really a bad thing," Abby finally said.

"Can't we find a name that implies handsome and strong?" It was another attempt at a joke.

She didn't even smile. "Maybe you were sent to change us all."

"I don't want to change anyone. I just want to join in and do my job. I just want to get to know someone."

She looked at him wistfully and stood. "I have to go now. It's late."

"Please. I want you to stay."

She leaned over him. "That's why I have to go." Her lips brushed his cheek, unexpectedly. "Goodnight, Enzyme. Maybe you'll change me."

Lewis sought out Norse the next day. Somehow he had to repair his social position at the station or go nuts. He'd become a snoop, a pariah, a suspect in a bizarre death. Getting involved hadn't helped him, it had made things worse.

Lewis was told the psychologist was out on the Dark Side, boxing Moss's things, so he hiked out to the astronomy building. He found Norse at the astrophysicist's workstation, Mickey's desk drawers half yanked open like an act of exposure. It seemed unnecessarily intrusive so soon after the funeral.

"Pillaging the dead?" He'd meant it like a joke, but it came out sounding sour.

The psychologist glanced up from a box he was filling with Moss's files. He looked patient instead of defensive. The man's calm might be his strongest asset but it could also be infuriating. "I'm shipping things back to the States. Cameron appointed me as the best person to bundle up the astronomer's personal effects and papers, suggesting the family and NSF would like them boxed before they're lost."

"The best because you're a psychologist."

"Probably the best because I'm new, like you. A little apart from the others. And used to keeping confidences."

"Right." Lewis hesitated. Maybe Norse *was* really as isolated as Lewis was. Maybe they did have something in common, the fellow fingies. And because of that maybe he'd understand. "I came out because I'm done playing detective, Doc. Case closed."

Norse slipped one cardboard flap under another, sealing the box. "Say again?"

"The meteorite. Looking for it now will cause more trouble than it's worth. With Mickey gone, there's no point. And I'm toast if I keep grilling everybody."

The psychologist nodded slowly. "Ah." He considered this and then pointed to the astronomer's old desk chair. "Sit down, Jed." It was the tone of a parent about to lecture, not unkindly.

Reluctantly, Lewis sat.

"You think Mickey's death has ended things."

"For me it has."

"I'm afraid just the opposite is true."

"How so?"

Norse took a breath. "Rod and I have been in communication with NSF and Mickey's home institution. Nancy doesn't have the training to do an autopsy now, but there's going to be an investigation into Moss's demise. Some of that is standard, and some is unusual because of the peculiar circumstances of his death. There might be people down here in the spring asking questions."

"I understand."

"I'm not sure you do." The psychologist pulled over another box and began dropping in files. "The most likely scenario is that Doctor Moss suffered an unfortunate accident while trying to retrieve his meteorite. It's possible an autopsy would reveal a heart attack or another contributing factor. Another possibility, however, is suicide."

"Abby's picture."

"Yes. I'm not at liberty to fully discuss that, but suffice to say there's some evidence that Moss had an unusual interest in younger women."

"I don't believe that."

Norse glanced at the boxes around them, as if they held compelling evidence. "Nobody is asking you to."

"Mickey Moss is not the kind of guy who kills himself."

"I'm talking about possibilities." The psychologist looked at him speculatively. "Look, you know what's appealing about the hard sciences? Their rationality. A handful of Greeks more than two thousand years ago said stop, we're not going to explain the world with supernatural miracles anymore, we're going to look for natural causes. It was almost a superhuman thing to do, embracing the scientific method, and for many scientists this rationality *is* their religion. Yet it's my contention that we're not wired to be rational, that superstition survives in all of us because that's the way people naturally think. Doctor Moss was a supremely rational man. But he was also a man, with all the freight of impulse and emotion and fear that any man carries with him. He might have been spooked. He might have been depressed. Who knows? It's completely unfair at this point to suggest anything untoward, but Abby and I have been discussing the situation. Please don't press her on it, because that could cause some real trauma in what in the best of circumstances is an emotional pressure cooker down here. Still, we all have to admit the possibility of the irrational."

"One more reason to put it all to rest, I think."

"Yes. We're really talking about the functioning of this group. Except there's a third possibility besides accident and suicide, you see."

"What do you mean?"

"Murder."

"Come on. . . ."

"It's possible that whoever took the meteorite and lured Mickey Moss into the old base pushed him down that pit."

"That doesn't make sense."

"Doesn't it? An esteemed scientist finds a meteorite? A thief takes it? As a search closes in, our culprit becomes desperate and decides to eliminate the one man he thinks might figure out who did it?"

"You're suggesting the meteorite could lead to *that*?"

"I'm suggesting that with five million dollars at stake, any rational person would consider it as a possibility. And if there's anything we can say about the scientists and engineers who run our little kingdom back in Washington, they are supremely rational. Positively anal about it."

"Well, I'm sure as hell not going to play homicide detective."

"Ah, but I think you have to."

"Forget it."

"Based on what authorities know so far, only one clear suspect has emerged." Norse looked at him with unusual intensity. "Which means, in your own defense, you can't stop looking."

"Now, wait a minute. . . ."

"Because that suspect is obviously you."

CHAPTER THIRTEEN

Lewis watched the first big storm of the winter season approach on his instruments as if he were tracking an armada of bombers, the barometer falling and the temperature actually rising slightly as the monster swelled up from beneath the horizon. Faxed satellite photos made the tempest look as vast as a pinwheel galaxy. Yet nothing happened at first, the atmosphere at the Pole seeming to hold its breath. He paced from his weather monitors to the windows, and from the windows to the monitors, curious and watchful, anticipating the storm but seeing nothing but gray blandness. He looked out at the other buildings on station and everything seemed still.

His wait was like the solitude of a lighthouse keeper. Lewis made people nervous now, since the discovery of Mickey's body, and people avoided him like they avoided Buck Tyson. No one had accused him of anything. No one had asked any questions. But when he was out at Clean Air no one telephoned, either. No one e-mailed. When he was out with his instruments, Jed Lewis was the last man on earth.

A murder suspect! Absurd. No one but Norse had said a thing and yet in every eye he now read suspicion and in every gesture a distancing. That e-mail! Galley chatter subsided at his approach as if he turned down a dial, and when he sat away it regained its volume. Not so much a snub as formal politeness. "Hey, Lewis." And that was it. No questions about *anything*. His isolation was exactly the opposite of what he'd expected at the Pole. His daily walk to Clean Air was a kind of voluntary exile, his trudge home one of dread at the caution he would encounter.

Every five minutes, Lewis cursed Mickey Moss.

He was reluctant to notify Cameron of his readings. It was difficult to talk to the man. The station manager had become remote since Moss's death, as if Lewis represented potential contamination. Cameron never visited Clean Air. In fact, he rarely left his office, where he was struggling with a report to Washington. His depression was dangerous. It affected the entire station. When Lewis suggested in a rare phone call to the station manager that Cameron stick his nose out of the dome once in a while, the response had been curt.

"I'm a little occupied, Lewis. We're still trying to hash this out."

"Hash what out?"

"Mickey."

Were they convicting him behind his back? "I'm tired of Mickey. I didn't have anything to do with him."

"I understand what you're saying. I'm sorry. I'm busy."

But as the approaching tempest swelled with power, Lewis was its first witness, and while he resented that all communication had to be initiated by himself, his duty was to warn the others. The storm would howl over the corpse of Mickey Moss, entombing him, and trap any human who hadn't scurried for shelter. In fact, the storm would do its best to snuff out the entire station, trying to push people back home where they belonged. Except at the end they'd still be here, burrowing out, and with them would reemerge his own problems, his own mystery. What was the astronomer doing in that pit?

He telephoned Cameron.

"Rod here." The tone was tired.

"This is Lewis. We've got a Herbie." The name was slang for storm and Lewis had picked up on it immediately, adopting the language of Antarctica.

"What?" Cameron came to life. "Where? When?"

"Greenwich quadrant. It will hit soon."

"How soon is soon?"

Lewis looked at the storm boiling up on his screens. "Within the hour. Maybe sooner. I don't know. I've never seen one before."

"An hour! Didn't you see the storm?"

"I saw it."

"I'm supposed to get a heads up!"

"I'm giving you one."

"Earlier! Why the hell didn't you call earlier?"

"The sucker brewed up out of nowhere. You know how fast the weather changes."

"I need more of a heads up."

The scolding irritated Lewis. "Rod, I haven't noticed a whole lot of interest lately in what I have to say."

There was silence for a moment. "Anybody else out with you?"

"No."

"You okay?"

"I'm talking to you."

"Okay, listen. I want you to stay there. I want you to clock the storm."

"The instruments will do that automatically."

"I know. I just don't want you wandering around until this blows through."

"That might take a while."

"Just sit tight. I've got to get everyone battened down. This is dangerous, Lewis. We need an early heads up. We need to get some warning."

"That's why I'm calling. Listen, nobody ever calls *me*."

Cameron hung up.

"Nice talking to you, Rod."

Lewis watched the sun wink out in the advancing wall of snow and then the ice plateau itself seemed to evaporate as the storm rushed forward, devouring ground. It was as if the world were dissolving. The dome was snuffed, the route flags jerked over, flapping, and then the blizzard hit his own research building with a howl. Clean Air lurched and then shuddered, its glass quaking, the wind rising to a shriek. Flakes streamed past the railings in parabolic swirls. The plateau below was gone, replaced with a rushing river of fogged snow, and the sky was equally obliterated. Here was the real Antarctica, powerful and malevolent. Lewis clung to the frame of a window, drinking in the magnificent violence. The building trembled under his hand like a frightened animal.

He thought again of his predicament, suspicion rubbing on his concentration like a rock in a boot. The damning e-mail had been traced to the Macintosh that Abby had fixed, someone using his log-on or, more likely, taking advantage of the fact that he rarely bothered to log off of the machine. Unless she'd done it! Abby had their passwords. But no. . . .

The problem was that Lewis had skipped the galley that night, electing to work out at the gym and take a packed meal to Clean Air afterward. Depressed by the feuding of Tyson, he'd purposefully been alone. Then he'd come back to his bed, leaving his computers on and unattended.

He had no alibi.

"Maybe it was Jerry Follett," he'd tried with Norse.

"Jerry?" The psychologist had smiled. "We both know Follett is a nerd's nerd. His idea of conversation is atmospheric chemistry. The station could burn down and he might not notice. No, Jed, Jerry Follett is an extremely hard sell."

"And I'm not?"

"*I* don't suspect you," Norse assured Lewis. "It's too neat. Too obvious to send the message from Clean Air. That's why I was against Harrison poking around in the first place. People jump to conclusions on fragmentary evidence. But you understand why you can't stop probing. We need to plumb the soul of every person on this base before this is over, Jed. We need to know who, how, and why you're being made to look like a killer. There's something really perverse going on and I'm worried it will only get worse."

"This is all a game to you, isn't it?" He was frustrated.

"No. I'm in greater earnest about this whole issue than any person on this base."

"Except me."

"Yes. Except you."

Well, that's just dandy, Doc, except I'm a damned fingie murder suspect in some kind of psychotic sinkhole where we don't even know if a murder occurred, he thought glumly. *Maybe you could speed up the analysis and give me a little hand.*

Lewis looked out at the storm now, the flakes rasping

his shelter. He knew that relatively little snow was falling. The polar plateau was a desert with only a few inches of precipitation a year. What produced the ice cap was the fact that nothing ever melted. The blizzard was made of the ice cap's skin, picked up by the wind and hurled like Saharan sand. He was in a world where the molecules all rearranged themselves fifty times a year. When the storm ended there'd be an entirely new landscape—and it would look exactly the same as before.

The telephone buzzed again. It was Cameron. "Lewis, you with Adams?"

"Who?"

"Harrison. He set off from the Dark Side to talk to you about something. Something he found on Mickey's hard drive. You seen him?"

"I told you I was alone."

"I thought maybe he'd gotten there."

"No."

"Shit. That means he's out in the storm."

"Maybe he's holed up in astronomy."

"No, I tried there but Bob says he's gone." Norse was still boxing up Moss's things. "This is why we need a heads up."

Dammit. "I gave you one."

"I got people all over station. We need that heads up." He clicked off again.

Why the hell did Harrison Adams want to see him now? Had he found something incriminating? He moved from window to window, watching them breathe in and out against the wind. There was no sign of the astronomer.

It made him uneasy. He'd been too moody, not sounding the alarm the instant he could have, and that meant another mistake. What pissed him off about Cameron was that the station manager was right. He should have alerted everyone earlier.

Suddenly he felt restless, unfairly cut off. He had no food, no water, no toilet. He didn't want to sit out the storm here. It felt useless.

Cameron called again. "Adams there yet?"

"No sign of him. Not at the dome?"

"No."

They were quiet, Lewis listening to the rising wind.

"I'm worried about him, Rod."

He could hear the station manager take an anxious breath. "Me, too. The guy's brilliant, but he couldn't find his way out of a phone booth."

"All he has to do is follow the flags."

"So why isn't he back yet? Next time, I want a heads up."

"You said that already!"

"I just don't want any more fuckups."

That made Lewis angry. "I'm going to go find him," he decided. He suddenly realized that Adams represented opportunity.

"What?"

"I'm going to find Harrison."

"No, don't!"

"I'll starve if I stay out here. Look, I'll follow the flags back, meet Adams, and make sure he gets back inside. You said yourself he's no good outdoors."

"Jed, the flags can blow out!"

"They're holding. I'll be okay."

"No! I'm ordering you to sit tight. Monitor those instruments!"

"You don't work for NOAA."

"I fucking run this base!"

"Do you, Rod?" It came out without thinking. "I'm going to get Adams." He hung up.

The phone began ringing. He ignored it. He knew that was impolitic but he suddenly felt trapped out in Clean Air, unable to influence his own winter. He'd come down to help, dammit. So, he'd help.

Lewis looked out the window at the drumming opacity of the storm and then at the satellite photos again. He was still green at meteorology but it looked to him like the blow was going to get bigger before it got smaller. Sometimes they clawed at the station for days. He wanted to get back to the dome where there were people. Food. Where they couldn't talk behind his back. Tyson was right. High school.

He wanted to find Adams and earn some goodwill.

The phone kept ringing and Lewis resisted it. He needed Cameron, needed his support. But he was tired of being suspect because he was new. He was tired of being the fingie. As the ringing stopped he began climbing into his polar gear. Somebody had to find the astronomer. Somebody had to act. Hell, he'd been in the snow before.

He was pulling on his mittens when the phone started ringing again, shrill and insistent. To fail to answer was a major violation of station policy. A portable radio squawked and Lewis shut it off, too, neglecting to put one in his parka. Another violation. "Line's down." Lewis stepped outside.

His picture-window view of the tempest did not prepare him for its energy when he pushed out the door. The wind hit him with muscular heaviness like the side of a horse, a blow that knocked him sideways and almost off metal steps newly slick with a rime of ice. The door banged open and he slipped and hurt his knee scuttling back to close it, barely wrenching it shut against the push of the wind. As it swung he had a glimpse of a small tornado of paper that the wind had kicked up inside. Storm noise that seemed exotic inside his metal cocoon was a deafening cacophony when he stepped outdoors. The blast yanked his hood off his head because he'd neglected to tie it and he was blinded when it flocked his goggles. He wiped them with his nylon mitten and then shed the hand covering to clumsily tie his hood strings. He was stunned by the violence.

It was the cold that was most surprising. Lewis had partly acclimated to the everyday freezerlike syrup of chill that seemed to coat every object with brittle rigidity. This cold was different. It wanted to reach inside his clothes and suck him out, swallowing all available oxygen as it did so. He couldn't see, hear, breathe. How was he going to find Adams? Only if the astronomer met him coming the other way. Lewis realized instantly that if he didn't follow the flag line briskly and alertly to the dome entrance, focusing every bit of his being into where he had to go, he'd be dead.

People have died a dozen feet from shelter, Cameron had said. *Use common sense.*

Common sense was to stay put. Well, he was beyond that, wasn't he?

He needed to take control of events.

Lewis leaned forward into the wind. The nearest flag was bent like a bow, its pennant flapping frantically. The nylon of his own clothes stuttered like a jackhammer. Feeling as if he were climbing a steep slope, Lewis began staggering toward the flag. When he reached it he stopped, turned his back to the wind, pulled down his gaiter, and gasped for air. The strain of pushing against the storm had left him breathless.

He pulled his gaiter back up and turned around again,

wiping his goggles against the sting. He could see the next flag! A couple dozen of the pennants and he was home free. With luck he'd find Adams staggering along the way. *This way to hot buttered rum, buddy! You got a problem with that, Rod?* Lewis bent and labored ahead toward the pennant.

Again, movement was like pushing through plastic. He was head-on into the wind. He made it to the flag and stopped, wheezing. When he turned around he saw the Clean Air building had already disappeared into the storm. Eerie. The dome couldn't be seen, either. It was just him and a bucking flagstaff in either direction. Everything else was white. He couldn't see the ground or the sky. His own body was erased at the waist.

Another stagger ahead. The noisy drum of the storm was like the hammer of a factory. Snow that found the crevice between his gaiter and his goggles burned his skin. His fingers were already stiffening. The pounding was stupefying. He'd skied bad days when snow spat like wet snot but that was nothing compared to this. A polar storm was beyond the pale. It was the literal end of the world. It was a head butt into tapioca, a struggle on the football line.

He began counting flags. Five, six, seven . . .

Then naming them, for amusement. Homer. Zeke. Jezebel. Hortus. Pygmalion . . .

God. How far was it? Wasn't he there yet? Had he somehow turned around?

Where the hell was Harrison Adams?

He stopped again to catch his breath, wiping tediously at his goggles. The snow crystals threatened to build into a mask of ice. His vision was blurring and he couldn't tell if it was the fogging of the goggles or the growing snow blindness of his own eyes. He realized his clothes were failing him. The wind seemed to be slicing right inside, robbing his torso of heat. It was like being knifed in the ribs.

"I've got to get inside soon."

The words were muffled by his gaiter, his cheeks and jaw slow to move, his tongue thick. *Ib ga ge iside soo*. Christ. How long had he been out here?

Cameron had been right. It was stupid to go into the storm.

Too late, mate. He had to be at least halfway, didn't he?

With no other choice, Lewis went on. Each thrust of his leg was like swinging a weight. His clothes buzzed in the wind, the fabric vibrating so fast that it might disintegrate. He felt dull, slow-thinking. The cold was freezing up his brain. Tightening his muscles. He kept his head down, trying to conserve heat.

An eternity passed, lost in self-pity. Why in hell had he ever come to the South Pole? Then Lewis remembered to look up. Nothing. He squinted. Where had the flag gone? He'd been aiming for it and now it had disappeared. He turned around awkwardly and when the wind struck his back it knocked him to his knees as if he'd been tackled from behind. He was tired. Dangerously tired.

No flag back there, either. He watched his own boot prints dissolving in the wind, covering up his passage. Somehow he'd stumbled the wrong way.

A vast dread began to overtake him.

Forcing himself to stand, he slowly turned in a circle, trying to recognize something. The universe was white. *Think, think!* Which way had he come? He'd been facing into the wind. But the wind kept shifting, and so did his path to the dome. How to get back to the trail?

He took a step, stumbled on a small drift, and lost his

footing. As he began to topple, the wind caught him like a sail. He actually flew sideways a few feet, coming down on his belly and skidding on the snow. His hood came off again, a tie broken. Even as he lay there the slashing snow began to drift on his windward side. Curling into a ball, half weeping, he found the ends of his hood tie and got it back on, the strap now tight and choking against his throat. For one perilous second he considered not getting up.

Then he worked up to his knees, trying to see. He felt dumbfounded. It seemed to be getting darker. He needed a flashlight, something to pick out color. But he'd left his light back at Clean Air.

Idiot. You've killed yourself.

Think!

Dully, he noticed the sastruga, the small drift he had tripped over. The sastrugi's tops had been torn off and hurled into the stormy air but their icier underlayment still existed, slowly being abraded by the wind. He'd walked over them every day and watched their wavelike pattern from Clean Air. Which way did they run? He tried to focus his mind. . . .

Yes. Yes! He remembered. Perpendicular to his path. And lower, smaller, in the lee of the dome. He could read them like sailors read the water, perhaps.

He struggled back up, desperate now. He hadn't much time. He was seizing up like the Tin Woodsman. *I'm rusting!* He set off, abandoning the flags as lost in the storm, betting all on his ability to run into the dome. He stopped for neither air nor rest, plunging forward, determined to bang up against salvation. Trudging on, hammered by the wind, trying to read the drifts, increasingly disoriented . . .

Nothing. How much time had gone by? As he looked down through the curtains of snow, he was increasingly

uncertain which way the sastrugi ran. It seemed they were
dissolving and re-forming before his eyes, curling into circles. No dome, no flags, no hope.

He turned around. His footprints had already disappeared.

He'd failed, he realized. Gambled and lost. Somehow he'd
missed a structure nearly the width of a football field. . . .

He was a dead man.

The wind lessened slightly and above the shriek of the
storm he heard a lower whine. Was he near the generators?
He struggled to place it. A butterfly, bright red, spun by, its
flicker like a flash of light. He was stunned. Butterfly? No,
it was cloth! Old Glory, still on the dome up there, because
they'd forgotten to take it in before the blow. The flag was
being shredded to pieces, its bits spinning past him like sparks
in the storm. He had to be close. Peering, he saw nothing,
and then suddenly there was a light, catching him in its blaze,
and a snowmobile snorted and charged up to him, a huge
hooded figure on its back like Death itself.

"Get on, you fucking moron!" Tyson yelled. "I'm half
frozen looking for the likes of you!"

Lewis's leg seemed enormously heavy as he tried to lift
it over the machine. He was on Jupiter, pinned by a cold
that had become equivalent to gravity. Yet he managed to
clutch the huge man in front of him, clinging to Tyson's
waist, and the snowmobile howled and spun off, Tyson following the weaving course of his own track.

"Rod made me come look for you, you dumb fuck! I
would have let you die!"

The dark wall of the dome loomed briefly out of the
snow as Tyson followed it, the snowmobile growling as it
jounced over confused drifts. Then there was a sudden bank
of snow, the machine lurched up it, and they were airborne.

"Aw, shit!"

Lewis was so surprised he let go and felt himself separate from the machine. He fell, his world gauze, then hit hard ice and snow, rolling, and finally skidded to a stop, breathless and stunned. The snowmobile banged down somewhere, coughed, and went silent. In the stunned quiet that followed, Lewis realized he was somehow more protected from the wind.

He was on the ramp that led to the dome.

Tyson skidded down, colliding with him. "Fuck, I thought I'd lost you again!"

"What happened?"

"Snowbank from digging out the ramp. Jumped the sucker and did a barrel roll."

"The snowmobile?" Lewis managed to mouth.

"It's trash."

They half crawled, half skidded down the rest of the ramp, skittering like hockey pucks against the closed metal doors. Lewis yelped when he hit, sore and gleeful. The smaller plywood emergency door was to one side of the main entrance and he pushed on it. Frozen shut. Stuck like glue.

Tyson shoved him aside and butted it. "See what I told you?" he shouted. "Sufficiency, man! You couldn't get out of the jam on your own!" The door popped open, slamming inside as the wind caught it. "You didn't have me, you'd be locker meat!"

Lewis leaned through and mittened hands grabbed him and yanked. Tyson pushed through, too. The door slammed shut behind them, a puff of flakes trapped inside.

Even the cold of the dome was immense relief because the wind was shut out. Lewis could still hear it howling, the snow rasping the protective shelter, but at least he could breathe and the wind didn't cut at him. He reached to pull down his goggles and had to break them loose from his forehead where they'd frozen. "Ow!" He felt blind in the gloom. His legs were trembling, his feet dangerously numb.

"Lewis, my God, you all right?" It was Cameron, pounding on him. "You damned lunatic, we thought you'd lost it! Why didn't you take a radio? Take a light?"

"Uh . . ." No words came.

"I'm going to thaw you out just so I can kick the shit out of you." He shoved him in the direction of the galley. The station manager turned to Tyson. "Good job, Buck. Norse just got back, too. But Adams hasn't showed."

Tyson's face was a mask of ice. "Fuck."

"He was going to see Lewis. I can't raise him."

The mechanic slumped. "I'm wasted, man. The machine's kaput. I can't go back out there."

Cameron turned to Lewis. "Jed, did you see him at all?"

Lewis shook his head. He remembered the argument between Tyson and Adams in the weight room. How anxious would Tyson be to look for him?

"We got another machine?" Cameron asked.

Tyson shook his head. "Not fired up and ready."

"How long? If I go instead of you."

"No way. It's suicide, man. Don't go."

"But if I did."

"Too long. Too long, in that."

Sickly, they looked at each other.

"I'm going up the ramp to fire some flares," Cameron said. "Maybe he can home in on that."

"You can't see for shit." Tyson looked as exhausted as a blown horse.

"I've got to try something."

"You can't see, you can't hear, you can't find. I just stumbled on the fingie with dumb luck."

"I've got to do something. I can't lose two."

CHAPTER FOURTEEN

The storm blew for thirty-seven hours, the snow crystalline and pitiless, driven so hard by the wind that it sizzled against the outside of the dome like grease in a frying pan. In that long cold twilight of noise and confinement, with no telephone or radio call for help, the winter-overs of Amundsen-Scott base became glumly convinced that Harrison Adams was also dead. In the midst of the storm Cameron led a party, roped and lit, out along the flag route to the Dark Sector astronomy building to look for him again. One flag was down, a bad sign, and they had to use GPS to bridge the gap. They searched the building, endured two hours in the blizzard going and coming back, and found nothing. Any further searching had to wait until the wind died down.

"I told everyone to stay put," Cameron said bitterly as he exhaustedly shed his parka, his nylon frozen over by a sheen of ice. "Why the hell didn't they stay put?"

No predecessor had ever lost two people before.

The great hush that marked the end of the storm came at what the clock said was morning. So much snow had drifted that when they opened the exit door to the ramp again, there was a chest-high wall they had to dig through to get outside. Tyson was told to warm up a Cat to bull-doze more blocking snow away and this time he complied without rebellion. The tragedies seemed to be sobering him. The others marched out in a platoon of orange and fanned out to look for Adams's body. Cameron passed out whis-tles to signal.

The clouds were gone. It was almost the equinox, the time when the sun would disappear completely from the Pole. The orb scraped the horizon, a trick of light making part of it seem to catch and drag behind in a blob of trail-ing fire, the brightness washed out by the rim of light fog that surrounded them. The haze was so thick and the light so low that the entire station already seemed shrouded in cold, sepulchral twilight. The temperature was seventy-three degrees below zero. During the storm the windchill had dipped to a hundred and fifty below.

Lewis searched for Adams in a mood of glum depres-sion. Maybe if he'd called about the storm at its first sign the astronomer might have made it. Maybe if he hadn't lost the flag route he'd have run into Adams. He was lucky he wasn't dead himself. Cameron had chewed him out for not staying at Clean Air as he'd been told. "Getting lost puts everyone else in jeopardy. It was a stupid, juvenile, fingie stunt."

Norse asked Lewis if he'd thought up anything new about Mickey's death. "Harrison said he was coming out to see you. I presume there was a reason."

"He didn't tell *me* that."

"People are pretty bummed out, Jed. We've got to get a handle on what's going on."

"Don't you think I'm trying? It's pretty tough to play

detective when no one will talk to me. Help me out on
this, will you?"

He grimaced. "People are shy about talking to me, too."

Lewis walked up the flag line now toward the astronomy building, trying to imagine where the missing astronomer might have gone. His own stumbling trek had
made him realize how easy it was to get lost. Adams had
obviously gone off course while trying to get to Clean Air,
for some reason choosing to talk to Lewis personally instead of simply call. Why? Once disoriented, his body shutting down from the cold, Adams would have sought any
shelter. Where?

The stark nature of the polar plateau created an illusion,
Lewis had realized. The base seemed simple and yet there
were more than a hundred separate buildings and structures
scattered around: observatories, storage shacks, vaults, telescopes, antennas, and long rows of stockpiled crates called
cargo berms. If lost, Adams could have stumbled into a lot
of places to seek refuge. Cameron and a few others were
already searching the electrical substation shack and telescope support buildings of the astronomy sector, digging
into the drifted-over plywood bumps one by one.

Lewis meanwhile squinted down the flag line, holding
out his arm to provide a makeshift straightedge. The flags
were leaning raggedly, but for the most part they'd held.
The astronomer should have been able to follow . . .

You didn't, he remembered.

And here there was a flag missing. Adams should have
retreated.

You didn't, he reminded himself.

Lewis walked to the gap where the flag had fallen and
slowly realized that the markers nearer the astronomy complex seemed slightly out of alignment. Going toward the

astronomy building the gap seemed hardly to matter: A straight walk from flag to flag would aim you correctly across the break in the route. But turned the other way . . .

Lewis backed up and sighted again. It was a subtle shift, hardly noticeable with the wind gone and the snow once more lying obediently in place. And yet he knew just how blind he'd been. Going this way, the last two flags would point at an angle that led off the main sled road, toward the white no-man's-land of the runway. A person walking that way would veer away from the dome, fail to find the next flag because of the gap, cross the skiway, and . . .

Had someone shifted the flags?

Suddenly certain, Lewis started by himself toward a cluster of shacks where the planes taxied. If Adams had gotten into shelter over there, it was possible he was still alive. People had seemed dead on Everest, stone cold, and yet had revived. Inside a shack, Harrison might have had a chance. . . .

A substation and storage shed were padlocked for the winter: No refuge there. But a warm-up shed, used by air crew to rejuvenate as they loaded and unloaded planes, had not been bolted.

"Harrison!"

No answer.

The building was nothing but a weathered plywood box with a shed roof and a round plastic bubble window to view the runway. Its portable heater was probably in winter storage. Still, it offered shelter from the wind. Lewis tried the door but it was stuck, frozen shut. When he pounded there was no answer. He went around to the window but it was smoked against summer glare and too scratched to see inside.

He studied the door again. A flat orange cord and a bar

of ice ran around its frame, thicker than was normal. If the ice had been present when Adams arrived, the astronomer couldn't have gotten inside. Yet why was there so much? As on other buildings, the cord was an electrical heat tape that ran around the jamb that was used to melt accumulating frost and keep openings from sticking. Somehow this one hadn't worked or had gone haywire. The ice had sealed the door.

"Adams!"

His shout drifted away in the cold twilight.

Something else orange caught Lewis's eye, poking out from the bottom of the wall near the door. A scrap of fabric. He stopped to inspect it, brushing snow aside, and slow dread began to settle on him as he dug. It was a mitten, a buried mitten. When Lewis tried to pick it up it wouldn't come because he felt something hard inside, stiff and clawlike.

Fingers.

Attached to someone's arm.

Lewis was holding Adams's frozen hand, reaching blindly out from under the wall of the warm-up shack as if the man were trying to dig his way out of a vault.

He dropped the mitten and backed away.

The arm was reaching out from beneath the shed wall in supplication, its hole too shallow for a body to squeeze through. The astronomer had tried to get out of the ice-locked shed through its floor, burrowing through the snow. He'd been stopped by the underlying ice.

Lewis's heart was hammering. Something had gone horribly wrong. He looked more closely at the ribbon of heat tape. The astronomer had gotten *inside*. Maybe in his confusion Adams might have cranked the tape temperature too high, melting so much snow that water ran down the frame to create a bar of ice, meaning he could no longer get *outside*. Yet why had the water then turned to ice? Why had the tape failed?

Lewis followed the cord down to the snow where it turned toward a junction box that supplied electricity. Orange wire came up as he would expect, winding, winding . . .

At the corner of the shack it was broken.

No. Neatly cut.

Harrison Adams had not died alone. Someone had followed him and effectively locked him in, snipping the tape and imprisoning him in ice.

This wasn't negligence, Lewis thought.

This was murder.

There was a gasp and he turned. Dana Andrews had come up behind him and was looking from the beseeching mitten to Lewis's own hand and the severed cord. Her head rotated from mitten to cord, back and forth, as if at a tennis match.

Then she pulled her plastic whistle out from her parka, put it to her mouth, and blew, and blew, and blew.

The winter-overs swarmed the warm-up shed like a crowd at an accident, looking in horrified fascination at the beseeching arm and severed tape. Everyone kept a wary distance from Lewis. Cameron strode up, puffing after a quick trot from astronomy, took in the scene in a moment, and brusquely ordered the others to leave. "I want Norse and Lewis only. The rest of you back to the dome. I don't want anyone thinking anything. Not yet."

But everyone was already thinking, of course, considering every dark possibility.

"Why us?" the psychologist asked.

"Because we've got some talking to do."

The others trailed off in a line of orange, looking curiously back at the remaining trio and the forlorn shack. Once they were back, their galley would buzz with speculation like a disturbed hive. Cameron, Lewis, and Norse watched until the others disappeared inside and then fetched a wooden beam from the cargo area to batter down the shed door. The ram made a dull, booming echo in the dusky morning, like the dirge of a bell. Finally the ice shattered in a spray like broken glass and the door burst inward.

Adams's last moments were heartbreaking. He must have stumbled inside in exhaustion, seeking a temporary refuge from the mind-deadening wind. The shack was insulated but had no heat. Eventually Harrison would have realized that he was still in subzero cold and had to start again for the dome, but when he tried to go back out the astronomer was frozen in. He'd have butted and kicked and screamed but no one knew where he was; no one could hear him above the howl of the wind. Eventually he must have panicked. With superhuman energy he'd somehow managed to rip up one of the plywood sections that formed the shack's crude floor, nails shattering in the cold. He'd sliced the nylon arm of his parka in the process and scraped his wrist. The floor was dotted with droplets of frozen blood. Then he'd burrowed, throwing a small heap of snow to one side of the room as he tried to dig his way out of his cold trap. The ice was too close to the surface to allow him to squeeze his way out. At some point he'd stopped, from exhaustion or defeat, helpless in a spasm of shivering, and then he'd fallen asleep as his core temperature plunged. Pain, and then no pain. At least his eyes were closed.

"I thought he took a radio," Norse said.

Cameron searched for one.

Adams had it in his pocket but its battery was dead. Someone had failed to recharge it. The astronomer probably hadn't checked.

"It looks like someone broke the heat tape," Lewis said dully.

"Cut it," Cameron said.

"What tape?" Norse asked.

Cameron pointed to the orange cord around the door. "You've seen these to keep the doorjambs from freezing?" He pointed to a dial at the bottom of the door. "Adams, or someone, cranked this tape way too high. It would have created a Niagara of meltwater around this jamb. Then the tape broke or was cut."

"I don't get it."

"If you wanted to seal someone inside an unheated shack at the height of a blizzard, that would be the way to do it. Melt some water, get the doorway wet, and then cut the heat off. The door would freeze as if it were welded." He looked at the other two.

"You're saying someone trapped him?"

"I'm saying I don't know how the hell else that tape broke."

"Maybe it was just an accident," Norse said. "Everything's brittle in the cold."

"Like Mickey."

"Yes. Two accidents."

"And what kind of luck is that?" Cameron's tone was bitter.

"Sometimes random chance clusters. You're a scientist and you know that. Unfortunately, the cluster fell on your watch. I'll be the first to testify you did all you can."

"Testify? At my trial?" The station manager gave a sharp laugh. "At my funeral?"

"I just mean when NSF asks questions about this. You've had bad luck, Rod."

"Jesus. One storm and I'm down two beakers. Is that some kind of record, or what?"

"Mickey didn't die in the storm."

"No, I lost *him* in clear weather. Christ Almighty. I wish I was the one who was dead." He looked gloomily down at Adams. "Can't someone pull his fucking neck gaiter up over his face so I don't have to look at him?"

Stooping, Lewis did so.

"Accident my ass."

"If it wasn't an accident, then why?" Norse asked.

Cameron looked grimly at Lewis. "That's the question, isn't it? Jed, why was Adams coming to see you in Clean Air?"

"I don't know. It's not like we were buddies."

"Why did you leave Clean Air after I told you not to?"

"To help find him! I couldn't last out that storm, I'd starve. I thought I'd meet him coming back to the dome. It was stupid to tell me to stay out there, Rod. I should have left before I did."

"Did you see Harrison in the storm?"

"No, of course not."

"But you saw Tyson."

"He saw me."

"You were riding with him. Tyson and you, together. The guy who doesn't like Adams."

"The guy who doesn't like *anybody*," Lewis said in exasperation. "Look, I had nothing to do with this! I couldn't even get from Clean Air to the dome! I would have frozen myself if Tyson hadn't found me. You know that. You saw what condition I was in. And I didn't have *time* to wander

clear over here. If anything, the storm proves I'm innocent." He looked expectantly. "Right?"

"It proves you're the one person who knew where the
body was."

"I *guessed.* Why would I go find the body if I killed
him?"

"To make sure he's dead?"

That one crossed the line. "Fuck you."

The station manager looked at the new man with frank
dislike. "Why are you always in the middle of things?"

"Because everyone else always puts me there!" He
pointed to Norse. "Why don't you question Bob? He was
out, too! Where the hell was he?"

"I know that," Cameron said quietly. "That's why I asked
for both of you to stay here with me, to hash this out." He
turned to Norse. "Did *you* see Harrison?"

"I already told you I did, at astronomy. I left just ahead
of the storm. I got back before Lewis did. Adams was going
to follow shortly."

"Were the flags intact?"

"They were when I passed them."

"So what do you think happened?"

Norse looked down at the frozen astronomer. "Why *not*
bad luck? A flag blows away, Adams gets lost, finds the
shack, the cord somehow fails on its own. It's almost broken through, Adams cranks it too high, the wind catches
it . . ." He considered. "Or not. Look. The only one with
any true mobility was Tyson, on the snowmobile."

"Do you think he . . ."

"I did see them arguing in the weight room," Lewis said,
and then instantly regretted having said it. He was doing
to Tyson what Cameron was trying to do to him. "But not
anything that would lead to this."

"Well, I damn well want to know what *would* lead to this!" the station manager suddenly shouted in frustration. "I want to know who's ruining *my* winter! This isn't fair, dammit! I'm sick of you, and I'm sick of Buck, and I'm sick of this damn job!"

"Rod!" Norse snapped crisply. "Rod, Rod. Cool it." His voice was admonitory. "Talk like that and you'll throw everyone in a panic. This is a time for leadership, not accusations. Rationality, not wild suspicion. Maybe it *is* all accidental. Certainly it's all circumstantial. We've got a small group and a lot of concern right now, even fear, consternation, sorrow, you name it. People will be feeding off each other. We've got to get them to the point of feeding strength, not weakness."

Cameron looked utterly depressed. "How do we do that?"

"First of all, you are the man. *The* man. Man of the hour. Everyone's looking to you for cues on how to respond. You've got to seem confident, unafraid, in charge. Get it together." Norse looked concerned.

The station manager took a deep breath. "I know. But to lose two of our top scientists, and then this bonehead here"—he nodded to Lewis—"wandering off in the storm . . . it's just hard, Doc. It's like being in the Navy and grounding a ship. They don't want to hear excuses. You just don't run aground."

"And when you do, you don't surrender. Listen, this is what the station is about. This is what our winter is about. Leadership! The ability of the individual to define the group! You're the keystone. The pivot. The rock."

Cameron closed his eyes. "Some rock." He thought a minute, his chest rising and falling, and then opened his eyes. "I know I've got to get my shit together," he said tiredly. "It's just a little much to take."

"It's a little much for everyone to take. That's why we need you."

He grimaced at his own explosion. "It's lonely at the top," he recited wryly.

"Everyone's alone. That's life."

"Okay." He took a breath. "Okay, okay. Listen. I'm going to ask NSF to send an investigator down here. They sent the FBI to McMurdo once. Maybe they can send somebody here."

Norse was surprised. "A cop?"

"I thought planes couldn't get in here," Lewis said. "If they can, I'm ready to go home."

"There's an outside chance for at least an airdrop," Cameron said. "They've done them in winter before. We've definitely got an emergency here. Maybe they can parachute somebody in. Somebody with a weapon and authority. Someone who knows what to do."

"That might be overreacting, Rod," Norse said.

"Overreacting? With two dead bodies?"

"Two *accidents*, until we learn otherwise. You put a cop in here and it becomes two victims. You define the problem in the worst possible light. You put your own stewardship in the worst possible light. And nobody will get any work done."

"Bullshit." He pointed at Norse. "Maybe they'll begin by investigating *you*."

The psychologist sighed. "I'd recommend it, actually, if you don't want to spook everyone else and screw up the whole winter. Concentrate on me."

"Is that a confession?" He was sour.

"Think about it. Suppose you get your G-man. He parachutes in and interrogates me. Or Lewis. Or Tyson. People are freaked out. A small group like this can turn on a person and make his life miserable. I've read about it. I've seen it. And then you've got somebody under a cloud, pre-occupying everyone, until spring. What are you going to do with them for the rest of the winter? How does anyone get any work done? I think we need to calm things down, not hype them up. And NSF is going to go ballistic if you turn an accident into a murder investigation. If you really need a fall guy, make it me. I'm not doing physical science. I'm not worried about what they might ask."

"I'm not looking for a fall guy! I'm looking to keep things under some kind of control! What do *you* suggest, Doctor Freud?"

"Just that we all cool off for a day or two. That we don't panic the bureaucrats in D.C. for a day or two. If one of us is a murderer . . . well, we're not going anywhere. We chill, and separate, and wait."

"What does that mean?" Lewis asked.

"Quarantine, Jed. There's going to be a lot of gossip and speculation about this, it's inevitable. Especially with you finding the body, after the e-mail to Mickey. I think you should stay out in Clean Air for a while longer, this time with a sleeping bag. We'll bring you your meals. You can collect your data for Sparco and be . . . safe."

"Under house arrest," Lewis clarified. "So everyone else feels safe."

"Temporarily. It's for your own good."

"Doc, there's not even a john out there."

"We'll bring you a bucket. Just for a few days, until we sort things out."

"I can't believe this! Is Tyson going to be quarantined?"

"Buck quarantines himself. Everyone's avoiding him like the plague anyway."

"Are *you* going to be quarantined?"

"Oh no!" He smiled. "Because this is what I came down for."

"To watch us," Cameron said bitterly. "Watch us go nuts."

"To watch the variable in the experiment once Jed is out of the way." Norse smiled thinly. "Who had mobility? Who had motive? I'm going to watch the habits and patterns and movements of Buck Tyson. And save your career by letting you solve this one yourself."

I Make My Decision

When the shit hits the fan there's no time to be polite to the weaklings. Fleming and Kressler had just killed themselves with their own reckless idiocy, Fat Boy had doomed himself by waddling off the rope against all orders, and the rest of the kids were sniffing and sniveling like a pack of whipped dogs. Somehow I had to find some spine in them if we were going to get out of this mess. I mostly felt contempt that they'd allowed themselves to be herded onto this ledge. That I'd allowed myself to be herded. And outrage that my life was at risk because of the incompetence and bad judgment of others.

I didn't deserve to die.

Still, I bit back most of what I wanted to say. I needed two of them, the two best, to ascend the cliff with me so we could belay the rest of the sheep back off the dead-end ledge my colleagues had led them to. I needed the remainder to break out of their freeze-up panic. The wind was rising, the snow getting thicker, but if we moved quickly, moved NOW, we still might get up to the saddle and descend the glacier on the other side before we became totally lost in a whiteout.

"They're dead but you're not!" I snapped at them about Fleming and Kressler. "Don't think about them, think about yourself! If you're going to survive this it's going to have to come from inside YOU! I need fire in your bellies or you're all going to DIE!"

More weeping and moaning. Jesus H. Christ. They were falling apart. Some of the kids were starting to shiver, a first warning of hypothermia, and we'd all lock up if we didn't get moving. So I had to be realistic. When the shit hits the fan, it's no time to tell fairy tales. It's triage time. Some were going to make it and some probably weren't. Fat Boy was dead meat, as far as I was concerned. He'd blundered, and was about to pay for it big time. The strongest of the rest of us had a chance. Maybe.

Women and children first is lunacy at a time like that, a sure invitation to disaster. I like girls as well as any man, but not at the end of a rope that's holding me to a crumbling rock wall. So the first decision I made was that the females stayed behind. They were supposed to be better in cold anyway, right? Epidermal layer and all that. If they huddled maybe they'd last through the storm if I could get back with help. If, if. The storm was building and help was a long time off. Nobody was helicoptering in, nobody was climbing back up, not until this little snow spat was over. Bad luck, but there it was. So the ladies would have to wait and hope for the best. I was taking the strongest boys. If the bucks remembered what they'd learned, maybe a few of us could make it.

Couldn't tell them the grim facts, of course. Sometimes when you're honest with yourself you still have to lie to the others. Especially if they might survive and tell stories about you afterward. So I told them I was leading the strongest of us to the top of the cliff and that we'd try to belay anyone else who wanted to come up if we could, and if we couldn't do that we were going to get help and they should all sit tight until we got back. Trust me! Hold on to each other and pray! We're all going to get through this!

Bullshit.

I took the two I thought just might make it. I truly did. Chisel Chin was a big-balled sonofabitch wise guy who had the endurance of any two of his classmates and was eyeing routes even as I tried to settle the rest of the herd. Carrot Top was jumpier and not as strong, but he was big and reasonably competent and hadn't spaced out like Ponytail Boy, the third candidate I had in mind. That one had developed a thousand-yard stare like he'd already seen the angelic choir, so I didn't think I could rely on his presence of mind. Maybe if we could really rig a rope to help the others, Ponytail could be the first to try to follow. I shook him, telling him that. Meanwhile, however, I'd have to rely on the other two.

We roped up, slipped on our packs, and readied ourselves to go back up the way we'd come down. What a moronic mess. Somebody asked about Fat Boy and I admit I was a little curt at that point, saying Fat Boy was just going to have to look after himself for a while and if he gave them any grief, they could just roll lard ass over the edge. They stared wide-eyed at my moment of honesty and actually shut up for half a minute. Gee, did I let a fart? What did they think was going to happen to Fat Boy? I loathed their innocence. I truly did.

So. I'd start the first pitch, hammer in a piton, fix a rope, and let Chisel Chin come up to me. Then I'd go on, my partner braced so that if I fell, the piton and Chisel Chin combined just might hold me in space. I might drop thirty feet before the rope brought me up taut, but that's a hell of a lot better than three thousand. Then another piton, another point, Carrot Top coming on, too, and we'd work our way up the cliff. Bing, bang, boom. Fleming and Kressler had taken too much rope, so we had to take all the remaining line from the others if we hoped to fashion a line all the way back up to the top. If we made it, great. If we didn't, the others weren't getting off that ledge anyway.

Just before we started I faced away from the weeping group, looked out to the gray eternity swirling all around us, and fumbled under my coat. I was mindful of what had happened to Kressler and Fleming and was determined that it wasn't going to happen to me. It wasn't prophetic. I was counting on those two kids, sure. But if you're going to survive in this jungle of ours you prepare for every contingency. You have to think ahead. Every time I've won in life it's because I've thought two or three moves down the road. A step ahead: That's the secret.

So I took out a silver commando knife, slipped it out of its sheath, and tucked it into a strap near my neck where I could snatch it out easily. Just in case. Then I turned to the others and actually managed a reassuring grin.

What a hero I was.

We started back up.

CHAPTER FIFTEEN

Flat gray clouds spoiled the final exit of the sun. There was a week of overcast, as dark and featureless as a pot lid, and when it blew away, the lingering orb was finally gone and the long polar night had begun. The sky was still dusk blue. A couple of stars popped out, tiny and cold, the first outriders of the glory to come. Instead of seeming foreboding, the approaching dark heralded a kind of peace to Lewis. The sun's scheduled disappearance meant it would reappear on schedule, too, and when that happened he would be near release from the Pole. Meanwhile, the ground had lost shadow and definition and the boundary between snow and sky became even more indistinct.

At first he didn't mind his isolation in the Clean Air quadrant. It spared him the necessity of trying to prove his own innocence. He didn't have to act some kind of normal relationship with a group of people half suspicious that he might be a murderer at worst and a bad-luck enzyme at best. Solitary, he called it, except that each day he had four hours in which orbiting satellites lifted high enough above the polar horizon to allow access to the Internet.

Lewis monitored world news that seemed increasingly remote, shopped for products he had no use for and couldn't
get delivered, and kept his mentor Sparco updated on his
weather measurements. He found himself surprisingly intrigued by the accumulating data points of temperature,
wind, snow, carbon dioxide, and ozone. Graphing the readings was like painstakingly sculpting a work of art. When
winds were calm he watched from the windows as Gerald
Follett launched his atmospheric balloons, observing the
quiet routine of inflation, rigging, and recording. The man
had declined Lewis's help, looking nervous when Lewis
even offered, but the regularity of the task was somehow
reassuring. Life went on. There was a purity to the science,
and a purity to the dry cold that Lewis found bracing. Meteorology itself was a constant dance of interwoven fac-
tors, like the twisted glass of a kaleidoscope suggesting
different global futures.

He'd found a better purpose.

His exile also spared him fevered group speculation on
the deaths of Moss and Adams. No theories, no rumors, no
jokes. It made him calmer. People were complicated but
science was not. The universe was designed to be understood. Only humans were an enigma.

Yet when his tasks were completed he was increasingly
lonely as well. The others brought him a mattress, a bucket,
and food as if he were a leper. His basic dilemma was that
day after day went by without mishap, according to
Cameron. There were no disappearances, no discoveries,
and no confessions, and thus nothing to turn suspicion away
from him. Lewis comes, and things go wrong. Lewis is
banished, and normalcy returns. No G-man parachuted in,
no conclusions were drawn.

A week drifted by, empty of real news.

Then Abby came, the first time he'd seen her since Adams's death.

Once more he detected her breath before he noticed her approach. A spike in his carbon measurements that he duly noted in the log. He stepped to a window and watched her walk the flag line, following a path of snow clumpy enough that she occasionally stumbled, a heavy daypack adding to her clumsiness in the dusk. He'd learned to recognize her from a distance: her quick, straightforward walk, the rather tight swing of her arms, her habit of sometimes tucking them around her torso as if to warm herself, bowing her head in thought like a bird at roost—and then popping up-right suddenly to peer around like a startled dove. It was funny how much you could tell from posture and move-ment. Everyone looked alike in their orange parkas and black bib pants and yet they didn't. A tilt of head, a curve of back, an angle of foot: stances as individualistic as fin-gerprints.

She clanged up the stairs, stamped snow loose in the vestibule, and came inside, swinging the backpack onto the floor with a soft thud. "More food, Enzyme."

Lewis grimaced. He was getting tired of hot-plate left-overs. "Bread and water?"

"Meat loaf and macaroni. A little junk food as well, for morale. Chemical preservatives disguised as cake, salt dis-guised as chips, sugar dusted with a little flour. Cueball promised he won't put in enough to poison you."

"Not without a group vote, at least." He meant it as a joke, but it came out sounding sour. "I'm sure everyone misses me."

"Forgotten you, actually." She shed her coat. "Too many troubles."

Trouble? He was shamelessly hungry for gossip. "A suspect unmasked?"

"Just bad feeling. It's turning into a pretty grim winter."

"Rod told me nothing's happening."

"That's because he doesn't know what to do. Tyson has gone nuts. He thinks everyone's against him, which we are. One shower stinks. Yet he won't back down. He's announced that since no one appreciates his contributions to our little society he's going to find the meteorite and make himself rich, and to hell with anyone else. So he's stomping around, ignoring his job, and even threatening to wig out of here on a Spryte or something—fixing those is the one thing he'll work on. Cameron blew up at him in the galley and said he's pulling Buck's bonus, as if he had any chance of getting it anyway, so then they almost got into a fistfight. It scared everybody. Geller fantasizes about putting a contract out on the guy, Pulaski is about to call Buck out, the beakers are bitching about not getting enough work done, and Bob is writing it all up like we're a bunch of lunatics. Which maybe we are. We're toasting at record speed."

"Jesus." Tyson was being pushed toward an explosion. Maybe Norse's plan of removing Lewis from the center of things was working after all: Bad feeling couldn't be blamed on him. Yet the tension sounded risky. "So you came to visit the only sane man on station?"

She looked at him warily. "Just to deliver groceries."

"Even though I might be dangerous. The mysterious fingie. The enzyme." Impulsively, he took a step toward her to see what she'd do.

"Doctor Bob actually suggested I deliver the food this time. Said it's good for you to see other people. And he said that . . ." She stopped, suddenly flustered.

"And what?"

"Nothing." She looked away.

"What?"

"He said we mesh well together."

He took another step. "I thought I made people nervous, Abby."

She'd stiffened, he noticed, not as sure of him as she pretended. "Not me. I'm not afraid of you, Jed."

Another step, very close now. "If so, you're the only one."

"Stop it. I'm trying to trust. Don't put everything to the test."

He stopped, feeling foolish. "I'm sorry. I shouldn't joke around. It's just that the whole situation is so . . . absurd. This place, this paranoia . . ."

"People are spooked. I'm spooked. We all just want to go home."

"And yet we can't."

"Yes." She slumped in a chair. "Stuck with each other." She squinted at him, slightly annoyed at his advance. Her lips were full, her neck high. Her hands were small, good for working with electronics. She was prettier than he remembered. He realized that he'd missed her.

"I like you, Abby." The bold confession surprised himself, and he was pleased at his own sudden boldness. "I like you a lot. I'm attracted to you. And I'm lonely. I'm glad you came out here."

She smiled wanly. "Just don't take an ax to me and make me regret it."

"You trusted me enough to come out here, right?"

"I guess."

"And I have to trust you, right?"

She looked wary. "I guess."

He sat in a chair opposite her. "If we're going to trust each other, we have to talk, I think. Too much has happened. You have to tell me about that photograph in Mickey's pocket."

She squirmed. "I don't know about that picture."

"But you know something, right? I saw it upset you. Abby, I'm a damned murder suspect. I'm in exile. I need help. What in the hell is going on?"

"I don't know." She looked away. "It turns out it's a photo from my personnel file. I checked and it's missing from the stuff NSF sent down."

"Mickey lifted it?"

"That's not what *he* said. Mickey brought it to me that night not long after the meteorite was stolen. He said he found it in Doctor Bob's room when you searched each other, that there was a wall panel with screws missing and it had been tucked in a slit there. He said that he didn't trust Norse, that he didn't like shrinks. He wanted to know what my photograph was doing there. He said if I was having a problem with Bob, he had authority enough to help me. He said he was prepared to be my friend."

"Jesus. Doctor Bob?"

"That's what I thought. So . . ." She faltered a moment, summoning courage. "So I went to Norse and told him I had some personal problems I wanted help with and needed to talk to him privately in his room. And then I went there, blabbering away, looking at the walls, and I didn't see anything like what Doctor Moss described. No screws missing, no gap in the panels. So I told Bob what Mickey had showed me and he suddenly got very concerned and agitated and warned me to stay away from the astronomer at all costs. I was just dumbfounded but he said there'd been past complaints from young women on the base about Moss coming on to them and worse, this old guy bullying and pawing them because of his power on station. That he invented excuses to get close to them; that he even researched the next group coming down, picking out the pretty ones. And that one reason Norse was sent down here was to check out those rumors. And that Moss probably suspected that and didn't like him because of it, and that possibly this whole meteorite thing was an attempt to distract attention." She said it in a rush.

Lewis was skeptical. "A geezer like Moss? Boy, I don't know. He was pretty regal. I can't imagine him coming on to anybody."

"That's what I thought. But then Bob had these files. I couldn't read them because of the confidentiality but he showed me a packet of what he said were complaints that had been filed . . . it was horrible! I didn't know what to think! And then Mickey dies. . . ."

"Suicide."

"Yes." She nodded miserably.

"He was afraid of exposure."

"I think so. I think Norse is some kind of investigator."

"Except Bob Norse told me he thought it could be murder. Or at least that's what NSF thinks, back in D.C. And for my own protection I'm sitting out here."

"Don't you see? NSF *wants* a murder. Or an accident. Anything but a big sexual scandal like Tailhook that's going to throw a wrench in their plans to get congressional money to rebuild this base. Reconstruction is going to cost a hundred million dollars and they can't afford to have their star scientist exposed as a rogue after Clarence Thomas and Monica Lewinsky and all that. So Norse thinks you're in danger, Jed. You're not one of the fraternity. You're just this oil guy down to make a few bucks over the winter.

They might try to pin something on you, to distract from any stories about Mickey. Nothing to file in court, because that would just make matters worse. Just enough suspicion and rumor to muddy the waters. To make you the fall guy, send you away under a cloud. Doctor Bob is trying to help you. That's why he encouraged me to come out here."

"What about Harrison Adams?"

"His death is probably a coincidence, but who knows? Doctor Bob is as confused as we are."

"This is too crazy. . . ."

"Which is exactly why he's here."

Lewis sighed, trying to think. Harrison Adams had been going through Moss's computer. Had he learned too much? Was there something incriminating he needed to discuss with Lewis? And if the deaths weren't back-to-back accidents, or a suicide-accident, then who was responsible? The only one he could see with a stake in the future of base reconstruction was Rod Cameron, who might be angling for a promotion in the NSF bureaucracy. But would Cameron kill to cover up a scandal? It was too far-fetched. You needed someone truly loony, or someone desperate for that meteorite.

He looked at her. "What do you think? Of me?"

"My heart tells me you're just unlucky—in the wrong place at the wrong time. My brain tells me not to trust anyone. But I'm here, aren't I? Maybe all this is nothing. Moss decided to go exploring, slipped, and fell. Harrison got caught in a storm. It happens."

He smiled ruefully. "So you risk bringing me dinner."

She looked away. "I'm attracted to you, too, Jed," she said.

The admission took him as much by surprise as his own.

"It's going to be a long winter. We both need a friend," she amended.

Her words filled him with longing. The tundra had been liberating, when he walked away from his oil job, but the aftermath had been lonely. He'd had no place he belonged, no purpose to his life. And now, suddenly, there was this woman.

"Abby, I think I need to kiss you," he decided.

She looked at him wryly.

"I'm going to go crazy if I can't kiss you right now," he insisted.

"You *are* crazy. We're all crazy. We just decided that."

"Yes. That's why it's all right to kiss you."

She considered it cautiously. "If we kiss, things change."

"Yes, like an enzyme. I want to change things with you. I know there's that other guy but he's not here and we are. He's not in this and we are."

"Then what happens?"

"I don't know. I just know it's important to do this now."

She looked at him: amused, impatient, uncertain. "I'm afraid I'll like it."

He grinned. "I'm afraid you won't."

She hesitated, as judicious as if reviewing a contract, reviewing her own instincts about him. Then she made up her mind. "Okay."

He knelt next to her and lifted his face to hers, struck by the green hazel of her eyes and the dark curl of her hair on each cheek. She coolly waited as he cupped the nape of her neck, bending her to him, but when his lips gently touched hers she shivered and closed her eyes. He came away and her lips parted slightly, revealing a glimpse of the pearl of her teeth. He kissed her again, more deeply this time, and she started to respond. Then she turned her head, sighing, and his lips brushed her cheek and ear and

followed the curve of her neck to the collar of her Ther-
max underwear. . . .

"That's enough." She stood up.

He remained kneeling, looking up at her. "No, it isn't."

"I like you, Jed, but too much is going on. I've got a
lot to think about." Her eyes were darting around the room,
betraying her confusion.

"You think too much, you know."

"Let's just leave it there for now."

He stood as well, grinning, savoring his small triumph.
He'd tasted her. She'd liked it. "I want to get to know
you."

"Yes." She said it in a tone that suggested she wasn't at
all sure that was a good idea. Yet she wanted to surrender,
he was sure of it.

"I'm tired of exile. I think I want to get back to the
dome."

"Yes."

Suddenly he was excited. Isolation out in Clean Air was
preferable to being ostracized inside the dome. But Abby's
confession of attraction made everything different. Here at
least was a friend. Ally. He'd work side by side with her.
Talk to her. Endure the winter with her.

"Go talk to Rod for me. Tell him to bring me in."

"I don't know if Doctor Bob thinks that's a good idea
yet."

"To hell with Doctor Bob."

"He's trying to protect you."

"Isolate me for his observations." He'd seen Norse con-
fer with Abby. Maybe the shrink wanted to put the moves
on her himself. His own exile was a convenience. "Screw
Norse. I want to be with you."

"Well, then *you* talk to Cameron. It will be embarrassing if I do it."

"Yes. Absolutely." He felt energized. She was receptive to a partnership. He could talk the station manager into anything.

"You'll have to call him but he's pretty stressed out."

"I will."

"Maybe in the morning. He's a little more rested then."

"Good idea."

"People are still pretty edgy in the dome. Snapping at each other. It's not going to be easy for you if you come back."

"I'll be okay if I can get to talk to you."

"That's all I'm promising."

"I know."

"Rod is pretty jumpy. Be patient."

"I will."

But when she left to do some maintenance work on the computers in astronomy he decided he couldn't wait. To hell with patience. To hell with tomorrow. He was sick of being isolated in Clean Air like some kind of germ. He went to the phone and called Cameron's office. There was no answer, so he dialed the galley. Pulaski told him to try a radio. "Our station manager is making his rounds. Can't it wait?"

"No, it can't." Lewis hung up and picked up the radio. "Enzyme to Ice Pick. Over."

After a few tries, Cameron's raspy, tired voice finally came on. "This is Cameron."

"This is Lewis. Where are you?" Anybody with a radio could listen in but he was too determined to care.

"Checking the fuel arch."

"Rod, can we meet to talk?"

There was a wary silence. Then: "I'm kind of busy."

"I'm going nuts in Clean Air."

"It's for your own good, buddy."

"I've been talking with Abby. Let me come back to the dome. She can keep an eye on me. Lock me in my room at night if you have to."

He stalled. "I'll talk about it to Doctor Bob."

"Doctor Bob has no authority here. You do. I've been exiled without charges. That's unconstitutional, isn't it?"

More uncomfortable silence. "I don't know. It's easier having you out there." The implication was plain.

"Rod, I think it was suicide. Suicide and an accident. You can't blame me and you can't blame yourself."

"Things are kind of messy, Jed."

"You mean Tyson?"

Cameron's voice was cold. "Tyson's a dead man. Don't bring him up to me."

"Don't blame *me* for *him*. Let me come over to talk. Let's meet privately, you and me. To talk."

Another long silence. "I have to check out these tanks."

"I'll find you there. We'll talk in private."

"Enzyme . . ." Cameron sounded besieged, reluctant. "Listen. Stay in Clean Air. When I finish this inspection I'll swing by and see how you're doing, okay?"

"Will we talk?"

"Yes." It was a sigh. "We'll talk."

"Talk about changing things?"

"We'll talk."

It was enough. "Roger that." He put down the radio, impatient and hopeful. Maybe with Abby Dixon he could find a way to live in this place.

I Choose Survival

Every once in a while you arrive at a point in life where you can't afford to make a mistake. Might be a job. Might be a romance. Might be a gamble or the way you choose to answer with a gun pointed to your head. Might be an icy road and oncoming headlights and that drink you had that was one too many. You can't know when or how it's going to come. But when it does, you have to get things right.

If you don't, you're dead, figuratively and literally.

My climbing companions didn't get it right.

For the first two hundred feet I was optimistic. It was difficult climbing but not impossible, even for relative amateurs. There were cracks and toeholds and chimneys enough to squirt our way upward, though the rocks we dislodged banged down and set off a fresh round of squeals and shouts from the kids below. Crash! Sorry about that. Hey, we were making it, inching back up, getting to a point where maybe everyone but Fat Boy could climb back out of purgatory, Chisel Chin and Carrot Top straining up to each piton, breathing hard, eyes wide, limbs trembling, yes—but making it. Our lives were at stake. The two kids were doing what they had to do.

I was feeling good about saving them. I was pulling us out of the trap.

To understand my choice you have to picture how piss-poor miserable it was on Wallace Wall. At first the light had strengthened as the sun rose, giving a crumb of encouragement, but then the storm blotted out any sight of Old Sol and the morning grew dim and murky. Snow was blowing horizontally, turning the rock slippery, and small puffs of snow broke off from the cornice at the top of the wall and rained down on us like sand into a pit, each of us tensing in case the drizzle heralded a larger avalanche. The gusts were up to forty, I learned later, and the wind-chill well below zero. Our mittens were off to allow us to grip but the rock was shredding our glove liners and our fingers were turning numb and bloody. The wall angle wasn't vertical but almost so, and it was a strain to stay glued. The farther we ascended, the more anxious I became. I could imagine the fear the two kids were feeling, the exposure, the helplessness. I kept remembering Kressler and Fleming pinwheeling off that cliff.

It was Chisel Chin who made the mistake. The first rule of climbing is to keep at least three of your four limbs in contact with the mountain at any one time. He was impatient and had both a foot and a hand reaching for fresh holds when a rock broke and both legs were suddenly churning in empty space. He hung for a moment on one exhausted arm, kicking in the air for substitute footholds he'd failed to locate first—I'd warned him!—and then with a grunt he dropped, all of this happening in the flash of a second. I had time to jam one forearm in a crack, almost breaking it, and braced against the shock. He fell to the limit of his rope, yelling, and it cinched on my waist so hard that I felt like I was being crushed against a wall by a car bumper, the impact expelling my breath and igniting my adrenaline.

With an experienced team we probably would have recovered. If Chisel Chin had a few seconds to dangle in space until he forced down his panic and found fresh purchase he could have taken the pressure off the line, we could have stabilized, and after a minute's shaky breathing we could have started up again. But when he dropped past Carrot Top the second boy jerked in surprise and panicked, coming off the wall for no reason at all, his wits gone in a blaze of shock. He dropped heavily, a condemned man through a trapdoor, wrenching at me, and then hung like a cow, both of them swinging and screaming and sawing on me with the weight of four hundred pounds.

"Grab something! Get the weight off me!" My own panic erupted and all I could see was that picture of Kressler and Fleming, tumbling lazily through empty gray air. The two kids were going to pull me off with them and we'd spend the last moments of our existence watching each other's sick dread as the glacier rushed up at us.

Or we could act.

"Grab, grab! I'm coming off the cliff!"

They kicked and twirled like the condemned.

When that life moment of split decision comes, you don't think but you react, and you react with instincts formed by all the thinking you've done before. I'm a strong man, but not strong enough to handle two heavily weighted climbers swinging across the face of a cliff, arms and legs flailing, rock peeling off, everyone roaring and cursing together. I can carry myself, but not the rest of the world with me.

So I reached for my knife.

If I'd fallen, every kid in that class would be dead. I knew that. I was their only hope in the world. The choice wasn't really about my survival, but theirs. Yet I had to think for myself, too. Think of myself.

I really did it for them.

I reached with my knife and slashed at the climbing line, even as I felt my other forearm being dragged out of its crack.

In memory there may have been just a moment's slackening of tension as one or both of the boys briefly grabbed back onto the rock. It was a confused experience and I'll never know for sure. Don't you think I've wondered, in the dark sweats of the night? But it was too late because I was already cutting, desperate to get free of them, and finally the rope parted and I slapped back against the cliff, making a woof, and then below me I heard long, terrified screaming.

I knew better than to look down.

From the ledge below there were more shouts, cries, wailing, terror as the students' two companions flashed past them. I ignored it all. That part was past me now, and there was nothing I could do. The surviving kids called to me like a wounded man calls for his mother and I ignored them, knowing that there was no second chance, that destiny had made its irrevocable turn. Instead I waited a couple minutes to catch my breath, my sweat freezing on my collar and hair. I still had presence of mind. I took the end of the cut rope and rubbed it against the rough igneous rock for the longest time, almost frantic, until I had frayed it into ragged string. I reached with my knife and put it into a deep crevice on Wallace Wall where it will never be found, I hope.

Then I resumed climbing.

What else could I do?

CHAPTER SIXTEEN

Dana Andrews shivered, and it wasn't just from cold. The shadowy fuel arch gave her the creeps, this dank tunnel that stank of petroleum and was so dimly lit. Accordingly, she started down the shadowy steel-roofed tunnel that held the station's petroleum supply with exasperated reluctance. Where the bloody hell was Rod Cameron?

Since coming upon the stiff, reaching hand of Harrison Adams, Dana had become more and more of a dome slug, clinging to the light and warmth of the galley and berthing floors like a child retreating to a bedroom. The winter was not beginning at all like she'd hoped. Thanks to Mickey's meteorite the station team seemed rent by suspicions and rivalries. Two deaths and the increasingly bizarre behavior of Mr. James "Buck" Tyson had smashed through the serenity she'd sought like a bus through a window. In reaction, Dana spent what time she could under the grow lights in the station greenhouse, helping Lena tend the hydroponic plants and trying to fight her own impending depression. God, it was claustrophobic here! Her work on polar atmospheric circulation was lagging to the point where she

might not gain the tenure at the University of Auckland
that she'd hoped to achieve by wintering at the Pole. She
needed Tyson to help her sled and service her instruments
pronto but it was impossible to get the mechanic to do anything unless he was ridden by Cameron, and the station
manager had avoided Tyson since the two had almost come
to blows two days before in the galley. It was an ugly situation. Cameron oscillated between bursts of annoying
spunk, in which he'd radiate false optimism in a pathetic
attempt to rally the troops, and a private gloom so profound he was becoming reclusive. Half the time he hid
himself in his office and the other half he set off on pointless inspection tours of the tiny world of the dome. Then
it would be up to the winter-overs to find him so they could
get some work done.

Like now.

The crazy Americans were wrecking her work! Wrecking her future! It was hard being a woman in science, and
she needed some good data, a solid discovery, to establish
herself. Some stroke of dumb luck like Mickey's rock.
Some commitment to the often mundane and tedious tasks
that made up the painstaking minutiae of modern research.
She needed logistical help and she needed to talk to the
station manager alone. Have it out with him. Get him to
snap out of it.

Their cook, who served as unofficial recording secretary
of the comings and goings at the base, had told her that
Cameron was checking the fuel that supplied the station.
The generators suckled off four hundred thousand gallons
of imported fuel kept in a chain of tanks in the arch behind Nancy Hodge's BioMed. The heat was as precious as
oxygen. Periodically Cameron or Pika walked the tunnel
to check the integrity of the valves and pipes as carefully

as the hull of a boat. The fuel arch represented survival, but it also served as an excuse for Cameron to disappear. He'd taken to inspecting it more than necessary.

"Rod!" Dana cried out impatiently. She was standing on a steel grate catwalk that ran the length of the tunnel, looking for some sign of the station manager along the line of tanks. The system was new, installed two summers before to replace rubberized bladders that NSF had feared were too susceptible to leaks or sabotage, and the new metal had the reassuring solidity of a battleship. It was also cold. Her call echoed off the tanks and bounced to the archway's far end, the wall there lost in darkness. There was no reply.

Dana hated the gloom of the arches, where cones of light from infrequent bulbs were separated by pockets of deep shadow. For a moment she considered returning to the galley and surrendering to a cup of tea. But no, she needed to get her project firmly on track and that meant talking candidly to Cameron in a place where they could have a moment's privacy. Tyson was lurking and wandering around like a perverse moron, eating slugs and hogging shower water and boasting he would find the meteorite and make himself rich, and he'd scared poor Gina Brindisi half to death by jumping out from behind a shed out on the Dark Side as if to make a joke out of the common belief he was ready to erupt. Everyone hated him, and hated the water rationing he had perversely imposed on them. Everyone feared him. Norse seemed like the only person able to even talk to him, but their conversations had little apparent effect. Tyson was two hundred and fifty pounds of coiled resentment, impenetrable to reason and uncaring of consequences. There was no sign he'd taken heed of the toast Dana had tacked to his door. The mechanic in fact seemed to enjoy being an outcast. Cameron had to reestablish con-

trol or the base would become dysfunctional. It was time
for Cameron to stand up to Tyson. Time to be a man.

Reluctantly she continued walking down the catwalk, her
boots making a rhythmic thud that repeated behind as if
someone were following her. Unable to resist, she turned.
No one there.

"Rod?"

She'd neglected to bring a flashlight and so couldn't see
well into the dark crevices between the tanks. Still, she
should be able to detect the movement of Cameron poking about. Nothing. Was he even here? Dana began walking faster toward the end of the fuel arch, impatient to
conclude her search and get out.

"Cameron, dammit, where are you?"

There! A dark shadow, moving ahead. Hadn't he heard
her? The figure rose and then sank as she followed. Her
boots rapped quickly.

"Rod!"

He didn't reply. Was the idiot playing hide and seek?

No, there he was again, popping up and dipping down.
A nonsense pattern. Was he circling around each tank? He
was going to make her walk all the way, she could tell.
Sighing, she went on, deeper and deeper into the cold
gloom. She could hear the tinkle of her frozen exhalations
crystallizing and falling away behind her.

"Bloody silly Yank."

Then a thought occurred to her. She stopped, her blood
thumping in her ears, and considered her situation again with
sudden doubt. What if the figure at the end of the archway
wasn't Cameron at all? What if it was somebody like that
Lewis, who always seemed to turn up in the wrong places?
Or Tyson, growling like a wounded bear? Here she was alone,
in this dark, spooky place, with no weapon, no escort. . . .

Nervously she reached inside her parka and pulled out the whistle she'd kept since finding Harrison Adams, the fingie Lewis standing there with broken heat tape in his hands as if he'd snipped it himself. She'd had nightmares about that one.

"Rod?" Her call was quiet, but still it echoed away.

Cautiously she moved ahead again, waiting for the elusive stranger to reappear. There! She stopped and he stopped, as if freezing. My God, who was it? Why wouldn't he approach? "Who's there!" Her weak challenge echoed away.

You can't run, she told herself. *Not if you're going to live here for seven more sinister, slogging, dome-slug months.* She edged ahead, cautious now, her whistle in one mitten. The figure moved upward and then slipped down and away. Damn, that was unprofessional! You didn't duck around like a silly jack-in-the-box! Not after all that had happened!

She was almost to the end and left the illumination of the last light, the archway like a receding cave. Her eyes were adjusting and she could make out dark shapes. The tanks sat in their trim, mute line, these farthest ones already empty. And yet she saw no one. No movement. She stopped, perplexed and frightened.

"Rod?"

This was weird.

Dana turned to retreat, her skin prickling under her parka. Something was wrong, she could sense it, and she felt a growing dread at being here. It was time to go back to the galley. Cameron was a lost cause, a supervisor who had no business supervising. Her data could wait. Global atmospheric circulation could wait. She'd spend the winter watching bloody videos if she had to, and try to pick up the pieces back in Auckland.

She strode back purposefully, fighting the impulse to

break into a clumsy run. And then there he was again, somehow having circled around her, rising up in front of her in the distance, elusive and ill-formed. . . .

She stopped. He stopped.

And suddenly it dawned on her.

"My shadow!" She glanced upward. As she passed under each light, the shadow of her form appeared and faded on the tanks ahead. Her elusive fugitive was her own advancing form. She'd been frightened of herself.

She laughed, the sound sharp and relieved. "Silly goose."

Her heartbeat began to slow, her sweat to cool her. She shivered again. Enough of this nonsense: Back to the galley! To hell with tea, she was ready for a tumbler of single malt! She walked again, quickly now, her boots banging as if she were on the boardwalk of a pioneer town, deciding firmly that her days of searching for her wayward station manager were over. Enough craziness! If Cameron wanted some research progress to show for the winter, he could damn well start working more effectively with the scientists. And if not . . .

She stopped again. There was something odd about the snow between two of the tanks, she realized.

Dana peered closer into the dimness. Coming this way, the shadows cast by the light made apparent what had failed to draw her eye in the opposite direction. The snow was heavily trampled, sprayed as if kicked. There was a geometric regularity down there in the scuffed area, she saw: a white curve against the dark paint of a tank. The curve of . . . a boot. A white bunny boot.

She glanced quickly around. No one there.

"Rod?"

Just leave it. Send someone else. But no, they'd think her a girlish fool.

Her pulse racing again, she climbed over the railing and down from the catwalk and walked unsteadily toward the boot. She could see a leg now, its black nylon windpants extending into shadow, and then another leg, knee up. The figure was on its back. *My God.*

She stopped, dizzy with fear. Why, why, why was *she* the one to stumble on these troubles? The whole winter was terribly unfair. She breathed a moment, closing her eyes, gathering her courage. Then she opened them again. The snow was blotchy and as she came near she realized that between the tanks it was colored red. Bright red.

Shaking now, she stepped in the gap, leaning unsteadily against one of the tanks. It was Cameron, sprawled on his back, his parka hood off, and his eyes screwed shut with pain. He'd frozen that way. He lay as if on a red disk, a platter of congealed blood. His parka was soaked with it, and a wisp of steam came from a ragged tear in his chest.

Rod hadn't been dead very long.

Feeling her gorge rise, she leaned closer. It appeared to be the kind of wound a sharp weapon would make. Something like a knife: a big knife. Cameron's mouth was open as if hollering as he went down, and so something was stuffed in it as if to cut the noise. A cloth, perhaps, to gag him. Smother him.

She knelt, reaching. But what had seemed like a cloth crumbled in a shockingly familiar manner and, trembling, she pulled a piece out and backed into the light where she could see what had been crammed down the station manager's throat.

It was a piece of rye toast. Exactly the same kind she had tacked to Buck Tyson's door.

Dana turned and threw up.

CHAPTER SEVENTEEN

The most important thing is to stay calm."

Robert Norse was magnificently calm, an inspiration, a pillar, an anchor. He was their nucleus and everyone else in the galley an excited, buzzing electron. The group was threatening to fly apart and the psychologist was the station's magnetic center. Norse hadn't been voted to leadership in the wake of Cameron's death and yet he'd quietly assumed it, with the backing of Nancy Hodge—her own authority established by her brisk, no-nonsense willingness to take charge of the station manager's bloody corpse. Norse's accession made a kind of sense. As a psychologist he was their odd duck, their voyeur, but he was also free of the everyday scientific allegiances and rivalries that might have made any other leader unacceptable to at least part of the group. He was a beaker and yet he wasn't. He conveyed sympathy and yet had a detachment that seemed to make him unflappable. Now the psychologist's eyes swept the room like a hose, trying to extinguish the panic that smoldered there. It was not just murder, but murder within a family: There was an incestuous nature to the stab-

bing that struck at the group's social core. Tyson! By going
after their station manager it was if the mechanic had van-
dalized their church, violated their taboos. He'd struck at
the station's head and heart. It would be all Norse could
do to keep the group from lynching him.

"We'll calm down when that murderous bastard is out
of here," Geller heatedly replied. There was a growl of assent. Fear was close to turning the winter-overs into a mob.

Norse held up his hands. "Please. I understand your emotion. I understand your fear. But our choices aren't easy.
We don't have a jail cell, we don't have a police force,
and there's a limit to what we can do."

"We don't have a gun and we don't have a good lock
and we don't have a sheriff," Geller added. "What we've
got is a psycho built like Hulk Hogan hiding somewhere
on station and not even a cap pistol to defend ourselves
with. We're in one hell of a fix, Doc."

"Is there any weapon on station at all?" Norse asked.

"Closest we come is the flare gun Rod used to try to
signal Harrison. It might hurt if fired into your eye but
short of that . . ."

"That's something, though. Let's start with that. Where
is it?"

"With the emergency stuff in the fire closet," said Hank
Anderson, the carpenter who helped coordinate fire teams.
"It ain't much."

"Well, I don't want Tyson to have it, either. Can you get
it, please, and deliver it here?"

"How about the fire axes?" Geller asked.

Norse shrugged. "Yes. Let's bring them to the galley,
too, until this is sorted out."

Anderson nodded and left.

"Okay," Norse went on, "I've contacted the National Science Foundation about our situation down here and I've asked Abby—at their request—to hold off on other e-mail or communication to the outside world for a while. We're going to keep this in-family."

"No!" Gabriella protested. "I want to talk to my friends!" There was a rolling murmur of support and anxiety. Nothing was more important than their electronic link.

The psychologist nodded again. He never disagreed. "You're right. Communication is what we need above all else. That's why we're talking now. And we'll reestablish contact to the outside world as soon as we can. But this is an explosive situation and people are trying to get a handle on it. We've got some circumstantial evidence, a volatile mechanic who's disappeared, and laws that say he's innocent until proven guilty. The folks back in D.C. need some time to sort this out and consider what our options are." He hesitated. "It was Rod's idea after Adams was found to ask them to send help down, like the FBI agents that went into McMurdo a few years back to pick up that cook who flew off the handle. I'll confess I talked him out of it as premature. I thought it would hurt his career. Maybe I was wrong. But even then it was too late to get a plane to actually land. It's winter, the runway is shut down, and the Guard crews who fly are long gone. It's dangerous to fly. It makes no sense to risk more lives if there's any other alternative."

"There is no alternative!" Dana Andrews shouted.

"Yes, let's open the damn runway!" astronomer Carl Mendoza agreed. "Get out the bulldozers! We'll figure them out without Buck. Plow without Buck. Put flame pots and flares out without Buck. We have to ship Tyson out of here before we lose the whole winter."

Norse kept nodding. "Absolutely. We're going to look

at every possibility. But right now NSF is asking us for three things. First, no panic. Okay? No panic. We have to keep a clear head. Second, no yelling to the world over satellite. And third, no rashness, nothing that will stain the reputation of the station in the future. Think! This is what you trained for. This is what you're paid for. Keeping things together, keeping it going. Okay? Can we lower the temperature here?" He waited for a response.

"Chill out," Hiro Sakura finally said. "It is easy to do at the South Pole." There was strained laughter at his thickly accented observation, a slight release of tension.

Norse smiled slightly, gratified at the help. "Okay. Now, what do we know? Dana found Rod's body with a stab wound. Someone had put toast on Buck's door, and the same kind of toast was in Rod's mouth. And Tyson's disappeared. It looks bad, but that doesn't mean we can be certain he's a murderer."

"Bullshit," said Pulaski. "We're certain he's a slug-eating, shower-hogging, work-shirking sonofabitch who's deliberately tried to scare the crap out of just about everyone in this room! Why not a murderer?"

"The bastard had it in for Rod from the beginning," added Mendoza. "He did nothing but complain and threaten. We all saw them almost get into a fistfight. He had it in for Harrison, too, and he was out the day Adams died. Him and Lewis."

"We all know Buck carried a chip on his shoulder," Norse cautioned. "We don't know he snapped."

"We have Mickey's death as well," Pulaski reminded. "Tyson didn't like him, either."

"Yes," Nancy Hodge chimed in. "Which could mean that Rod learned something about those deaths that the killer didn't want discovered. He panics, they fight . . ." She shrugged. "It could happen."

"It *did* happen." Alexi Molotov stood up. "Listen, Doctor Bob, I appreciate your efforts to keep things as, what you say, sensible. We are scientists, that is how it should be. But we have had three deaths. Three deaths! In our tiny group! And now this angry mechanic who makes knives is hiding somewhere and we have no weapons and maybe no chance of help from the outside world." He looked at them expectantly.

"What are you saying, Alexi?" Norse asked quietly.

"That we hunt him down before he hunts us. Like the Russian wolf."

"Hunt him down?"

"String him up," Geller said, only half jokingly. "First tree we find."

"No, we are not executioners," Molotov said. "Let your authorities investigate when they can, but you are right, it will not be until spring. In the meantime, he has to be quarantined, confined, so the rest of us feel safe."

"Like Lewis was."

"Like Lewis still should be," Dana said. Lewis wasn't there, having been ordered to stay out at Clear Air for his own safety. "I don't trust him, either. He's the one who started all this."

"That's unfair," Abby said, coming to his defense. "He's just new."

"You're sweet on him, Ice Cream, but he gives the rest of us the willies. Besides, where was *he* when Cameron died? I heard he was on the squawk box setting up a meeting with our dead leader."

"Yes," Molotov said. "He radioed. We heard it."

"Right," Abby retorted. "And if he was going to knife

him, would he broadcast a rendezvous?" She was angry. "Where were *you*, Dana? In the arch with the victim, as I understand it. Maybe you killed him, and made it look like Tyson."

"That is so completely out of bounds . . ."

"Enough!" Norse raised his hands. "Enough, enough, enough. Let's deal with Mr. Lewis later. He stays in Clean Air until we sort this out."

"How can we sort it out when he's never here to defend himself?" Abby protested.

Norse ignored her. "We think we have our killer, so let's not go off the deep end pointing fingers at others. The problem is Buck. The issue is Buck. Where can we keep him when we catch him?"

"*That's* the problem," Calhoun spoke up. As the other station carpenter, he was one of the most familiar with the construction of the station. "This base has no real locks worthy of the name. You can pry apart most of the walls with a can opener. The habitable parts he could break out of, I'll bet. We could bolt and weld some kind of coop, but how to heat it, plumb it, feed him? Jails are complicated."

"How about sticking him out in Bedrock?" suggested Geller. Bedrock Village was the nickname of the station's emergency shelter Quonset huts, called Hypertats. They were a bright blue cluster several hundred yards from the dome with their own generator. "Put him at a distance, like Lewis."

"And how do we keep him out there?" asked Calhoun.

"Guard him."

"How? He's so big you'd need at least two of us, both men, three shifts a day, seven days a week—come on! We can't lock him and we can't guard him and we can't feed him. Unless we want to spend the rest of the winter just doing that."

"The only practical solution is to ship him out of here, Robert." It was Nancy Hodge, and it was odd to hear her call Norse by his formal first name.

For the first time, Norse looked mildly exasperated. "They can't land a plane, it's too cold. Anything below minus fifty-five and the hydraulics freeze up. You know that."

"We know we're facing the worst emergency this base has ever encountered and we need something done before we all go nuts. *Doctor.*"

Norse looked annoyed. He didn't like criticism from another professional. The others shifted uncomfortably.

"There's one other solution, of course," Pulaski said grimly. "We try him, and do to him what he did to Rod Cameron."

"Fuckin' A," Geller said.

"No way!" Linda Brown protested. "Wade"—her tone was scolding—"we're not executioners. We have no legal authority. We have no moral authority."

"We do when our lives are at stake," the cook said quietly. There was no reply. Pulaski looked dangerous, the old soldier. "Sometimes it's you or him. Kill or be killed."

"Whoa. Come on, people." Norse raised his hands again, wearily. "Let's not go off the deep end. Cueball, I understand your feelings but try to keep them in check."

"Just don't go off by yourself," Pulaski told the others with a growl. "Not until we find the bastard."

Norse nodded. "Okay. Good advice. Stay together. Stay alert. But before we go on a manhunt let me talk to NSF. It's off-hours in D.C. now but I'll call when I can. I'll stress the dire nature of our situation again. Maybe they can find a break in the weather to somehow parachute an agent in here."

There was cautious hope.

"Or maybe I can think of something else."

Tyson jerked awake in the dark and sat up, banging his head. He heard the sound of the grate to the cramped utility tunnel being removed and someone dropping down into his burrow. He brought an arm with a knife out of his sleeping bag and extended it toward the entry to his hideaway, his wrist betraying an irritating tremble. If a mob came for him he was going down fighting, but he felt trapped. Hunted. Outnumbered. Doomed. "That you, Bob?"

"It's me."

The answer came as a relief. He'd left a note for Norse when the commotion started. The shrink was the only one he'd been able to talk to in this zoo. The only one he trusted. Then he'd hid here, fearing for his life. The psychologist had whispered through the grate that he would come back after a station meeting. Now it was two A.M., he saw by the illuminated dial of his watch, and Norse had dropped down into the man-sized conduit for wires and pipes that ran from the garage all the way to the fuel arch. Most station personnel didn't know the utility tube existed, and that was buying him time. Tyson was hoping he could camp there until things cooled down.

"What's the verdict, Doc?"

Norse kept his voice low. "It's not looking good."

No, it wouldn't look good, would it? He'd never exactly been Mr. Popularity with the grab bag of nerds and cretins they'd assembled to endure this insanity. Tyson could just imagine what kind of a fair hearing he'd get from them now. He'd told them all what he truly thought, never a great idea, and now it was payback time. One-on-one he could take any of them, but a group would hamstring him like wolves. *Jimmy, you are well and truly fucked,* he told himself. *Should have practiced that shit-eating grin.* "It hasn't looked good since I left North Dakota," he said aloud.

Norse actually chuckled for a second. He switched on a small penlight, providing them with a beam of illumination. "And how good could it have looked there?"

"It's better than its reputation. I had room, back home."

The psychologist nodded. "And that's what you need now. Room."

"What are they gonna do to me, Doc?"

"Nothing, if you're not here."

The two were silent for a moment, Norse giving time for this statement to sink in. He was also waiting with his next question. "Did you do it?" the psychologist finally asked point-blank.

"Hell no." That was simple enough.

Norse studied him, probably looking for the twitches and ticks that he'd been told in shrink school would reveal a liar. Well, let him look. As far as Tyson was concerned he was trapped in the looniest of loony bins, and Norse was the asylum's Big Nurse. The psychologist's professional opinion was worth about as much as the cheap tools they gave Tyson that kept snapping in the cold. When he dropped the phony psyche bullshit, however, Norse wasn't a bad guy. He listened. Kept in shape. Looked after himself.

"You're too obvious, aren't you?" Norse finally said. "Too angry, too mouthy. So obvious that I don't know if I believe it. It's the kind of crime that seems blood simple. Too dumb. You're not dumb, are you, Tyson?"

"Dumb enough to come down here."

Norse smiled. "That could be said about all of us."

"What's going to happen to me, Bob?"

"The ideal would be to ship you back. Let people sort this out in the States where emotions are a little less raw. The trouble is, I don't think they're going to get a plane down here. It's cold and it's getting colder. We've got at least six more months of isolation. You want to spend six months in this tunnel?"

"I don't want to spend six months in this whole fucking base. You know that. I've made no secret of it. I just want out."

"You and everyone else about now."

"That's right. And I'm as scared as they are. I didn't kill nobody. I'm being set up, maybe by that fingie Lewis. All the trouble started when he came. The only thing I'm guilty of is saying what I think. They crucify you in this world if you say what you think."

"Amen to that."

"It's like we talked about, Doc. The importance of self-reliance. The fucking *duty* of self-reliance. Everyone pays lip service to this touchy-feely group shit but that's only because they hope somebody like me will carry their load. Do the shit work. Until you won't do it for them. Then they turn."

Norse betrayed nothing. "My concern is that you get a fair hearing."

"Well, I ain't gonna get it here."

"I know."

"So what the fuck do I do now? They won't listen to me. I can't fight them all. I didn't want their bullshit commune and now I'm the bad guy. It's because I won't play the game. It's like that movie where the island kids go crazy. That 'Lord' thing, what was it?"

"Flies. *Lord of the Flies.*"

"That's what it feels like. Like I'm the only sane one. Is that crazy?"

Norse grimaced. "It may be the only rational reaction to this base. My fear is that humans aren't meant to be in a place like this. So cold. So bleak. It does things to them, physically and mentally. We evolved in Africa, for Christ's sake. Coming here is an act of hubris. Greek hubris. The pride that goes before the fall. So I sympathize with where you're coming from. I admire your insistence on being an individual."

Tyson nodded. "You gotta keep them away from me, Doc."

"I've been thinking about your situation," Norse went on carefully. "We had a meeting and the mood was ugly. I calmed them down for a while but six, seven more months? I don't know. I can't hide you that long. I can't keep the others functioning that long, not with you tucked down here like a troll. A few of them want to try and execute you."

"Jesus H. Christ." The mechanic was quietly frightened.

"About your only hope would be another killing while you're locked up, taking suspicion off you, if you're telling the truth and the killer is someone else. Otherwise, it all points to Buck Tyson. The new totem of evil. Unfair, perhaps— I wouldn't be in this hole with you if I thought you truly dangerous—but very human. So I've come to suggest a long-shot chance, one you once suggested to me when we were looking for Mickey."

"What's that?"

"Vostok."

"What?"

"I think you should seek asylum. Go to another base,

winter over, and surrender to the American authorities in the spring. By that time the situation may have cleared up a bit, who knows? Otherwise it's a risk that something might trigger a mob mentality and you find yourself in Salem as Witch Number One. You get my meaning?"

"Yeah, but holy shit, trying to get to Vostok . . ."

"No airplane is going to get in here like a magic carpet. The others are fantasizing that there's a chance but there isn't any, not really. You're going to have to flee overland. The closest refuge is the Russian base. Seven hundred miles but it's fairly flat going across the polar plateau. No crevasses, no mountains. Bad food, good vodka, and better company than you'll find here the rest of the winter. It's a risk to try to reach it but I don't know what else to offer. Obviously, I think the risk is even higher if you stay here."

"I can't fucking believe this."

"My idea is you take a Spryte like you said. If anyone can do it alone, you can. You've trained for survival. You're prepared to tough it out. And we can survive without one of the machines. Pull a sled loaded with fuel and food and take along a GPS to help you navigate. With minimal sleep and decent weather you could reach Vostok in several days. If you have to hunker down for a storm you can take enough along to survive for a few weeks. If the engine doesn't break down, you can make it. And if it does . . . well, you're our best mechanic, right?"

"Me and Pika."

"Right. So we have Pika to keep things going here, and you keep your Spryte going out there."

Tyson groaned. "But if I completely break down, I'm fucked. A couple hours at a hundred below . . ."

"And you go to sleep." The meaning was clear. There were worse ways to die.

Tyson took a breath, considering the stark choice. He knew he couldn't stay there. "Will the others let me do it?"

"I haven't told them. I'm not going to ask them. We have to move now. Fait accompli. Their disappointment at losing a Spryte will be more than mitigated by their relief at losing you."

"Thanks."

"I'm giving it to you straight, Buck."

The mechanic nodded glumly. "A mob or the plateau."

"When you don't have any friends, you have to rely on yourself."

They waited, Tyson mulling it over. If he got a hole in the weather it should be possible. He had the skills to earn his way at Vostok. . . .

"Or we can go face the others in the galley now," Norse said.

The mechanic shook his head. *Fuck those bastards.* "They *want* it to be me. That's the problem."

"You can rely on them or rely on yourself."

Tyson hesitated, gathering his courage. There was a certain hopelessness in his eyes, a realization of having made an irrevocable wrong turn. Then, fatalistically: "I'm out of here."

"It's for the best, Buck. Best if you leave soon."

"Don't worry about *that*. If I'm leaving I ain't going to let the screen door hit my butt on the way out." He unzipped his bag, suddenly anxious. "You gonna help?"

"I've taken the liberty of doing that." Norse backed up, removed the grate, and crawled out. The mechanic followed him. They stood in the gloom of the garage, looking at the vehicles. "The Spryte is fueled, the sled loaded, you're ready to go. It's best to be well away before morning, just in case some self-righteous sheriff gets it in his head to chase after you with a snowmobile."

"Agreed." Tyson looked at him curiously. "Why you helping me, Doc?"

"I've found myself thrust into a curious position of responsibility. My profession is people, and I know what they're capable of. You ever hear of the *Swordfish*?"

Tyson shook his head.

"It's classified, but word gets around in professional circles. Nuke sub on a long, secret mission under the Arctic ice. There was a quarrel, a popular ensign was killed, and there wasn't a chance to surface or return. They were sitting off a Russian base, for Christ's sake. They did a quick court-martial but there was no brig, just like here. You know what they did with the offender?"

"Do I want to know?"

"Loaded him into a torpedo tube and fired him out. He was kicking, screaming, pleading, crying, it didn't matter. He'd made no friends and everyone was around the bend with tension anyway. There was hell to pay when they got back, of course, and a few careers ended. But at the time, ejecting him into the Arctic Ocean seemed the right thing to do. That's what I'm worried about here. The right thing to do."

Tyson nodded dumbly.

"I'm gambling on this one, Buck. Gambling on you. So punch on out of here and hope you make friends with the Russkies. Your boots and parka are in the cab."

Tyson looked at the Spryte, resignedly determined. "I'll make it. What are you going to tell them?"

"That I helped you go. If I get blamed for it, I'll tell them you pulled a knife on me."

"Adding to my reputation."

"Until winter's over and the truth comes out. I have to live here, too."

Tyson stepped up on the treads of the Spryte and looked back at Norse. "If I didn't do it, who did, Doc?"

"I'm not sure you didn't do it. I'm just praying it doesn't matter. Because with you gone and convicted in abstentia, any other murderer escapes suspicion. Which means he has good reason not to strike again."

CHAPTER EIGHTEEN

Pika Taylor always woke first to check the generators and walk the archways, surveying their safety. It was he who discovered the open garage door and the missing Spryte. So much snow had blown into the entryway that he couldn't close the bay and had to fetch help to shovel it clear. His shouts woke the survivors.

A group filed into the garage and gaped at the opening and the tread tracks going up its ramp as if it were as miraculous as Jesus' tomb. The temperature in the vehicle shed had plunged, coating the workbenches and machinery with a flocking of frost. The winter-overs worked rapidly to clear the drifting snow, melt a rim of ice, and shut the bay door against the night. Then they went outside.

The darkness was deepening. The cloudless sky was beginning to spot with stars and the horizon had only the faintest of blushes, the blue there as eerie as the glow of Cherenkov radiation in a nuclear fuel rod pool. The snow glowed silver. There was no wind but it was bitterly cold. The tractor and sled tracks steered for the horizon as straight as the wake of an autopilot boat, the Spryte's message as plain as a telegram. Tyson was pointed toward Vostok station. Their nemesis had fled.

His escape was received as deliverance. The monster was gone. No longer did they have to fear him, hold him, or prepare the runway to export him. Their water crisis was solved in an instant. His blustering hunt for the meteorite became a bad dream. He left behind only the nervous disorientation that follows a nightmare, an emotional tingle as barely contained panic gave way to mutual reassurance. They'd survived! They straddled the tracks in numb relief.

That Norse must have had a role in Tyson's disappearance was quickly assumed. Despite the excitement, the psychologist didn't emerge from his room to follow them out into the snow and he didn't join in the wildfire of announcement. It was as if he already knew what they'd find out there. Rising later, he admitted nothing, nor did anyone pronounce it. Still, he hadn't talked to their bosses at the National Science Foundation and had gone to bed late the night before as if the problem were solved. Norse's equanimity about the mechanic's escape told the rest all they needed to know. He was calm, where Rod Cameron had visibly battled depression. Robert Norse was their rock.

"I wonder if Tyson took *the* rock," Geller said happily at a late breakfast, working through a celebratory stack of pancakes. "Maybe he found it. Maybe he's the one who took it all along."

"Good riddance if he did," Calhoun opined, forking a sausage.

"Maybe he'll hock it. Maybe we'll meet him years from now on a beach in Hawaii, tanned and retired, still sipping mai tais from Mickey Moss's meteorite. Maybe he's smarter than any of us and got Doctor Bob to help send him to the Russians."

"So?"

"So, it would be ironic if dumb old Buck got exactly what he wanted."

"If I survive this freezer and get back to a beach in Hawaii to see him, do you think I'll give a flying fuck?"

"Alexi," Geller asked with his mouth full, "you think Vostok will take him?"

The Russian shrugged. "Why not? He brings his own car, maybe his own food—even his survival scraps will be better than theirs. They'll radio: Who he is? We'll say a what, a . . . defector, just so they don't fear him and send him back. He'll work or he'll starve at that base. It will be worse for him than jail here. And he'll find some companions even scarier than he is. Only the hard-core icemen still survive at Vostok. The real Russians." He grinned. "They chew leather and pound nails with their foreheads."

"The Brits up at Faraday *wear* leather and paint their nails," Dana said. "And their women are even kinkier." She'd rediscovered her spirit as soon as she blearily woke to find Tyson gone.

"I hear the Kiwis nail their women and leather their foreskins," Geller remarked.

"Well, the Argentines at Esperanza—" Calhoun began.

"Make fun of the Chileans at Bernardo O'Higgins who tell jokes about the Poles at Arctowski who long for the Chinese food at Zhongshan," their psychologist interrupted, sliding into a seat with a cup of coffee. Norse had come into the galley quietly. "It's a wonder any work gets done in Antarctica at all."

"We were just wishing Tyson the worst, Doctor Bob," Geller explained. "We figured the Russians would give it to him."

"He's given it to himself. The plateau at Vostok is a half

mile higher than the Pole. The world record low was set there—minus 128.6 degrees." Norse said it as if the precision gave him pleasure. "And traveling seven hundred miles is like driving from Berlin to Moscow. He'll be doing well to get there without losing his fingers and toes."

"He brought it on himself."

Norse sipped somberly. "That's the question, isn't it? What *was* Buck's choice? The central conundrum of psychology. How much of what we do is free will and how much is genes and conditioning? How responsible are we for our actions?"

"One hundred fucking percent," Pulaski said, bringing a bottle of syrup from the pantry to replace what Geller had depleted. "If you don't believe that, then society doesn't work because nobody's responsible for anything. Don't give *me* the behavioralist song and dance. Tyson was a mean sonofabitch who scared everyone here and deserves every inch of frostbite he gets. The feds are going to have a lot to answer for by not taking him back to begin with, when he started grousing. The Pole is no place for malcontents. Uncle Sam better hope Rod's relatives don't find a good lawyer."

"Lawyers. Now, there's a scary bunch," said Geller.

"I happen to agree with you, Wade," Norse told the cook. "You can't have freedom without accepting free will, and all the risk and responsibility that goes with it. Buck believed that, too. He just wasn't very adept at fitting his philosophy into a group."

"He was damn antisocial," said Calhoun.

"He refused to follow but he also refused to lead," Norse corrected. "He tried to isolate himself in a place where that was a physical impossibility. He had to either change the

Pole, change himself, or leave. Rod's death made him realize that, and he left."

That struck Abby, who was listening, as a little too neat.
"You're saying he should have tried to take over?"

"I'm saying that just as the natural world is an evolutionary struggle of species against species, society is an intellectual and emotional struggle of ego against ego. You
conquer or you submit. You impose your own will or you
labor under someone else's. You lead or you follow because life's a dance. Mere rebels, like Buck, simply hang
or go into exile." The psychologist sipped his coffee again.

"I thought the whole point was to work together," Abby
said. "We're a team. That's what makes the Pole work, our
working together."

"Or not work when you have a malcontent. Then it boils
down to leadership. I was hoping Rod would come to terms
with the need for leadership, or at least I was observing
his struggle, and then . . ."

There was quiet, everyone thinking about the murder.

"You did the right thing to get rid of Buck," Dana finally said. There. It was out in the open. She'd said what
everyone knew.

Norse's mouth twisted wryly, not trying to deny it. "He
had a knife but . . . I just gave him a choice and he got rid
of himself. It's not a light thing, you know. More like ban-
ishment in the Middle Ages. Back then everything was kin
and clan. Being forced out was being forced into poverty.
No family, no land, no equivalent of social security to take
you into whatever old age you could manage. Exile was a
kind of death sentence. Down here, with our feudal cluster of bases, maybe it's not so different."

"Don't be so grim, Doc," Pulaski said. "The research
stations help each other, they don't besiege each other.

Tyson will survive if he can make it. I'm not sure the bastard deserves to survive."

"That is the question, yes?" said Molotov. "Will he make it?"

"No, the real question is how we're going to celebrate his leaving," said Geller. "I propose a thank-God-I'm-still-here dinner and a polar cocktail contest."

"Here, here," Dana said.

"The pig!" Pulaski suggested.

"The what?" Calhoun asked.

"I had one shipped down for our winter solstice party. I'm thinking maybe we need it now. You know, Hawaiian luau? What do you think, Doc? Good for morale?"

"Good for my morale."

"Yes, bring on the mai tais!" Dana said. "And an initiation session into the Three Hundred Degree Club!"

"Is it cold enough?" Geller asked.

"Didn't you feel it this morning?" she asked. "Breathing out there was like drinking Drāno."

"The temperature's getting down there," the cook agreed. "We'll have to get an official reading from Lewis out in Clean Air. Assuming he gives us the time of day. That fingie has been treated pretty rough."

Norse looked at the New Zealander. "You ready to accept Jed, Dana?"

She sighed. "I don't know. When I saw him with that severed cord, and Harrison's hand reaching through the snow . . . I thought the worst. Unlike Abby, here, I can't warm up to Lewis. He's quiet, hard to read. But yes, we're down to just twenty-two now. Buck's escape points to Lewis's innocence, right?"

"Let's assume so," the psychologist said. "I don't think they were Butch and Sundance. Bonnie and Clyde."

"God, I didn't even consider if the killer had an accomplice!"

Norse looked at her evenly. "Or if Tyson was the wrong man."

She looked uncertain. "We still don't know for sure, do we?"

"We never know for sure on anything. In a courtroom or down here. All the important things in life remain a mystery. So, your verdict on Jed. Your responsibility. Your choice. Your call."

She glanced at Abby. "Bring him in." She sighed. "It *was* Buck. Or I'll go crazy."

"Call Lewis up, Cueball," Norse told their cook. "Find out if we're going to get weather severe enough to let we fingies join your club."

Every tribe has its initiation, Lewis thought. *This is mine.*

The temperature at Clean Air had actually registered only ninety-eight degrees below zero but he'd promised Norse that it would keep on dropping and then altered the thermometer link to the dome to make sure the reading on the galley television screen fell to minus one hundred. The slight subterfuge seemed justified after all he'd gone through. This was his way back into the fold.

Pulaski, who'd done this once before, briefed those who assembled outside the sauna. "First of all, this club—short of having walked on the moon—may be the most exclusive on the planet," he told them. "You've gotta be at the Pole when it's a hundred below, which means you've got to be here in winter, which means you've got to be stupid enough to sign on for eight toasty months of cheerful isolation." There was nervous laughter among the group.

"Accordingly, it may also be the most *foolish* club on

the planet. There's some polar plunges into the Antarctic ocean at Palmer, and dips into the frozen lakes near Mc-Murdo, but for sheer idiocy I think *we* take the cake. This is a story you can tell your grandchildren about—and if you do, they'll have you institutionalized."

The tittering had an edge to it.

"Exhibit One is this temperature gauge." He pointed to the dial registering the temperature inside the sauna. "As you can see, our cedar box is crawling upward to two hundred degrees *above* zero, just about enough to let me slow-roast some meat. That's you." He gave his best evil smile, the lights glinting off his bald head. Cueball could look scary when he wanted to.

"Exhibit Two is your appearance. This is the South Pole, people, and you look like you bought tickets to Tahiti." Laughter again. Thirteen of the twenty-two survivors were bunched outside the sauna door, men and women segregating into separate groups. All were wrapped in towels, had tennis shoes on to protect their feet, and clutched balaclavas, scarves, or gaiters to cover their mouths at the critical moment. Still, there was more bare skin on display than they'd seen for months. Their bodies looked pasty in the fluorescent light, like shelled oysters. The clumped flesh was as depersonalizing as a military haircut.

"Exhibit Three is the goal: to endure the heat until it hits the two-hundred-degree mark, to drop your towels, and then to sprint stark-raving naked except for shoes and head covering to the South Pole marker, or as close to it as you care to go, given safety and screaming common sense. A three-hundred-degree-difference shock to the senses. For those of you hoping for an erotic experience, let me disappoint. We dim the lights for privacy, and subzero temperatures have a way of diminishing—and I do mean diminishing—any sexual ardor. Nature attacks any and all appendages. I urge you to listen to your body and retreat prudently: We had a case of genital frostbite one year and it was not a pretty sight. Nipples, noses—anything that sticks out."

"Jesus, they got more encouragement at Omaha Beach," Geller muttered. "You're not exactly getting my spirits up."

"That's just what I'm saying, George. Don't get *anything* up."

"Or don't get it up around me," Nancy Hodge added.

"I shrivel every time I have to see *you,* Doc."

"Yeah. I noticed."

"Ooh, that hurts!" the men hooted. "That's more painful than the cold!"

"Who *does* get it up for you, Nurse Nancy?"

"If this is an issue for you, George, there's some new drugs in BioMed that might help."

More moans and laughter.

"Okay, enough anticipation," Pulaski interrupted. "Doctor Bob can take care of all your Freudian problems while you're packed like Pringles in the sauna. I'll open the door to let you out after it hits two hundred. Move briskly, but not recklessly. Don't fall on the ice and break your leg."

"Or anything else, if you're on Nancy's drugs!" Calhoun called.

Pulaski turned to Lewis, still standing a little apart from the others. "So, fingie. You glad we brought you back to share in our secret society?"

Lewis managed a grin. "Didn't know what I was missing."

"Damn right. Last night we all set fire to our hair. Tomorrow is electric shock therapy. Okay, in the sauna! Go, go, go! Get pumped! Get psyched! Get hot! Sweat! Snarl! The night is just beginning!"

They crowded into the dimly lit box with their towels, laughing and cracking jokes. "George, you're poking me!" someone said in a falsetto voice. The door closed and there was only dim red light. It was initially claustrophobic, a mesh of flesh as intimate as a crowded elevator. The box was already one hundred and fifty degrees. For the first minute or so, the heat felt good, like an enveloping blanket. Then it began to seem cloying. Skin scraped unfamiliarly on skin. It was a tangle of bodies, hard to make out who was who, which sex was which. And yet Lewis felt the terry-cloth press of a breast against one arm. Long dark hair. Gabriella.

He glanced around, looking for Abby. She was on the lower bench, looking down again as if lost in thought. She'd given him a shy glance in the corridor to acknowledge his return from Clean Air but showed nothing of the flirtatious familiarity he'd expected after their kiss. Cameron's death and Tyson's flight had gotten between them, leaving her troubled and remote. A shadowy, powerfully muscled man, probably Norse, sat behind her.

"This is what sets humans apart from the animals," someone said.

"A reckless thirst for experience?"

"Sweat."

Lewis felt light-headed. There wasn't enough air for this many occupants. His skin tingled as his pores opened, an almost forgotten experience after the dry cold of the Pole. His nose filled with the scent of their bodies, the perspiration and musk. The hot steam of the air heated his lungs. In a way the press of the bodies reassured him. After the fear that had divided it, the community was coming back together. The bizarre initiation implied a certain trust, an implicit friendship.

"I'm toasssssssting . . ." someone wailed like the dissolving witch in *The Wizard of Oz.*

"I'm riiiisssssing . . ." Geller rumbled.

"Don't listen to him," Nancy Hodge assured. "You couldn't tell the difference with a surveyor's transit."

Everyone laughed.

"Do you like hot weather, Lewis?" It was Gabriella, whispering in his ear.

She made him nervous. "I'm a moderate."

"No, you're not. I know about you. Working for the oil companies. Always going to extremes."

"That's just where the oil is."

"There's oil in other places, too." Her breath raised the hair on his neck.

"Do *you* like hot weather?" He was staring at Abby but she wouldn't look up. She was more embarrassed by this intimacy, he guessed.

"I like sensation." Gabriella's lips were brushing his ear. Incongruously, he thought of the load master shouting into it, the day he arrived. The tale of the doomed fly.

"Gawd, I'm going to suffocate before I freeze," someone said.

"Almost there!" Pulaski called through the door.

Lewis leaned back, pressed against someone's body, leaned away. He was roasting, unbearably hot. His concern about dropping his towel was fading; he wanted release! He was looking forward to the cold! Sweat ran in tributaries down his temples, in rivers down his back. His belly was sticky with it. He wanted to make the Pole. He wanted to shed his newcomer status. Gabriella brushed his arm with her own. Both were slick, as if oiled.

Despite himself, his pulse quickened at her touch.

"Once I read that everyone's lonely," Gabriella whispered. "That what we want is to fuse with each other."

Lewis tried to joke. "Well, we're sticky enough." He was feeling dizzy.

"That hell is being scattered apart. Heaven is coming together."

"I thought heaven would have more oxygen." He felt drugged.

"That everybody wants reunion."

She was arousing him. He wished she'd be quiet.

"That all the parts try to become one."

He was saved when the door finally swung open, the light in the hallway killed to give a measure of privacy. There was a gush of cooler air. "And they're off!" Pulaski yelled.

Everyone stood, jostling like passengers anxious to get off an airplane. Towels dropped like shadows. It was so crowded and dark there was nothing to see. People began shoving out the door, breaking into an awkward run. Gabriella moved in front of him, her towel slipping away, and he got only an impression of curved form, lithe and smooth. Then he was carried with the crowd out the door, a jostling of elbows and knees like people squirming through a fire escape. They spread out in the corridor, darting through the exit and out under the dome's interior like a swarm of ghosts. Everyone was whooping and screaming with fear and excitement. Lewis felt like he was running on a beach, his core so hot he didn't yet feel any cold.

When they hit the chill of the dome their sweat flashed to steam. They ran in a river of fog, so dense they couldn't see each other's nakedness. As they sprinted out past the archways to the exit ramp, Lewis pulled his gaiter over his head and down around his mouth so his lungs wouldn't burn. The lining of his sinuses had already frozen.

When he burst outside he could feel a further temperature drop. It was like hitting a cold pond, his breath jerked away.

He could hardly see. He blindly followed the yells and laughter and howls of the others up the ramp and then across the sastrugi drifts toward the Pole marker. Some were already hurrying back the other way, he realized, stunned by the cold and turning for shelter well before reaching the taxiway. It was an act of self-preservation. He had no sense of who was who anymore, it was just a shuttle of bodies, a scene from a medieval triptych of hell.

His sweat was freezing on his skin. It had crystallized in his hair. His fingers were already numb. His testicles had shriveled. He was grateful it was as dark as it was.

"Come on, fellow fingie!"

It was Norse, loping ahead of him as if on an early-morning jog. He could make out the silhouette of the man's powerfully broad shoulders and slim hips. The psychologist was built like a Greek god, fit and vain. The steam had left them now and the other runners were gone, too. They were the only two loping across the runway for the distant stake. Lewis felt his muscles tightening. What if he cramped up out here?

With the steam gone it was dazzlingly clear. Glancing around, Lewis realized it wasn't as dark as he'd first thought. The structures of the research base were geometric sculptures in sharp starlit relief: the Dark Sector, Clean Air, the snowy hump of the summer Quonset huts that were winterized now. The sky was on fire, he realized: the aurora australis! It shimmered, a spangle of colors, as hallucinatory as a curtain to another world. The Pole had never looked so beautiful and for a revelatory moment he grasped the magnificence of being allowed to be here, of being given this glimpse of astronomical beauty. A rare privilege of time and space! And it was killing him!

Lewis was wheezing. His lungs ached with cold, despite the frost-shrouded gaiter over his mouth. His energy was evaporating. He stumbled, almost fell. He should turn back. He was risking frostbite by staying out so long. But there was the polar stake! Norse had paused at it, watching him. "You can do it, Jed!"

Lewis staggered to the Pole and looked back. Everyone else had disappeared inside. The dome looked impossibly far away and he realized he'd misjudged. This was insane! He was naked at a hundred degrees below zero and his sauna warmth was leaking away like a reservoir from a ruptured dam. "I think I'm dying," he gasped. He was looking up at his own ephemeral existence: the aurora!

"Not yet." Norse reached out and seized Lewis's arm, jerking him back in the direction of the dome. "Double time!" They jogged together, their goal rocking in his vision, the psychologist's hand like a vise. "You can do it!"

"It feels like my shoulders are freezing up. I can hear them cracking."

"You've got to sprint, man! Sprint to save your life!" He seized Lewis's hand and the two began awkwardly running flat out, nude, intimate, two earthlings cast off into space, barely keeping their balance on the skittering of snow. "Go, go!"

They saw Pulaski at the crest of the ramp, waving them in like an orange-clad angel. Stars began dancing in Lewis's eyes. "I . . . can't . . . do . . ."

He fell, skidding on powder, his chest painfully burning on the firmer packed snow just underneath. Then he was being pulled up off the snow by one arm, the stars swinging crazily and his consciousness dazed, Norse dragging him forward like a wounded man. "We're almost back!" The psychologist leaped over the crest of the ramp, howling at the cold, yanking Lewis over its lip with him, and then they fell and slid down it together in a tangle, scraping their skin again. Pulaski ran and hauled them up. Snow stuck to them like flour, their skin flushed red. "We made it, Cueball!" Norse gasped in triumph. "Made it to the Pole!"

"Now you have to make it inside!" The cook pushed the pair through the dome door and slammed it shut and they staggered on, utterly frozen, back under the dome toward the sauna.

Lewis had no memory of the last minute or so across the dusky dome. Just the wooden door, a blast of heat, and then falling into the welcoming arms of the others who'd crowded back into the sauna before him, snatching at towels and coughing and swearing and shouting with victory from the cold that had seared into their lungs.

Three hundred degrees!

Now he was one of them.

CHAPTER NINETEEN

The pig is on fire. Repeat. The pig is on fire."

The warning over the galley public address system penetrated a haze of post-sauna alcohol and set off an explosion of consternation and amusement. Pulaski had arranged for an entire pig to be flown down for a midwinter luau, planning it to occur at the June 21 winter solstice, the darkest time at the Pole. But by general consensus the darkest time was *now*, with Rod's death and Tyson's flight, and so he'd decided the group needed the pig in order to recover equilibrium and fraternity. He'd constructed a crude barbecue out of scrap sheet metal and concrete blocks in the archway near the gym, fed it with propane, and lit it up soon after the disappearance of Tyson, putting the pig to roast before the Three Hundred Degree Club even met. As the animal turned, their cook deputized assistant pit chefs to check it occasionally after ritually donning a Hawaiian shirt. Now Hiro, with his heavy Japanese accent, was delivering an apocalyptic message in his scientific monotone, informing them that their luau was in danger of turning into a cremation.

Laughing and hooting, several of the men spilled out of the galley with fire extinguishers and flame blankets to rescue their meal. Pulaski, sprinting after them, just barely managed to deflect an enthusiastic but ill-thought-out blast of halon before it contaminated the meat. He smothered the flames in a blanket instead. "This is our dinner, morons!" Then he examined the blackened hide with a jeweler's squint. "No harm done." The pig was elevated above the gas flames to keep it above the flash point and the rescuers trooped back to the galley with mission accomplished, Lewis among them, the pungent smell of cooked pork making the men salivate in anticipation.

"The pig has been extinguished!" Pulaski announced, the women dutifully applauding this act of male prowess.

It had taken Lewis a full half hour in the sauna to thaw himself from the brutal run, coughing uncontrollably for several minutes from the bronchial rape of raw polar air. Then fifteen minutes more to convince himself that none of his parts, public or private, were seriously frostbitten. He was the last to limp out from the cedar box, dehydrated and exhausted, and was ready to collapse into bed when others seized him, gave him water, pushed him into the shower, and then told him to join the survival party in the station galley. It was a camaraderie he was unaccustomed to. Now he savored it. He saluted the cook along with everyone else, hoisting a cup of dome-brewed beer.

The Three Hundred Degree Club had purged the group of tension. The participants were pink and relieved, the veterans welcoming and inclusive, and the suspicions and speculation had been, for the moment at least, erased. "Tyson fled for our sins," Geller belched. A shadow had passed and the polar night had been symbolically rolled back. The survivors desperately needed psychic relief and couldn't go

anywhere but inside themselves to get it. A rock anthem
was playing, haunting and accumulative as it built in volume, a fossilized pulse from planet Led Zeppelin, a world
back across the edge. *"Cliiiimbing a staiiiirway to . . ."*

"Hey, all the way to the Pole, man!" Geller, gleeful and
drunk, slapped Lewis on the back. "You're lucky your dick
didn't fall off!"

"Heaaavennnn . . ."

Lewis grinned modestly. "I'm not sure it didn't. I got so
cold I'm still looking for the damn thing."

Geller laughed. "Check out Gabriella, dude. She'll help
you find it."

Their Gal Friday had put on a skirt, short and tight, a
garment more extraordinary at the Pole than a bathing suit
or sarong. She wore a tank top, its straps tangled with those
of the lacy bra underneath like a DNA helix. The outfit revealed an upper arm tattooed with a ringlet of flowers. Her
dark hair had been released to cascade down to her shoulders, its color matching her black, liquid eyes. She was beginning to sway by herself in time with the music, her hips
hypnotic as she did so, her look demurely downward but
her entire being intensely aware of the attention she was
drawing to herself. She had a smoky intensity, as if she,
too, could burst into flame.

"That's almost scary," Lewis confessed.

"Not after a couple margaritas, man. Carl is mixing up
a batch in honor of Cinco de Mayo. You'll be ready for
her then."

"It's not even May yet."

"It's any day you want it to be, former fingie. It's luau
night, Mexican Independence Day, the Lord's birthday, and
Halloween rolled into one. We're alive, my friend, the North
Dakota boogeyman is gone, and we're all so thoroughly

toasted that tonight might as well be the first insane night of the rest of your life. Cheers, brother! Heeeee-haw!"

The pig was deemed ready by Hiro's watchdog replacement, Alexi Molotov. A group of men went outside again and brought it back slung on a pole, chanting as Pika kept time to their march by knocking together two pieces of wood. The pig's head was still attached, mahogany brown, shiny and squinting, a red rubber ball stuck in its snout in lieu of apples long since eaten. The preposterous animal filled half a galley table. There was hot fresh bread, canned fruit salad, yams with brown sugar and pecans, mashed potatoes, olives, baked beans, peas and onions, cheeses, Jell-O, chips. The other tables had cloths and lit candles and coupled bottles of red and white wine.

A memorial to the dead had been pinned up near the galley tray table. Pulaski had posted pictures of Mickey Moss, Harrison Adams, and Rod Cameron. "They live on in our memories," a small banner read.

Norse was looking at the pictures as if they might reveal something that had eluded him.

"It makes me want to cry," said Lena Jindrova, who unconsciously carried with her the perfumed scent of the tomato plants she tended in their greenhouse. She'd come up beside Norse.

"But you're not crying, are you?" the psychologist replied a little coldly.

She took it as a criticism. "Well, I have accepted them not being here. Does that sound mean?"

"It sounds human," Norse conceded, his manner softer. "Do you know what I was told in college?"

She shook her head.

"That society does nothing better than close ranks and

move on after the death of its members. That *that's* what society is all about."

"That is awful! Don't you think?"

"Or ruthlessly realistic." He turned and regarded the others. "Everyone here will be gone someday and the world will go on. What will give their lives meaning?"

"What they are. Were." She pointed. "Like these three."

"What they learned," Norse corrected. "Or rather, what the world learned from them."

They feasted and Lewis felt as if his own body were on fire, electric from survival of murder and cold. He shuddered uncontrollably a couple of times as he continued to warm, his skin prickling, his senses taut even as he felt a deep, purging exhaustion. His brain was effervescent with its own chemicals. He felt high, as if Hodge had sprinkled some kind of pixie-dust drug from BioMed on all their food. He could hear everything, see every color, smell every scent. The women were all beautiful, the men his comrades. Suddenly, overwhelmingly, he loved them all.

I've had too much to drink, he scolded himself. He poured another glass of wine.

After the eating, they cleared the food and plates, some helping with the washing, and moved the tables aside. The dancing began. Carl Mendoza brought out a slush tub of ice, lime, tequila, and triple sec, putting on a CD of salsa music. The celebrants yipped and sang. Dancers bumped and swirled, some clumsy, some sinuous. Gabriella writhed. Abby stood against one wall, sipping a drink. Lewis hadn't talked to her since their kiss at Clean Air.

He made his way to her with some difficulty. Geller stumbled against him, badly drunk, and Linda Brown, who'd skipped the Three Hundred Degree Club because she'd joined the year before, clipped him with her ample hip. "Oops! And shake it all about!"

Abby smiled stiffly at Lewis's approach. The exhibitionism of the Three Hundred Degree Club had slightly embarrassed her and she'd been one of the first to turn around during the run. It had been a ritual to get through, not an experience to be savored.

"Did you like the run?" He had to half shout above the music.

She looked at him over the rim of her glass, holding it like a bandit's mask. "It reminded me of what they say about jogging. It feels so good when it stops."

"I thought I was going to freeze out there!"

"I didn't notice the cold at first. It was so beautiful. Then it hurt."

"I wish I'd stopped with you." It was odd to have burst outside naked with this woman. He couldn't remember what she looked like. He couldn't remember having really even seen her. They'd shared it without really sharing it at all.

"You looked half dead when you got back to the sauna. I think Bob saved your life."

He hadn't quite thought of it that way but it was true, the man had pulled him in. "Sort of." He'd never heard her call Norse just "Bob" before.

"He's holding us together."

"I suppose he is."

"Now you're not the fingie anymore. You're in the club."

"Yes." She was looking past him at someone, which annoyed him. "Look, do you want to dance?"

It brought her back to him. "All right." She put her glass down.

They moved out into the swaying thicket of bodies. The fluorescent lights had been turned off and incandescents warmed the dancers with their yellow glow. The bulbs were usually discouraged because their heat could cause a fire, so feared at the Pole because all water was frozen and all wood was tinder dry. Acquisition of a regular light bulb was a sign of station rank and moxie: the "bulbed" and "bulbless." More high school, as Tyson would say. The table candles, also allowed tonight because the crowd would keep an eye on them, danced in the hum of warm ventilation.

Pika Taylor was passing a magazine back and forth in front of a lamp in one corner, creating a primitive kind of strobe effect. He seemed perfectly content to be their mute automaton. It was hot like the sauna, musky again, animalistic. Abby began to move, her hips undulating, turning a slow, careful circle. She'd acquired a new gravity since the deaths of the others and her movements were still too tentative to be entirely silky. She seemed lost in thought, remote and unobtainable.

"I heard you defended me in front of the others after Rod's body was found," he tried. "I want to thank you for that."

"Just from Dana." The two women weren't fond of each other, he knew.

"I liked what happened between us at Clean Air. Now that the trouble's over I hope we can be friends. Good friends."

"Now that it's over." There was doubt in her voice, and a strange detachment. Lewis wanted to be Enzyme again, agent of change, but he suspected she was still focused on that mysterious photograph. Less persuaded than any of them that Tyson was the easy answer to it all: Why had Mickey died with her picture near his breast? Lewis had to break through to her. Calm her fear.

"Everyone's come together. This is the real start of the winter," he told her.

"I hope so," she murmured.

"I'm glad the group wanted me back."

She looked at him then, the old mischief in her eyes. "Just so we could keep an eye on you."

The jibe made him feel he was getting somewhere. "That's okay. It's a relief, fitting in."

"What are you fitting into?"

Before he could reply, a muscular arm landed on his shoulder. "How you doing, sport?" Norse shouted it into his ear.

"Warmin' up."

"That was some run, wasn't it?"

"Nothing like it."

"What a rush!"

The squeeze of the arm had stopped Lewis's modest attempts at dancing. "It was. Hey, thanks for pulling me through there."

Norse laughed. "Naked as jaybirds! Don't tell that to my Freudian friends!"

Abby was eyeing the psychologist shyly.

"At least we had shoes," Lewis said.

"Yes, and I'm even growing back my hair!" The psychologist smiled, his teeth big and perfect, running his hand across what was now a crew cut. "I can almost feel it coming back. My strength, like Samson." He hammered his chest with his fist.

"You're doing good with our group," Lewis congratulated. "You've held things together."

"But you've got the prettiest partner." Norse smiled at Abby, making no move to leave.

Lewis felt dominated by the help he'd had to receive.

The older man had established a hold over him somehow, like a big brother. He had to counter with his own help. "Cut in, if you'd like."

"Never give an opening as easily as that." But the psychologist took Abby's arm and lifted it, tugging at her wrist and letting her twirl underneath. She shrugged at Lewis. Norse moved with catlike grace, interposing himself, maneuvering her backward. "I want to talk to you," he whispered at her. Involuntarily, Lewis had to step back.

Abby was looking up at her new partner with a mixture of expectation and fear, a fly to a spider.

Lewis stood, momentarily at a loss, looking at them dance. Abby avoided his eye.

Then someone bumped him from behind. "You can dance with me."

He turned. Gabriella had her arms up, wrists together, her tank top lifting to show a slice of belly as she shimmied, laughing. Her arms squeezed and lifted her breasts, revealing her cleavage, making her look more naked than when she'd been nude.

"We've already sweated together," he joked evasively, glancing around at Abby.

"Yes." Gabriella twirled, her hair flying. "Let's do it again."

They danced, she expertly steering him away from the other two and losing them in the shadows, pushing suggestively up against him as Pika's makeshift strobe provided a peekaboo privacy. He felt himself flushing, growing hard, and he turned slightly so that she might not see or feel it. Geller's prediction had been right.

She laughed at him, slithering away, then coming back, her body quivering as she shook it. "I feel the power of the Pole, where all lines converge!" He almost stopped dancing as he watched, astonished at her suppleness. She laughed again and stopped, taking his hand, her point made. "I'm thirsty from all this sweat. Buy me a margarita?"

The drinks, this night, were free.

"To Mexico and freedom," Mendoza slurred as he scooped them two glasses.

"Carl, you were raised in Fresno," Gabriella said. "What do you know about Mexico?"

"I lost my virginity in Puerto Vallarta." He leered. "Or was it Modesto?"

She took Lewis's hand again and led him to a corner, where they sipped and watched. Abby was still dancing with Norse, moving more easily now as if she'd been cajoled out of her moodiness. So Lewis and Gabriella returned to dance more and then drink more, the music and the movement and the talk blurring. His partner was losing all inhibition, writhing like a snake, flashing her thighs and a glimpse of her panties as she moved. The music had given her the fluidity of honey.

Lewis glanced desperately about, feeling himself shunted to the wrong track. He wanted to talk to Abby, but she and Norse had disappeared. He was alone with temptation.

"Life is good, isn't it?" Gabriella asked over the music.

"What?"

"Being alive and not dead!"

He nodded, hypnotized by her body. She was grinning at him.

"I feel more alive at the Pole," he slurred. "But more dead, too."

She ground against him, mocking him. "Not that dead."

Lewis felt embarrassed. "I'm getting too drunk. I've got to sit down." His reentry into the group was going too fast. He hadn't sorted out his feelings for everyone.

"Sure." She took his hand again, both their palms moist. "But not here."

He thought again about Abby. She was with Norse! The man she'd said had saved him! Pictures flickered though his mind of the two dancing, talking, whispering. He felt humiliated by the psychologist. Dominated. Irritated. Somehow he'd barged into Lewis's life. "Okay."

They slipped out of the galley module, getting a quick blast of cold air under the icicles of the dome. It sobered him. Was she taking him to her room? Would he regret it if she did? No, they ran into the heat of the communications building. She led him up the steel stairs to the library and glanced inside. "All clear." She pulled him in.

It was dark, the air musty with that faint paper-and-paste smell of books. There was a couch they bumped against and he jerked to a stop, dizzy. She kissed him, quickly and hard.

He broke away. "In the library?"

"There's no one here. They're all at the party." She kissed him again. "I like it in places like this."

"What if someone comes?"

"I like the danger."

He glanced around. What the hell? He kissed her back this time, letting his tongue glance off her lips, her teeth, her tongue. He could feel the sting of alcohol there. His head reeled with the smell of perfume and perspiration and musk. "Jesus."

"It's not good to hold your feelings in. It backs up on you." Her hands were running from his chest to the back of his thighs. "Then it blows up, like Tyson."

"Gabriella, I like you, but I'm not sure this is a good idea yet. . . ."

"I want you, Jed. I want you to want me."

He wanted it, too, even though he felt nothing for this woman. It was just that she was a woman. Her beauty inflamed him. She crossed her arms and lifted off her top in an instant and then, with a twist of her wrist, dropped her skirt. The lace of her underwear revealed shadows, of her nipples and delta of hair. Lewis groaned. She was pulling at his own long-sleeved thermal shirt and he helped pull it off. They kissed again and he unfastened her bra. It slipped away, her nipples like tarnished coins, the tips engorged and hard. He was just as hard and she pushed against him excitedly. Then she broke free and turned, looking back at him coyly, and slowly wiggled her panties down. It was dark but he could see light reflected off the curve of her hips. A topography of shadow led to the darker mysteries beyond.

"Take me on the couch," she whispered, crawling over the arm of it.

He thought of Abby as he swayed unsteadily. She was the one he liked, dammit. "I'm not ready for this," he tried, slurring the words.

Gabriella twisted onto her back, reached up, and snagged the end of his belt, tugging her to him. Her hand brushed his jeans. "Yes, you are."

He let her pull him as if on a bridle. He didn't know this woman! But he wanted her, wanted her badly. It had been a long time.

She reached up to grapple with his pants. He was fearful he was going to simply explode. She was gorgeous, a chocolate candy melting in the dark. He felt himself starting to plunge toward the pool of femininity beneath him.

Then there was a gasp.

He jerked around, Gabriella's hand still at his belt. Abby was in the library doorway, something bright on her cheeks, a tear that glistened in the dim light. She looked wildly from Lewis to Gabriella, taking in the moment.

The other woman looked at the intruder angrily, her knees up, her thighs parted. "We're busy."

Abby gave a low moan. "Why didn't you wait?"

Then she vanished.

"Abby!"

There was a hand on his leg. "Forget her, Jed. She's gone."

But he was jerking away, awkward in his drunkenness, suddenly frantic to break free of this woman holding his leg. He didn't want this!

"Damn you, take me!"

He pushed Gabriella's nude body back down to the couch, his hands marveling despite himself at the smoothness of her skin, every fiber of his being screaming regret. Her hands slipped along his forearm as he pulled away and suddenly she looked despairing at his abandonment, her act broken, her seductiveness punctured, her knees pressed together. "Please. . . ."

"I'm sorry."

"Don't leave me like this. . . ." There was a hollow hopelessness.

"I have to go!"

"I just want . . ." It was a groan. She was pleading.

But he'd already lurched out of the room in his bare feet, banging down the cold metal stairs and stumbling out the door into the chill of the dome. The snow burned his soles. Like a drowning man, straining for breath, he whirled around looking for Abby. Nothing! Frantic, he made his way to the berthing building where she slept. Everything was terribly wrong.

"Abby!" The call echoed down the corridor. What did he care what people thought?

Her tried her knob but her door was locked. He hammered on its surface.

"Abby! . . ."

But if she was behind it, she didn't answer his mournful pounding.

CHAPTER TWENTY

Amundsen-Scott base came awake with a collective hangover, wrung out from alcohol, the temperature extremes of the Three Hundred Degree Club, and emotional depletion. Clouds had moved back in, the outside was ink, and the temperature rose to eighty-nine below and settled there. Norse sent a message to Washington, D.C., explaining that Tyson had disappeared and that the base was in the process of recovering its emotional equilibrium. Some of the research would slip for a day or two. In his professional opinion, the survivors could still endure the winter. Personal e-mail and satellite telephone messages were still on hold until the group completed its catharsis.

Their mood was fragile. They needed time.

Lewis lay awake for most of the night and then fell into an exhausted sleep that lasted until early afternoon. He woke feeling wearier than when he'd gone to bed, and he scratched morosely at the frost of the Ice Room. He supposed that with four people gone from the base he could move to an interior berth, but the thought of occupying the space of a dead man seemed ghoulish. He sat on his bunk, euphoria replaced with depression. *I have no friends.* Norse had undercut him by pursuing Abby. Abby he had betrayed. Poor Gabriella he'd abandoned.

He dressed and went to the galley, dreading meeting either woman. Fortunately, neither was there. He ate a few leftovers without appetite, his mouth like cotton, and then went outside into the dark, hoping to assuage his guilt and regret with the rote labor of collecting data. The cold was bracing, a sharp reminder of where he really was. The surroundings were so black that the meteorology building looked like a hovering spacecraft as he approached it. He climbed the stairs, shed his parka and boots, and duly recorded every decimal point: a robot on assignment. Lewis wished he had the control of a robot. He'd been welcomed into the fold only to drunkenly embarrass himself in front of the person he cared about most. Now that he'd made the club, he'd become a fool.

Why was connection so difficult? He'd learned the superficialities like anyone else: the hearty hellos, the solicitous sympathies, the psychological bargaining of favor and position that made up casual friendship. It was true communion that eluded him. Honesty brought a wary reaction and confession seemed regarded as weakness. Sex seemed the enemy of love. Lewis had hoped that by coming to the Pole he'd find an isolated commune in which barriers would shatter: a forced encounter group in which the environment would encourage people to share their souls. Nothing of the sort had happened. If anything, people seemed to grow thicker shells to protect precious privacy. The nicknames were armor, signaling the role each had been chosen to play through the false dance of winter.

If he couldn't make connection with another human being, he thought, he was going to go crazy.

*   *   *

"Well, Buck, old boy, it's time to find an Exxon station."

The gauge on the Spryte still showed a quarter tank of diesel in reserve but Tyson had been thinking of refueling for the last twenty miles. He'd just been putting off getting out in the cold. The cabin altimeter showed the plateau had swollen to eleven thousand feet here and the thermometer read one hundred and three below zero. Inside the machine it was a relatively cozy sixty-three above, a cocoon of habitability maintained only by the full-blast roaring of the cabin heater. The wind was beginning to pick up, too. Pretty soon it might blow hard enough that he'd be fighting ice on the windshield.

Damn, it was lonely.

Beyond the pool of his headlights he could see nothing. Tyson checked his GPS again. A compass was so useless down here that he'd thrown the damn thing away, but the satellite readings were faithfully keeping him on track. According to his latitude and longitude beamed from space, he'd come about two hundred miles from the American base and had five hundred to go. Vostok! Better than being lynched by a bunch of polar nutcases, perhaps, but just barely.

Someday they were going to know his innocence. Someday they were going to find the real killer and wish they had big bad Buck Tyson around to help bring him down. But right now he was out on Pluto, the underworld, hoping hard as hell that he could get back someday to the green hills of earth.

He knew Norse didn't give a shit about him. The shrink was just trying to keep the lid on and prevent everyone else from going loco by flushing Mr. Unpopularity away.

And old Buck? He'd have a right jolly time with the

Russkies the rest of the winter, eating pickled herring and black bread and counting the seconds until he could get out of collapsing Commie-ville. Get back to clear his name.

"Not until you gas up, Bucky-boy." He stopped the rig, letting the engine idle.

Grunting in the tight cab space, he pulled on his parka and ski gloves and face mask and goggles and pulled the lever on the cab door. It had frozen shut, natch, so he had to pop it with a hard butt of his shoulder. "Ow!" When he stepped down to the metal footrest, the cold squeezed him like a frozen lake. *My balls are going to implode.* As quickly as he could he slammed the door shut and peered back inside at the cabin thermometer. The interior had plunged fifteen degrees from that brief blast of cold air before steadying. Wouldn't take long to freeze up completely if his dear old diesel stopped chugging. Well, he'd babied that mother for weeks, now. It should tick like a clock.

Tyson dropped to the snow and apprehensively looked around. He couldn't see shit. The only thing visible was a curtain of knee-high blowing snow, rippling at him out of the dark and zipping on, waving goodbye to the lights of the Spryte. Beyond was dark and profound as a cave. Five, six more months of this insanity before the light returned. Jesus, he'd been stupid! Yeah, he'd needed the money, but *this* place . . .

He walked to the sled he towed behind, stiff from sitting and awkward from the thick clothes and the cold he involuntarily shrank from. They'd used the sled to drag construction materials on base and Norse had commandeered it for Tyson's escape. It was loaded with fuel in five-gallon jerricans. The mechanic grasped one, feeling the cold of its metal even through his gloves, and tugged.

It was like pulling on bedrock. Everything was frozen to everything else.

"Fucking Antarctica."

He trundled back to the Spryte and shoved open its tool-box, kept marginally warm by its proximity to the engine. He took out a ball peen hammer and pointed tire jack and went back to the sled. A few whacks broke the outermost container free enough that he could yank it off. It took more hammer blows to get the metal screw-top loosened, everything clumsy in the cold. Finally he had it off and a fuel spout screwed on. Grunting, he lifted the can and began emptying its contents into the tracked vehicle's gas tank. The process was excruciatingly slow. At this temperature, the fuel was like syrup.

When the can was empty he unscrewed the spout and heaved the empty container away. The garbage would mark his spot, like a bobcat pissing on pine needles. Like that stuff they left on the moon. Puffing, cursing, he went back for the next one.

Christ, it was cold! His lungs were raw, his head aching. Despite the exertion he felt like he was stiffening up. He stopped after fifteen gallons and climbed back into the cab to warm up, letting the ice on his face mask melt before he ripped it down, gasping. He sipped some water to battle dehydration. Cameron had told him once that studies showed everything at the Pole took three times longer to do than normal. Then the asshole asked him to do things three times faster than they reasonably could be done.

"Rest in peace, you sonofabitch." No one deserved a knife in the chest but jeez, he'd been an ineffectual prick. He wondered who murdered him. Half the base would qualify, near as Tyson could tell.

He climbed out again and went back to work. The hammer shattered like glass on the eighth can, its metal brittle from the incredible cold. Tyson wearily got a spare from the toolbox and went back to work. Glug, glug, glug. Terrible task, but this stuff was his lifeblood. Without fuel, he was a dead man.

At forty-five gallons he called it a pit stop. The tank was still slightly shy of full but he couldn't take the cold anymore. He'd drive several more hours, nap, and fill up again. As long as the plateau stayed flat and featureless, he'd be drinking vodka toasts in a few days. Until then, stay calm, stay focused. Stay alive! He climbed back aboard the rumbling Spryte.

Tyson gave himself a few minutes to warm up, savoring the heat of the cab, and finally stopped shivering enough to take off his parka and gloves. He gave the engine a couple of experimental blasts with the throttle, slipped the vehicle into gear, and set out with a lurch. The scattering of empty jerricans slipped away behind to be quietly entombed by the snow.

An hour of dark tedium passed. It was like driving a submarine across lightless mud. Except this was far colder than the deep sea. He was right, his windshield was beginning to ice up, so he turned the defrost higher and beat at the skin with the feeble scritch-scratch of the wipers. Not that there was anything to see!

Then the engine coughed.

Don't scare me like that, you cheap-ass hunk of machinery.

It coughed again.

Tyson chilled. A breakdown out here could be lethal. These diesels liked to run until doomsday, once you got them warmed up. What the hell could be wrong?

The engine began stuttering, as if something were caught

in its throat, and he goosed the throttle to clear it. It roared, gagged, clattered wildly. Then, as if drowning on its own phlegm, it guttered out.

"Shit!"

He crawled behind his seat and lifted an access panel. There was nothing obviously wrong. No smoke. The fluids were normal. He checked the oil and there was plenty of that, too. It sounded like there was water or some other contaminant in the fuel.

Had that moron psychologist given him the wrong stuff?

Reluctantly, he opened the cab again. The wind had risen, and although the temperature had climbed ten degrees with it, the cold's bite was worse than ever. Tyson was instantly chilled. He slammed the door shut and looked longingly back inside. Again that fifteen-degree drop, but this time there was no heater blowing to maintain cab temperature. Even as he watched, the mercury continued to slowly descend. Have to hurry!

If it was the fuel, the two filters should bleed it out. Maybe they needed to be emptied of water. Maybe they'd iced up. He crawled under the machine with a flashlight to open a panel and check the fuel line, muttering imprecations at every mush-minded beaker he'd ever met. Norse wouldn't know a carburetor from a camshaft, he was sure of it. Shining the light around, he was momentarily puzzled. Where the devil were the filters? It was like he'd never seen this machine before.

Then he looked closer and realized. The filters had been cut out of the line. Excised like a bad appendix. Snip, snip. The breaks had been bridged by tubing.

Dread realization began to descend. *Well, well, Doctor Bob. Savior of the Pole. More mechanically savvy than I gave you credit for. And, with a little tune and lube, my judge, jury, and executioner.*

If he got going again, he'd turn around and strangle the bastard.

Tyson crawled back out and stood in the wind, trying to think. He had to not just fix things, but fix them fast. He had to get that engine going before he froze.

He boosted himself up on the step and looked back in the cab. It was down to forty degrees. Tyson opened the door, fished out some chewing gum from the console, and shut it again. Then he dropped back to the snow.

His only hope was that the other fuel was good. How many cans could the fucker have doped? Tyson had no tubing to siphon the bad stuff out, and no drain hole. His only choice was to make his own. He opened the toolbox, took out a cold chisel—*now, there's an appropriate name,* he told himself—and placed it against the fuel tank. Then he swung with a hammer. It took a furious set of blows, which had the advantage of warming him, before he punched a hole through the dented tank. Diesel began running out onto the snow in a pulse like a cut artery, warmed by its proximity to the engine. Once it hit the snow it congealed.

What had Norse put in it? Water? Sugar? Some weird chemical shit?

He took out the gum, having to painfully bare his hand to unwrap it, and stuffed every stick into his mouth, chewing furiously. Then, slipping his glove back on, he began to break the other cans loose from the sled. Even if these worked, were there enough to get back to Amundsen-Scott? Would the others help him if he got there?

Cursing, clumsy from the cold, he got one top off after another. The wind kept rising, biting at him. Frantic, he left off for a minute to check the fuel tank. It was still emptying in a now-sluggish stream. He stepped up on the Spryte to look at the thermometer inside the cabin.

Eighteen degrees above zero. Heat was leaching from his survival capsule like gas from a balloon.

At last the fuel tank emptied. The area under the machine was slick with it, half frozen, a petroleum lake. He took the gum from his mouth and wedged it, steaming, over the hole he'd made. The gum wrapper went over that. Shit-poor work, but the cold instantly hardened his patch like putty.

Then he began lugging the newly opened cans to the opening and pouring them in. Diesel spilled on the side of the tank, streaming into the snow, and he didn't care. If he could light the damn diesel he'd get warm in a hurry, and that sounded almost pleasant right now. *Baby will you light my fire. . . .*

He could hardly feel his damn feet.

But he couldn't afford a bonfire. He needed every drop to get back for a little counseling session with Robert Norse. *You saved 'em all, didn't you, Doctor Bob? Talked to me with sympathy just before you pushed me off the plank. So what's going to be your solution when there's another murder and you realize that, oops, Buck Tyson didn't do it? What happens to your tidy little social theories then?*

At fifteen gallons he left off. Had to get the engine going before he froze. Once he had respite with the heater, he'd dump the rest in. That's if the engine *started.* If *this* crap wasn't as poisoned as the other batch. If just *once* in his pathetic life he'd get a single fucking break.

Tyson climbed in the cab and slammed the door. It was a relief to be out of the wind but the temperature inside was already close to zero. It was like escaping to a meat locker. Without hesitation he turned the key. *Please. Please please me. . . .*

It cranked, stuttered, died.

He turned it again. The cab light dimmed as the engine labored.

And again.

Duh-duh-duh-duh.

He looked at the cab thermometer. Zero! Even with his body heat the temperature inside was falling like a rock. He needed heat, and fast.

It occurred to Tyson to use the radio. Not for rescue—there was no possibility of that—but just to inform Norse's many admirers at Amundsen-Scott base just how well and truly the psychologist had fucked over naive Dakota farm boy Buck Tyson. Wouldn't they like to hear about Norse's therapy in action? Of course, maybe they'd cheer that their ex-mechanic was about to turn into USDA-grade frozen—gee, the Doc sure took care of *that* little social problem—but they should at least *know* what their paranoia had led to, just to interrupt their slumber at night. And so he picked up the radio. *Hello, this is your old buddy Buck and I'm about to die. . . .*

Click. Nothing. Not even static. He wormed under the dash. All the wires had been cut.

Checkmate, Jimmy. And you can't even flip over the game board, can you?

He flicked off all the lights and turned the key and cranked. And cranked. And cranked. There were a couple pops and snorts, just enough to give him a moment of cruel hope. But the damned engine wouldn't turn over. Wouldn't even properly fart.

Finally the batteries died. It was quiet and dark.

He turned on the flashlight kept close to his chest to

avoid the cold draining its D cells and took another reading. Minus eight and still falling. Going for equilibrium with the great outdoors.

Well, this was it, then. His nowhere life had come to ground in nowhere.

He began to shiver.

Tyson knew his body would shake only so long. Then it would be out of energy like the Spryte's batteries, his core temperature dropping, a surrendering drowsiness taking over. How many hours of torture before that sleepy relief? Minutes, if he opened his coat. Which was worse?

Or he could find a match and try to light the mess outdoors. A quicker, more painful, pyre.

"What's it to be, Bucky? Fire or ice?"

Norse! Does that fucker have any idea what horror he's inflicted?

"Yep, Doc, you saved 'em all."

Tyson considered, trying to think clearly. If he didn't burn himself up, they'd find him someday. Maybe piece together enough to determine what had happened. Maybe even catch that slimy psychologist and make him pay.

Maybe. Or maybe give Norse a medal.

He slammed open the door, letting the last of his heat escape. Best to get it over with.

Then he closed the cab again and settled deeper into his parka, trying by muscle strength to control his shivering. He couldn't, of course.

One last peek at the thermometer. Minus twenty-eight and accelerating. Plunging downward to match the bottomless cold outside.

Even at the bottom of the world, solitude can be interrupted by the telephone. Lewis's at Clean Air rang with buzz-saw insistence, as harshly demanding as a baby's cry, and his guilt over ignoring Cameron's calls at the onset of the blizzard made him habitually pick it up now. His reverie of isolation, watching the lonely ice cap as fire lookouts once held vigil on their mountaintops, was shattered. "Lewis here."

"Got a minute?" It was Norse.

"I'm busy, Doc." The reply was sullen. The psychologist was the last person he wanted to talk to. He'd moved in on Abby. Started this mess, really. And it was beginning to annoy him that Norse carried his air of authority, of leadership, so easily. Annoy him that he'd let the man establish unspoken rank.

"You've been hiding out there."

"I've been working."

"Even the weather takes a break."

"Data to catch up on."

There was a pause as Norse thought about what to say. "Look, I called because I figured you might be sore about the other night. Abby, the party. Guilty as charged. Trouble is, she isn't attracted to me. I guess it caused some trouble. We were all drinking too much."

Lewis, his pride wounded, thought any apology was condescending. "You can dance with whoever you want. We weren't a couple. As near as I can tell, she doesn't like me, either."

"That's where you're wrong, sport."

Lewis was curious what had led Norse to say that and was not about to admit it. "And don't call me sport. Or friend, or son, or buddy, or sweetie. I don't like the Father Superior act."

"No offense meant." Norse's voice crackled over the phone. "Just trying to repair the damage."

"Why?"

"Because today's the first day of the rest of our lives. The post–Buck era. Remainder of the winter. All for one and one for all."

Lewis inwardly frowned, knowing he'd voiced the same thoughts. Had Abby repeated them to Bob?

"Look, how about a meeting on neutral ground?" Norse went on.

"What do you mean?"

"The KitKat Club after dinner tonight. I've got an idea to help continue patching things back together under the dome. There's a bunch of crap out there that people leave behind. Hobbies, toys, eccentric gear. It's stored there. Might be something good for morale."

"You're recreational director now?"

"I'm just trying to keep the station on keel."

Lewis knew he was sulking. "I've never even been out there."

"That's the whole point. It's the station's start-over place."

Lewis thought about it, fighting with his pride. "Who said I need to start over?"

"Okay, maybe I do." Norse waited.

"You're a manipulator, you know that? You manipulate people."

"Of course I do. Any effective person does. But that doesn't mean I'm not your friend. I'm trying to help, dammit."

"Help what?"

"Help the winter progress. Help make up for my own mistakes."

Lewis was mad at Norse because he was still mad at himself. "So why *did* you take her away at the party?"

There was a long silence. "Look, I said I fucked up, okay? I cut in on you, I came on to Abby, I was feeling cocky that people were turning to me, and high that Tyson had split. I was drunk. Conceded. But it was a game to me and Abby saw through that and she shot me down. She told me she liked *you*. I should have known better. I *did* know better. And I woke up hungover like everyone else and not feeling too good about myself. So now I'm trying to move on from here."

Lewis was silent. He was jealous of this man trying to hold things together. Jealous of Norse's glib rationalizations. *Grow up,* he told himself. *He's trying to apologize.*

"I'm a shrink and I've wound up as temporary, de facto . . . point man. Okay?"

Boss, Lewis thought.

"That's not a recipe for popularity, and I feel pressure like anyone else," Norse continued, "but we need each other and we need to get through the winter. Together. I think Abby really cares about you, Jed. She knows that other thing with Gabriella—she knows that was bullshit. So give me a chance to fix things. Manipulate, like you said. That's not always a bad thing."

Lewis sighed. "I just feel this whole winter I've been jerked around, with the meteorite and everything else. I'm tired of it."

"This isn't easy for me, either, you know. If you haven't guessed yet, I've got quite an ego. When push came to shove, she chose you. That stung. But you, me, her—all of us getting back together is the right thing to do."

"The right thing? I'm losing my bearings on that one, Doc."

Norse laughed at himself. "Okay. The best plan I have at the time." There was a click as he hung up the phone.

CHAPTER TWENTY-ONE

The KitKat Club was a two-story plywood balloon-launching shack, obsolete and abandoned, that an enterprising station carpenter had remodeled in his spare time into what he had jokingly proclaimed as "a penthouse pad of pleasure." Actually it was the top floor that had been turned into an unofficial storage attic for base personnel, crammed with cast-off junk. The bottom had been insulated, carpeted, papered with travel posters, and heated. While it was just three hundred yards from the dome, the building—named for the decadent nightclub in *Cabaret*—had become a place of physical and psychological separation and escape, the one refuge that didn't have a job attached to it. Neutral ground, Norse had called it. When its carpenter-creator left after one season, his shack became a place for parties, sexual trysts, verbal showdowns, and therapeutic solitude. Station managers like Cameron diplomatically ignored its existence because of its value as a pressure relief valve. Fingies were introduced to it after station and social acceptance. It was a perk, like visiting the abandoned base. Winter-overs thought of the KitKat Club, like the Pole itself, as theirs.

When Lewis arrived, Norse wasn't there. He flicked on the lights to look around while he waited. Small windows had been shuttered for the winter but smuggled incandescent bulbs behind a screen of colored paper, violating all fire safety regulations, gave the room a warm glow. There were two surplus single mattresses covered with unzipped nylon sleeping bags, a ratty and torn couch surplused from the dome, crates and a cable spool that had been liberated for tables, and makeshift shelves that held drifts of dog-eared books: Tolkien and Grisham, Shackleton and Byrd. A hot plate, an espresso maker, a small fridge. An old boom box and a shoal of CDs. The walls were a mosaic of posters, clippings, cartoons, and bumper stickers: *He who dies with the most toys wins.* It seemed unintentionally macabre after what had happened.

Maybe the psychologist would put him on the couch. He felt like he needed it about now.

He heard the crunch of snow outside and considered again what he wanted. Some kind of equality, he decided, some kind of mutual respect. An acceptance of who he was and an end to Norse's incessant observation. The shrink's real problem was that he didn't have enough real work to do and so dwelled on everybody else. With so many lost, they needed a reallocation. . . .

"Hello?" It was Abby outside the door, sounding uncertain.

Just her voice was enough to get his heart to slip sideways off its track. Surprised, by both her presence and the strength of his own reaction, Lewis opened the latch.

She was startled. "It's you," she said, blinking.

"What are *you* doing here?" he replied.

Great beginning.

She glanced past him to see if anyone else was inside. "Bob . . ."

Of course, it was always Bob, wasn't it? "Come on in," he said gruffly. "We're letting out the heat."

It was too cold for indecision. She stepped inside and he shut the door. Abby took a deep breath, letting warmth settle back inside her lungs, and then looked at him warily. "I didn't know you'd be out here."

"I think we were set up by Norse. He sent us on the same mission."

"Mission?"

"To find some toys, right? I thought he was coming out, too, but . . ." *Meet on neutral ground,* Norse had suggested. He hadn't said with whom. Quite the matchmaker. "Look, I didn't plan this, but I'm glad you came out. Really. I'm surprised but . . . please don't go." Somehow he had to make things right.

She remembered she was angry about Gabriella. "If Bob did this, then I'm mad at him, too."

"Please." He lifted his arms to take her parka. "It's a long winter." His conciliatory tone softened her. Hesitantly, she let it slip off.

"I thought I was meeting *him,*" Lewis explained, hanging her coat on a peg. "But maybe not, if he sent you, too. He said it's all for station morale."

She looked cautious. "I don't know whether to believe you."

"Really, he's playing with us both. We're just another experiment."

"Which I'm fed up with. I don't need his help. Or yours."

"That's what *I* said. Except . . ."

"Except what?"

"Except maybe we *should* start over. Here, on new ground."

"You thought or Doctor Bob thought?"

"Abby, I got drunk and screwed up the other night. That's not an excuse but it wasn't what I wanted to happen. I wanted things to happen with *you*. I'm frustrated. Frustrated at how things haven't gone as I planned. Frustrated at myself."

It was apology enough to get her to reluctantly sit, let him help her shuck off her snowy boots, and, with that, concede that she wasn't immediately leaving. "We're all frustrated, Jed," she admitted. "It's been a hell of a winter."

"Yes. So now that the bad stuff is over, let's have a truce, okay?"

"What about her?" She'd be damned if she'd say the name.

"There is no her! That's the whole point. I ran after *you*. Didn't you hear me?"

She glanced away, letting her eyes roam the room.

"I haven't even seen her," Lewis added. "I think she's embarrassed, too."

"Well." Abby was looking for a way to answer without answering. "Welcome to the club, then, if we've both been sent here by our group therapist." Her voice was quiet, resigned.

He smiled. They were going to talk, at least in a general way. "How many clubs does this place have, anyway?"

She considered the light question seriously. "The entire Pole is a club, I guess. So's Antarctica. The science community itself. This is a sub-branch."

"Half hippie hideaway, half slumber party."

"It's not *Architectural Digest*. I think of it as a den, or burrow." She allowed a slight smile. "I've always liked it. If anything ever goes wrong, I've thought this is where I'd come to wait for the end."

She meant the generator but he had to laugh. "If anything ever goes wrong! You should have camped out here weeks ago!"

"You know what I mean."

"Yeah. It's cozy."

"And hot. How high did you crank the heat, anyway?"

"Enough to get the rest of your stuff off."

She looked at him skeptically and he grinned.

"It's part of my plan, make it a sauna and watch 'em strip. Works with all the girls."

Abby snorted at that joke and shed her nylon bib overalls, keeping on the fleece pants and vest underneath. He enjoyed a glimpse of her stretching and bending even while pretending to politely glance around elsewhere. Men called her Ice Cream because they wanted her to melt. Yet while Abby was attractive, she didn't make him uncomfortable the way Gabriella did. Somehow her presence made him content, like the beauty of a flower. She hung up the overalls next to her parka, water from her boots pooling on the plywood by the door. "Why would it matter where you waited?" he asked her.

"I'd want to die at home."

"Jesus. Let's not be morbid."

"How can we not?" She meant the deaths, the makeshift graves.

"It's been hard, hasn't it?" he said.

"Nothing like what I hoped."

"But it's over, I think. So we should be friends again."

"We've never not been friends. You can be angry at a friend and still be friends."

"So you're still mad?"

She sighed, her look one of exasperation, but an exasperation as much at herself as him. "Yes, but I don't have an excuse for my anger. No claim to you, I mean. I know that. I admit that. I'm trying to be honest about things. I've been thinking a lot about what's going on."

"And?"

"And I'm not doing very well handling it alone."

"We *do* have Doctor Bob." It was meant as a kind of joke, but his frustration was portrayed in a sarcastic tone that popped out before he could control it.

"Are you jealous, Jed?"

It took him a moment to admit the truth. "Yes. He's . . . smooth."

"I pulled away from you because I was afraid how I felt about *you*, not Bob. I don't have the same feeling about Norse. He's *too* smooth. And that's what I've been thinking about."

Now Lewis was curious. "Maybe we'd better sit more comfortably."

She nodded, pointing him to the torn couch. He sat, sinking in a squeal of springs. Instead of sitting next to him she plopped cross-legged down on one of the mattresses, facing him. "Have you noticed what's been going on?" she began.

"The dying?"

She shook her head. "The Pole. What it feels like here."

"Cold." It was flippant, an attempt to lighten things.

"No, our perspective. We're so low to the ground that we can't see very far. It's almost like treading water. And then as the sun set the horizon kind of shrank in on us. We went from seeing little to seeing almost nothing, on the really dark nights. Step beyond the lights and you step into a void. It's like we're floating, which in a sense is true, since we're on this ice. And at the same time the sky is so clear we're not just looking at the atmosphere but beyond it, out to the universe. It's exactly as if we've blasted into space."

"Doctor Bob again."

She shook her head. "His focus is on the compound, the way all us little bits glue together or fall apart. He's a social scientist studying a spaceship. But to me we're individual atoms after a Big Bang, flying away from each other while maintaining this faint gravity. That's how the station makes me feel, anyway. Maybe it's that all these people here are *too* close, physically, and so as the winter closes in it forces you deeper inside yourself just to get away. If you're not careful the Pole starts to take you over. Like the monster in *The Thing*, except it's the Pole itself. Your sleep cycle, your appetite, your hormones, your periods, your energy, your habits: Everything begins to slide out of whack when the sun leaves. And the more you try to run after yourself, the more you seem to fall into yourself, leaving everyone else behind. Do you know what I mean?"

"Sort of."

"It's isolating. We know each other but we don't know each other because if we all admitted what we're feeling it would create this kind of psychic whirlpool which might suck us all down. So we're wary. But some people reach out: you, Bob, even Gabriella."

"But not you."

She took a breath, hesitating, then plunged ahead. "A woman learns to be cautious with men. Guys want to pretend everything doesn't matter, but it does. This thing with my picture baffles me. *You* baffle me, that a geologist would really want to go to the Pole. It's like a biologist going to the moon. So I chickened out. I'm not afraid of relationships but I'm a little afraid of *you.* I know another guy, too, I told you that, but I wasn't ready to commit to him, either. I came down to think things through."

"I respect that, Abby."

"It was escape. But it's not working out as I planned."

"These deaths haven't exactly created a retreat atmosphere."

"I'm just trying to explain that I haven't been trying to be a jerk, even if it seems like it. I like you, and because of that I'm afraid of getting hurt. I'm not teasing, I'm just . . . incompetent." She looked defeated.

"Abby, everyone's incompetent. It's a fact of life."

She looked at him hopefully. "Do you think so?"

"At that stuff they are. Look at the gossip columns about the rich and famous. It's one constant litany of incompetence. The more confident they act, the more frightened they feel."

She smiled. "I don't know if I believe that. If that's true, then Norse must be very frightened indeed. I've never seen anyone so confident under such pressure."

"I think that's because it's good for his damn study."

"Or he's rising to the occasion."

"He thinks that's what the best people do. And I admit he's got a weird charm. I don't really blame you for leaving with him at the dance. I don't have a claim to *you,* either. We just never seem to get very far."

"There's just been too much going on."

"Too much pressure."

"Bob and I talked about that picture of Mickey's. He's easy to confide in. A talker. A professional. Charismatic, even. He invited me to take a bottle of wine and to go talk, so we did, but then he came on to me."

"You're an attractive woman, Abby."

"I wasn't offended. I didn't think it was some breach of professional ethics. It's not like I'm in therapy. But when he began touching me I stiffened up, no matter how hard I tried not to, and this terror—this irrational terror—took over. I broke away and he accused me of being dishonest, with him and myself, and I saw something. . . ." She shivered. "Suddenly he looked very analytical. It was so dispassionate he frightened me. Like his warmth is a disguise for his cold. So I left, looking for you, but you'd left the dance, too, and then I found you. . . ." She looked hopeless. "I pushed you away."

"We both screwed up."

"Yes."

"We wound up with the wrong partners."

"Yes."

"So forget about it. It's over. This is the first day of the rest of whatever." It amused him to quote Doctor Bob.

She looked depressed. "You're so much better at getting over things than I am. All men are."

"That's not really true."

"You function. Compartmentalize. I can't even function."

"Women get paralyzed. Men go out and do something stupid. Start wars and things. I'm not sure one's better than the other."

Abby grinned ruefully. "I guess what I'm admitting is that I *would* like to kind of start over. Now that the bad stuff is past, or at least I hope it is. That I'd like to know you, just so I can tell myself I know *somebody* on station in some kind of meaningful way."

He looked at her with hope. "Can't you sense how alike we are? I'm incompetent, too. I got into rocks because they were as unlike people as anything I could find. Then I joined this industry that seemed to be just about money, disposable conscience, and transience. Nobody belonged anywhere, it was all just oil. Ruthless competition. So then I ran away from *that*. I ran here, to the Pole."

"To become the fingie. The outsider."

"If Buck Tyson hadn't run away I'd have gone nuts from being ostracized. His disappearance saved my winter." Lewis studied her, trying to decide what to do. He wanted to kiss her again but feared it would drive her away. He wanted to take her in his arms and feared she'd evaporate if he did that, too.

"Can we make it through?" Her voice held doubt.

"That analytical hardness you saw in Bob Norse isn't entirely a bad thing. He's held things together by staying levelheaded. He's trying to prove we can all sail to the stars."

"I was bad to him, too."

"Abby, did it ever occur to you that you weren't bad to anybody? That it's your prerogative to have doubts, to say no, to change your mind?"

She shook her head. "No. You're supposed to be nice."

"You're supposed to be honest."

"You're supposed to be some mix of those two things and that's where I always foul up." She flopped backward on the mattress, her hands over her eyes. "I know I make things harder than they are."

He laughed at her. "I'll say."

She lay there, her hands over her eyes, her legs stretched out and stiff, her chest rising and falling. He slid off the couch and knelt beside her. She didn't move. He bent, admiring the sculpture of her ear, the barest down on her cheek, wondering if he had the right to kiss her again after what had happened. Still she didn't move. So he kissed her, lightly, brushing her lips.

She slid her hands down to cover her mouth, her eyes watching him with deep seriousness but without surprise. Then she reached up to put her arms around his neck, pulling him down to her, and kissed him again, fully this time. It was sweeter than with Gabriella, less wanton and more affectionate. Softer. He held her, going again to her cheek and neck, and she cuddled into him, shivering slightly as he nuzzled her. He was content for the moment to just hold her, his fingers on the fine bones of her back. Ivory on a piano.

They lay quietly for several minutes. Finally she spoke. "What are we doing down here, Jed?"

He was drowsy in her heat and embrace. "Trying to understand the universe," he mumbled. "That's what Mickey Moss said. Buck Tyson argued for realism. He said everything but the paycheck is a pose."

"To come so far?" She sounded doubtful. "To a place this bitter?"

"We're adventurers, Abby. People are driven."

"No." She shifted restlessly. "We misplaced something and we've come down here to find it. We came down here to take it back home. Our real home."

"Misplaced what?"

"Hope. That we can make things right again."

He lifted on one elbow, looking at her lazily, more contented at her quiet intimacy than he'd have guessed, more contented than at any time since he'd come to Antarctica. "Make things right how?"

"By finding the best in ourselves."

He grinned. "I'm starting to find the best in you. Let's explore some more."

She considered, then rolled away. "No. Not yet. Not now."

He fell on his back, the picture of rejection. "Forget what I said about the honest part. Go back to nice."

"Let's make sure we truly like each other first." She was too shy to say *love*.

"Now, *there's* the difference between men and women."

She laughed ruefully at herself. "I am a complete tease, aren't I?"

"No, but I'm not sure you recognize how attractive you are. The effect you can have on men."

"That's sweet. I'll remember that."

"So let me kiss you again."

"No." She held out her hand to pull him up. "Come on, Enzyme. We've started over, and we'll see how things go. Doctor Bob sent us for a reason."

"Dang." He looked wistfully at the mattress.

"People store stuff upstairs. Oddball stuff that they've smuggled down and then don't want to bother taking back. Musical instruments, obsolete stereos, leftover hobby kits, ancient laptops, even a Foosball set. Our mission is to bring back something fun."

"Even if it's other people's stuff?"

"It becomes our stuff when we sign on, like an inheritance. We share it."

"Like Santa Claus?"

"Maybe we're anti-Claus, since we're at the South Pole. Gathering data is fine, but we've got to have something more at the end of the day, right? That's what our shrink said. Bring it back to the others. Become *The Waltons*. Or *Little House on the Prairie*."

"Oh, yuck." He looked around. "Instead of hauling stuff

out of the attic, maybe we should just have a party out here. Not a scientific instrument in sight."

"It's too small to fit everybody and we need everybody right now. We need to lighten up the galley."

"I've still got a hangover from the last party." He looked at a ladder that led to a trapdoor and shook his head. It reminded him uncomfortably of the entrance to the underground base. "It's got to be freezing cold up there, Abby. Let's pass for now and just go back to what we were doing."

"No. We'll never get to it." She stood. "I'll go first." She marched to the ladder and pushed up on the trapdoor, letting it fall over and bang down with a thud on the plywood floor above. Light from below gave a pillar of pale upward illumination but the room, jammed with junk, was mostly shadow. "I need a flashlight."

"You're letting in the cold," Lewis grumbled, feeling the draft. He went to his parka to get a light.

Abby glanced around as he fetched it, letting her eyes adjust. It was fun, like peeking into Santa's workshop. There were boxes, a guitar case, an improbable single-speed bicycle. Old skis and snowshoes, skates and a runner sled. What could they bring back for the others? There was a trombone: That might be fun. In one corner something white and shapeless hung like an old dress, moving slightly in the column of warm air that was wafting up from below. Next was a broken Universal gym, a driving wood, an unstrung racket. . . . It was bitterly cold in the unheated upper floor, a deep freeze as effective as a time capsule. Frost spotted the boxes but there was no rust, no decay. It was too dry.

Then Abby realized what she'd seen.

Shadows can confuse the mind's eye. Sometimes one sees what isn't there. Sometimes one misses what is. Her head was turning back, her brain reassembling the patterns even as Lewis handed up the flashlight. It was with growing dread that she suddenly swung back to that white form in the corner.

It had feet.

She turned the flashlight beam on and jerked so violently she almost dropped it. Then screamed, "Oh my God!"

"What, what?" Lewis shouted from below. He was climbing up next to her, trying to get past her.

Her blood was a roar in her ears, her vision dazed. She forced herself to play the light across what was hanging there. The body was ghost-white, all right, the head tilted, the tongue purple, everything waxy and elongated and sad.

"Abby, what the hell . . ."

"It isn't over."

"*What* isn't over?"

"The bad stuff." She forced herself to look, sickened. The toes were small and pointed down, like the broken wings of a bird.

Jammed in next to her, Lewis took the flashlight and aimed it. The face that stared back at him had been made hideous by strangulation, completely transformed by a cruel death. A naked and forlorn Gabriella Reid hung limply from a ceiling crossbeam, turning slowly in the current of warmer air.

"Ah, Jesus."

He finally forced his way past Abby and stepped up onto the floor. The body was frozen by now, a noose around its neck. He approached it cautiously. Suicide?

No, of course not. There was a sign around her neck. He played the light across it, reading block letters that had been cut and pasted from a magazine like a ransom note:

YOU KNOW WHO YOU ARE. YOU KNOW WHAT I WANT. GIVE IT, OR EVERYONE WILL DIE.

I Go for Help

*By the time I topped the cliff the visibility on the moun-
tain was down to a hundred yards. I could no longer
hear the wailing of the kids on the ledge, which was a
considerable relief, and instead the only sound was the
stutter of my clothing as the wind blew over the saddle.
The ripple of fabric was welcoming, reminding me that
I was alive. Alive! And off that damned wall! Because
I'd acted for myself.*

*Snow was falling heavily, which meant avalanches
were likely sometime soon. I had to get over the hump
and down the glacier as quickly as possible. I had to get
a rescue team back up to the rest of the class before it
was too late. I had to refine my story. So I untied the
rope and put it in my pack. It would raise too many questions to abandon it and answer some if I could point to
its frayed break. You have to understand that I no longer
had any means to haul up the others. I had no choice
but to walk out on my own.*

I had to hurry. The storm was getting worse.

*I made good time. Freedom! Without a team of blun-
dering neophytes in harness I felt release. I was tired but
electrified with adrenaline, my thighs chugging like pistons and my torso warm from their burn. I made the crest
of the saddle in near-whiteout conditions, acutely aware
that it would be easy to repeat the blunder of Fat Boy
and go down the slope in the wrong direction. But I'd
been up the main route several times and I felt an un-
canny sense of direction. Maybe I was being directed!
Maybe all of this was fate! Maybe Fat Boy was some*

kind of agent of my own destiny! Or maybe I was simply the victim of blind bad luck, saved from hideous misfortune by my own skill and fortitude. Maybe—and this is what I really felt, as I stood on the shoulder of that white volcano with snow swirling around me—I had been granted a revelation, an understanding of how the universe really operates. All is cruelty, except whatever you can draw from yourself. There's nothing Outside, no angel of mercy. The goal of life, its test, its meaning, is survival itself—and survival is a lonely thing, harsh, merciless, and the direction of any herd of sheep is set by the few individuals who recognize this cold reality and set a sensible direction. Most people are carried, the victims of mass delusion. The visionaries carry them. And if some lambs are lost along the way ... well, it's no loss, is it? It weeds and strengthens the remainder. What had just occurred on Wallace Wall was an act of natural selection. I was its evolved product.

I chose my direction and prepared to glissade. It was as if I could see through the snow, so certain was I of my direction. I'd never felt so powerful! I sat on the steep slope, my ice ax ready as a brake, and began to butt-skid down the mountain, flashing down in seconds the elevation it had taken us long painful minutes to slog up only hours before. I was exhilarated. Ecstatic! I was alive, forged in the fire, and newly capable of seeing through the bullshit of existence. I was reborn, really. Born again, as they say! I felt the breath of an uncaring, implacable divinity as I careened down the glacier, the breath of a monster I had bested, snow stinging my face like a joyous shower, and I dropped through the clouds until I popped out of their lower reaches and could see a good mile or more down the glacier, the smudge of the first dark trees far below me. I'd escaped the dark god.

The glacial slope began to bottom out and my easy ride came to an end. I stood, a bit unsteady from the emotion of the last hours, and began to walk. Our tracks were gone, erased by the new snow, but I swear I could have found my way in an unfamiliar cavern. It was as if I could seè through the fog. I'd been purged of fear and doubt. I had direction! I got off the ice and removed my crampons, descended down the snowy moraine to the tree line, and then into the trees to the cabin where we'd spent those few hours of uneasy rest before the midnight climb. The walking was gray and ghostly under the trees, quieter away from the wind, and in the stillness I began to imagine shapes behind the shrouded firs as if someone were watching me. No one was, of course. Still I hurried, mindful of those kids stuck up on the ledge. Mindful of how this must all play out.

I got to the university van, found the key where its magnet case stuck it to a wheel well, and unlocked the frozen door. My pack inside, the scraper out, my mittened hands brushing the snow from the windows. I climbed onto the cold vinyl, pumped the accelerator, got the engine to turn over, and waited a few minutes while the vehicle warmed. As I sat there it occurred to me I might need tire chains in the storm and rooted in the back until I found them and began putting them on. The engine exhaust was choking me and so I had to stop to shut the van off again and then went back to the chains. I wasn't very practiced and I was cold and tired and had to take a moment for a candy bar and some water, so it took me a while. I checked my watch: forty-seven minutes. There might be questions about things like that later *on, so it was smart to know. I couldn't be too precise, however, or I'd sound too calculated. Then I started the van again, put it in gear, and began driving down the mountain. The snow was slippery and deep and I had to go slow at first. Being all alone, I couldn't risk going into a tree!*

At the junction with the main Forest Service road the snow was turning to wet slush and mud and the chains were clanking. I stopped the van and took them off. Eleven minutes. I hurried. I hurried! Smeared myself with mud, making me look like I'd crawled through the trenches. And then back in the van and down toward the main highway. . . .

They asked me later about a cell phone but it went over in Fleming's pack. I had to get down to a telephone.

Astonishingly, it was only nine in the morning. With the storm and season, there was no mountain traffic. I had the roads to myself until I got down to the Mountain Highway. The first telephone I could find was at Beedle's Store, which wasn't even open. The phone was in a weather hood but otherwise open, wet, and cold, and I remember the chill of its plastic and metal as I dialed 911 to report what had happened. I have no idea what I sounded like except that a dispatcher reported afterward that I sounded like hell. Kind of numb, she said. Shell-shocked. Incoherent. Still, I conveyed the emergency. The tragedy! The plan was to meet the assembling search and rescue team at the Forest Service headquarters eight miles down the road. I drove there and was welcomed with alarm and concern.

What followed was long and grim. I was too exhausted to go back up the mountain but I knew the terrain well enough to pinpoint to the experts where the rest of the class was. I explained the fall of the other two instructors, my decision to climb out alone to get help, our heroic efforts to rescue Fat Boy, and so on. I neglected to mention the fall of the other two kids. I was distraught, anxious, demanding, all the things I imagined I was supposed to be. It took until noon to get a team assembled, another hour to get them to the trailhead, another hour up to the cabin, and still the snow was falling. I made it to the cabin with them before collapsing. They went on up themselves, trudging up the glacier, but stopped at four P.M. as they neared the cirque below the saddle and heard avalanches rumbling in the clouds like the crack and thunder of artillery. One slide came down out of the mist and erased the tracks where they'd just been. It was getting dark and still snowing heavily and if they pushed on they'd risk an even greater disaster. Prudently, they retreated.

When they came back down I refused to leave the cabin for the comfort of a room down below. Those were my kids! Those were my kids! I would spend a second night.

The storm blew through during the dark hours and when the rasping trees began to hush I finally fell into what I pretended was a troubled sleep. They left me alone. The rescuers started up again at dawn and a helicopter was launched at the same time.

I sat up and managed to get down some coffee. Everyone was somber. Hope was slim. Two reporters hiked up to us as we waited and I haltingly went over the story again, how Fleming had let Fat Boy wander off in the wrong direction and we'd done our best to rescue him and I'd been left to go for help. I covered for the other two instructors as best I could, giving them the benefit of the doubt, mourning their loss, but the resulting stories painted me in a pretty sympathetic light. By God, I'd done my best! I was haggard with sorrow. Distraught. Exhausted.

The helicopter report came in an hour later.

Avalanches were still spilling down Wallace Wall, rinsing it clean. The pilots orbited the area for miles in all directions.

The ledge was empty. Fat Boy and all the others were gone.

CHAPTER TWENTY-TWO

The winter-overs gathered in the galley like a convocation of the damned, their faces revealing the underbelly of the human psyche. Dread. Anger. Suspicion. Depression. Their illusions about escape had been buried with Gabriella's body, her snowy grave marked by another bleak cross of black plastic pipe. It was months before the winter was over, and already everyone looked like toast. Several staff members had come in carrying makeshift weapons: lengths of pipe, knives, an improbable hickory-handled hatchet brought down for some long-forgotten purpose. Pulaski arrived with a six-foot length of galvanized water pipe that he'd sawed off at a sharp angle to make the point of a spear. In a society with no guarantee of safety, people were arming themselves as best they could.

Robert Norse had looked the night before like a faith-shaken priest, his shell of infectious confidence cracked by the discovery of Gabriella's body. The news of her death left him haggard, his eyes sunken, and he'd refused to help take down the forlorn corpse. "I can't deal with the rest if I have to do that," he'd said, his voice hollow at the news of her death. "I have to function. One of us has to function." So the dead woman had been laid to rest with no ceremony, her cross the fourth in a row, the gravediggers chilled and spooked and anxious to finish the task and get back inside to the light and warmth of the dome. Whoever had hanged Gabriella might be lurking somewhere out there in the dark of the plateau, waiting for the next one to pick off.

By the following day, however, Norse had collected himself. The disquieting breach in his calm had been repaired. In fact he seemed newly confident, newly knowledgeable, and he came around the tables to tell them all to stay after supper. It was important that they all talk, he said. Important that they use this to grow stronger. Important that he find strength to feed theirs. So they stayed.

When he stood up to speak, it was so quiet they could hear the drone of the ventilation and the burble of the drink dispenser. Their ranks were visibly thinner. It was awful, how small their gathering looked.

"I'm afraid I have some more disturbing news," Norse began.

You could hear the sound of their breathing.

"I've radioed the Russian base at Vostok. There's no sign of Buck Tyson. He never arrived. We have no idea where he is."

There was a long, despairing quiet.

"Don't we?" Geller asked.

Dana Andrews gave a low moan.

"We can't assume anything." Norse looked at them soberly. "*Anything.* We don't know it's Buck. And somehow, until we come through this, we've got to combat panic. Panic will kill us faster than anything. Distrust will kill us. Paranoia will kill us. I think we're going to have to reach inside ourselves and find the core of what's there. This is a test—a test of what we're made of."

"Cut the psychobabble, Doc," Geller replied. "I'm panicked and distrustful and paranoid as hell. I'm freakin' ready to jump out of my skin, and I'm freakin' ready to call it quits for this winter. I didn't sign on for the Chainsaw Massacre. I want to get out of here before that North Dakota madman annihilates us all."

There was a buzz of assent. If there'd been anywhere to run to, they'd have bolted.

Geller's complaint focused the psychologist on him. Norse looked resolute. "*You* cut the fantasy, George. We're not going home. We can't go home. *This* is home, for six or seven more months. You know that."

"So we just go about our little data-collection duties, waiting for Tyson to pick us off one by one?" Mendoza asked. Since the discovery of Gabriella's body he'd refused to hike out to the Dark Sector to continue his research. The other studies were also on hold. The plants in the greenhouse were yellowing, Lena too morose to tend to them. Their routine was breaking down.

"Why are you so sure it's Tyson?" Norse replied.

That startled them. They looked at the psychologist uneasily.

"I was never certain myself. I sent him away for his own safety as well as ours. He could still be traveling. His radio could be broken. He could have gotten lost and died. But coming back *here,* to prey on us, seems particularly risky. Where's his Spryte? Where is he surviving? Does Tyson really make sense?"

The survivors looked at each other.

"Who, then?" Hiro Sakura asked.

"My bet is Lewis," Alexi Molotov spoke up.

Abby turned to glare at him.

"Goddammit," Lewis groaned. Yet when he looked around the room for support, everyone except Abby shifted uneasily. Pulaski was staring resolutely away, the butt of his new spear on the floor. Lewis had a sense of foreboding. Something wasn't right.

"Lewis," Molotov insisted. "Who just happens to find all the dead. Who can never account for his whereabouts. Who started all this when he came down here. Who was going to meet Rod when our station manager was knifed. Who has some kind of falling-out with poor Gabriella. Who knows everything about this mysterious meteorite."

"If I was the killer would I lead the way to my own victims?" Lewis retorted.

"Yes, because you know where they are!"

"I didn't find Cameron! Dana did! And I'm tired of being suspected just because I'm the newest! Suspect Doctor Bob! He's almost as new as I am!"

Molotov shrugged. "He didn't come for the meteorite."

"That doesn't make me a killer!"

"Maybe you are innocent. But you do not belong here, because you do not really fit. A geologist doing weather, it is absurd! You are not even a real scientist, you are an oilman. A prospector. A fortune-seeker. You should go, go find Tyson, go to Vostok, go and try to get to McMurdo. Just get out of here before our little group shrinks down to nothing." He glanced around. "Do you realize we have lost five people?"

"Go how?" asked Hank Anderson, the carpenter. "I ain't giving him the last Spryte."

"I would," Dana said.

"Hold up here. Let's not run ahead too fast," Norse cautioned. "No more Sprytes, no more disappearances. We need to consider things slowly, rationally. *Was* Jed the one who led us to Gabriella's body?" He put the question to Abby.

She looked uneasy. "I found it. You know I was going to the attic to find some stuff to entertain us, and Jed didn't . . ." She looked suddenly confused, remembering his reluctance in going up the ladder.

"Did Lewis pick the KitKat Club to meet?" Dana asked.

"No," Abby said, looking at Norse. "Bob did."

"That's right," Norse agreed. "I suggested to Jed and Abby separately that they go out there. I was trying to bring them back together. I wanted to give them a chance to talk on neutral ground."

Lewis was grateful for the candor.

"So it wasn't Jed's choice to go there at all," Dana clarified.

"Which means he *could* be the killer!" Geller reassessed wildly. "He put the body there before Bob suggested he go there!"

"George . . ." Norse began wearily.

"Jed didn't kill Gabriella," Abby insisted. "I'm certain. He's incapable of murdering anyone."

"How do you know that?" Molotov replied. "Are you listening to your head? Or your heart?"

"I saw how shocked he was when we found the body."

"Maybe you remember good acting."

"What about that sign?" Geller interrupted. "That sign around her neck. *You know what I want.* What does that mean?"

"It means somebody's got the million-dollar rock and should put it out where Tyson, or Lewis, or whoever, can get it and leave us alone," Mendoza said.

"It means somebody in this room can end this!" cried

Dana. She jumped up, looking at them wildly. "*You know who you are.* Who is it, then? Who knows what he wants? For the love of God, let's stop this insanity and give it to him!"

"Maybe it's you, Dana," said Steve Calhoun, just to quiet her down.

"And maybe it's you, Steve!"

A babble of voices erupted, angry and afraid. People began pointing.

Norse watched them evenly and Lewis wondered what the psychologist was thinking, watching his little laboratory of rats. It *was* Norse who directed them to the attic. And yet Norse had made no secret of it and had seemed more disturbed than anyone, more surprised than anyone. . . . Where was he going with this meeting?

What was Robert Norse really down here for?

The psychologist held up his hand until the group quieted. "Science, people," he suggested. "Our enemy is unfounded fear and suspicion, and our ally is science. Science! Just like it's been for our kind since the ancient Greeks. Rationality, right? Isn't that what you represent? So, we're going to be rational. We're going to beat this with rationality."

"Doc, this whole situation is completely *irrational,*" Geller said. "That's why we're freaking out. We can't rationalize it."

"Can't we?" Norse asked softly. "That's the issue of our winter, isn't it? Can rationality handle the irrational?"

Lewis looked curiously at the psychologist. Wasn't this the issue he'd mused about over beers in the bar when they first met? Hadn't Norse been anti-science? What did the man truly believe? *Good acting,* Molotov had suggested. Yet what motive did Norse have? What motive did anyone have? How was Gabriella a threat to anyone? Geller was. right. It was all irrational.

"Let's play scientific method," Norse went on. "Let's play by the rules that drive this whole place."

"Bob . . ." Nancy Hodge groaned.

"Hypothesis and experiment, right? Logical progression. And maybe at the end a workable theory that we all agree on, one that lets us decide what action to take. Are you with me? Can we do that?"

The others looked at him uncertainly. Except Pulaski. He was nodding.

"So. What are the possibilities to explain what's going on down here?"

They hesitated like a classroom. "Lunacy," Geller finally mumbled.

"Greed," Mendoza added.

"Some kind of weird vendetta," Dana said. "Terrorism, sort of."

Norse nodded. "Good. Very good. Logic, people, logic. Let's consider the body. Gabriella is found dead, hanged. Suicide?"

"Not from that height," Mendoza said. "No chair to stand on. And why naked? She was probably dead before she was strung up. I say murder. Maybe rape and murder."

"Nancy?" Hodge had inspected the body.

"No semen. She was bruised, scratched. Maybe an attempted rape. I say she went out with a fight." The crowd murmured.

Norse nodded. "Any chance of making an I.D. with clues? Hair? Blood?"

"Not with the instruments I have down here."

The psychologist nodded again, taking a breath. "Okay,

suspects. Possibility one: Tyson somehow came back and did it, for reasons unknown."

"Because he's bloody Jack the Ripper of Amundsen-Scott base!" Dana said.

"Possibility two: Tyson didn't come back and we have a different killer."

Several people looked at Lewis. He looked squarely back at them in disgust.

"Who?" Hiro prompted. He was a scientist. He liked this step-by-step.

"It could be a single killer is responsible for all the deaths: either Tyson, or Tyson was never responsible in the first place and we exiled the wrong man. Alternately, it could be we have a second killer, a copycat killer. It could be the deaths are some weird mix of murder, accident, and suicide."

"They don't seem linked," Geller said. "That's why I say it's a fruitcake."

"And which one of us is that, George?" Mendoza asked lightly.

"I'd say we're all a little balmy," the maintenance man muttered. "Just for being here." There was nervous laughter of agreement.

Norse nodded again. "Other possibilities? What are they, people? Come on, hypothesis."

"Jealous lover," Linda Brown said softly. "She slept around too much. Someone finally got mad." The idea seemed to give her a certain satisfaction. Nobody was sleeping with Linda Brown.

"Okay. So, we consider who slept with her."

"Who didn't?" Calhoun cracked.

"I'll bet you didn't, you horse-faced nail pounder," Gage Perlin said.

"You'n me, Gage, we're the only ones homely enough to be left out! Every other male is suspect!" Calhoun laughed.

The other men said nothing, not wanting to admit or deny a relationship.

"What else?" Norse said.

"Someone trying to sabotage the base," Lewis spoke up. "A foreign agent." He looked at Molotov. *Take that, Russian finger-pointer.* "Maybe Mickey or somebody stumbled on something strategic."

"Someone chasing the meteorite for something other than money," Lena Jindrova suggested. "Maybe it has evidence of Martian life. Something philosophical. Theological."

"Hmmm, interesting," Norse said. "Dana, you read the Bible. Does life on another planet threaten your view of our world?"

"My beliefs are compatible with science. And *I* didn't kill anybody."

"The government playing with our heads," the postdoc Gina Brindisi suggested. She pointed at the psychologist. "They sent you down here to watch us all go nuts."

Norse shrugged to concede the point. "It's true I'm in shrink nirvana. As George said, we're all balmy and getting nuttier by the minute." Uneasy laughter again. "But at this point I'd rather have you sane."

"Maybe they're faking everything," spoke up Gerald Follet. "It's a hoax. They want us to panic, like that radio broadcast of *War of the Worlds.*"

"Except the bodies are real," Geller said glumly. "Take a walk out to Boot Hill if you don't believe that."

"Opportunity," Abby suddenly said. "You've got a score to settle and people are dropping like flies. What better time to murder? It's lost in the crowd."

"That's good," Norse nodded. "I like that one. It could be any of us, taking revenge on anyone." He scanned their faces. People were looking more confused than ever. More wary and suspicious than ever. Lewis didn't like the way the meeting was going. How was this a help?

"What good are these ideas if they're not testable?" Hiro interrupted as if reading Lewis's mind. "We can speculate our way into the grave."

"Good question. Ideas?"

"Somehow figure out who really boinked Gabriella," Geller suggested. "Who was lover enough to care, to be jealous."

"Oh please," Dana groaned.

"No, really. To eliminate some of us."

"That doesn't eliminate anybody," Mendoza said with exasperation. "Maybe it was someone she *wouldn't* sleep with. Maybe it was a jealous woman. Maybe it had nothing to do with her love life."

"Well, then eliminate people who couldn't have been around the victims. Make a spreadsheet of our whereabouts."

"So where were *you,* George, when these deaths occurred?"

"I don't know."

Mendoza threw up his hands in exasperation.

"What about your files?" Abby asked the psychologist quietly. "Don't you have basic information on all of us? Didn't Rod? Doesn't Nancy? Don't you have suspicions?"

Norse opened his mouth as if to speak and then stopped a moment, as if considering the idea for the first time. "Not from the files. You all left the box next to 'Are you a murderer?' blank on your application forms. Making someone a murderer on the basis of a psychological screening test is a little reckless, don't you think?" There was a slight edge to his voice as he replied to her, this woman who'd turned him down.

Abby looked unsatisfied. He hadn't denied having a suspicion.

"I don't see that this discussion is getting us anywhere," Molotov complained. "I have *my* suspicion, which I have voiced." He looked again at Lewis. "But unless someone wants to confess, we are no closer than before. It is a nice try, Doctor Bob, but you cannot rationalize what makes no sense."

"You can't rationalize without *information*," Norse corrected. Now he looked directly at Lewis. Suddenly he was the teacher, a lesson about to become apparent. "I've led you through this speculative exercise to demonstrate the dangers of jumping to conclusions, but I've also done a little investigation of my own. Since the shock of finding Gabriella I've considered all the possibilities you just voiced, thought of all the ways a murderer might leave clues. Everything we know is circumstantial, but in our desperate situation maybe that has to be enough. Wade?"

Pulaski stood up. He had positioned himself between Lewis and the door. The cook stood with his legs apart, as if bracing for attack, and looked somber, even sad, his new spear his staff. "You all know what good little recyclers we are," the cook began. There were smiles and a few snickers. They were supposed to separate all trash into labeled containers in the cold of the dome. Miscreants who dropped things into the wrong bin brought a regular outburst from Linda Brown, who was in charge of the recycling program. She'd threatened to kill one or two. Hyperbole, of course, but the bins had been one more source of casual tension. "We have no incinerator at the Pole. We have no dump. Everything that flies into the Pole eventually flies out of it. Every bit of garbage we've generated this winter is still here."

He paused. They were quiet, waiting.

"The sign around Gabriella's neck was made from letters cut from a magazine. So I looked in the paper bin for its source. What I found at the bottom was this." He held up a copy of a popular science and environmental journal. "It has an article on meteorites." He flipped it open, showing ragged pages. "And a lot of letters cut out from the middle."

Norse was looking at Lewis. "And where's the cover, Wade?" he asked the cook. "Where's the address label that will tell us whose magazine it was?"

"It was Jed!" Dana gasped. "I've seen him read that. We all have!"

"From the library . . ." Lewis objected.

"Torn off and missing," Pulaski said. He nodded at Dana. "So I checked Jed's room. Couldn't find a thing except . . ."

"Yes?"

"There were ashes in the soup can I'd given him the first night to use as a chamber pot. He'd never bothered to give it back."

Lewis stood up, his head dizzy, dumbfounded by a combination of outrage and fear. He was being set up. "That's a lie," he choked. Everyone was looking at him. Even Abby looked confused.

"I've bagged them for lab analysis in the spring," Pulaski said, holding up a baggie. "Maybe the lab people can tell if they came from the magazine stock. In the meantime . . ."

"This is absurd, those ashes could have come from anywhere."

"I saw you reading it!" Dana yelled.

"The magazine must have been stolen—"

"See! This is what I am telling you!" Molotov shouted. "Lewis, Lewis, Lewis! Every time it is Jed Lewis!"

"The hell it is!"

"What do you propose we do, Alexi?" Norse asked quietly.

"If there is only one more Spryte, then I agree, I don't want to give it to a murderer. If we cannot send Lewis away, then I do not want him wandering around. We need to lock him up. I don't trust him."

"Dammit, I'm being framed! That's no proof!"

"There is no proof of your innocence, either."

"Guilty until proven innocent, right, Alexi?" Lewis said heatedly. "Like Tyson? Is that how you did it in the gulags?"

The Americans shifted uncomfortably.

"Prove that you did *not* do it," the Russian insisted. "Everyone saw you with Gabriella. No one saw her since."

"I did *not* cut up that magazine," Lewis insisted. "Wouldn't I hide it? Would I leave the ashes in my own damn room? Think, dammit!"

"This is what we are doing, thinking about what has happened!"

The silence was thick, a congealing presumption of guilt.

"So we put him in the sauna," Pulaski suddenly summed up. He'd thought this through. "Just to be safe. It's our thickest box. We can put a crossbeam outside the door. We keep him locked down until this is resolved. He's right, it isn't proof, but we can't prove he didn't do it, either. Or anyone else. So I say safety is priority one. No more wandering around. No one leaves the dome. No one even goes down the archways to the generators or the fuel. We block up the entrances so no one can exit the dome and no one can enter. We search every inch of this aluminum beanie. We watch each other. We enter a state of siege."

"That sounds like a police state," Mendoza said.

"No, Carl. A state with police. A citizen militia. Us. So no one else has to die."

Mendoza frowned, considering it.

"Another thing," Pulaski said. "That means the science goes on hold."

"NSF isn't going to like that," Norse pointed out.

"Fuck NSF. If they're not getting their data, maybe they'll figure out some way to resolve this thing. Send in an FBI agent like we've talked about. Get us the hell out of here. Something."

There was a murmur of approval. Enough was enough.

"This is a radical decision to lock Lewis up," Norse said. "To lock the rest of ourselves in. I think it has to be a group decision."

"What about our work?" Lewis protested. "I thought we were all down here for the research. What about Jim Sparco's data? Global warming? We won't get anything done with what you're proposing!"

"And I say no more victims," Pulaski responded. "No more sacrificial sheep. This is a state of emergency until we can get out of here, get help, get something. If we block up the entrances no one can get us from outside. None of us can wander off to be picked off. We arm everybody. I train everybody. If a killer strikes, I want it to be a fight. I want noise. I want screaming. I want the attacker so bloody punctured with wounds that there's no question who did it. And then I want to fry him myself." He looked at them fiercely.

"It's liable to feel a little claustrophobic," Norse cautioned.

"Winter's already claustrophobic," Pulaski said. "Better claustrophobic than dead." Most of the others nodded. It was time to bar the door. It was time to pen Jed Lewis. The geologist looked around for support and saw none. Abby was looking morosely at the floor, outnumbered, alone, and confused by doubts.

"You can make a fight of it or you can cooperate," Pulaski told him. "*I'm* not saying it's you. I'm saying we won't know it's *not* you until we remove you as a variable. Like we tried to do at Clean Air."

"Except he goes in the storm when Harrison dies," Molotov said. "Calls Rod when Cameron dies."

Slowly Lewis sat down, dizzy with fear.

"Another thing," Geller said. "I say no more censorship. No more e-mail cancellation, no more radio silence. It's time the world knows what's going on down here, not just the bureaucrats at NSF. It's time we screamed bloody murder."

"Damn right!" Dana said.

"I understand what you're saying." Norse looked uneasy. "I know we need help. But before we get on the horn, hollering our heads off, let's cool the jets a minute. We've got a new polar base planned. We've got a hundred million dollars riding on how these events are characterized in the media. If you guys get on the net and start yelling for your mothers, it's going to sound like Charles Manson."

"So?" Geller asked.

"The whole polar program could be in jeopardy."

"And with our lives at stake, how many of us give a rat's ass about the polar program right now, Doctor Bob?" Pulaski demanded.

Norse waited, letting the question add weight. "I don't know," he said softly. "How many?"

People shifted uncomfortably. "It's survival, Doctor," Dana said quietly.

"What do you propose to say to your friends? Who can help you? What good is it to contact them right now except to worry them needlessly?"

"I'll bet they're worried already by not hearing from us," Dana said.

"I'm just suggesting we give NSF a chance to handle this."

"Screw that," said Geller. "They should've parachuted an investigator in the minute Mickey disappeared. They've left us swinging in the wind. I say we tell the world what's going on."

Norse's eyes polled the room. They were against him on this one.

"All right," he surrendered. "Broadcast your panic. Destroy this station. Maybe *that's* what the killer wants."

"We're bottled up," Pulaski said defensively. "We need release."

"You're also professionals. I thought."

The two men looked at each other.

"I can't stop you," Norse said. "I know that."

Pulaski hesitated. He was a cook, not a beaker. Norse had unconscious rank. Norse was looking at a bigger picture. "Okay, then how about this," he said reluctantly, looking at the others. "We have leverage, people. Leverage! It's like Doctor Bob says—we broadcast this in the right way and we can turn this station into a fiasco. Too unstable. End all funding for it. Close it up and send it packing. And that's our stick with NSF! Let's call them, and tell them what we've discussed, and give them twenty-four hours to figure out a way to get us out of here. I don't care if it's the space shuttle or a dog sled, we deserve to go home. And if they can't do that, *then* we talk about this to the world. The world! Let the chips fall where they may."

"Twenty-four hours isn't much time," Norse said.

"They've had time and done nothing."

The others nodded.

Norse took an unhappy breath. "All right. Deal. Let me talk to them on the phone when the satellites come in view. I agree, they need to know how antsy we all are. I'll talk to them about Lewis, about Tyson, about everyone. Let me think of what I want to say and we should be ready to phone in"—he looked at his watch—"an hour, say."

"I want to hear what you tell them," Geller said.

"And I don't want to talk as a committee. They'll get a babble and things will be more confused than ever. Give me a chance, okay? A chance to save the winter. One day. Clyde Skinner will be helping and he can listen. Okay, Clyde?" Skinner was their radioman.

He nodded.

"Meet me there in an hour to fire things up," Norse said.

It was enough. Everyone appeared to agree on this compromise.

"Jed goes into the sauna, at least for the time being. And Cueball, why don't you start figuring how to lock us in, like you said? Our world shrinks down to this dome. Spaceship Pulaski." Norse looked at them and took a breath. The group was still under control. If nothing more happened, maybe they could make it.

"I'll do my best to resolve this thing," Norse promised.

CHAPTER TWENTY-THREE

The explosion was so muffled that at first it was more puzzling than alarming, sounding in the galley like a flat, mysterious *whump*. Then the alarm began ringing. Fire! It was the one deadly threat they constantly drilled for: In the dry air of the Pole, combustibles could flash into fire like gasoline, and liquid water to douse them was in chronic short supply. Reaction was instantaneous and automatic. People jerked to their feet, chairs toppling over, a coffee cup spilled. This was no overcooked pig, it was the real thing! Not bothering to dress, they crashed out the galley door and sprinted for assigned extinguishers and hoses. There was a haze in the air of the dome.

"Where's it coming from!" Pulaski yelled.

Smoke was drifting out of one end of Comms, he saw, its aluminum wall bulging like a blister. The radio room! The cook called for help and then waved their dead run to a halt, feeling the outside of the metal module for heat before cautiously opening a door. A gust of smoky gases rolled out, stinking and ominous. From inside came an agonized screaming.

"Christ," Pulaski muttered, shining a flashlight into the murk. "What more can happen? Was Doctor Bob in there?"

Everyone looked around. Norse was nowhere to be seen.

Gina Brindisi had the presence of mind to run around the end of the building to a crack where the building had split like a swollen can, and then spray fire retardant through the hole into the communications center. Pulaski, Geller, and Calhoun donned fire masks and pushed into the corridor, squirting halon and hunting for survivors. The screaming was horrible. When they reached the radio room it was dark and smoky, illuminated by spurts of sparks. Puffs of chemical from the extinguishers made the last orange flames snuff out and then their flashlights and headlamps swept the wreckage. Pulaski dropped to the floor, groping for Norse, and touched a body. A wounded man was writhing in agony with his hands over his face, his skin burnt off from an explosion of acid. The cook gripped the man and leaned close, peering through his mask. It was Clyde Skinner, their radioman.

"I'm blinded!"

"What happened, what happened?" Pulaski kept shouting the question through his mask but it was obvious Skinner was in no condition to answer. What breath he could suck in was used to scream.

"Oh my God, I can't see!"

The communications center was destroyed. Its bank of lead batteries had exploded, shattering the equipment and spraying the room with acid. The explosion had caught Skinner full force, dissolving his face. It was almost unlucky he was alive.

Nancy Hodge pushed into the room, took in the wreckage at a glance, and knelt beside Skinner. She looked sickened. "Where the hell is Bob?"

"We don't know."

"Well, help me get Skinner to sick bay! We've got to wash him!"

The trio of men lifted the radioman and carried him out to the cold and clear air of the dome. Someone came at them with a bucket to douse Skinner and wash the acid, but Hodge stopped it. "Not here! It will just freeze on his face!"

"I'm blind! Oh, how it hurts!"

Everyone was looking at him in horror. "He'll be begging for more morphine than we have," Nancy said. "More relief than we can give. Go on, get him into sick bay!"

Skinner's screams faded like a disappearing train as they carried him off.

"Now I'm really getting pissed," Pulaski muttered, glowering for a culprit and finding none. Lewis was already locked up. "Really, really pissed."

"You can't blame Jed for this one," Abby told him.

"Really? Let's figure out what happened first."

"We found Doctor Bob!" someone shouted.

Norse was sitting on the floor of Cameron's old office next to Comms, dazed and coughing in the lingering smoke. He appeared to have been knocked unconscious in the blast. Furniture was awry, papers on the floor like snow. "I was getting ready to make the call!" he choked. "What the hell happened?"

"The worst, near as I can tell," Pulaski told him.

"Clyde said he had to crank up the radios!"

"He cranked them up, all right."

They lifted the psychologist to his feet, Norse blinking from the concussion of the blast. Losing him would cut them from their last anchor. They led him back into the radio room, where everything stank of burnt plastic and rubber. At a glance it was apparent their normal connection to the outside world had been wiped out. "I don't understand what happened," Norse muttered.

"The batteries blew up," said Charles Longfellow, their electrician.

"Yes, but why?"

"They were probably charging. You told us to pull the plug on this place during the communications blackout and the batteries ran down. Clyde had to bring them up again with the generator. Charging always creates hydrogen and oxygen gases, which is the stuff that blew up the *Hindenburg*. Normally it vents off okay but a spark or a match . . ."

"Clyde didn't smoke."

"No, something else. . . ." Longfellow was leaning over the wrecked radios and computers, looking for a clue. "There, maybe."

They looked. Two crossing wires, now blackened and bubbled, had frayed down to metal. "When Clyde flipped the radios on, the current could have caused a short," the electrician pointed out. "If the gases weren't venting, then . . . bang. But I thought the battery compartment had a vent."

They went outside. A sheet of plywood had been shot outward by the explosion. Longfellow kicked it. "This could have been leaning up against the hole," he said, "blocking it."

"Deliberately?" Norse asked.

The electrician just looked at him.

"And the wires. Don't you check them?"

"Twice a year," Longfellow said. "At the beginning and end of summer season. They were fine. There's no reason for them to be abraded like that."

"So what happened?"

He looked at the ruptured building. "Someone wanted this to happen. The bastard didn't just destroy our radios, he shorted out the linkages to the machines and radios on the rest of the station. This place was a hub. Now we're deaf and dumb."

"But why?"

"Someone planned this before Clyde ever threw a switch to recharge the batteries. Someone wanted to destroy our communications. Someone doesn't want us talking about Jed Lewis."

They were panicked now, their vulnerability to accident or sabotage made clear. No one slept for the next twenty-two hours as they fortified their enclosure from a threat they didn't understand. There was no sun anyway, no natural clock, and no place to escape to. Only a suffocating paranoia that seemed to settle on the dome with the weight of the polar night. Pulaski had become transformed by the explosion, a metamorphosis that shed the cook and returned the old soldier. He was Crockett at the Alamo, girding for battle. The garage was ransacked for metal, wood, welding torches, and tools. Brackets were welded in a shower of sparks and beams were placed against the bay doors. Latches were fastened for the smallest doors and fastened with wire, cutters issued to sentries. Their greatest points of vulnerability were the fuel tanks and the generators, and so the fuel arch behind BioMed and the opposite arch leading to Pika Taylor's machines were walled up completely. A frame was built across both half sections of tunnel, and sheets of plywood and metal were nailed across it to prevent any kind of access at all.

"*I* still know how to get in," Pika said quietly. "No one else has to know. No one else has to get to my machines."

He looked from face to face, a slight grin as he regarded them. "You kill *me,* you die."

The work went in shifts, one group hammering and welding while another warmed up in the galley and gulped down coffee to stay awake. No one was sleeping until they were certain Antarctica was walled off: that Buck Tyson or some malevolent ghost wasn't somehow sneaking into the dome to wreak murder and sabotage, revenge and psychic terror. That some traitor in their midst was not plotting a final catastrophe. The rest of the station was to be abandoned for the time being, the Dark Sector and Clean Air left to slumber in the snow. "We're a turtle," Pulaski explained. "We're drawing into our shell."

The cook insisted that everyone, without exception, be armed. Tyson's old locker was broken into and the knives he'd made were distributed to whoever didn't have one. The recipients regarded them a little dubiously.

"Amundsen-Scott Base," the blade of one read, the legend bracketed by penguins. There wasn't a penguin within eight hundred miles.

"What if we start going after each other with these things?" Gina protested. Like everyone else, she was so cold and sore she could hardly move. The frenzy of getting the dome sealed was holding off their terror but they were also close to a breaking point. Losing Comms had wrung them out. The damage to their communications would take days to repair, especially with Skinner blinded and Abby morose.

"I am a little concerned about arming people to the teeth," Norse admitted. He'd deferred to Pulaski's military expertise in locking up the dome but seemed uneasy with the cook's new martial authority. It had eclipsed his own. "Tempers are short. People are jumpy."

"And so far no more of us are dead," Pulaski answered grimly. "We tried it one way, with all of us wandering around like blind sheep and getting picked off one by one. Now let's try it another way. Strategic deterrence, people. Mutual assured destruction. You take a predator like a mountain lion and they'll back off if you fight back. They don't want to risk injury. They *can't* risk injury, because if they get hurt they starve. If our murderer is someone other than Lewis, then he or she can't risk injury, either, because they'll be found out. You get jumped, make sure you draw blood. Die if you have to, but scream bloody hell first."

"Jeez, Cueball," Geller said. "Enough drill instructor dramatics, okay?"

"You people are almost asleep on your feet. You need some dramatics."

"I just don't know that we're up to stabbing people," Dana said tiredly.

"Well, someone might be up to stabbing *you*. That make a difference?"

The New Zealander looked at him gloomily.

"Come here, Dana," Pulaski suddenly said.

"What bloody for?"

"Come here." It was an order and she complied against her own wishes, walking over to the cook. He turned her around to face the others. "You're my Raggedy Ann for a little knife lesson."

"Oh please," she groaned. "I just want to go to my bloody bed."

"Now, listen," he said to the others in the galley. "The whole point of this is that you *don't* get attacked. That any killer knows that open season is over. But if you *are* attacked, you don't want to pussy around, right? You want to stop an assailant so they can't stop you, cut them so they can't cut you, make them go down and stay down so you can run for help. Right? Otherwise all you do is piss them off."

They looked at him with exhaustion.

"Stay here a moment," he told Dana. He went to the kitchen and came back with a jar of spaghetti sauce and a basting brush.

"Wade, Jesus Christ, come on—"

"Stand still. This might save your life. Our lives." He dipped in the brush.

"Please . . ."

He dabbed a splotch of red under her nose and she started. "Hit them here, under the nose. Try to break it. Try to push it upward. It will hurt like hell. If you're lucky, the cartilage will be shoved into the brain and the frontal lobes will bleed and they'll go down permanently." He dipped again and painted her throat. "Hit here. Under the Adam's apple for men is a good pain point. It can chop off air for either sex. With a weapon you can cut an artery, with a blow you can collapse the windpipe. Don't screw around! Don't give your opponent time to do it to you! Not unless you want to get laid out in the snow with Gabriella Reid."

Dana looked at him with distaste.

He dipped again and aimed toward the hollow behind her clavicle. "Next pain point—"

"No." She stepped away, raising her own knife. "Enough. Stay away from me, Cueball. I'm not some damned American killer mercenary."

"Excellent reaction, Dana. Get that knife up. This is *exactly* my point. I want to *make* you a damned killer mercenary."

"So I declare my graduation. Enough with the sauce."

She walked away and slumped in a chair, throwing her knife with a clatter on the table.

He turned to the others, pointing with the brush. "The solar plexus, right under the rib cage. The abdomen. Breasts if it's a woman, balls if it's a man. The eyes. The ears. Anywhere you can inflict pain. Any way you can get the other guy to hesitate, back off, go down. Listen, I know it's grim, but I'm tired of people dying like rabbits. You gotta look after yourself. I've climbed, I've rafted, I've jumped, I've shot. Look for yourself. Check your own chute. Sharpen your own bayonet. Lock and load, people."

"You're scaring me with all this army stuff," Gina said. "You're going to make us fear every man and woman on this base."

"That's right, Gina. Fear is the one thing that might just keep you alive." He looked at the others. "At the end of the winter, that's all that counts."

"Is that all?" Geller asked wearily.

"No. When we finish boarding things up, I think it would be smart to search each other again as well."

Lewis was dreaming of Arabia. He was on a flat plain, stony and hot, looking for oil. The sky was white, the horizon watery, and he was uneasy because if he didn't find his prize soon he'd lose his job. The oil was under one of the rocks, he knew, but every stone looked alike. Each was the shape of a potato, burnt and glassy, and he was having to turn them over one by one to find what he was looking for. Finally he turned one over and was startled to see a face looking up at him. It was a woman, buried in the sand, her long hair made of strands of quartz and mica. He stepped back in surprise and she rose up out of the desert, robed, her gown made of silicon. It was a gray, shimmering, translucent thing, her body perfect beneath it. The woman was looking at him boldly and he heard himself think, *I don't know you,* and then the gown turned to sand and slid away, leaving the woman naked except for specks of quartz on her shoulders and thighs and breasts like a scattering of glitter. The merciless glare from the sun turned a cool blue directly above her, a small dark circle giving her a column of shade. Except the woman was now Abby, her hair shorter and her expression shy, and the glitter wasn't sand, it was specks of ice.

Lewis awoke groggily, his dream penetrated by a tapping. The sauna was pitch-black and stuffy, the bench where he lay hard and uncomfortable. He sat up. Someone was knocking at his door. It was the latest in a series of noises that had bewildered him—an explosion, alarms, hammerings, drills, saws. Despite his shouts, no one ever came to explain what was going on. It was like he'd been locked in the sauna and abandoned. It was like being buried in the old base. It was like freezing to death in the pit where they'd found Mickey Moss. His claustrophobia had come back to him.

"Who's there?" His voice was thick, doped from sleep.

"It's Abby. Can I talk to you?"

He was frustrated and embarrassed at his plight. In the end she'd stopped trying to defend him. In the end she hadn't known who to believe. "Go away."

"Jed, please, we're in danger. You've got to let me in."

He didn't answer.

"I'm sorry that I didn't say more in the galley. I was quiet because I had to think things through. I had to trust, first."

"Trust what?"

"Trust who to believe."

He sat there brooding tiredly, feeling angry and frustrated. There was no chance to prove anything to anyone now, locked up in here.

"I decided to believe you," she said.

"Well, hell." He flicked on the sauna light. Pulaski had barred the door from the outside as he'd promised, preventing Lewis from escaping his makeshift prison. But he'd also left the latch working on the inside, preventing anyone from getting in that Lewis didn't want to see.

"We can't afford a guard to protect us from you, and we can't afford a guard to protect you from us," the cook had growled. "I don't want some vigilante coming in here and beating the crap out of you until we know what's going on. So lock the damn door from the inside and don't open it up for anyone but me. Okay?"

Lewis had nodded. He wasn't even going to open it to Pulaski until he was so damn hungry and thirsty that he had to face the cook. Until then he wanted to be alone in his depression, willing himself mentally ten thousand miles from the Pole.

Yet did he? He felt so isolated. And Abby . . .

He cautiously opened the door, fearing a mob behind her, but it was only the woman. She quickly slipped inside, latching it behind her.

"Jed, I need help," she whispered.

"*You* need help? What the hell is going on out there, anyway?"

"We're completely cut off from the outside world and we're making prisoners of ourselves. Comms blew up and—"

"What?"

"The batteries exploded. They think it was sabotage. It knocked out the power grid to the outside buildings and everyone's gone nuts. They've barricaded all the entrances with beams and bolts and they're building walls to block off the fuel arch and the generators because that's where we're most vulnerable. We can't get to the fuel and we can't get to the gym and garage anymore. Only Pika knows how to get around them; he's the only one mild enough that everyone trusts him. And *he's* become some kind of hypochondriac, running off to BioMed all the time like he has a case of the runs. The rest of us are in prison, just like you. They're walling us in against a boogeyman nobody is really sure is out there, until they rebuild the communications hub. It's like a kettle coming to a boil and they've screwed down the lid. I'm worried the whole place is going to explode. I'm worried we're building a firetrap."

"Jesus." He rubbed his head wearily. "What the hell am I supposed to do about it? I'm locked up."

"I've been thinking about things and I think I need to unlock you."

"Escape?"

"Reconnoiter. Get out to a computer that works and try to figure out what's going on. Before it's too late."

"What do you mean?"

"Pulaski has armed *everybody*. He gave a class and painted poor Dana with glops of spaghetti sauce to show where the lethal parts are. He said we're all warriors, we're all deputies. He said it's like the arms race. People are strutting around like gladiators and someone's going to get hurt. Hiro *did* get hurt: He was tired and got in a quarrel with Alexi and the Russian cut his hand and now it's all bandaged up and Alexi is in a funk about the whole thing because it's just the kind of craziness he's been accusing *you* of. Hiro's terrified of him. All the rooms have been searched again, this time throwing everything into the open. There's no privacy left, no dignity. If something more happens, I'm afraid they'll come looking for a scapegoat. Looking for you."

"They can't blame anything on me when I'm in here."

"Some people already have. Someone prepped Comms to explode before it happened. Something to do with the wires and batteries. It was a booby trap, and Clyde had his entire face burnt off. He might even die. So who did that?"

"Not me."

"The same somebody who killed Gabriella."

Lewis shut his eyes in weariness. "Does Norse know you're here?"

"No." She glanced sideways as if he might be watching. "He led the others into sealing you off, and I think it's deliberate. He doesn't want me talking to you. Or you talking to anyone."

"Why?"

"He called me in after you were locked up, after the explosion, and said he understood my support for you but that Gabriella's death had changed everything, changed his own thinking. Then he showed me the note."

"*What* note?"

"He said he found it in Rod Cameron's desk drawer. It says Rod can save his career by giving you the meteorite, and it's signed . . . by you." She was watching him.

"Come on. I didn't write that note."

"It had your name."

"It's a forgery, Abby. It has to be. This is all so crazy! Norse, or Rod, or someone, is screwing me. They're out to turn us against each other."

"He said he hadn't shown it to the others yet but if more bad things continued to happen they might have to ask you some hard questions."

"Hard questions?"

"Jed, I think he wants to interrogate you. Break you, somehow."

"To hell with that."

"I'm just telling you that you can't stay here waiting for things to play out."

Now he was suspicious. The paranoia was infectious. He looked at her narrowly, suddenly wary. "Bob put you up to this, didn't he? He wants me to try to escape. He'll use it against me."

"No! But he wants to turn your head around, just like what's happening now. He twists everything. He objects to Pulaski in public and then confers with him in private. He's playing him. Playing you, playing me. There's something wrong—"

"Wait a minute! I did sign it!" Lewis had remembered.

"What?"

"A piece of paper, the first day I came here. We were joking around about psychology and handwriting analysis and Bob had me sign something. . . ." His eyes were distant, trying to recall what Norse had done with the paper. "I *did* sign it. What the hell, has this been a setup from the beginning?"

Abby looked intrigued. "You think he planned this?"

"I don't know what to think. That far ahead?"

"What if Mickey was right and it was Bob who took my picture?" she asked. "That's what I've been thinking about. What if *he* planted it on Moss?"

"But why?"

"To confuse us. Make us think Mickey might have committed suicide. Put pressure on me to see how'd I react."

"You think Norse is responsible for all this?"

"What do we really know about him? He's a fingie just like you. He came down at the last minute just like you."

"To figure us out."

"Or bewilder us."

"But he's been holding things together."

"Has he?"

"Jesus." He thought a minute, trying to go back over events. Norse had admitted he'd heard where Mickey might have hidden the meteorite. Norse had been out in the storm when Adams died. Norse had helped Tyson flee. . . ."But why?"

"That's what you've got to find out. You're the one person who can sneak out of the dome right now and not be missed. The one person with time to wait for the satellites and get on the Internet. The one person who will ask who Robert Norse really is."

"I thought you said the radios and the computers are down."

"The hub at Comms is destroyed. But if you could get to another source of power and shunt some electricity to Clean Air, you could still use the machines out here."

"*If* I can get to another source of power."

"There's an emergency generator at the Hypertats at Bedrock Village."

"Can I start it?"

"You could try. I think it might work. I think that's why Bob has allowed Pulaski to wall up the dome. He doesn't want us getting out there, calling out. All the doors are locked now. The perimeter is patrolled."

"So how the hell am *I* going to get out there?"

"That's why I came here. Look, everyone's exhausted. Almost everyone's asleep. They've been up for hours and hours, locking us in. I'm blitzed, too, but I was going crazy, thinking about Bob, thinking about you, so I couldn't sleep and got up and wandered outside and I just sort of collapsed in the snow under the dome, utterly defeated, just lying there, and then a snowflake hit me in the eye. You know how that feels? Between a kiss and a sting. So I stood up and then all these little snowflakes were sticking to me...."

He looked at her in wonder. It was like the image from his dream.

"Then I realized what we had all overlooked."

Error of Judgment

For three days I was a hero. Then the weather cleared, recovery teams ventured out on the ice below Wallace Wall, and the bodies began to be recovered. Some goober of a deputy sheriff, who probably watched too much Columbo *and talked like a Mayberry hick, started to yodel about the neatly clipped end of the line still attached to the corpses of Chisel Chin and Carrot Top. I professed shocked innocence—I'd left both fine young men on the ledge with the others. Just why the devil they were roped and how they'd fallen (were they trying to climb out on their own?) was a mystery to me. But then why was my own line broken? There were the beginnings of awkward questions of just who had been roped to whom. I expressed grieving outrage, of course, at any implication of negligence or wrongdoing. I had risked my life to save those kids! To save that whale Fat Boy! But the holier-than-thou crowd wanted to know why I had saved myself. Slow-talking Deputy Goober wouldn't shut up about it, even though he didn't have the balls to go down the cliff himself and look for evidence—like a knife secreted in a convenient crevice. Finally the university had to exert some pressure on the sheriff because of fear of a lawsuit. The matter of exactly just what did happen on the mountain was not-so-quietly dropped, despite the confused bleating of bereaved parents. And that was that. I'd done my best and was prepared to get on with my life.*

Except my application for tenure was denied.

They wouldn't let it drop.

They wouldn't let it drop!

Barney Fife, deputy dipshit, kept nosing around. The whispering started. The peer reviews of my research papers began to get very much more pointed, very pointed indeed. They started murmuring about me in the campus coffee shop—I could feel the stares!—and plotting against me in the department. They denied it, of course, but I knew what was happening. I knew it! The file cabinets that were locked, the meetings called without notifying me they were being held, the evasive looks, the papers turned upside down on desks so I couldn't read them, the hollow sympathies. God, did I know it! Friends became distant. A woman I thought I felt something for became chillingly remote. No charge was ever brought and no charge was needed—my life had become intolerable. I'd been sentenced without being charged. So one day I just walked away.

Let me be perfectly clear about exactly what happened on that mountain. An act of individual and immature foolishness by a single overweight student led to leadership miscalculation, group panic, and a brutal winnowing based on skill and common sense. The strongest, clearest thinker had survived. It was as pure an experiment in natural selection as one could hope for. So don't call me lucky! I was not blessed! I was realistic. Brutally, coldly, and rationally realistic. No one was going to save me, so I saved myself. Once my companions slipped, I didn't have any chance of saving the others. With their trust in each other they had all doomed themselves. The ropes that bound us together had proved to be gossamer threads long before I brought out my knife. I am merely the surviving witness to the fragility of society. Any society.

*Do you see my point? We are alone in life. We can't
know another person. We can't join with another person.
We are islands, made of either rock . . . or sand. Anything
else is delusion.*

I found that out when everyone turned on me.

*I acquired another position and began to labor to doc-
ument this point. I plowed into psychological and sociological research and combed through history. Cooperation
comes only through coercion. It's so obvious when you
look at the literature! Everything else is a fraud. Progress
is achieved by the natural selection of the superior individual, and it is individual vision that drives or destroys
the group.*

*No one would listen, of course. My realization col-
lided with their cozy dreams of group comfort. Social security! The American myth of democracy, teamwork,
compromise. The whispers followed, the looks, the suspicions. I saw it everywhere: in the supermarket, at the
bank, in my office. Everyone looking at me strangely,
thinking the worst of my quite defensible actions, blaming me for having the courage to survive. I saw it!*

*So. How to prove my point? How to demonstrate that
I really had no choice?*

*Imagine a small society in a harsh environment. Imag-
ine one that could be kept in experimental isolation for
eight long, dark months. Imagine applying sufficient
stress that group solidarity is tested. Imagine forcing each
individual to realize how completely alone he or she
really is.*

*The National Science Foundation ignored me, of
course. They dismissed my carefully constructed application. They really had no clue as to the significance of
the social experiment they had unwittingly constructed*

*at the Pole. It was all astronomy and climatology to them,
instruments and data. No vision of the future, no understanding of our grim evolutionary future in the cold black-
ness of space.*

*So. Everyone ignored me. My papers went unpublished.
My grant proposals were rejected. My every step dogged
by ugly rumor. I was broke, desperate, humiliated.*

And then, destiny.

*Can you possibly imagine what an arrogant, boorish
prick Robert Norse really was? I met him at a professional conference when he was boasting of his assignment to Antarctica. His assignment to the Pole, precisely
the place where I wanted to go! He blathered on mind-
lessly, gloating, stuffed full of himself, not having even
the merest pathetic clue of just how unfairly his own good
fortune had erased my own. He was going to a place he
didn't begin to understand. And along the way, he was
trekking in New Zealand.*

A few months later, I read about his disappearance.

*Do you believe in miracles? I'm a rational man, a
man of science, and yet sometimes opportunity presents
itself in so deliciously glorious a way that one can't help
but wonder at the secret workings of the universe. The
dark wood. It occurred to me that if I could not compete
with Robert Norse, I had to become Robert Norse. I had
to act decisively, just as I had on that cliff. And everything after that just . . . happened.*

I acted on the best plan I had at the time.

CHAPTER TWENTY-FOUR

This is completely insane," Lewis said.

"Which is why it just might work in a place like this," Abby replied.

It was past midnight and most of the winter-overs were asleep with whatever dreams plagued them, wrung out from their frenzy to barricade the dome. Only Gage Perlin, their plumber, was making hourly rounds as the designated sentry of the witching-hour watch. In preparation Abby had raided Jerry Follett's crate of atmospheric sampling equipment that was tucked against one wall of the dome, taking a small weather balloon and a gas canister. She'd filched and concealed a 150-foot length of sturdy rope, a lighter tether line half that length, a pack with a flashlight, two ice axes, and a coil of wire. Now she crouched behind the ruptured Comms building to fill the balloon while Lewis used first tape, then wire, and finally rope to bind the two ice ax prongs at right angles to each other. More tape fused the handles. The result was a crude approximation of a grappling hook. Tied to the climbing rope, it would be hoisted aloft by the balloon.

"What if somebody sees us?" Lewis had worried.

"They're worn out. Besides, how much more locked up can we be than we already are?"

In a grave, he thought, but didn't say that. There was a fierceness about Abby now that he found exciting. Infectious. Her own decisive energy had ignited his own. They weren't even sure what they were fighting, but they were at least beginning to fight back.

The pair peered around the corner and heard and saw nothing. "We have to do this quickly," Lewis said. "Maybe twenty minutes before Gage comes through again."

They briskly walked across the snowy floor to the center of the dome, pulling the bobbing balloon behind them. The gas bag was tied to a tether line that in turn was fastened by a slip knot to the makeshift grappling hook. The climbing rope hung from the hook. It was a bizarre plan made necessary by their bizarre entrapment. Norse and Pulaski had sealed every entrance to the structure except the most obvious one: the opening at the top of the dome that Jed had seen on his first day, left permanently open like a smoke hole in a kiva to allow air circulation. Looked at from below it was like the eyepiece of a telescope, giving a glimpse of a few bright stars and the outside world.

Lewis let the medicine-ball-sized balloon go, holding on to its light tether. It shot up faster than he expected and the line writhed like a flagellum until Abby grabbed it and controlled its ascent through her fingers. Then hook lifted off and the two lines uncoiled upward together at a steady pace, swimming in the night.

When the helium orb bumped against the icicles overhead a few broke off and fell, forcing the pair to duck. Fortunately, the frozen spikes plunged noiselessly into the snow in the center of the dome instead of banging against

the roof of the modules. They stuck out from the ground
like knives.

"Careful!" Abby hissed.

"Help me pull it over."

They gingerly tugged on the lines to lower the balloon
slightly and bring it under the hole. Then they let rope out
again and the orb popped free. Once the gas bag was above
the crest of the dome, the wind took it like a fish after bait,
the ropes yanked taut. When their grappling hook was carried to the lee side of the opening they hauled sharply
down, letting the ice axes wedge against the outside of the
roof. As the pair threw their weight against it the aluminum
bent slightly, snugging the ax heads tightly against the rim.
Lewis jerked on the tether to free the slip knot and the balloon lurched upward and soared away into the night, the
tether snaking up and out of sight. Remaining were the hook
and its climbing rope, hanging downward from the vent
hole. He sighted up the line's length, trying to judge its bite
on the roof. It just might hold.

He gave her a kiss of partnership. "I'll be back before
Pika wakes up to check the generators."

"Just get up the rope first."

Scaling a rope five stories high by grip alone required
considerable strength and risked a bad fall. Lewis instead
used a trick he'd learned years ago while mountaineering.
Two loops resembling hangman's nooses and called Prusik
loops were tied with light line and hung on the main rope
with slip knots, so they could be pulled up or down the
main line. He slid one two feet above the snow and slipped
his boot into its loop. As he put his weight on it, stepping
up off the snow, the slip knot tightened and friction held
the loop firmly in place like a foothold, giving him his first
short ascent. He pirouetted slowly as he held on, watching

the rope turn under the grappling hook and waiting to make sure it wouldn't twist off. "Hold the bottom to help keep me steady," he instructed Abby. Then, balancing on the loop, he stooped and caught the second Prusik loop with his glove. He slid it two feet higher than the first and put his other boot into that. Again, the knot tightened and he stepped upward. He wiggled his first boot out of the first knot, loosening its grip, bent awkwardly to slide it just under the knot he was standing on, and transferred his weight yet again. By keeping his weight on one loop at a time, he could slide the knots steadily up the rope and keep climbing.

"I think this is going to work," he said, already breathing heavily.

"What if Gage comes?" Abby asked.

"Seduce him."

The first twenty feet were easy enough. It helped that Abby steadied the rope. Once he got high enough that a fall might seriously hurt, however, his worry about the security of the hook increased. He looked upward, trying to see what was happening in the gloom, but could tell nothing. What if the whole contraption unraveled?

Then this damnable winter will be over, he told himself.

He climbed higher. As he ascended he began to feel a slight breeze from the chilly opening and the stars seemed brighter. Progress! It was like climbing to the mouth of a well. Up, up, up. He was panting from the exertion and awkward in his winter clothes, but he'd need them once he was outside. Abby had become very small below. The roofs of the housing modules formed a geometric pattern, their tops dusted with snow.

He paused for breath again, braced on one trembling leg, glancing below to make sure no one was watching. Gage would probably wander around again in about ten minutes. Even with Abby holding on below, the rope twisted slowly, rotating him slowly first one way, then another. It was too bad in a way the others weren't awake: He was putting on quite a show, a damned circus. The dome seemed higher and higher as he climbed toward its apex, his perspective changing.

Then he felt an ominous jerk, the rope vibrating. The hook was shifting! He froze, waiting with dread for it to slide free and cause his own long plummet to the ice below. But no, the movement stopped and he was still hanging in space, sweating, his body tense, the rope trembling like a plucked string. So much for stopping. He began hauling himself upward again as fast as he could manage.

His glove touched the taped ax shafts and he could hear the moan of the wind across the top of the dome. He slipped the top loop as high as it would go, boosted himself up, put out one hand, and grasped the rim. An aluminum tube ran around the four-foot-wide opening, slick and cold and hard to hang on to. He awkwardly leveraged his head upward and a blast of Antarctic wind hit him like a slap. As claustrophobically cold as it was inside the aluminum dome, the windchill outside was twice as bad. Once more its power sucked his breath away. Yet that way promised release. If he could just lever himself up a few more feet . . .

He leaned against the rim and began twisting his boot, trying to work it out of the final loop. The damn thing worked like a snare. He came loose awkwardly, catching his boot tip on the line and tangling himself. He grunted in fear as his legs and weight abruptly dropped free. His fingers clenched on the aluminum rim and his body snapped straight as he hung on his gloves, swaying back and forth like a pendulum, with the hard white floor five stories below. Abby's upturned face was a white oval, the hook somewhere behind him. Dammit! He dangled a moment, collecting his wits, and then, muscles straining, Lewis worked his way hand over hand around the trim to the grappling hook, grabbed it, and got his feet wrapped around the main climbing rope again, sliding the Prusik loops down out of the way. He pushed upward with his legs, shoving himself back up into the wind and the darkness outside the dome, and worked high enough to get the leverage he needed for a final desperate lunge that would let him belly-flop onto the dome's slick roof. It took a second to catch his breath. Then he squirmed around to a sitting position and looked down through the hole.

Abby was gesturing wildly. Perlin must be coming! She'd already tied the end of the rope to his pack of supplies. The rope was deliberately more than twice the length needed to reach the top of the dome and he hauled the slack up quickly. Finally the pack itself jerked off the snow and began to dance upward as he pulled, while Abby ducked behind Comms. And here came the plumber, cold and hunched, walking again with a crude spear made from a knife lashed onto a sawed-off mop handle, ambling across the point where they'd just been standing, without noticing the fresh scuffle of snow.

Perlin never looked up at the backpack oscillating silently over his head. Striding to check the barricaded entrance by the archways, he disappeared from view.

Lewis pulled the pack up the rest of the way, put it on, reversed the hook, and pitched the climbing rope down the outside of the geodesic structure. Grasping it and walking backward, he gingerly made his way down the face of the dome to the snow, the aluminum making a faint hollow pop as it flexed under his weight.

It became so steep that he had to let go and drop the last few feet, rolling into the drifts that mounded against the dome. Then he bounded up, shaking himself like a dog. He was out! The freedom, after being locked in the sauna, was exhilarating.

Lewis looked around. All exterior lights had been shorted out in the explosion and the base was dark. A ground fog of blown snow skittered waist-high across the plateau. Yet above this miasma he could see surprisingly well. The stars were a shoal of diamonds, the Milky Way a brilliant white arch. Their galaxy! He'd never seen so many stars, so close and so brilliant. They were a swath of luminous paint. He tilted his head back to drink them—bite them, as Sparco had promised. The glory of it stunned him with the force of belated recognition: Yes, I'm a part of *that*. He stood for a moment gaping, oblivious to the cold.

"This is why I'm down here," he murmured.

Then he began walking toward the dark blue huts that marked Bedrock, the emergency shelter that housed a small auxiliary generator. He had about three hours.

The Hypertats were modest and modern Quonset-shaped huts that had been installed as an emergency refuge in case the dome somehow failed. Insulated, modern, and cramped, they were designed to keep people alive until rescue could be organized. As winter deepened they were drifting with snow, and no one, so far as Lewis knew, had been inside them this season. Behind them was an emergency generator building. This shed was deliberately unlocked and had clear instructions posted inside so that any survivor would be able to start the machine. Still, it took Lewis fifteen minutes to push aside snow blocking its door. Inside, the machine was brittle and cold, ice crystals glittering as his flashlight played over it, the fuel like jelly, and with the grid down the batteries had lost much of their charge. There was enough to start warming the cylinders but then the batteries petered out and it took another twenty minutes of hard labor for Lewis to hand-crank the diesel to get it going. Each reluctant chug that died increased his sense of desperation. Just as he was thoroughly frustrated by its mule-like reluctance, ready to scream with resentment, it coughed and rumbled and gave him the first real hope he'd had for some time. Energy! A source Norse and Pulaski had overlooked! The roar seemed cacophonous inside the shed but he knew the generator's modest chug couldn't be heard from the distant dome. Yet it was enough to make electricity for the Hypertats, and power was power. This juice was going to let him reach the outside world.

Bedrock's small generator was never designed to power the other outlying buildings. Yet it connected to a substation shack with an electrical panel and, if switched and rerouted as Abby had instructed, it could shunt electricity away from the emergency shelters and out to Clean Air. He trudged to the shack, butted it open, and searched with his flashlight for the right switches. He hesitated only a moment. If he threw the wrong ones he could short out the entire system. But no, they were clearly labeled, and one by one he flipped them over as the woman had instructed. No sparks flew. No circuits shorted. He looked outside. Hallelujah. A deck light had come on at Clean Air.

Abby knew her stuff.

The light would alert anyone watching, but no one should be watching. The others had blinded themselves by barricading the dome.

Lewis set off for his workplace, boots crunching in fresh crust. It was eerie how dead the rest of the station looked.

Everything was in silhouette under the stars, the antennas mute, the telescopes blinded. It was like walking a ghostly ruin. The snow was a frozen sea, an undulating series of drifts he strode up and down like a boat, his trail leading from one half-buried flag to the next. He wondered about the distant future. Would humans stay at the Pole forever or retreat someday? Would everything they had built eventually become as ghostly as the abandoned Navy base?

While fairly confident he wouldn't be missed until morning, Lewis flicked off the deck light once he clambered up the metal steps to reach Clean Air. He also didn't take the chance of turning on a light inside his old workplace. Instead he flicked on an auxiliary heater and used his flashlight to pick his way to one of the computers, dragging some furniture over to block its glow from the windows. He didn't want to be interrupted by pursuit. Only then did he turn the machine on. There was the familiar whir and bleep, and a faint crackle as photons danced in the tube.

Lewis checked his watch. The satellites that tied them to the Internet cleared the horizon at intervals of eight hours. The next one was rising now.

The temptation to simply sound a cry for help was powerful but was unlikely to bring any meaningful response. He couldn't stay out here to wait for a reply because he'd be missed in the sauna and a hunt would be on. And even if the National Science Foundation decided to dispatch the Texas Rangers at his strange SOS it would take at least days—and more likely weeks, in winter—to mount the logistics to fly to the Pole. All the military transports were back in the United States, their National Guard crews had dispersed, and their cold weather gear was stored. The Pole was designed to be self-sufficient until October. The winter-overs were facing a danger they'd have to deal with themselves, and before they could deal with it he had to understand what their peril was.

There was now one person of uncertain past, one person leading them to an even more uncertain future. Lewis launched a web search.

Robert Norse.

He started with the usual string of search engines: Alta Vista, Yahoo, AOL, Google, MSN. The results were frustrating because the name was too common. There were scores of references to Bobs and Norses, but none obviously fitting their psychologist. He turned up *Robert's Rules of Order* and a reference to Norse mythology, a link to a Warhammer game and a construction company in Minneapolis. "Come on. . . ." There were even puzzling references to New Zealand, referring to outdoor hiking trips there. What the hell was that about? "Damn brainless Internet clutter."

He tried searching professional journals but quickly became lost in a bog of poor indexing and the ceaseless accumulation of academic publication. So much stuff that no one could read it, and so dense no one could understand it. Brilliant people in a cocoon of irrelevance. He didn't have the vaguest idea who Norse might have written for anyway. And what would an academic study prove?

Stymied, he decided to try news media databases instead. The *New York Times* and *Wall Street Journal* came up empty, but a *Los Angeles Times* brief from two years before mentioned Norse as a visiting lecturer at San Diego State University. The sentence came in a story about a psychological conference on human adaptation to extremes. It said Norse was planning polar research. "We're looking at the adaptability of people to stressful conditions," he'd told the reporter. Well, that made sense. Frustratingly, there was nothing more. The university web site had no listing for Norse: no picture, no biography, no vital statistics.

The city's newspaper?

The *San Diego Union-Tribune* electronic archive turned up "Norse" sixty-two times, in stories that ranged from a football lineman for the Chargers to a feature on Scandinavian cooking. It was near the end of the list that he found a two-paragraph news brief and whispered, "Bingo."

It was dated February 5 and datelined Christchurch.

LOCAL MAN FOUND IN NZ the headline read. The story began:

Robert Norse, a southern California research psychologist affiliated with San Diego State as a guest lecturer, survived two weeks in the southern New Zealand wilderness and walked out under his own power on Friday, New Zealand authorities said today.

Norse was reported missing on January 23, having disappeared from a guided walk in Mount Aspiring National Park. Searchers had given up hope when the American reappeared, hungry but in good shape, more than 30 kilometers from where he'd become lost. Refusing medical help, he left immediately for Christchurch where he is overdue to join an American scientific contingent assigned to Antarctica. Authorities said he gave little information about his ordeal.

There were no follow-up stories and no article in the archives about Norse's original disappearance. Lewis began trying other communities in a widening orbit around San Diego, hunting for their newspapers and trying their electronic databases. It wasn't until he'd broadened his search

to the *Orange County Register* near Los Angeles that he
hit pay dirt again.

ORANGE COUNTY MAN MISSING read the headline.

> *Robert Norse, an American scientist scheduled to con-
> duct sociology studies at the South Pole, has disap-
> peared during a hiking tour of New Zealand, a tour
> company reported yesterday.*
>
> *A rare summer snow squall in the high country had
> obscured a popular trek route and Norse apparently
> lagged behind during bad weather. A search for him
> the following morning proved fruitless.*
>
> *New Zealand authorities are continuing to look in
> the rugged area.*
>
> *Norse, who is single, is a self-employed psycholo-
> gist, writer and social theorist who occasionally
> teaches at area universities. Authorities said his most
> recent appointment was at San Diego State Univer-
> sity.*

So: Norse was what he said he was—a psychologist. And
he'd mentioned something about New Zealand. Yet he'd
never talked about being *lost* in New Zealand, even though
everyone on station had depleted their life stories by now.
It must have been a traumatic experience to be lost for two
weeks. That was a hell of a long time in the woods. Yet
Norse never referred to it? Odd.

What if his disappearance was intentional?

Lewis felt a rising excitement, that prickling that comes
on the edge of discovery.

But why? What could he have wanted in the New Zealand
wilderness? Some kind of personal test? Some validation
for his theories of individual survival?

Lewis pondered, glancing at the clock at the bottom of the computer screen. It had taken him half an hour to hike to Clean Air from the Hypertats, fifteen minutes to get some heat and fire up the computer, several more to get a connection. . . . Pika would be up soon. In half an hour he needed to race back to the dome if he didn't want to set off an alarm. The satellite was drifting out of range again anyway. Yet he was no closer to an answer than before.

There seemed no other obvious avenues to pursue on the Internet and so he considered the station's databases. The hard drives of the victims had been corrupted by a magnet, Abby had reported to him, the killer apparently smart enough to scramble any potential clue there. Even if there was an electronic link to Norse or anyone else, the culprit had squelched it. Lewis tried logging on to the station's uncorrupted astronomy database but found no reference to the psychologist, which was not surprising given the astronomers' attitude toward Norse and his trade.

What else? What else?

There were always the station personnel records. This was mundane stuff, not the more intimate information known only to Rod Cameron, Norse, and Nancy Hodge and available only on paper, not on-line. Still, maybe the routine logging of the logistical comings and goings of base employees would reveal *something*. Its compiler was Gabriella, whose job had been the arrangement and recording of flights, rooms, counting heads at meals, tracking cargo and luggage.

He scanned quickly, looking for Norse's name. Had the psychologist brought something weird or unusual in his gear? Not really. There was a reference to *hby tscp*, which Lewis assumed was a reference to the telescope the psychologist had brought down to build. Appropriate project for a six-month night, as Norse had said.

Nothing else, however. No bombs, no meteorites, no knives, no nooses. Everything Gabriella Reid had written down about Norse was utterly tedious. Most of his winter-over gear had been shipped ahead of him, but that was normal: The Guard stockpiled personal gear in Christchurch and tucked it into the transports when there was room for an extra load. The winter-overs themselves arrived with a single duffel and found the rest of their things waiting for them. Much of it never went back home, as the storeroom at the KitKat Club testified. Norse apparently followed the routine.

He was just one more fingie, rotating in on tour.

Lewis sat back, frustrated, rubbing his eyes. He was missing something, something obvious, but he was damned if he could figure out what it was. His time was almost up and except for the New Zealand adventure he knew little more about Robert Norse than when he'd climbed out of the dome. Maybe he was investigating the wrong man. Maybe their paranoia was driving them to convert friends to enemies, enemies to friends. In any event it was time to drop back into imprisonment, since he still had no ammunition to secure his own release: no revelation, no smoking gun. Lewis flipped the computer off and stood up. Now what?

Nothing made much sense.

Norse was a scientist, just like him. Arriving late, just like him. . . .

Then it hit him, the thing that had been staring him in the face and he'd been too blind to recognize. The discrepancy! He abruptly sat back down and fired up the machine again. That whir again, and the laborious chug. Beep, bop, boop. *Come on.* . . . There was the familiar blue glow and he typed madly, getting back to Gabriella's station lists. Yes, there! *1-29. Auckland.* That was the day Norse had checked his telescope and other gear with American authorities in the New Zealand capital, shipping it through to the staging base at Christchurch and then on to Antarctica.

1-29!

Norse had signed the necessary forms. He had allowed inspection of his gear. Which meant, according to the records of Gabriella Reid, that Norse had been at the Auckland airport, dealing with logistics, at the same time the newspapers said he'd already disappeared into the country's wilderness.

Yet Norse hadn't emerged from his ordeal for another week. How could he have been lost at Mount Aspiring and back in Auckland at the same time? How could he have been in two places at once?

Had he gone astray on a vacation hike, popped out to check in his luggage, and then disappeared back into the woods again? Damn unlikely.

What else, then?

Lewis stared at the number. *1-29.*

What if there were *two* Robert Norses, one going missing on January 23, another checking his gear six days later? Odd coincidence. Maybe the newspaper stories he dug up referred then to another man entirely. . . .

Two Robert Norses going to the Pole?

No way.

How did Antarctic authorities know a person was who he said he was? Nobody had asked Lewis for I.D. once he'd cleared customs. He'd shown up in New Zealand, identified himself to warehousing authorities, been checked off a list and issued the necessary paperwork and polar

gear. Was the second man really Robert Norse? Or someone *claiming* to be him? And which Norse had emerged
from the New Zealand wilderness two weeks later, too
rushed to answer any questions?

What if the man under the dome wasn't the real Robert
Norse at all? What if the hiking disappearance had allowed
an impostor to take his place, that somehow their Norse
had followed the other Norse to New Zealand, cleared customs under his real name and passport, made sure of Norse's
disappearance, assumed his role, boarded the plane to the
Pole . . .

Lewis flipped off the computer and stood up, dizzy, excited, and still bewildered. Who, then, was Doctor Bob?

And how to prove that he and the real Norse weren't
the same man?

CHAPTER TWENTY-FIVE

Bob, I've got a problem."

Norse looked at Abby quizzically, his powerful fingers splayed to hold down something he was writing on his desk as if it might somehow blow away, the cursive letters hidden as he did so. In an instant he went from the distraction of his thought to focusing intently on her, a cautious smile on his lips, alert, ready. Once again she felt his peculiar magnetism. There was a strength to him that she found disquietingly alluring, and with his hair coming back he was more handsome than ever. There was also a strain to his gaze now, the kind of weariness she'd noticed in Rod Cameron. A pain to his slight smile. The Pole wore on you. It was wearing on all of them.

She'd seen it in the others, of course, a closing up like the petals of a flower at dusk. Nancy Hodge had retreated to BioMed, taking her meals there and tending to the burnt Clyde Skinner. For the first time since arriving on station she'd locked its door, insisting that anyone else needing help must knock first.

Several of the men had camped in the library like a squad

from an occupying army, sprawling on the couches in sullen encampment while they watched a marathon stream of fuzzy video movies, a distracting blur of car chases and explosions and half-dressed women that they napped through in depressed exhaustion. Their talk was in monosyllables, their concentration wandering. Mostly, they tried to sleep.

Linda Brown was allowing the galley to slip toward disorder, a glacial backlog of unscrubbed pans grinding toward the sink, their food consumed without being logged.

Gina Brindisi was lost in old letters in her room.

Dana Andrews was typing in the computer room at a terminal that didn't work, its hard disk shorted out in the Comms room explosion, explaining the clack of the keys was helping her memorize the damning report she planned to write when everything was over.

And the greenhouse had been clear-cut. Abby had gone there after Lewis's exhausted return, confused by his discoveries and seeking inspiration for what to do next. Instead she found its benches covered with a brown carpet of withered leaves: Lena Jindrova had snipped the yellowing plants off at their base or hauled them out of their hydroponic tanks, leaving them dry and dead. The last greenery had been snuffed out.

Fearing for Lena's well-being, she'd found the young woman sitting in a corner of the galley with coffee, staring morosely at the station dartboard, which had been covered with some kinds of paper.

"We are either leaving this place or we are dying," Lena explained dully when Abby asked what had happened to the plants. "I didn't want them suffering from neglect."

"Plants don't suffer."

The young Czech used her finger to cut patterns into a

coffee ring on the Formica of the galley table, alarmingly depressed. "Do you think not, with no sun and no warmth? Do you think these pretty plants are happy way down here, in the dark and the cold?"

"The dying is going to stop, Lena."

"I do not have that feeling. It is just beginning, is the feeling I have."

"We're going to learn what's going on," Abby insisted. "People are going to come together over this."

"No, people are abandoning hope. Did you see the board there?"

"Somebody covered it."

"No more games. No more matches with the Kiwis. Because no more radio, because the fixing is not going so well. So Dana and Carl got drunk last night and taped their research proposals to the board and threw the darts at *them*. They have given up because we are alone down here and we are forgotten."

"We aren't forgotten! I'm sure the rest of the world is wondering what happened to us. Trying to contact us. We'll get Comms up and running."

"No, we are forgotten. We are not people to them, I think. Just some name. Some file. Some record. We are trapped down here and so now I am done with my plants."

Name. File. Record. And with that Abby suddenly had an idea what to do. How to follow up Lewis's discovery. So now she was in the office Norse had taken over from the dead Cameron, trying to mask her own nervousness in approaching the enigmatic psychologist, trying to act casual in seeking something that could save them all.

Norse looked at her warily. "I hope you're not here about Lewis. I know you don't believe he's guilty but keeping him in the sauna is the only thing keeping him safe."

"No, it's not about Jed," she said. "I know you have no choice. I'm not sure myself that he is who he says he is." She watched Norse closely when she said this but he showed no reaction. If the man was a liar, he composed his emotions like a schedule. "My problem's more mundane," she went on. "I've got a toothache."

Norse frowned. Dental problems could become a real hazard in the isolation of the Pole. Everyone had thorough exams before coming down because bad teeth could produce either agony or, in summer, an expensive evacuation. "Have you talked to Nancy?"

"Yes, and she suspects it might be a problem with a loose crown. She needs to see my X rays. Apparently they're in the office here."

"I thought she had her own set."

"The one she has is fogged. Maybe it went through an airport detector."

"And there's another here?"

"Yes." Nancy knew that Cameron's old office had a storage closet that included a complete set of dental X rays for every winter-over at Amundsen-Scott base. They were required of all American personnel in Antarctica. One reason was to screen for problems that could be crippling in a remote camp. Another, more morbid rationale was to have on file a means—if aircraft crashed and bodies were burnt—of identifying the dead. For safe redundancy, two sets came down, one sent by medical authorities and the second hand-carried by the winter-over.

"I don't even know where they are," he confessed. "Haven't had time to poke around."

"Nancy said Rod kept them in boxes in the closet."

He glanced over his shoulder at a storage closet behind him. "You want me to find them?"

"I'll get them."

He looked at her speculatively. Here was an opportunity to repair a relationship, perhaps. She'd been avoiding him up to now. "Okay."

The woman nodded her thanks.

"We've been through some rough times, Abby," he tried. "It's important we all come together in a situation like this."

"I know." She looked a little impatient. She'd said her tooth was hurting but he couldn't help but plunge ahead. Abby, his failure with her, represented a rare defeat. It gnawed at him.

"I realize you've been upset about Lewis but I don't know what else I can do for him until we get Comms up and running and some of this sorted out. I . . . I know I came on a little strong with you at the party. I wonder if we could at least be good friends."

She swallowed. "We *are* friends, Bob. Just not that kind of friend."

He got up from his desk and moved around to her. "The group worries me, frankly. It's weaker than I was expecting. I'm trying to hold people together but there's a real chance someone's going to get in a fight or try to run away or get emotional and do something dangerous. The beakers are the worst because they have the least to do, now that the grid is down. If there's trouble I'd like to be able to count on you."

"Of course you can."

He took her right hand in both of his, enclosing it. The grip was not tight but the power there was unmistakable. It emanated from him like a force. "If anything bad happens I'd like you to stay by me. I'm thinking of assigning pairs, a kind of buddy system, and I'd like to partner with you. Boy-girl, mostly—I think each gender has its strengths and could help look after the other. And I know it's a little sexist, but I'd like to think I could help protect you in a crisis. Do you understand what I mean?"

She smiled more bravely than she felt, actually confused by what he meant. What crisis? "I guess so," she evaded. She needed to get to that box. "I *would* like to know you better, Bob. That's one reason I came down for the winter, to get close to people. With Jed locked away I'm learning how important that might be."

He was looking at her with an intensity she found unnerving. She wished he'd sit back down. "Are you?"

Abby pulled out of his grip. "But not right now, not with a toothache. Let me get Nancy to look at this and decide what we can do. After I get fixed maybe we can talk. Maybe you can tell me more about yourself. I'm very curious. You're kind of mysterious, you know."

She got a glimpse of his annoyance at her elusiveness and then his face masked over. "Everyone's mysterious. Even to themselves."

"Well, my mystery is my own dental work. I'm going to dig out that file."

He shrugged, stepping away. "Of course. I hope Nancy can help. Get you a painkiller or something." Obviously dissatisfied, he sat down and went back to writing. It looked personal, like some kind of diary.

Abby went around the desk and into the storage closet, finding the cardboard box that Nancy had described. Lifting it down, she began rifling through it, praying he wouldn't come help. She could feel him glance over occasionally to watch her. "I'm surprised you can think to write after all that's happened," she called. "Even concentrate. What is it?"

There was a long silence. Then a shuffling of paper. "A

narrative of an important time," he finally said. "Explaining things to myself."

"That's what writing does, doesn't it?"

"That and explaining things to the world."

She found what she was looking for, slipped it into her own file folder, and put the box back. "It's too bad Clyde was burnt in the explosion," she commented as she went back past his desk, clutching the X rays. "The repair work would go a lot faster with his expertise."

"Awful," Norse said. He straightened a little. "Yet disaster can bring out the best in people as well. It's a kind of test, I think. Being cut off from communication from the outside world has forced us to rely a little bit more on ourselves. Like you and me. It's terrible to say so, but the trauma has given a real edge to my research."

She smiled. "Hoping for the worst?" She tried to keep it light, without any edge to it. "Shrink nirvana?"

"Sounds awful, doesn't it?" He shook his head at himself. "I find myself in an awkward position between participant and observer. Victim and beneficiary."

"Our leader, now."

"No, no. Camp counselor, maybe."

"Our director."

His look was sardonic. "No matter how well you plan things, everything comes out differently. You make things up as you go along."

"And how do you know where you're trying to go, Bob?" She seemed genuinely interested.

"I'm a psychologist. Inside instead of outside. Soul instead of stars. At some fundamental level I'm not sure they're all that different. The goal of any life is to justify yourself to yourself. Or at least explain yourself."

"That sounds like what a shrink would say."

"That's what an honest man would say."

She left and he watched her go with a concealed hunger: her slim back, the nape of her neck, the curve of her hip, that coy primness he wanted to possess and violate. Her presence was tormenting him like a hunger, inflating his desire. The more she put him off, the more he wanted her.

But he couldn't let that interfere with the experiment. Couldn't let that interfere with himself! Still, Norse allowed himself the luxury of pondering her for a while, considering their encounter. She'd been more receptive this time, he thought, as if she were thawing. Ice Cream! Getting Lewis out of the way had helped. Getting rid of him entirely would help more. Too bad there was just one more Spryte, but he needed to reserve *that* for himself. . . . Norse imagined triumphing with her, he her only hope of survival, getting her to do the things he needed. Too bad she had a damn toothache.

Maybe in the end they could leave together.

He looked at what he had just written. *I acted on the best plan I had at the time.*

Adaptable, yes. But always a step ahead. Always a step ahead.

It really would be quite the brilliant paper. He took up his pen again.

It wasn't until later, much later, that another possibility occurred to him and he stood up from his desk, suddenly alarmed.

"Damn her!"

He wrenched open the closet door, threw down the box Abby had pawed through, and flipped frantically to his own folder, cursing as he did so. He opened it.

His dental X rays were gone.

She was taking them to Nancy Hodge.

*   *   *

There were red droplets on the snow between the galley and BioMed, a bright disturbing trail that announced more trouble. Abby followed them at a trot, the X rays in her mitten. The door to the sick bay was locked and she groaned inwardly. She remembered that the increasingly paranoid Nancy Hodge was locking herself in, and the need to knock was maddening. Every second seemed vital. Norse was no fool, and Abby feared he'd come storming out from his office at any moment. She needed Nancy to make the X ray comparison so they could get the others to help.

"Nancy, open up!" She pounded anxiously with the flat of her hand.

There was a pause, then a reply muffled by the door. "I'm busy."

There wasn't time to be busy! They had to learn the truth about Norse! Abby hammered on the door again, impatient and irritated. "Hurry up! It's an emergency!"

"I've got an emergency in here!"

"Nancy, please!"

She heard a muffled oath and the bang of something being shut, then the quick clump of footsteps. The door opened and Nancy looked out, her eyes looking tired and harassed. "You'll have to come back later. I'm treating Gina."

"Please, I've got to talk to you now."

"Abby, I've got blood all over the place in here."

Abby stepped up to the level of BioMed and peeked past Nancy to the examining room beyond. Clyde Skinner was lying on the lone bed, his eyes bandaged. Gina Brindisi was sitting on the table, her face white and scared looking, her pants on the floor. One of her legs was smeared with blood, a slashing wound on her calf looking partly sewn up. "My God, what happened?"

Nancy looked back over her shoulder at Gina. "She tripped over some damn pike or battleax Calhoun made. We're all going to poke each other's eyes out with those things. It's crazy. I've got to finish up these stitches to stop the bleeding."

"Can't we talk for a second first?"

"Abby, she's leaking all over the damn table! Are you hurt or sick?"

"No."

"Then come back later." She started to close the door.

"Wait!" Abby thrust her boot inside, preventing its closure. "It's about everything that's happening!"

"I'm trying to patch up everything that's happening! I'll talk to you later!"

"Please!"

Nancy was annoyed now. "Get your foot out of my door! Damn you and damn this place anyway!"

Abby was thinking furiously. How much time before Norse figured out what she was up to? She couldn't wait until later, not if she was going to try to get into Norse's room for more evidence. She needed to be in two places at once! And now Nancy was distracted.

"Listen to me!" Abby hissed urgently. "Listen, or we're all going to die!" Her determination interrupted Nancy's impatience, piercing the doctor's anger. For just a moment the medic was listening. "Norse is not Norse," Abby insisted in a low voice. "Do you understand? Bob is not Bob. He's someone else, some impostor, and that means he could be behind all this craziness that's been going on. I can't come back later, I have to find the one thing that will convince the rest of you, so I'm going to send Jed over here instead, okay? I'm going to send Lewis. He can explain."

Nancy looked wary, curious, fearful. "He's locked up."

"I'm going to let him out. It's important. Nancy, you have to trust him. You have to trust me. It's our only chance."

The doctor shook her head. "I don't trust anyone anymore."

Abby thrust the folder of X rays at her. "These are Norse's dental X rays. You've got another set here. I need you to compare the two as soon as you stitch up Gina. Hurry, before Bob comes!"

"Abby . . ."

"Just do it! You'll see! I'm going to send Jed to fill you in and then I'm going to come back if I find what I think I'll find. Then the three of us will go to the others."

Nancy took the folder uncertainly. "I don't understand. . . ."

"Just look at the two sets! See if they match! Please, Nancy, I think you're our last chance!"

"Last chance?"

"To get away from the Pole alive."

Lewis darted across the snow under the dome like a wraith for what he hoped was the last time, carrying as a crude defense one of the ice axes he'd used as a grappling hook. He had descended like a spider back into the dome the night before, pausing on the roof to untie the hook from the rope and thrust it in his belt. Then he doubled the rope around one of the framing braces on the dome. Its ample length allowed him to descend back into his imprisonment on the doubled line and then retrieve the entire rope by pulling on one end, reeling it in until it slipped out of the

dome brace and fell down on the snow. He hid the rope
behind Comms and tucked the axes in a maintenance closet
near the sauna. Then he'd waited in his cedar jail in an
agony of impatience, anxious to see if Abby could figure
a way to follow up on the mystery.

She'd finally come to him panting like a sprinter, gasping out the tale of her acquisition of Norse's X ray and its
delivery to Nancy Hodge. The doctor had been too busy
to listen, Abby said hurriedly, because she was bandaging
up Gina, but now Nancy was waiting for him in BioMed
and Abby was about to pursue a hunch about what she
might find in Norse's room. It was all hunches now, a gamble that they could save all their lives by uncovering the
truth about one. Yet what if he was wrong? Then the only
alternative might be the kind of desperate escape Tyson
had resorted to, stealing the other Spryte and setting off
for McMurdo. Probably dying in the attempt.

Now he looked around carefully to avoid interception
but, surprisingly, no one was around. Eating? Moping? Arguing? Maybe Norse had started some kind of bizarre encounter group. He slipped into the archway, surprised at
how easy this was, and went to the door of the medic's
module. He reached for the freezerlike door handle and
stopped. It was hanging askew, its lock apparently broken.
Hadn't Nancy said they didn't lock the sick bay? Why was
it pried open now? Hesitantly, he knocked.

No reply. The door creaked open a quarter inch.

"Nancy?"

No answer.

He pounded harder. "Hodge? You in there?" Again, silence. "It's Lewis! We need to talk!"

Then a faint moan. "Help. . . ."

It was Clyde Skinner.

"For God's sake, help. . . ."

Where was Nancy? He shoved open the broken door and stepped inside, shutting it against the cold. "Clyde?"

"Who is it? Who is it?"

It was Skinner, all right, the burnt radioman. He was lying in the sick bay bed with his face swathed in bandages, blind and helpless, clutching his sheets.

"It's Lewis. I've come to help."

"Lewis?" His voice betrayed dread. "You set the bomb."

"No, I didn't, Clyde. Someone's setting me up."

The man lay quietly, looking afraid.

"What happened? BioMed was locked. Where's Nancy?"

"You've come to kill me, too, haven't you?"

"No! No, no. I'm trying to help. What the hell happened?"

"Where's Abby?"

"I don't know."

"Nancy told me to talk only to Abby."

"Well, where's Nancy?"

"I don't know, I don't know. There was a noise, like something breaking, and Nancy yelled, someone inside, and then lots of banging around, and then it went quiet. I thought you'd all abandoned me. I thought you'd left the station and left me behind."

Lewis glanced around. BioMed was a mess. There was blood all over the examining table: Gina must have really been cut. More ominously, drawers hung half open, cabinet doors were swung wide, and medical supplies had cascaded onto the floor. Notebooks had spilled a glacier of paper. The place had been ransacked. Where the hell was Nancy?

The storage door in back was cracked open.

He went to the entrance and tried to push open the door,

but something was blocking it. He shoved enough to get an arm through the opening and turned on the light to see what was in the way.

Legs.

Lewis felt a sick dread. He pushed harder and something heavy skidded aside, allowing him to squeeze through. He stumbled inside and looked down in grim confirmation at Nancy Hodge, her eyes rolled back and mouth open, a hypodermic needle jutting from the back of her neck. A set of X rays was resting on her body. He knelt and glanced at a manila folder. It read, "Abby Dixon."

The assailant was still confusing the trail.

He felt vainly for a pulse. Their doctor was dead. There were no obvious cuts and bruises, but not even junkies injected themselves in the nape of the neck. It was obvious that someone had crept up behind her and injected her. Killed her before she could talk about the X rays. Killed her before she could talk about Norse.

No escape. No radio. And now no doctor.

No proof.

He glanced around. X-ray records were upended and the storage cabinet against the rear wall had been shoved aside, exposing a metal panel screwed to the wall, scratched and dirty. Lewis slowly stood. They were doomed. Except . . . someone had been searching BioMed. And that searching meant maybe Nancy had hidden the two sets of X rays. What if Norse hadn't found them yet?

Another faint tremor of hope. The shifted storage cabinet appeared to hold nothing but medical supplies. The panel behind it required a screwdriver. So he moved out into the main sick bay and began his own search.

"What's going on? What's happening?" Skinner asked

from his bed, his voice fearful. It wasn't just his pain. It was agonizing not to see.

"Nancy's dead, Clyde."

"Oh my God!" he moaned. "Not her, too!"

"It wasn't me who killed her. You have to believe that." Skinner was silent.

"Did you see anything?"

"Is that a joke?"

Lewis grimaced. "Sorry."

"Dead how?" His tone was hopeless.

"An injection. Maybe murder. Was Norse here?"

"No voice. Just funny noises. Like what you're doing now."

"But who was it? Who was here before me, Clyde?"

"I don't know." There was a tremor in his voice. He was afraid.

"Think! I might need your help!"

"Please don't kill me, Lewis. I didn't see anything."

"Christ." He gave up on Skinner and turned to the drawers. The room didn't take that long to search. Nothing. "He took them," Lewis muttered.

"Took what?"

"Something Nancy had."

"Does it matter?"

He stood, despairing. How could he convince the others? "It matters because it means that I am well and truly screwed." He looked back at Nancy's body, frustrated and depressed.

"And that's the first intelligent observation you've made since you came here," a different voice said.

It was someone at the doorway. Lewis turned.

Norse!

The psychologist stepped inside and turned to address a

group of men behind him. "We finally caught him in the act," he announced.

Pulaski, Geller, Calhoun, and Perlin followed, crowding one end of BioMed. A posse rousted from the videos in the library, bleary and belligerent. The open door let in a freezerlike chill, the spilled papers shifting in the draft. Abby's X rays slid off Nancy's still chest with a sigh. "It wasn't me," Lewis tried.

"It's never you, is it, Jed?" Norse replied softly.

Lewis picked up his ice ax in instinctive defense, trying to buy a moment's time, composing what he had to say. But before he could speak, Pulaski shot forward in sudden assault, the cook's flying tackle hurling Lewis backward against a set of wall shelves, the air whooshing out of him and the ice ax spinning into a corner. The shelves gave way, crashing down around his head. Dimly he realized Geller and Calhoun and Perlin were charging, too. "Wait!" he yelled.

Pulaski butted his face with his bald head, bloodying Lewis's nose, and one of the others struck him in the stomach. Lewis couldn't breathe. He feebly tried to rise but the cook gripped him in a wrestling hold, twisted his arm, and expertly flipped him onto his belly. Other strong hands caught his wrists and ankles and twisted electrical cords around them.

They'd trailed him to BioMed. Waited while he scampered across the snow. Crept up while he was discovering the body.

Geller grunted and stood up, stepping over Lewis into the storeroom beyond. "Nancy's dead!" he confirmed.

Lewis had been hit so hard he was seeing stars. It was difficult to think. "No," he wheezed. "I found—"

"Clyde, you all right?" Calhoun asked Skinner.

"What's going on? What's going on?"

"It's Doctor Bob," Norse said. "We caught Lewis preparing to kill you."

"Oh my God. Where's Abby?"

"We're looking for her, too. You seen her?"

Skinner said nothing. He was shaking with fear.

"She comes here, you notify us, okay?"

The blind man went rigid, as if waiting for a blow.

Norse crouched by Lewis's head, looking disgusted. "Who let you out?"

"X rays . . ."

"It was Dixon, wasn't it?"

"Ask Clyde . . ."

"Jed Lewis," he said solemnly, "by the emergency powers confirmed to me by the agreement of our peers in an emergency situation, I place you under arrest for the murder of Nancy Hodge."

He was choking, trying to get the words out. "Bastard . . ."

"And for the murders of Gabriella Reid, Rod Cameron, Harrison Adams, and Mickey Moss. Perhaps manslaughter for the flight of Buck Tyson. For the blinding of Clyde Skinner. For terrorism and emotional assault, for theft and false witness, for stalking and betrayal. You've jeopardized the very existence of Amundsen-Scott station."

Lewis's lower face was a mask of blood, his throat hacked, his ribs sore. "Lie!"

Norse stood. "You all saw it," he told the others. "We caught him in the act this time. He broke into BioMed after I'd ordered Nancy to lock it for her own safety. But we're not savages. We're going to have a trial."

"What can we do with him even if he's guilty?" It was Gage Perlin, looking at the trussed Lewis with frank fear.

"He already busted out of the sauna. It's like he never stays put. He gets out, and something happens."

"It's my fault this occurred," Norse said. "I wouldn't listen to the rest of you. I wouldn't act when the rest of you wanted to. I wanted to go slow. But this time I *am* going to listen to you. This time we're going to end this nightmare once and for all."

"No," Lewis coughed. "He's not—"

Something in Norse snapped. He kicked Lewis, knocking the wind out of him again. It was as if he were furious with himself for having been blinded by the man's ruses. "Shut up, Lewis! Just shut up!"

He turned to the others. "We need to locate Abby—find out what her role was in all this."

Lewis closed his eyes and spit out some blood. He writhed helplessly on the floor, his cheek on cold linoleum, his vision a cluster of white polar boots. *Abby,* he thought, *don't let them do this to you, too.*

CHAPTER TWENTY-SIX

I think all of you believe in the rule of law," Norse began to the assembled winter-overs in the galley. "All of you believe in unity. All of you believe in fairness. And no one has tried harder than myself to keep a rein on our emotions, to counsel moderation, to avoid irrevocable actions. But in a truly extreme situation, extreme measures become inevitable, and an extreme situation is exactly what Jed Lewis has put us in."

Lewis sat in a chair with his hands and feet tied, Pulaski standing over him. The geologist was bruised, dried blood on his face, his hair in an unwashed tangle. His look at Norse was of sullen amazement, anger, and disbelief, but he once more felt overmastered. The fear and the hostility the others directed against him were as heavy and oppressive as the stickiness before a thunderstorm. He'd become the new Tyson.

"We don't have any communications," Norse went on. "We obviously don't have a proper jail. What we *do* have is a seductive, glib psychotic who has not only killed our only medical doctor but has been mocking us and toying with us from the beginning." The psychologist looked intently at the others. "We're ten thousand miles from home, stranded without help at the darkest, coldest place on earth. A quarter of us are already dead. A determined saboteur could doom us all. It's time for the group to come together, for the *group* to decide how we're going to get rid of a murderous infection."

"He's lying," Lewis spat, his voice thick and slurred after Pulaski's head butt. "He's not who he says he is! *He's* the one who's psychotic. Ask him who he *really* is."

Norse ignored this. "No one was fooled more than I was. No one liked Jed Lewis better than I did. I was his first friend! I ran with him in the Three Hundred Degree Club! But we found him today with the body of Nancy Hodge and with that even *I* had to admit I'd been wrong about our fingie. Did we see him kill her? No. But we have to act on what we know, and what do we know?"

"We know he has a connection to every bad thing that has happened on this station," Molotov growled. "That all this started when Lewis came."

"I was looking for the X rays, dammit! Ask him about the X rays! That's the key to this whole thing!"

"We know it was Mr. Lewis who put a value on that meteorite," Norse went on, "and that shortly afterward the meteorite went missing. He apparently saw where Doctor Moss hid it. Was he the thief? I can't prove it. You'll remember that Cameron told Jed about the abandoned base and that he asked us about it. Then Mickey Moss died down there. Does that prove anything? No. Does it disprove anything?"

"He went last when we crawled to that pit where we found Mickey," Geller remembered. "The farthest from that hole. Like he knew it was there."

"He sent the e-mail!" Dana shouted.

"Listen to me," Lewis groaned. "Norse came to New Zealand at two different times. You're listening to an impostor."

They looked at him with disbelief. Their attention was on Norse and his recital. They'd stopped listening, because they wanted their nightmare to stop.

"Dana's right," the psychologist went on. "Remember what happened. Harrison Adams found someone had sent Moss an e-mail about the meteorite from Jed's computer in Clean Air. I thought a killer would be more careful than to use his own machine, but perhaps not. During a blizzard Lewis leaves his post despite orders from our station manager to stay there. Adams disappears at the same time. Who finds his body? Lewis. Who's holding a cut heat tape? Lewis. And here's where I made my mistake. I proposed a simple quarantine instead of confinement while we investigated the situation. I wrongly focused on Tyson. And so who asks to meet with Rod Cameron, who was continuing to investigate the two deaths? Lewis. And Rod ends up dead."

"I never even saw Cameron! I never went to the fuel arch!"

Norse looked grimly at a group transfixed by this history. He was reciting what they knew. He was preaching to the choir. "It wasn't until later—*too* late, in fact—that I was exploring Rod's office after the explosion and found this letter." He held up a sheet of paper with Lewis's signature on it, the same one he'd showed Abby. "It promises that Rod can save his career if he lets Lewis have the meteorite. He thought Cameron might have it, and was still determined to get it any way he could."

"It's a forgery! He tricked me into signing that!"

Norse passed the letter around.

"We thought it was Tyson, but wasn't it with Lewis's arrival that our animosity towards Buck began to grow? Did Jed foster that? Frankly, it's difficult to remember. But Tyson fled because he feared he couldn't get a fair hearing, not with Jed Lewis in this group. And now he, too, is probably dead."

"I had nothing to do with—"

"So we welcome Lewis into our little fraternity. We party. Something goes wrong between him and Gabriella. And again, he is on hand for the discovery of her body. The cut-up magazine to make a note, the ashes in his room: We've been through this already."

"Think!" Lewis pleaded. "Why would I lead you to my victims?"

"You're not the first murderer to do so, Jed." Norse's observation was dispassionate, sad.

"Shut up and let Bob finish," Pulaski added. "Then it's your turn."

"So we lock him up," the psychologist resumed. "But before we can ask the authorities back home what action we should take, our communications center explodes from an apparent booby trap, blinding one of our key individuals. Lewis could have created the conditions for that explosion at any time after we curfewed our communications. Yet despite all this a young woman—someone Lewis has been seducing from the beginning and who has apparently been blinded herself by infatuation—springs him from his cell. Now *she's* disappeared, and perhaps with good reason. Within minutes, hours at most, our medic is dead as a result of Abby Dixon's romantic foolishness. And again, Jed Lewis is discovered with the body. Is Abby an accomplice? Or has he now killed Abby Dixon as well?"

"I told you he's a bloody psycho," Dana muttered.

"This is admittedly circumstantial," Norse went on, weaving the prosecution case. "Lewis has been careful to cover his tracks and to strike unobserved when his victims are alone, or at least when any witness is too blind to identify him, like poor Clyde. Yet sometimes victims can strike back from the grave. Nancy Hodge was drugged but before she died she pulled out the one piece of identification that pinpoints her assailant. There was a folder on her body."

"Yes, Abby's," Lewis said impatiently. "Does that make *her* the killer?"

"Nancy was smart and the murderer was in too much of a hurry to look at her folder," Norse went on. "It was a grave mistake. Because when we looked at the X rays . . ." He glanced at the cook.

"They were Jed's," Pulaski concluded quietly.

The group began to buzz like a disturbed hive. What had Lewis been mumbling about X rays? Lewis felt dizzy. The cook pulled out the film of his teeth and it began to be passed around the room like damning proof. Everything had gone horribly wrong.

"I'm sure you can appreciate how embarrassing this is for me," Norse said sadly. "I came down here thinking I was a pretty good shrink. I thought I was a decent judge of character. I bet that Jed Lewis could be trusted. I told *Rod* he could be trusted. I stuck up for him when the rest of you were suspicious. But I was wrong, dead wrong, and I mean dead in the most literal way. I don't expect you to forgive me. I certainly won't forgive myself. All I ask is that we act, and act now."

"Act how?" Gina Brindisi said in a small voice.

Norse took a breath. "Jed Lewis appears to have directly or indirectly killed six people. Maybe seven, if he's

butchered Abby. It's not for me to say if we know that beyond a reasonable doubt. It's for *you*. But for our own survival and peace of mind, we can't wait out the winter. We
can't wait for distant rescue. The final say has to be a group
decision, but . . ."

"You want to execute him?"

Norse looked at Gina sadly. "I don't want to execute
anyone. None of us does."

"But what, then?" Geller asked. "Where can we keep
him?"

"I want Antarctica to do it."

There was a long silence as they realized what he meant.

"You mean put him outside the dome," Pulaski clarified.

"Where he can sabotage even more!" Dana objected.

Norse shook his head. "I want him tied out on the snow
until he can't do us any more harm. If we remove most of
his clothing it won't take very long. It's not that cruel a
death. He'll shiver and go to sleep. And none of us have
to be the executioner."

They looked at Lewis uneasily: hateful, fearful, sad.

"He's a shrink, dammit!" Lewis shouted. "He's playing
with your minds!"

"All this trouble started when Jed Lewis arrived," Norse
summed up. "I predict it will end when Jed Lewis is no
longer a factor. I don't want to risk anyone else. We're facing a catastrophe and have only each other to rely on. I
won't do it alone, but I'll do it with you. We'll do it together, as a group, in unity. And then it will all be over."

"If we freeze him can we reopen the station?" Mendoza
asked. "Get back to work?"

"We can if you believe he's your killer."

"Listen to me," Lewis groaned. "Norse is not Norse!

He's an impostor! He's manipulating you! He's playing
with the station for some kind of sick experiment!"

"Is that so?" Pulaski asked. He shook his head, wondering what fantasy Lewis would weave next.

"I called out to learn about him and nothing adds up."

"You dialed up from the sauna?" Geller said derisively.

"No, no-o-o," Lewis said. *How to get through to them?*
"I got outside the dome, went to Clean Air! I started the
generator at the emergency camp and rerouted some
power—"

"Bullshit. The dome's sealed."

"I went out through the vent hole, at the top."

"How? With a stepladder?"

"I used one of Jerry's balloons. Ask him, one's missing."

They turned to Follett, who looked puzzled. "A balloon?"

"To carry a rope up to the top of the dome. I know it
sounds crazy but it worked."

"How did you get my balloons?"

"I stole one," Lewis said, less desperation in his voice
now. At least they were paying attention.

"So you're a thief." It was flat confirmation.

"To get out!"

Follett waved his hand dismissively. "I don't believe a
word you say."

"Go count!"

"Count what? I've lost track of my balloons. It proves
nothing!"

"Damn right, it doesn't," Geller said.

"You've heard Bob, now hear me," Lewis insisted desperately. "Everything he's told you is backward. Everything
he's told you has been twisted around. There's a psychologist named Robert Norse who got lost in New Zealand.

Who died, I think. And our Norse followed him and took his place and came down here to, to . . ."

"To what?" Pulaski asked.

"I don't know. To screw us up somehow. But that's not the real Norse." He pointed to Bob.

"Who is he, then?"

"I don't know."

The others groaned. Norse had a pitying smile.

"No, listen! He came to Auckland after the real Norse had disappeared on some hike or climb! Gabriella had the date. Nancy Hodge was going to compare the dental X rays Norse sent in advance to NSF with the ones this impostor brought down with him. But when I went to see her she was already dead! Think! Why would I kill her?"

"Because maybe *you* are the impostor," Molotov said slowly. "You, the geologist doing weather, which makes no sense. You who show up at the last minute. You, who knew about the value of the meteorite. You, whose X rays are on the dead body."

"Norse planted them there! Why would *I* leave them?"

"Because we found you before you looked at them," Geller growled. "Just like Bob said."

"What Jed has just told you is completely absurd," Norse added unnecessarily.

"He's looking for some chance to escape," Dana said. "Some chance to kill again."

"Dammit, I'm trying to save the rest of you!"

"Then where are these X rays you claim incriminate me?" Norse demanded. "Let's see this supposed proof!"

"I don't know," he admitted more quietly. "I don't have them."

"And I don't have them, either. I looked for my X rays after we captured you and they've disappeared. Very convenient, isn't it, for you to remove any chance for me to prove my own innocence? Your whole story is tissue, Lewis. I don't even believe you got out of the dome."

Inspiration struck. "Really? Because I can *prove* that part to you! The rope I used is hidden in the snow behind Comms! Would I have put a rope there if I'm not telling the truth? Go out to a working computer like I did! Use the satellites like I did!"

"And look for what?" Mendoza said. "People with the same common name?"

"Just do it and draw your own conclusions, Carl."

Norse looked uncertain. "Maybe you planted that rope as an alibi."

"Come on, you know that's crazy! I didn't plan this! Look, let's go out into the dome if you don't believe me!"

There was an uneasy silence. They wanted it over. They just wanted it to be him.

"Let's look," Steve Calhoun, the carpenter, finally said, standing up. "I'm not exposing anybody until I'm certain. I don't know what a rope proves, but if it's there we can at least see if it's long enough."

"It's long! I doubled it, in a loop, so I could pull it back down!"

"Maybe long enough to hang you, if it comes to that," Pulaski warned.

"If I'm telling the truth, will you look into the rest of it?"

They were wary, but here was something easy to check. The assembly pulled on parkas and boots and went outside, circling behind Comms.

"There! I buried it there!"

Several moved forward and dug with their mittens. Nothing.

Lewis was confused. "No, it was there somewhere! Dig more!"

He watched them with growing hopelessness as they dug and kicked.

The rope was gone.

"Everything you've ever told us has been a lie, hasn't it?" Pulaski said quietly. "All this slaughter for a damn meteorite?"

Lewis felt dizzy. He was exhausted from fighting them. Everything he tried made things worse. He slumped on his knees on the snow. "Then ask Abby," he groaned.

"We can't find Abby," Dana said.

"Please. Lock me up if you don't believe me. Just check out Bob before you put me out in the cold." His gaze flickered from one face to another, looking for an ally. Several looked away.

"We tried that," Geller told the others. "And every time we do, another of us winds up dead."

CHAPTER TWENTY-SEVEN

They unwired and unbolted the smaller door that led to the dome ramp, breaching their fortress for this one grave duty. Then they filed upward to the plateau like a hooded procession of monks, Lewis bound and hobbled. Everyone was there because Norse insisted that everyone be there, that they make this decision together, that they unify as a group. "When we explain that we did this to save the station, it has to be unanimous," he told them. "Beyond a reasonable doubt."

Several looked sick. But they came along.

The night outside was green and gold and red, a shimmer of auroral light caught by the earth's magnetic field. Lewis was going to die under the colors of Christmas. The stars had added their illumination to the starlit glow of snow, and the plateau was a silver mirror of color, a spangle of galaxies. They glittered above and glittered below, like the spark of Mickey's neutrinos. The survivors marched on a platter of stars.

A long metal tube used for ice coring was solemnly screwed into the snow at the South Pole stake until it was as rigid and strong as a fence post. They would tie Lewis there. The temperature was almost a hundred degrees below zero again, the air still. "It's kinder than what he did to our friends," Pulaski told the others, to help stiffen their resolve. "He'll go quickly and then it will be over."

They wrestled Lewis out of his parka and slit open his windpants, the sting of the invading cold instantaneous. They disregarded his wince. Their souls were as frozen as the Pole now, their mood vengeful. They'd had enough. They were going to extinguish their own fear.

"You're killing an innocent man," Lewis gasped as the cold hit him. "When I'm gone it will all start again and then this will be on your conscience, too."

"Can't we gag him?" Geller asked.

"He's trying to divide us," Mendoza added.

"No, let him talk," Norse said. "Let him predict. So that when it does end, after he's gone, you can all take heart in the knowledge that you did the right thing."

They looked at Lewis, waiting for him to say more, and in the end he didn't know what more to say.

When they lashed him to the coring tube it burned through his thermal undershirt like hot iron. He writhed against it, struggling to think, already in mental shock because the absurdity of his dilemma was overwhelming. He'd come to the bottom of the world for companionship, and his companions were about to kill him. He'd come for purpose, and instead had found death. The sky was the most glorious he'd ever seen and he was about to see nothing ever again.

It was insane.

He wanted to weep, but his tears had frozen, too.

"How long will it take?" Lena Jindrova asked, her voice trembling.

"He'll be lucky to last half an hour," Pulaski replied.

"This doesn't feel right," she whispered.

Norse put his arm around her. "It's right if we do it together."

The coring tube was high enough that it was impossible for Lewis to slip his bonds over the top of it. They stood in a semicircle around him and watched for a moment, sickly fascinated, but he was beginning to shiver and no one wanted to watch this death for very long, the slow freezing that all of them unconsciously feared.

"Do we really all have to be out here?" Gina Brindisi asked.

"It has to be unanimous," Norse said. "So there's no finger-pointing afterward. So we can come together afterward."

"I'm not taking any satisfaction in this," she said.

"I am," Geller muttered. "I hope it fucking hurts."

"When the shivering stops, so will the pain," Pulaski promised. "His brain will shut down pretty fast." He finished his knots and stepped back.

They watched Lewis clench against the cold and then go into a quick spasm of shivering, his stare hollow now and far away. Then he'd shake again, rattling against the stake like a husk in the wind.

"I'm leaving," Gina threatened. A few others nodded.

Norse turned away as well, addressing the others. "This is pretty difficult for some of us. A hard choice, hard to watch. Hard for me. We don't need any more nightmares. Can you stand watch, Cueball? You've been a soldier. I'd like to take the rest of us back to the dome. We've got some healing to do."

The cook looked at the hopeless Lewis. "Go heal."

They turned, a depleted platoon, Lewis hanging from

the coring tube as if he were about to be shot. Six dead,
a seventh dying. Abby missing, Skinner blinded. And
months of isolation to go. It had been a disaster to allow
the fingie to come at the last minute. A disaster not to have
screened him first, not to have incorporated him from the
beginning, not to have learned something about his warped
personality.

A disaster to trust.

Their next job was to find Abby, deal with her, and then
somehow piece the station back together. Endure the dark
winter. Wait again for the first blush of sunlight, and with
it their distant rescue.

"Goodbye, Jed," Gina said sorrowfully as they began to
move away.

"Good riddance," Calhoun amended.

They started to follow their own boot prints back to the
dome.

And then a shout from the crest of the ramp, two figures stumbling toward them. Again they had the anony-
mous hoods up but the one in the lead was obviously Abby,
struggling over the sastrugi drifts of snow because she was
bent with some burden on her back. Her left hand was extended to her companion, who could only be Skinner.
"Stop!" she shouted again. Her high voice drifted, a crys-
tal note, a bell on the stillness of the plateau. "Let him
go!"

"Don't listen to her!" Norse warned. He'd stiffened.

But they did stop until she stormed up, gasping for breath,
her gaiter a white beard of ice. Straightening her back, she
rolled something off that looked like a squat mortar and
let it fall with a plop on the snow. Skinner stopped beside
her, swaying unsteadily, goggles missing but his eyes swathed,
his head cocked at an angle toward a sky he couldn't see,

so that he could hear better from one ear at the edge of his hood. He looked stricken.

"Are you all insane?" Abby challenged, pointing past them to Lewis. "Get his damn parka back on!"

"It's too late, Dixon," Norse said coldly. "You let your lover out to kill again and he went after our most important member, our doctor. The group has made a decision to put an end to this nightmare. You've got a lot to answer for yourself. Push things now and there'll be *serious* repercussions."

"Is that a threat, Bob?"

"If you like."

Abby turned from the psychologist. "So now he's got you to do his killing for him?" she asked, her eyes sweeping the group. They huddled like uncertain deer, newly bewildered by her arrival, depleted of their certainty by her own anger. "Get his clothes back on him, Carl!" she told Mendoza. "You're executing the wrong man!"

"You're bewitched by Lewis, Abby," Dana tried.

"I'm an admirer of a man struggling to do the right thing. By God, get some clothes on him! He's going to get frostbite if you don't move! Give some time to hear me out! I've got proof! Proof that you're all being set up! You've got all winter to execute him if I'm wrong!"

"But you let the killer out of the sauna!" Dana accused. "Maybe we should tie you out there, too!"

"I let *Jed* out of the sauna. And who's killing who, Dana?"

There was an uneasy silence, people shuffling in the cold. The awful irrevocability of what they were doing began to sink in.

"Let's put his clothes back on," Pulaski finally muttered

to Mendoza. "She's right, there's time. What if we're wrong? Let's sort this out."

"No!" Norse snapped, suddenly furious. "Carl, don't you dare!"

The astronomer blinked in surprise. The psychologist's loss of cool was unaccustomed, and his implicit threat opened a wedge of doubt. It wasn't like Norse to snap at anybody, especially a beaker. Hesitantly, Mendoza took a step toward the stake.

"Don't you touch those ropes!" It was a hiss.

They all looked at Norse uncertainly now, surprised by his emotion.

"It wasn't Lewis!" Skinner suddenly hollered. "You're freezing the wrong man!"

The winter-overs jerked at this loud pronouncement. And that was enough to suddenly make the astronomer stride to the stake, cursing at everyone and everything, and begin untying Lewis. "Start talking, Abby," he said fiercely as he worked clumsily. "Start talking, and if you don't make your case I'll strangle this bastard with my own hands."

The ropes began to fall on the snow. No one moved to stop what he was doing.

"You're making it worse," Norse warned, his voice trembling slightly. He was tensing, his eyes flickering from the object Abby had dumped in the snow to the others around him. "When you remember the truth, the execution will be worse."

"The killing stops now," Abby countered.

Lewis was mumbling incoherently, uncertain what Mendoza was even doing, his mind already numb from the cold. He was disoriented. Gina began to sniffle.

"Yeah, start talking, Gearloose," Geller said. "What the hell is that?" He pointed toward the mortarlike object.

"It's Doctor Bob's telescope kit," Abby replied. "Fat suckers like this are called Dobsons—hobbyists use 'em, right Bob?"

"You stole that from my room." His voice had a quiet menace.

"I broke into your room because I was looking for evidence to set things straight. Couldn't find a thing. Not even my picture. You're careful, Bob, I give you that. But then it occurred to me to lift up your telescope."

"She's in love with Lewis," Norse told the others. "She's gone crazy herself. She's trying to twist things the same way he does, but she's not dangerous like him. We don't need to kill her. Just get her some help."

Abby ignored this. "Nancy Hodge did leave us a clue, Bob, but not Jed's X rays. Why do his teeth prove anything?"

He looked belligerent. "How do you even know about Jed's X rays?"

"Oh, I was listening to your kangaroo court from above, from behind the bar."

He started at his own failure to check above the galley and frowned, furious with himself for not apprehending her. "We caught him in the act, Abby," he blustered. "Give it up."

"You caught him in the act of discovering the body of a woman you'd already killed," Abby corrected. She glanced past him to where Lewis was slumping forward as the bonds came free. Mendoza began to help the shivering man into his parka. "Your silly recitation of evidence did give me an idea, though. I knew Nancy had no reason to pull Jed's X ray and put it in my folder—you did that—but I did think she might have successfully hidden the ones that really counted. Like you said, Hodge was smart. So while

you assembled your lynch mob I went back to talk to Clyde
here. You wouldn't let anyone talk to him because you'd
been in BioMed just before Lewis and were afraid of what
he might say. So I talked to him. And do you know what
he was lying on?" She held up the sheet in her mitten, which
they now saw was photographic film. "Your dental X ray,
Bob. The one I took from Rod's files, the one you brought
down to Antarctica with you. The reason you couldn't find
it is because Nancy had already hidden it under Clyde's
pillow. She'd also hidden the earlier set sent down by NSF.
Two dental X rays, supposedly of the same man." She
looked past him to the others. "They don't match."

"I had some work done," he bluffed.

"You sure did. You gained four molars."

There was a murmur of confusion, and then slow realization of what the X rays might mean. One set sent by
NSF of the original Norse, a man perhaps still lost in New
Zealand. And a second brought by his replacement, showing a different set of teeth. Lewis was being dressed, Mendoza pulling the clothes onto his trembling limbs as if Lewis
were a young child.

"Who are you, Bob?" Abby asked. "You're not the Robert
Norse the National Science Foundation selected to come
down here. He disappeared in New Zealand. Six days after
he went missing, you followed him into the woods. Then
you materialized in Christchurch and flew to Antarctica before too many awkward questions could be asked. Are you
even a psychologist at all?"

"That's a lie!" he shouted to the others. "She's covering
up for Lewis!"

"You're the liar!" Skinner hollered, his ear turned to the
debate because his eyes were bandaged. "I heard you in
with Nancy before she fell! You blinded me, you sono-

fabitch, but you didn't kill me, and that was your first big mistake. I smelled you, Doctor Bob! I wasn't sure just who was who but Abby brought your aftershave from your room and I remembered it! When you lose your eyes, your nose starts to remember! I smelled your aftershave! I smelled your fear when Nancy died!"

"That's absurd," Norse snorted. "A couple days of blindness and Clyde is some kind of bloodhound? To a scent Dixon brought him? Come on! What kind of aftershave does Lewis use?"

"Lewis stinks," Calhoun drawled. "He's been in jail." Someone barked a laugh and with that Norse realized he was beginning to lose them. The spell was breaking.

"Nancy mixed up the X rays," Norse tried. "This is all a misunderstanding. Don't let this woman set the killer loose where he can attack you all!"

"I'm going to get him back inside," Mendoza said quietly, the astronomer's manner embarrassed and subdued. "I'm going to get him warm." Putting his arm around the shuddering Lewis, he began walking him back to the dome. Nobody made a move to stop them. The group's righteousness had deflated. A growing dread was replacing it.

"I knew I needed something better to convince the rest of you," Abby went on, ignoring Norse and addressing the others. "Not circumstantial and confusing, like a pair of X rays. Evidence that was absolutely rock-solid, right? So I've been desperately thinking. It was the meteorite that started things. The meteorite that disappeared. Have you stopped wondering where it went?" She kicked the Dobson telescope with her boot and something clunked inside. "When I picked this up it was heavier and noisier than what I expected. So I brought it out here on a bet. Alexi, you're the one who's always accusing Jed. Go ahead and look through it at the sky. Tell us what you see."

"Leave it alone!" Norse yelled, stepping to block the others from it.

"Just give it a try, Alexi."

The Russian hesitated, then stepped forward, brusquely pushing the psychologist aside. Kneeling in the snow, he set the Dobson telescope upright and bent to the eyepiece, cranking its focus first one way, then the other. Finally he looked up. "It is dark. I cannot see from this thing. The telescope of Bob does not work."

"That's because it's not finished yet!" Norse said with exasperation.

"I don't think it's a telescope at all," Abby went on. "I think it's a box, a hiding place, a way to smuggle down things that might otherwise be illegal. Something that can't be opened and thus something where no one would ever look. And I'm betting if we cut it open anyway we'll find a missing meteorite inside it."

The group shuffled curiously forward, making a half circle around the telescope. Skinner unzipped his parka and withdrew a hacksaw he'd carried out.

"Don't you dare destroy my telescope! I've spent a hundred hours on the damn thing!"

"I'll make you a deal, Bob," Abby said. "If I cut into this and I'm wrong, you can tie me to your sacrificial stake out there. Because right now I'm a threat to your life. But if I cut into it and I'm right, then you're the one we strap to the coring tube." She knelt beside the telescope. "Deal?"

"Wait, wait!" He looked at the others with increasing panic and confusion. Mendoza was disappearing down the ramp with the stumbling Lewis. The ropes that had tied Lewis to the stake were in a tangle around its base. The group was extending its own enclosing line, flanking around him. "All right, all right. But let me cut it open. For God's sake, maybe that way I can at least repair it when you see how wrong you are!"

Abby hesitated, holding the hacksaw. Norse reached out and snatched it from her.

"Okay?" he asked the others.

"Hurry up," Geller growled. "It's cold out here!"

Norse began sawing through the fat telescope tube. The Dobson was only two and a half feet long but as rotund as a small keg. Its simple mirror arrangement collected huge amounts of light and was a cost-effective astronomy tool for amateurs. It could also hold a lot inside. As the psychologist cut, the top of the tube sagged down. Finally it split, the front lens falling away, and something the size of a large potato rolled down onto the snow.

It was the meteorite.

"Bloody hell," Dana whispered.

"She planted it in there," Norse tried.

Nobody believed him.

"Why?" Gina breathed. "Why kill so many?"

Norse glared at her then, with a look so contemptuous and malevolent his face was transformed. In an instant he went from reason to unreason, from the solemn light to the hateful dark. He was a man consumed by demons, a deep inner rage. He put his glove into the split shell of the telescope. "You've been killing yourselves," he said ominously. "You've sabotaged your own little commune with fear, mistrust, blind faith, and group delusion. And once again, I'm the one who's going to survive."

Suddenly he sprang to his feet, stiff-armed the unprepared Clyde Skinner to bowl him over, and grabbed Abby, his forearm around her throat. It was fluid, an action that had been mentally rehearsed, with the quick grace of an athlete. She went rigid and yelled.

"Get him!" Pulaski roared.

But before the survivors could rush, Norse lifted his other arm.

He had a pistol, its muzzle gaping like the twin barrels of a shotgun. It was crude and homemade, with no apparent magazine or revolving chamber, but was as black down its twin barrels as the bottom of the world. They presumed the gun held at least two bullets. "Back off or I kill some more," Norse growled.

They stopped, frightened by the weapon.

He grinned at their acquiescence, pinning Abby tighter. "I told you not to open my telescope."

The Things We Share

Amundsen-Scott base was built by a nation that guarantees the pursuit of happiness. A good psychologist will tell you that all of us chase that elusive and torturous goal by seeking four things.

The first is freedom. Freedom? Mine had been robbed by Fat Boy, whose blundering mistake had bound my destiny to his and left me to drag his disgusting ghost of quivering blubber everywhere I went. With his death, choice collapsed in on me like the dirt of the grave.

Security? The kids and the mountain had robbed me of that, too. When I came down off that glacier I could never rest. Never rest! My career became migratory, my jobs makeshift, and my savings sifted away. I had no home, no institution, no identity, except as the man they whispered about. I'd whirl sometimes to catch them and they'd look at me like a curiosity, pretending that they hadn't been judging, but I knew better. I knew better! I'd been stripped of every certainty except my own moral innocence.

Recognition? All my life I've longed for respect. My ideas are significant. My insights are creative. My mastery at the Pole is a demonstration of ability already displayed a hundred times. Yet I was continually passed over. Snubbed. Outmaneuvered by lesser men and women, the victim of gossip and innuendo and condescension. It worsened after the climb. Every rejected paper was a rebuke. Every missed invitation was an accusation. I'd been shorn of all respect, judged guilty without trial. Damned for my own survival!

So at the very end I longed for the fourth thing the shrinks say we all need, response. For love, and if not love then at least friendship, and if not friendship then at least companionship, and if not companionship then at least acknowledgment, the comfort of knowing your words are listened to, your comments receive response. And at the South Pole I thought I'd found that. In the Three Hundred Degree Club I thought I'd found salvation.

The women shouldn't have betrayed me. They shouldn't have betrayed me!

I was ready to stop. You have to believe that. I was ready to stop. Tyson had fled, and it would be child's play to let all suspicion remain on him. I had a case study to prove my point and a valuable meteorite to give me freedom and security. I was on the very edge of happiness, I'm sure of it.

Yet Dixon couldn't see my possibilities. She'd been blinded by a lesser man, Lewis, and at my moment of triumph she ran to a man of clay.

So when I went to help the weeping Gabriella that night, I expected we could find some kind of solace with each other. Some kind of consolation. What I wasn't counting on was her anger, her fury at herself, her foolish longing for love, and her irrational focusing of her own poison on me.

She turned me down. The slut, after her rejection by Lewis, turned me down! Suddenly she wanted self-respect!

I found myself out of control without understanding why I even cared. Damn her! I was fighting with her, holding her down, my hands somehow around her throat—I'm not that kind of man at all!—but ordained

*by God, it seems, or doomed by the devil, to finally take
the station down with me. I really didn't plan to end it
this way. I simply wanted to choke out every hateful thing
I ever imagined people saying.*

*And as she died, her eyes bulging, her frantic bucks
becoming more feeble, her look became an accusatory
question.*

Had I become a coward on that mountain?

If I'm to have any peace, I have to erase them all.

CHAPTER TWENTY-EIGHT

*B*ut *the hair on his head began to grow again. . . ."*

Norse's voice crackled over the galley intercom as condescending sermon, the paternal recitation of a school principal. The experiment had been conducted and its meaning was about to be revealed, so his own particular collection of winter-over lab rats had been ordered at gunpoint to stay in the galley while he announced his intentions from Cameron's old office in the other module, next to the radios he'd destroyed. Abby was being held hostage to ensure their compliance until he completed his lecture and his preparations to leave. The rest listened with gloomy apprehension.

"Then he pushed with all his might, and down came the temple on the rulers and all the people in it. . . ."

"He's gone balmy," Dana Andrews whispered.

"He always was," Pulaski said grimly, angry at himself. "The more we listened to him, the more over the edge he went. It fed him. *We* fed him."

"What the hell is he talking about?" Geller asked.

"I think it's stuff from the Bible," Lewis said, beginning

to revive from his near-execution. He had just enough frostbite to make his nose and fingers sting like fire and his shudders were receding only with the help of some soup Pulaski had microwaved. The pain as his skin warmed helped keep him from collapsing. "He quoted some to me when I arrived. It's the story of Samson, destroying the temple of the Philistines."

"I ain't no Philistine. That's something bad, right?"

"It is if he pulls down our temple."

"My God, is he going to destroy the bloody station?" Dana asked.

"He might if we let him. He gets off on toying with us."

The intercom crackled again. "We've finally been stripped of pretense, haven't we?" Norse broadcast. The disembodied sound had an eerie power and Lewis realized that the psychologist had done what Lewis had asked him not to do: Norse had gotten into their heads. It wasn't just a voice, vibrating in air. His presence reverberated in their minds. "*I'm* revealed as Oz, puppeteer of souls. *You're* exposed as a thin biologic film on the petri dish of the Pole, as easy to erase as a smear of mold. You joined a society that can't protect you. That can't even recognize its own internal danger. How does that make you feel?"

There was no way for them to reply.

"I've been giving you an experience similar to that which I faced once," Norse went on, a teacher to his students. "In the face of group incompetence I had to rely on myself for salvation. I've been punished for it ever since. So the question is, was my misfortune simply a fateful tragedy of bad luck? Or is it modern civilization, the Age of the Committee, that is to blame? Are there so many of us now, in so many clubs and consortiums and families and clans and boardrooms and unions and seminars and societies, that we've forgotten how to think for ourselves? Act for ourselves? *Be* ourselves? What happens when the lemmings lead us to nuclear Armageddon or a stock market crash or global climate collapse or starvation from overpopulation or off the edge of a cliff? Will it be the feel-good commune that saves us? Or will it be individual preparation and reliance and free will? When I acted for myself was I exhibiting the worst of human nature? Or the best? I think evolution suggests the latter. I think we've been so cushioned by mere numbers that we've forgotten what evolution demands."

"He is a Nazi is what he is," Molotov said grimly.

"Do scientists have even the slightest idea of the human hardness that's going to be required now to explore the extremes of the universe or survive among the evolving brilliance of machines? Just how strong is your collective? Not very strong, is it? You panicked. You abandoned your work. You locked yourself in. You armed yourself. You quarreled. You turned on each other. You were ready to kill each other. The one who finally woke you up was Lewis, the fingie I set up as the outsider."

There was noise in the background, a scrape of furniture. "Shut up," Norse muttered. They assumed he was speaking to Abby.

"Civilization is a fraud," he resumed, his pontificating reminding Lewis of Mickey Moss. "It's a blip in time, a blemish on a million years of humanoid existence. *Society* is a fraud. They always fall, always break down. And when they do it comes down to individual survival. When something new is built in the ruins it's the strong individual, the visionary, the freethinker, who points the way. I followed the most fundamental of human instincts: survival. And they hounded me for it! So I came down to their little jewel, their farthest place, the place of night and hypothermia, to test social utopia. And you snapped like a cord in this cold."

"You wouldn't have survived thirty minutes by yourself, you deluded bastard," Pulaski muttered. There was no answer, of course.

"I hope you realize that you've made things far more terrible than I intended them to be," Norse went on. "I wasn't planning much more than an embarrassing psychological paper on station dysfunction, illustrated by depression and mistrust. But God had more in store for us, it seems: He planted an apple in Eden! Mickey was so greedy to get back his meteorite. And so pathetic at the end that he followed it, and me, right into the pit. He begged to be let out again. Let out? Was Lucifer let out? He fell from grace! He'd chosen his own fate! But the rest of you wouldn't stop. You wouldn't stop! First Adams, and then Cameron. It was you who turned on Buck Tyson, not me. You who mistrusted Lewis, not me. You who missed every clue and misplaced every doubt. I used Carl's candle to make a wax impression of Buck Tyson's knife locker lock. I didn't forge Lewis's name, I got him to write it for me. When I wondered how Lewis had escaped the dome, all I had to do was look down at the icicles stabbed into the snow, guess what he'd done, and find the rope to confirm it. I wanted to humiliate your little society, not destroy it. I'd made my point! But you wouldn't stop!" He took a breath.

They waited. He didn't mention Gabriella.

"So. At last it stops. How to end my little demonstration? Closing down an experiment can be as difficult as starting it. I think the best solution is that I leave, alone. I'm at my best alone. I'll give Miss Dixon here a final choice on her fate. She can save herself by coming with me or cast her lot with the morons. I'm indifferent either way."

"Let her go now so we can test your little experiment, tough guy," Pulaski said to the speaker. It was pointless. He was talking to a machine.

"As you saw, my telescope kit allowed me to smuggle down the necessary components of a gun," Norse went on blandly. "You might take *me,* sure, but I'd be sure to take more of *you.* Frankly, however, I think there's been enough violence. So this is what we're going to do. I need one hour. One hour to make my preparations! At the end of that time I'll commandeer the remaining Spryte. I'll take my chances on the polar plateau, just as Tyson did. And if you go telling stories to our Vostok friends, well, let's just say that I have a story of my own prepared. I can be quite convincing."

No one bothered to answer this time. They were depleted, defeated by their own mistakes. Spirit had been sucked out of them. It was difficult for them to even look at Lewis, the innocent man they'd almost executed.

"I was the serpent, people, and when I came you had no individual strength to resist my temptation. Look around at those so-called friends of yours. You have none. You have none! You'll all despise each other the rest of your short, miserable lives! Lewis, look at the people who just tried to kill you! And then credit *me* the path to inner strength. You came ten thousand miles for a family. Which meant you came ten thousand miles for a mirage."

More noise in the background. Then: "Shut up! Shut up!" A long pause.

He resumed. "One hour. One hour and I'm out of your lives. Remain in the galley until I'm on my way. I see that galley door open and the agreement's off. Don't forget, I have Abby."

The intercom switched off.

CHAPTER TWENTY-NINE

They sat in the galley in sick indecision, listening to the hum of the ventilation system and half expecting it to go off as the power died. If they hunted down and confronted Norse, they risked Abby. If they didn't go after him, they might risk themselves: How did they know the psychologist wasn't sabotaging the station? Yet they were emotionally depleted. After the near-disaster with Lewis, none had the stomach to sacrifice Abby for the group right now by confronting the psychopath. A showdown might prompt Norse to somehow not just shoot her, but damage the fragile machinery that kept them alive. Maybe it was safer to wait. Maybe he would simply keep his word and drive away.

It was a depressed silence, each of them profoundly alone, a cataloguing of misgivings and second guesses and confused doubts. Norse had robbed them of their own self-confidence. He'd drained them of purpose.

"I don't get it," Pulaski finally said. "How can a man hate all of us like that? Hate his own kind?"

Lewis was in no mood for philosophy. "Easy. By hating himself."

"And if he hates himself, why? What the hell did he do?"

"Who knows? I think he lost it completely when he strangled Gabriella. Before that maybe it's something he *didn't* do once. Something he's been trying to justify to himself."

"Justify by killing people."

"By getting us to act like the fools he thinks we are. Maybe we'll find out someday, if we get through this."

"It would have to be something pretty bad, wouldn't it? Something to really make you feel terrible about life?"

Lewis looked at the cook for a long time and then let his gaze drift around the room. Geller. Calhoun. Dana Andrews. Alexi Molotov. Accusers. Executioners. "Yes," he finally said. "Like tying an innocent man to a stake at the Pole." He couldn't hide the bitterness.

Everyone looked away.

He should have bit it back but Norse's taunting had hit home. Lewis was angry, sore, depleted. He'd lived, yes, but some vital part of him seemed to have gone: He felt that he'd died a little just by being strapped to that stake. He wondered if he'd ever get that part of himself back. Basic optimism. Trust.

He'd come looking for community and they'd been willing to dispose of him. The harder he'd tried, the worse things seemed to get. So here he was, the woman he was falling in love with in the hands of a madman, without a friend and without a future. *Welcome to the Three Hundred Degree Club, buddy.*

Sitting in a metal box, waiting like dumb poultry for their fate. That's what Norse would have predicted, wouldn't he?

Predicted that, at the end, none of them would be talking to each other.

He'd played with them.

What if he was *still* playing with them?

It was the first thought to jolt Lewis out of his depressed apathy. What was Norse's game now? They had nothing but the word of a killer that he'd ever let Abby go. That he wouldn't damage the station. There were, what? He counted. Seventeen of them. Abby, the eighteenth, and then Norse. Six dead, assuming Tyson had succumbed. And . . .

Where the hell was Pika?

The little man was so quiet he was easy to miss.

Lewis stood up, suddenly terribly concerned but not certain what he was concerned about. The lethargy! They had to shake it off! Norse was counting on it to give himself time to get away. Get away with Abby. Get away with . . . what?

Seventeen against one.

What the hell were they sitting there for?

The others were eyeing him uncertainly.

"Cueball, did you get a look at his gun?"

Pulaski shrugged. "Barely."

"Is it real?"

The cook looked at Lewis speculatively, his own energy pricked slightly by the geologist's. "It looked real to me. Won't know unless we jump him."

"How many shots does he have?"

"Well, a real gun would have been picked up in the detectors when he came down here, so his looked pretty crude, a bunch of homemade parts." Pulaski thought. "I saw two barrels, which suggests there's no chamber for extra bullets. Probably just two shots, like a double-barreled shotgun, until he has time to reload. Who knows how many bullets? What are you thinking?"

"That we've been letting him control events since the

winter began. And that we're still letting him, by sitting here."

The cook looked doubtful. "You want to risk Abby, Jed?"

"You think she's not already at risk? After all that's happened? Norse says he's going to leave, but how?"

"The Spryte," Geller spoke up. "Like Tyson tried. Norse was curious about it from the beginning. Load a sled with food and fuel and take off across the plateau. It's risky, but he knows he's dead if he stays here. If we'd killed you, maybe he would have gotten away with the whole thing, but not now. His only chance is to go to the Russians and try to bribe his way off the continent with the meteorite."

"Norse is a good talker, but it doesn't make sense. It's him against eighteen or nineteen witnesses, and he knows we'll get the radios back up sometime, that we'll alert NSF and the Russians."

"He's crazy, Jed," Calhoun offered.

"Is he? If Norse takes that Spryte, he not only gets away with murder, but he takes away our only emergency exit in case something goes wrong. What if he's screwing up the base right now, sentencing us all?"

"He can't get to the fuel or generators," Pulaski said. "We sealed those up."

"So how is he getting to the garage to get the Spryte? When you sealed off the generator room you sealed off the garage, too, didn't you?"

That stopped them.

"Maybe he's breaking in or something," Geller said. "He'd have to. Pika is the only one who knows a way to get in. Who has a key."

Lewis let his eyes scan the room. "So where's Pika?"

Heads turned, their apathy becoming alarm. Had Norse kidnapped him, too?

"If Bob is planning to bring down the temple like some kind of deranged Samson, we need him alive to tell us how to defuse whatever he's cooked up. Don't we? We can't afford to let him set off for Vostok because then he's free to pull the plug on *this* place. Booby-trap it, like the batteries in Comms."

"Set a fire," Pulaski said. "Cut a cable."

"We're sitting like hams in a can, waiting for him to do it."

They looked at the galley door. What if Norse had anticipated this very conversation? What if he was outside the door, waiting for one of them to test his threat? Or was he already firing up the Spryte, the station generators about to explode?

"Maybe we need to get out of here and into emergency shelter," Dana said quietly. "Run the bloody hell to Bedrock Village."

"If it comes to that. But I'm not sure I'm willing to write off the rest of the station for this guy. Willing to sit out *there,* hoping for the best."

"I hear you on that," Mendoza said.

"If he's got Pika's keys, or Pika himself," Lewis reminded them, "he can go anywhere, do anything. We're letting a lunatic roam the station."

"And if we go charging out there, we're not only going to get some of us killed, but Abby, too," Linda Brown warned. "If we just wait maybe it will be over."

"Or not. Maybe his experiment hasn't stopped. Why should we believe it has?"

Everyone was looking at Lewis uneasily, suddenly restless, suddenly uncertain again. Every choice seemed risky.

"I care for Abby more than any of you. But Norse is counting on us to react, not anticipate. That's been his expectation from the beginning. He's counting on us to be a step behind him."

"He said if we go out that door—" Linda began.

"That's my whole point. *He* said."

"But what do you want us to do?"

Lewis stopped. What should they do? He thought a moment. "If he sees us coming, he's got more chance to hurt Abby or hurt the station. We need to take him by surprise. If he's really fleeing, then he has to already be in the garage gassing up. Right? He's got to be getting ready. So he *can't* see us. There's only one of him. Let's go outside, circle around to the garage doors, and jump him when he comes out."

"What about the generators?" Mendoza said. "What if he's rigged them to blow when he leaves? Blow if we come at him?"

Lewis paused. "Is that possible?"

"Who knows? He seemed awfully sure we won't survive long enough to sic the authorities on him."

"Okay, how about this? A few of us should go that way— sneak into the garage the back way in case he tries to retreat. Check for any sabotage. Take him from behind with the rest in front. We'll surround the bastard."

"How do we get in?"

"The same way Norse did, I hope. I just remembered something. Pika's been going to BioMed like a horse to a feed bag but there's no sign he's sick. When I found Nancy in the storeroom there was a cabinet askew, a panel behind it, and I'm wondering now if there's some kind of utility access there to the arches. I'd like to take Longfellow through in case there's some electrical thing Norse has rigged to booby-trap our power. You, too, Carl. See if we

can find Abby before he takes off in the Spryte, and get
her safe. Then the rest of you can block him."

"He's got a gun!" Linda Brown reminded.

"Homemade, we think. With two shots."

The others looked queasy, apprehensive, but with a
slowly hardening resolve. They'd lost all sense of control.
Maybe, following Lewis, they could somehow get it back.

"If any one of us tries it alone we'll be killed," Lewis
said. "Any two of us, maybe. But with all of us, everyone
distracting him . . ." He shrugged. "We win."

"With casualties," Pulaski warned.

"But not as lame victims."

Geller was nodding, too. He stood up. "I agree. We're
sitting here like sheep."

"So we give him a shot at us?" Linda asked.

"*We* ambush *him.*"

Others were nodding now, too. The idea of doing something, acting together, was beginning to reenergize them.

"I just want him to go away," Linda moaned.

"No. Because if he gets away, he wins," Lewis said. "He
leaves us like lab rats, pressing levers and chasing cheese.
Don't you see? Norse wants to erase everything Mickey
Moss built by making us give up on it ourselves."

It was disorienting listening now to Lewis, the man they'd
almost killed.

So it was Clyde Skinner who ended the last hesitation.
He unsteadily stood.

"I don't want him to get away with my eyes."

Lewis stepped out of the galley first, bracing for a shot
despite the bland certainty about Norse's movements he'd
conveyed to the others. What if he was wrong?

But no shot came. The shadowy dome seemed empty, a

soft slough of wind audible through the hole at the top of
the dome. He heard nothing else, saw nothing else. So he
stepped down to the snow and waved the others out, watching them pour silently like a line of emerging bees, trot-
ting across the snow to the junction of the archways where
the ramp was. Still no Bob. To the left and right were the
barrier walls they'd erected to seal off the fuel supply and
generators. They hadn't been breached, and the door to the
outside was still bolted and locked. If he was in the garage,
Norse had followed Pika's way.

"Okay, there has to be some kind of tunnel or corridor,"
Lewis told the others. "Go outside and get in position, we'll
push from behind. Stay low, but move fast once it starts.
With luck, we'll surprise him."

Pulaski unlocked the dome's smaller side door and the
winter-overs began filing out into the night, going up the
ramp as they had before to stake out Lewis. This time, if
Lewis was right, they'd stop the Spryte. If wrong, they'd
retreat to the emergency camp at Bedrock and regroup. Pulaski had told them that the galley suddenly seemed like
the worst kind of trap.

"Unless Bob wants us to abandon the galley," Hiro muttered.

"We Yanks had a general named Grant once whose officers were always spooked by a general named Lee," Pulaski told him. "Grant told them to stop worrying what Lee
was going to do and start thinking what *they* were going
to do."

"What happened?"

"They won the war."

Lewis turned with Longfellow and Mendoza to BioMed.
The trio studied the sick bay module, which stood on stilts
a foot above the snow. Crouching, Lewis could now see

there was one point at the rear where a metal culvert led from the sick bay floor down into the snow. Stepping back to view its roof, he noted there was a tube of utility piping that reached to the arched ceiling above, conduits spreading like branches. Some kind of artery ran up the back of BioMed like a spine. It was here, he was certain, that Pika went in and out.

With everyone suspect, no one had been trusted to have access to their power supply. The necessary exception had been their generator mechanic. Norse must have coerced him into showing the way. Coerced him into getting the Spryte.

BioMed's door was half open; the snapped lock had made it impossible for the fugitive to secure it after himself. The three men went inside. It was much as before except that Skinner's bed was empty. Medical supplies remained scattered, drawers askew, the shelves where Lewis had been tackled were still toppled. The cold had invaded, and broken liquids had frozen into thin platters. Lewis went to the rear room. Poor Nancy Hodge lay in the wreckage of her life, her corpse stiff from cold. In the confusion that had followed the murder, her body had been shockingly forgotten. Now she'd have to wait even longer for commemoration. Lewis stepped over her to the cabinet he'd seen dragged askew.

He saw the panel in back of it was now removed. Cold air swirled into BioMed from the dark air beyond. Had Pika been forced to show this entryway to Norse?

Lewis poked his head in and looked downward. No light, but a faint glimmer from spaces beyond. He couldn't risk his own light. If he came upon Norse, he wanted it to be a surprise, which meant claustrophobic gloom again. "I hate tunnels," he murmured to Longfellow.

"Well, it can't be a very long one. I'll go first."

"No, I will, because it was my idea. Just in case he uses that gun."

Taking a breath, he climbed into the shaft and dropped down the short ladder inside it, finding himself in a utility culvert that led in both directions under the archways. Pipes ran here, more than he'd ever suspected existed. The station was as complex as a spaceship. He wondered if Tyson had hidden in here somewhere after Cameron was stabbed. There was enough light from the opening overhead to dimly see and he considered for a moment which way to go. In the direction of the fuel arch it was dark, with a sound like water running. Unlikely Norse would go that way: It was opposite of the garage. Back under the other archway, toward the generators and Spryte, there was a dim light of another opening. He began crawling in that direction, Longfellow and Mendoza following.

It was a tight, grubby, cold place, the thing Lewis hated most. But Pika must have come this way on his regular rounds to keep the plant running. Had Norse and Abby passed here, too? It occurred to Lewis that maybe the psychologist had known about this escape hatch all along. That maybe that's why he'd agreed to Pulaski's determination to seal up the archways, to lock them in the dome. But why would Pika tell him?

Lewis came to an opening overhead that light issued from and could hear the reassuring drum of the generators beyond. At least Norse hadn't cut their power. Cautiously he poked his head up and glanced around. As expected, he was in a corner of the generator room. No one. He pulled himself out of the tunnel and crouched near the reserve generator. The electrician and astronomer came up beside him.

"You see anything out of the ordinary?"

Longfellow crept from machine to machine. The middle one was drumming faithfully. No wires, no bombs, no monkey wrenches. "I think he's left them alone."

Lewis was surprised. Maybe Norse didn't care if he left witnesses. Maybe he was tired of killing. Maybe there was some booby trap they couldn't see.

"We have to make sure," Mendoza said.

"We do that by catching him," Lewis replied.

The three men began cautiously moving toward the gym and garage, giving the others time to circle around in the snow.

Suddenly there was the sharp pop of a gun. Lewis reflexively dropped at the bang, flinching from the expected whine of a bullet. Had Norse spotted them? The others fell with him. But there was no buzz, no thud of a projectile striking a hard surface, and he realized the bullet would have reached him before the bang anyway. The shot had been aimed at someone else. Had Norse gotten in a struggle with Abby? His stomach tightened at the thought of it. "Come on," he hissed. "Let's rush him." Determined to risk a confrontation, he moved forward. The others scuttled after him. Ahead there were footsteps and the slam of a door.

The gym was dark, the door to the garage beyond closed. Lewis trotted ahead and then tripped on something in the gloom, sprawling. Damn! Raggedy Ann, the CPR doll? He reached around. No, someone still warm and sticky. His heart hammering, he moved his hands along the head and body. Despite himself he felt a flood of relief. It wasn't Abby.

"Turn on a light," he whispered.

Longfellow felt along the wall until he found a switch,

all of them blinking in the glare. The body was Pika's, they saw, sprawled as he tried to run back toward the generator room. His arm was outstretched, as if trying to score a goal, and his back was bloody. Norse had cut him down in midflight, the poor little bastard. His other arm was tucked under him and clutching something rough and heavy as tightly as a football. Lewis reached under and tugged it free.

It was the meteorite.

Then they heard the snort and roar of a revved-up Spryte.

CHAPTER THIRTY

Norse didn't open the bay doors that allowed him to exit the half-buried garage, he crashed through them as a precaution against surprise. Always a step ahead! His Spryte burst through in a blaze of light, spraying snow and plywood fragments like a tug butting a wave. The machine's headlights momentarily blinded the ring of winter-overs who'd hunched against the icy darkness to wait for their tormentor, and the violence of the breakout startled them. The machine lurched over the lip of the garage ramp and rocked back down, jerking a sled of fuel and supplies behind it. The engine's howl and the clanking of the treads made it sound like half dinosaur, half tank. When the beams finally swept by them and the cab was silhouetted against the stars, the ambushing group could see there were two people inside, Abby swaying uncertainly and Norse hunched at the wheel. It was obvious the psychologist planned to charge through the station and head toward Vostok as quickly as possible. No pause to say goodbye.

Pulaski was the first to stand up, running to take position in front of the lumbering tractor like a matador in front

of a bull. The old soldier's blood was up now, his opponent finally plain and visible. "Come on!" he roared to the
others. "Help me stop him!"

One by one the rest of the group rose out of the snow
with their crude spears and clubs, rushing to surround the
rumbling machine.

Norse sounded the horn of the Spryte at Pulaski's challenge, an angry, elephantine trumpeting, and then acceler-
ated to run the determined cook down. The diesel snorted
with power, its exhaust a black cloud. The commando
waited until the last second, crouching as if willing to be
hit, and then darted to one side as the machine ground by,
running back along its length in his heavy boots, snow
kicking up in lively spouts. A flying leap threw him upon
the fuel and food sled that Norse was towing and the other
pursuers roared at the sight. Then Pulaski regained his footing and sprang forward like a cat, a boot dancing on the
trailer hitch until his gloved hand could catch a handhold
on the main cab. If he could stop the Spryte the others
could help him swarm Bob. Clenching a vent opening, he
swung himself firmly aboard the snow tractor and worked
along the driver's side, a hammer readied in one fist. The
rest of the winter-overs were pursuing now like a pack of
wolves, yelling and whooping.

Because they hadn't come through the tunnel, none of
this group knew that Norse's gun had already murdered
Pika.

The cook got to the cab door and Norse snarled sound-
lessly at him, swerving the tractor in a vain attempt to
throw his attacker off. Pulaski hung on and swung the hammer. Heavy glass shattered, breaking the Spryte's cocoon
of warmth, and the cook reached inside to either fumble
with the door lock or drag Norse bodily out through the

window's splintery teeth. The others would never know for sure.

The breakage gave Norse a clear shot. There was another bang.

The bullet cuffed the cook off the cab and sent him flying. There was something graceful to his arc, like a backward dive off a board, but when the old soldier fell into the snow it was heavily, his body instantly still. Now it was Norse who howled, an animalistic cry of rage and triumph, and he gunned the machine even harder. Jouncing across the sastrugi drifts toward the summer camp, his Spryte was well on its way toward leaving the Pole.

Dana and Geller reached Pulaski first. The cook's hood had been thrown back and the crest of his head had turned molten where the bullet had hit him. Hot blood steamed like acid into the snow.

He was dead.

A few of the others threw things, the clubs and spears banging off the sides of the Spryte as harmlessly as if it were an armored car. Then it was beyond them, red taillights a taunt, driving on into the night.

Norse was getting away.

"Always a step ahead!" he roared.

Suddenly there was a different snarl, a coughing rumble that rose to a whine, and another, single headlight blazed over the rim of the snow at the entrance to the garage. Snowmobile! It burst up through the wreckage of the garage's bay doors as if catapulted, leaping a drift and coming down in a wild skid, its treads biting and its single ski pointing toward its quarry. It was Lewis, in hot pursuit. Longfellow and Mendoza came charging along after him on foot.

The others began running again, too, trying to catch the

churning tractor. "He's got Abby!" Geller roared at the geologist as Lewis shot by him. "He shot Cueball! Stop him and we'll finish it!"

The blinded Skinner was dancing from leg to leg to the sounds of pursuit, howling in the cold. "Get him, get him, get him!"

The snowmobile was far faster than the Spryte and Lewis pulled up alongside the machine quickly, eyeing the cab, trying to decide what to do. Norse pointed his gun out the window and Lewis fell back. How many shots did he have? One for Pika, one for the cook, but if he'd reloaded . . . Lewis hefted the meteorite as he decelerated, considering. What choice did he have? He swerved around the back of the sled and came up on the machine's other side, where Abby was riding, praying she'd jump at what was coming next. Pulling alongside the galloping treads, he chose a place to aim and then, with grim deliberation, threw the rock into the gearing.

There was another bang, a squeal of metal. The rock caught in the bogie wheels of the tread and jammed it so the Spryte swerved wildly, the other cab door popping open. There was a spurt of dust as Mickey Moss's jewel was crushed into powder. Even as the meteorite disintegrated, a broken tread slithered off one side and the snow machine spun helplessly. Abby was thrown clear and flopped onto the snow, apparently stunned or killed. The Spryte's one working tread sent it wheeling in a tight circle like a dog chasing its tail, the trailer tipping over and the hitch snapping free. The machine was mortally wounded: a window shattered, a tread gone, its extra fuel lost. The others ran up as it careened, surrounding it. Norse was wrenching with the controls, cursing in frustration.

It was like a boat without a rudder.

Then the psychologist realized the inevitable and sat back suddenly, cutting the engine so the Spryte ground to a stop. Its lights dimmed. Lewis cut the snowmobile, too.

It was quiet.

Norse was trapped.

The others stayed back several yards, wary of the gun, their lungs laboring in the bitter cold, surrounding the broken Spryte like hunters around a mammoth. Lewis got off his machine and ran for Abby, fearing she'd been shot. Falling to his knees in the snow beside her, he gingerly turned her over.

It was Raggedy Ann, the CPR doll.

Norse was laughing at him.

The psychologist had climbed out of the cab of the machine and was standing on the Spryte's roof, his parka hood back and his head lit by a halo of stars. He had his crude homemade pistol pointed casually outward, well aware that the others had recollected their hurled weapons and were in a circle around him now, arms poised to throw. He might get off one shot, maybe two. Then it would finally be over.

"Where's Abby?" Lewis called as he shakily rose, trying to catch his breath.

"You didn't do as you were told," Norse replied.

It was quiet again, the only sound the hiss of lightly blown snow slithering over the drifts. Lewis took a step toward the Spryte.

"I didn't really expect to get away," the psychologist finally went on. "I knew that when I was forced to eliminate Gabriella. The game had gotten out of control. But I've made my point, haven't I?"

"Where's Abby?"

"I didn't want to kill anybody, not really." Norse turned slowly, facing each one of the surrounding group in turn, still strangely in command with the force of his personality. "I wanted to kill the pomposity. The pride. The hubris! The academic arrogance, the smugness, the indifference. It was the *station* that killed you people, not me! The delusion that a place like this can work."

Lewis was trembling with impatience and outrage, desperate to know what had happened to the woman who'd saved him. But he had to communicate with this man, and that meant tolerating him for a few moments longer. "It's over, Doc," he tried, his face battered, his voice hoarse. "Give it up and maybe we can get you help come spring."

Norse looked down at him, remote, lordly, distracted. "What possible help could I get from *you*?"

"Learning how to live."

Norse shook his head, snowflakes dancing past his brush of regrown hair. "You still don't understand, do you? I already died. Long, long ago."

They were quiet then, watching each other.

"What did you put in the tractor treads?" Norse finally asked. The quiet of the group, their will against him, was unnerving him.

"The meteorite," Lewis said.

"And it's gone?"

"Yes."

"Destroyed?"

"Yes."

"Fitting, no?"

"Good riddance," Lewis said. "I hate that rock. Everyone does."

"Where did you find it?"

"With Pika, where you murdered him."

"He betrayed you, you know. We can't know anybody, can we?"

"Where's Abby, dammit?"

"Did you know that Pika sold you out for a few pounds of space rock? Quiet little Pika, who never seemed to know what was going on? Yet when I offered him the meteorite he showed me the way past the barrier into the fuel arch. I told him I was just fueling the jerricans to escape. I told him I was going to take him to Vostok. He ran away from me to try to fix things with *you* when he learned the truth. But it's always too late to fix things. That's what I've learned."

Lewis had a growing feeling of chill dread. "What truth?"

"That I'm still a step ahead of you, Lewis. That I've *always* been a step ahead. And the fact that you've cornered me out here, brought me down like a pack of yapping mongrel dogs, means *nothing*. Because I've already erased all of you."

"Did you kill Abby?" His voice was hollow. He felt sick.

"I *loved* Abby. *She* failed at loving *me*. So I'm giving her the quicker end. I opened some valves and the fuel level is rising in the arch, creeping up her parka where she's tied, and she'll either drown in jet fuel or ignite like a torch when it flashes into fire. Either way it's relatively quick and really quite merciful compared to freezing to death in the cold. I'm just letting her think about her rejection of me before her death comes. Believe me, you'll envy her—in your own last hours. I lied about what it would have been like if we'd left you on the stake. Freezing is a terrible way to go."

"Bob, it's not too late," Lewis tried. "Tell us what you've done. Help us make it right. We *can* fix it."

"The arch is filling with spilled fuel." Norse nodded solemnly. "The dome is becoming a bomb. If you'd left things alone you would have incinerated in the galley before you knew what was happening, which was the mercy I had planned for you. Now you can watch it from out here, your shelter vaporizing. The living will envy the dead."

The group looked up at him in disbelief. "But why?" Dana finally asked, her voice quavering.

"Because people don't work. Because it all falls apart on the way to Pluto."

There was a low keening sound as the winter-overs began to comprehend what he must have done. An enveloping dread at their own fate.

"Unfortunately, you didn't give me time to stop and destroy the generator at the Hypertats so there's a chance you can linger for days, maybe weeks. So I'm really leaving you with a final choice. The dilemma is my final gift to you. You can go back into the dome and try to save Dixon and risk dying with her. Or you can retreat to the emergency camp and try to save yourselves."

He reached in his parka and they stiffened, but it was only to pull out a sheaf of paper. "As you're freezing to death you might read some notes I made. It explains why you'll choose to save yourselves. Why our collective failure was inevitable. Why your mistake was in trusting each other. Trusting anybody! Every one of us is selfish at the final moment. So don't pity Abby. Pity yourselves." He glanced at his watch. "I'm guessing the rest of you have about thirty minutes."

"Tell us how to shut it off, dammit!" shouted Geller.

"This way," said Norse. And with that he turned the gun, pressed its twin barrels against the roof of his mouth, and fired.

CHAPTER THIRTY-ONE

The top of the barrier that sealed off the fuel arch had been crafted enough to keep out intruders but not to keep out air. There were cracks to see through and enough of a stench of petroleum to announce the explosive danger. The surviving winter-overs had spilled down the entry ramp to the archways and were bunched at the makeshift fuel arch wall, puddles leaking ominously from its base and the barrier groaning at the weight of the rising fuel behind it. The group boosted Lewis up to a crevice so he could shine a light into the gloom beyond. He reeled from the fumes, shouting down to the others to break out the fire masks. Then he took a fresh breath, held it, and aimed his light inside.

The sight was sickening. The fuel arch had become a black combustible lake, the tanks emptying to fill the Quonset-shaped structure a third of the way up its walls. Partway down the tunnel he saw a slumped figure tied to some of the tank plumbing, the fuel lapping at her chest. Abby!

Something was bobbing in the fuel beside her. He played his light across it and recognized a half-inflated weather balloon. What the hell? Wires went every which way into the fuel and above it, and just as lines of longitude converged at the Pole, the wires converged upon some small implement hung above the rising lake. He shone his light on that, trying to figure out what it was.

With recognition came fear. The flare gun! Lewis dimly recalled Norse asking it be brought to him.

What fools they'd been.

As the fuel level rose, the balloon was rising with it. One of the wires leading into the ooze was slack but as the balloon floated upward . . .

Norse had turned the entire station into a time bomb.

Lewis pulled his head back, dizzy from the fumes, thinking desperately. Then he told the others to let him down.

"Did you see her?" Molotov asked.

Lewis was coughing, nauseous from the poisonous fog. *One step ahead,* Norse had claimed. "She's there, and I can't tell if she's still alive. The whole arch has become a lake of fuel with gases above it. Norse wasn't lying; he opened some valves. The fuel's rising and I don't see how we could find the valves in that goop to shut the flood off."

"Jesus," Geller said.

"Listen, that's not the worst of it. The bastard has rigged some kind of trigger, I think. I'm not quite sure how it works, but one of Jerry's weather balloons is floating on the fuel and as it rises a wire is tightening on the trigger of the flare gun."

"What?" Dana cried.

"When the fuel level gets high enough, I think, the flare goes off."

"Oh my God," Linda gasped. "It's some kind of trap!"

"A simple one," guessed Gage Perlin, their plumber.

"Like the way a float in a toilet tank rises high enough to trigger a valve to shut off the refilling water." He was thinking. "A wire from the trigger goes to a pulley at the bottom and up to the balloon. . . ."

"However he rigged it, Norse has been thinking about this for a long time," Lewis said. "He wants us to abandon Abby. He wants us to abandon the dome." He looked at the others. "He wants us to give up."

"What else can we do?" asked Hiro with resignation.

"I don't think we have a choice, Jed," Mendoza added.

"Yes, we do," spoke up Molotov. The Russian looked grimly resolute, glancing up the wall in speculation. "There is always a choice. I made a choice when I wrongly accused Lewis here. I made a choice when I helped create this mess. Now I make another choice. You Americans go back. I will break inside and swim to her!" It was the growl of a bear angry at his own mistakes. The decision of a man eager to either make up for the past or be annihilated by it.

"Wait," said Lewis, thinking furiously. "Isn't that what he's counting on us to do? Treading fuel when the gun goes off? What we need is to keep the toilet tank from filling. If we can spring a leak in the arch, the fuel will start draining out as fast or faster than it's pouring in from the tanks. Right? It stabilizes, drops, and *then* we go get Abby."

"Jed," objected Longfellow, their electrician, "a single spark . . ."

"It's risky as hell. Even if we get Abby we may lose the fuel, unless we can somehow pump some of it back in. But if we don't . . ."

"We lose the dome," Geller said.

They hesitated.

"We lose more than that," Dana said.

"You mean we lose another person," said Lena. "That is what I am thinking. That I am tired of losing people."

"No, that's crazy," protested Linda. "I know it's terrible but we'll lose *everyone* if we stay here."

"Damn right," Calhoun warned. "We go up in flames. I'd rather freeze."

"Would you, Steve?" asked Dana. "Norse said that's worse."

"Well, we go to the emergency camp, then. At least it's a chance. We lose us all staying here."

"I think if we don't try here, we lose our soul," Dana said. "I agree with Alexi. I was wrong, too. I want to save what's left."

Calhoun groaned but didn't reply. They could hear the sound of swirling fuel.

Lewis looked at the others, their hesitation, their despair. Half determined, half panicked. "The archway is buried in snow," he reminded. "The only real exit for the fuel is right here, where we're standing. I'm proposing releasing it in here, letting it dam up against the generator wall and the outside ramp, and building a temporary dike to keep it out of the dome proper. Then I go in after Abby."

There was a long silence, an unspoken debate.

"That's just crazy," Linda moaned.

"Yes. Like running naked to the Pole."

The others glanced around, starting to make mental measurement of what they had to achieve. "Well, if we're going to do it, then let's do it!" Mendoza finally said, grimly determined. "Come on, amigos! Six of us with me to build the dike! The rest of you breach that wall!"

Most of them began to move. Calhoun and Linda still hesitated, watching the others.

"Ah, the hell with it," surrendered Calhoun. "At least it

will be quick." He pointed up the wall. "All right, start with that beam there. That will give access to this panel."

"There's enough weight from the fuel that it will help pry 'er loose!" Geller added.

And at that Linda Brown blinked and acquiesced. "I know some crates we can drag to help build a dike," she said fatalistically.

"Then drag!" shouted Dana. "We don't know how taut that wire is!"

Masks and tools were passed out. Extra gloves were stuffed in to make a barrier between prying crowbars and bare metal, in hopes of minimizing sparks. The large ramp-way doors were dragged open, letting in the sharp outside cold but helping to dissipate the fumes.

The removal of Calhoun's beam started a small breach in their barrier. Fuel from the arch began spraying out in a ghastly plume, spattering the snowy floor of the archway intersection behind them. Pools of congealing petroleum began to form. The work stopped for a moment, the winter-overs uneasily eyeing this new fountain and its rich stink.

"Hurry up, dammit!" Geller roared. "We've got to move!"

They started again with new ferocity. Bolts were screwed out and a panel of plywood began to bulge, pulling its own nails, squealing as it bent. As it did so, the flow of fuel turned from fountain to pulsing flood, its weight pushing aside the barrier and pouring out onto the snowy floor in a dark river, swirling past BioMed and reaching the far generator wall, where it splashed as oily surf and began pooling into a new lake. An entire panel came off and the flood quickened, an artery of syrup. Their lake deepened, even as the rise of the one in the fuel arch began to re-verse. They were wading in a petroleum sea, oily waves oscillating back and forth in their enclosure. The fuel lifted

BioMed off its foundation and sent it floating, bouncing, and scuttling against one wall. The spreading fuel would have poured into the dome proper if the makeshift dike hadn't delayed it. Small rivulets broke through that thin barrier and ran toward the galley and the science building.

As the pool spread, Norse's triggering balloon bobbed in place a moment and then began to sink. Lewis played his light over Abby, wondering if she was still alive.

"How taut is the wire?" Geller yelled.

"We're still here, aren't we?" Calhoun grunted.

The fumes built, half poisoning them. Lewis was increasingly terrified there'd be a spark. "Okay, we've got a breach, that's enough!" he decided. "The rest of you retreat!" They didn't have to be told twice. The survivors threw down their tools and waded for the ramp, the fuel swirling around their thighs, a combustible fog roiling ahead of them up into the night. If it ignited, they'd be vaporized. They splashed up the slick ramp, falling and grunting, crawling up the oily beach into the dark and cold of the outdoors, soaked from fuel and coughing and woozy as they pulled off their masks. Their reddish black patina grew gummy in the cold and began to freeze.

"Smoking or nonsmoking?" a coughing Calhoun tried to crack.

Lewis watched them go, waiting for the tidal current swirling out from the fuel arches to subside as the two pools equalized. The flood became sluggish, its overall depth cut in half. More oil was breaking through their hasty dike, running into the dome, but that served to keep the fuel from deepening again as the tanks continued to drain.

Still no explosion.

It was time. Lewis waded to the breached wall. The fuel was thick and syrupy with cold, fogged and tarlike. It was a prehistoric swamp, viscous and evil. He pushed past the break and shone his light around. The archway walls glistened with the sheen. "Christ, what a mess." With their tanks emptying he didn't know how they were going to survive the ice, but at least they'd so far evaded the fire. He could plainly see the trapped woman.

He pulled his mask aside for a moment. "Abby!"

There was no answer.

He waded into the fuel arch and felt his way to the catwalk, mounting its stairs and pulling himself along it where the fuel was now just ankle deep. He could see the high tide mark of the petroleum on the walls, the liquid dripping, the balloon like a distant buoy.

He counted the tanks off as he advanced, coming to the one where Cameron had been killed. It was here that Abby hung like a tired scarecrow. The balloon was sinking beside her, the wire to the trigger of the flare gun slacker now, but a board with another, tighter wire was floating beside it. The contraption looked more complex than it had to be.

He vaulted over the rail into stomach-deep fuel and waded toward the woman. She was limp as if dead, fuel having stained her to her chin, her body looking small and wilted. The flood had stopped an inch from her mouth.

"Abby?"

No response. He slapped her.

She jerked into crude consciousness and began coughing. He unstrapped one arm, then another, and she fell into his arms. Lewis had never seen anything so implacably heartless as this insane execution. He dragged her to the catwalk, pushing her up onto it and leaning her against the railing. She doubled over and vomited. When she came up gasping, he put an extra oxygen mask over her face. Abby sucked in air, reeling, tears streaming down her face.

"Where did he turn the valve? Where's the valve? We need to save what fuel we can!"

She shook her head.

"Where? Which pipe?"

She pulled away the oxygen mask, gasping to speak. "The wire! The flare!"

"I know! We got the fuel level to go down! We beat his clock!"

She shook her head vigorously. "No! Two wires! One if too high. A board if too low! It drops, pulls wire . . ."

Lewis saw what she was pointing at. Norse had anticipated them again. A second wire on the trigger was tightening as the fuel level fell and its board sank with it.

Good God. He'd brought nothing to cut it with.

"Run!"

She put on her mask and he pushed her frantically down the catwalk. The grating was slippery but the fuel had drained below it now. Gripping the slick rail, they ran as best they could, banging into the sides of the arch, looking back at the poised and hanging flare through a stinking fog of petroleum fumes, the slack wire growing tauter as the board pulled down.

Then they descended the catwalk stairs and went through the breach, wading across the petroleum pond to the ramp leading outside. It was molasses, clinging to them, beseeching them to stay. Behind them fuel was running across the hard-packed snow toward the modules, its fumes curling upward to the roof of the dome. It was a gray haze in the dome lights, the generator still chugging obediently behind the other wall.

The pair crawled up the slippery ramp, both slick with

stinking fuel, the wetness beginning to freeze on their clothes.

"Go, go, go!" Lewis shouted to the others. "Get as far away as you can!"

Someone screamed. They were running.

Then a reflected flash as the flare gun went off, releasing red light like a glimpse of hell. With a gassy roar, the fuel arch blew up.

The shock wave of the blast kicked Abby and Lewis the last few feet up the ramp and knocked the scattering group as flat as a strike of bowling pins. The violence hit an instant before the sound did, and then for another instant everything at the Pole was noise. The pulse of superheated air that was now beyond the flattened winter-overs kicked up a wall of loose snow that expanded outward across the station like the penumbra of a star, an expanding blizzard, rushing a half mile in all directions before puffing out.

The snow over the fuel arch erupted like napalm, its wall of flame shooting skyward in an upside down curtain. Bio-Med disintegrated instantly, its fragments spewing into the entryway. The opposite wall guarding the generators blew inward into kindling and a gout of flame and plasma gases seared into the generator room like the exhaust of a rocket, melting the electrical connections and setting the gym ablaze. In an instant, power to the dome was snuffed out.

Fire leaped over the crude dike and flashed through the dome itself, the gases igniting and the resulting energy punching vents in the dome as if it were made of foil. Smoke and heat shot up through the ventilation hole at the top of the structure in a volcanic plume, spattering the complex with a rain of debris. Thousands of icicles broke off and rained down on the arena below like breaking glass, a maniacal tinkle against the thunder.

The fireball knocked the habitation modules askew from their foundations. Pipes were torn off, electrical cables snipped, and each metal box was seared with flame, roasting from orange to black in seconds. Crates flared into torches, banked ice cream flashed into steam. For a minute, the entire dome was an inferno.

Yet the explosion was a mere spark in a universe of implacable cold. Antarctica, for a brief moment punched aside, imploded back inward once the shock wave passed. The ice was determined to reclaim its dominance. Snow turned to steam and slush. The most volatile gases had vaporized and what was left began to burn more sluggishly as the heat consumed itself by turning a tinder-dry environment into a melting one. The blast had created a stinking lake. Fuel leaked down into the ice cap and spread into the surrounding snow. Flames roared, smoked, melted, and sputtered out. The ruptured tanks burned fiercely, sending a column of smoke boiling a mile high into the sky, but the blaze retreated to its heart almost as swiftly as it had expanded. With it went the stored energy that was to have kept them alive for the rest of the winter. There'd been a flash of oily violence, and now a grim guttering.

Their lifeblood had been consumed.

Shakily, the survivors stood. Miraculously, none had been seriously hurt and none had caught on fire. The searing heat was already a dim memory, replaced once more by relentless cold. They shivered.

Their spaceship had been destroyed.

Wordlessly, Geller handed over to Lewis some papers he'd snatched from Norse's dying hand.

There was some kind of scribbled account of a moun-

tain climb, Lewis saw as he leafed through them. And a
cover sheet with a scrawled message:

*Thus Samson killed many more when he died than
when he lived.*

CHAPTER THIRTY-TWO

The dying fire lit their way as the tiny tribe trudged wearily back toward the Spryte. They were silent in their weariness, Skinner using the shoulder of an exhausted Hiro to guide him back across the snow. So many had been lost! More than a third of them. The rest alive, staggering like blackened zombies, exhausted, shivering. Left to what kind of fate?

When they got to the snow tractor Geller climbed up on it and caught the corpse of Norse by the boot, dragging him off the cab roof without ceremony. His blood was frozen so there was no trail. His limbs were already stiff. He toppled like Raggedy Ann into the snow, and man and mannequin lay together.

"I'd leave the sonofabitch for the buzzards but there ain't buzzards down here," the maintenance man said bitterly.

"It's just his shell," Lena whispered. "The demon is gone."

Lewis stooped to look at the tractor treads. Gears were bent, a sprocket broken. The track had snapped. Still, the basics were there. "Can we fix it?"

The support personnel clustered around. "Maybe," Calhoun said. He glanced back toward the burning dome. "Maybe the garage escaped the worst of it. With some tools, if we can get the generator at Bedrock running—"

"What the hell for?" Geller interrupted. "Why the hell try?"

Calhoun shrugged.

"I mean, can you fix the Spryte to run a thousand miles?" clarified Lewis. "Towing that sled, and maybe another, with a shelter and some food and tents. Drive to Vostok, like Bob was going to do. Or better yet, drive to the Americans at McMurdo."

Calhoun looked at the rest of them, emptied by the struggle. "It's winter, Jed."

"I know it would be hard."

"More than hard," Mendoza spoke up wearily. "Some of us are banged up pretty good. Clyde's blind. Abby's half dead. We'd have to melt drinking water, ride out storms. Winds can hit two hundred miles per hour on the Beardmore glacier. Windchill is, what, two hundred and fifty below? We'd be dependent on a single engine."

"I know it would be risky."

"But six or eight of us in the cab, in shifts," Dana said, coming to life at the thought of escape. "The rest towed in a covered sled. Better than Scott had."

"Scott died, and that was summer."

"Better than Amundsen had, then. He lived."

Several of the others were nodding at Dana. Escape!

"Yes, but not McMurdo across the mountains. Vostok," Molotov said.

"Suicide," countered Hiro. "We would have no chance."

Lewis looked at the huddled group. They were as haggard as war refugees, spent, fearful. It was calm now, but the next storm would be along soon enough. Yet the emergency Hypertats appeared to be intact, and with them the generator. That meant heat, and some food. Norse was dead. The immediate emergency had passed. They had time to repair the Spryte. Time to try to rig a radio and computer from the outer buildings. Time to make a less exhausted decision.

"We can't agree now," he said. "We can't think straight now. There's no need to decide now. The first thing to do is get warm."

"What are you saying?"

"That we need to get back to Bedrock."

They staggered toward the emergency camp, arm in arm, body leaning on body. Skinner kept his hand on Hiro's shoulder, stumbling after him. Lewis half carried the woozy and nauseous Abby and kept thinking covetously about the wounded Spryte. It hurt to even walk away from it. Maybe they could rig a radio to let everyone know what had happened and to alert potential rescuers of their plan to attempt escape. Maybe the rescuers could arrange some airdrops along the route. It would be wildly desperate, but it was a chance to go home.

Home. It was hard for Lewis to remember what it looked like. Smelled like. The scent of earth, grass, flowers. He ached for it, could hardly remember it. Home! He imagined being in such a place with Abby, not the stricken woman he was dragging but the bright, funny, optimistic woman he'd first met.

What would that be like?

Yet just the quarter mile to Bedrock was endless. Every step was leaden, every footstep sidelighted by the oily flames still burning in the arch. The majority stumbled into the huts while Molotov and Mendoza called on the last of their reserves to help Lewis start the generator again. It was easier this time, having been run by Lewis not that long before, and the generator's cough and rumble was like the restart of a ruptured heart. Their own blood surged at the sound of it. Heat and light were the gift of life.

Then they went inside.

Logistics expert Linda estimated that they probably had enough fuel and food at the camp for a month. Survival after that would require an airdrop. They'd lost their cook, their doctor, their two best mechanics. They'd lost much of their clothing and supplies.

The survivors broke open a cache of emergency clothing and began to shed their oily garments and toss them outdoors for later cremation. Water was heated. People exhaustedly stripped, washed, and redressed without self-consciousness or modesty, helping each other numbly, small kindnesses enough to bring a tear of gratitude. Most were shaking from cold and shock.

Some granola bars were passed out, and hot tea.

Then they slept for twenty hours.

Slept as if dead.

Lewis came awake first, nestled next to a drowsy Abby. He couldn't remember their falling asleep next to each other. He couldn't remember much of anything. His life had become a blur. Around the pair the others were jammed onto the floor of just one of the huts, clustered in their need for human proximity. Cave dwellers must have been like this, he thought, huddling together against the cold of the night. Prehistoric! That's how far they'd fallen.

Abby shifted, too, nuzzling against him, her body warm, promising a future that still seemed tenuous and remote. "Did you dream?" she whispered sleepily.

He shook his head, still groggy. "Of home, I think."

She was silent for a long time, clutching to him, their

chests rising and falling in unison. "Where's home, Jed?" she said softly.

He lay there, listening to the breathing and snoring of the others, and thought about her question. Where indeed? He had no family, no house, no address, no sense of place. He lay there in darkness, thinking first about her and then about himself. Where could they make a home?

She fell asleep again, resting against him.

He gently got up, swaying a bit from lingering exhaustion, and carefully stepped over the prone forms of the others. Some were half awake now, some exhaustedly asleep, but all were quiet, lost in their own thoughts or dreams, waiting to see what was decided next. A head or two rose up at his passing but no one spoke. At the end of the hut he dressed. The ritual that Cameron had taught him at a simpler time, which seemed eons ago: the layers of clothing, the boots, the hat, the mittens. He stepped into the Hypertat air lock, closed the inner door behind him, and, taking a breath, opened the outer one. He stepped outside into the midnight cold of the Pole.

The temperature hit him again like a slap, little different than when he'd first walked off that airplane. And yet it wasn't alien anymore. Just a new edge. He'd come to a place where people didn't belong and now, perversely, was used to it.

Lewis filtered cold air through his gaiter, filled his lungs, and looked around. The fire was out, the plateau lit by galactic milk. The station was a ruin of silvers and grays, as soundless as the moon.

What had he hoped for? A place uncomplicated. Pure.

Lewis slowly turned, taking in the geography of the battered station. They had no thermometer registering temperature anymore and so the cold was simply cold: embracing, leaching, and yet not as savage as that night when they'd all run from the sauna. He was surprised once more by the light: how the night could repeal itself and become less threatening. The galaxy was a banner of illumination, the snow fluorescent in its gleam. The base was wounded, unlit, stark, and yet even now the Pole was one of the most lovely places he'd ever seen, astonishing in its cleanliness. Spangled, ethereal, crystalline. As long as they lived there it was still a spaceship, drifting through space.

The aluminum dome still looked whole in the pale starlight and of course it mostly was. Perhaps the worst breaches could be patched, or the galley module stripped of food and parts. Like Crusoe, they had a wreckage of supplies to pillage. There were the cargo berms, the mothballed Quonsets of summer camp, the science buildings. It would be hard, but there was an enormous residue of equipment and dozens of structures with which to eke out a winter. Perhaps they could stick it out if enough food and fuel were parachuted in. Aid, as distant as it seemed, was over the horizon.

People had endured worse.

They could also freeze, he knew. Just one generator now, their last Spryte crippled, their two best mechanics dead, their quarters claustrophobic, their unity far from certain. Norse had mocked a group that had never really congealed.

Had they finally become a club?

The bigger question was where he belonged. Lewis had come to the Pole looking for some kind of fulfillment: escape, and an end to escape. Bizarrely, he may have finally found it in the station's near-destruction. In the heart of a nightmare he'd found a woman to love, tentative acceptance, life-changing experience, meaningful work. He actually cared about the damn place. He still cared about his weather readings.

He looked at the sky. Was the world warming? Hard to imagine, down here.

Still, he wanted to know. Wanted to help others know.

If they stayed, maybe he could record more readings. Send them to Sparco when the winter was done. And someday toast poor old Mickey Moss, the things that had made the astrophysicist human and the things that had made him special enough to push for this base.

Lewis looked across at the Spryte he'd recaptured with a certain melancholy. It would have been more fitting, perhaps, if the psychologist had finally made it to Vostok and eventually faced a realization that would have tormented him for the rest of his life: that the others had stayed, and lived, and come out of everything Robert Norse had thrown at them stronger than before.

That the Three Hundred Degree Club really worked.

"Maybe I busted up a five-million-dollar rock for nothing," he whispered to himself, half smiling at the bitter thought.

But then maybe Norse *had* come to the same dread realization, just before he'd pointed the barrel of his pistol into his own mouth. That the flaw wasn't in society, but in himself.

It was a gamble to continue the winter, Lewis knew. Their position was precarious.

It was a bigger gamble not to.

He came back inside, slowly undressed, stepped over the drowsy forms of the others, and lay down next to Abby. She snuggled him to herself with her arms, warming him, drowsily awake herself again.

Lewis kissed her hair.

"Maybe this is home," he murmured.

She squeezed him. A tight hug of fear and hope.

ACKNOWLEDGMENTS

This book is a mix of fact and fiction, and the men and women who have wintered at the Pole will likely disagree with each other on where fact leaves off and fiction begins. Many of the physical details of the Pole and polar life are true, taken from interviews, research, nonfiction books on polar psychology (I can recommend *Bold Endeavors* by Jack Stuster and *Antarctic Psychology* by A. J. W. Taylor), and my own visit to Amundsen-Scott station. The abandoned base still exists, the Three Hundred Degree Club is an annual ritual, the KitKat Club is real, and the strain of serving in Antarctica has resulted in several sociological studies. None of them, however, have been conducted by a psychologist like Norse!

The plot is fiction, of course: There has never been a serious crime at the Pole. While my description of the polar base is generally accurate, I haven't hesitated to take liberties with its details. And the replacement of the decaying Amundsen-Scott station that I allude to is already well under way and should be completed by about 2005. The dome will likely be gone and the modules this story takes place in replaced with new, more modern quarters. The result will be more habitable for researchers. Novelists, alas, will find it less spooky.

Because just over a thousand people have actually wintered at the South Pole since a base was established in 1958, it is necessary to stress that none of the characters in this book are intended to represent real polar veterans. Despite their occasionally colorful eccentricities, the record of polar personnel has been that of serious, sustained, and cheerful professionalism in the face of physical and emotional adversity. To serve a winter at the Pole is an astonishing opportunity and real sacrifice. The people who do it are as remarkable as astronauts.

While the National Science Foundation was uneasy with the subject of this novel, the federal agency deserves thanks for giving me the opportunity to visit the South Pole as a science journalist in 1994 and for sharing invaluable information on the current station's layout, logistics, and routine. Those curious about the real Pole are encouraged to explore the journals, photographs, and science descriptions posted on the Internet. Of the many people who provided information, special thanks go to Lynn Simarski, Beth Gaston, John Lynch, Jerry Marty, and Erick Chiang at NSF; to David Fisher of Antarctic Support Associates; to winterovers Katy and Rod Jensen and Lisa Beal for interviews and correspondence; and to sociological researcher Dr. Lawrence Palinkas of the University of California at San Diego. Of the many notable and outstanding scientists I met at the Pole, Marty Pomerantz deserves special mention: When I interviewed him, the solar astronomer was seventy-seven and had been coming to the Pole for thirty-five years. He represents the best of the pioneering spirit of the place.

Whatever is accurate and true about this novel comes from the generosity of experts like these. The fictions and horrors are entirely my own.

Once again I must thank the patient and encouraging guidance of my editor at Warner Books, Rick Horgan, and the support of my agent at International Creative Management, Kris Dahl. And, as always, I am indebted to the partnership of my wife, Holly, whose encouragement and insight were once more invaluable in getting me through the dark winter of this particular yarn.

WILLIAM DIETRICH won a Pulitzer Prize for science and environmental writing at the *Seattle Times*. He is the author of two nonfiction books, *The Final Forest* and *Northwest Passage*, as well as the acclaimed adventure novels *Ice Reich* and *Getting Back*.